THE
HANNAH
DOCUMENT

LAURA SWAN

Paperback: ISBN 978-8-9925203-1-6

E-Book: ISBN 978-8-9925203-0-9

Book Cover by Get Covers.com

First edition 2025

CONTENTS

Preface

TO THE READER

Midrash, which roughly translates as"searching," "seeking," "questioning," or"asking," is an ancient Jewish tradition of sacred storytelling where scholars investigate meanings behind sacred texts, particularly The Torah (the first five books of the Bible) that allowed rabbis to seek ways to reconcile biblical contradictions and enrich biblical content with new meanings. Midrashim are creative explorations of troubling texts. Thus, in the story ofAbraham (found in the book of Genesis) taking his young son Isaac to the region of Moriah to offer sacrifice to God, Isaac wonders where the ram is, andAbraham responds, "God will provide." Abraham builds the fire and binds his son before God stops him. A contemporary version of Midrash retells this story from the ram's point of view, and a new perspective emerges (that it's a story of God's rejection of child sacrifice, which was common in the Middle East at that time). The parables of Jesus in the New Testament are examples of Midrashim. Frequently, Midrashim are presented to invite the reader to consider new perspectives. And to consider, "Whose voice is needed here?"

I invite my reader to consider Sofia's ultimate discovery as a contemporary form of Midrash.

ONE

2 012 CE

MOR GABRIEL, SOUTHEASTERN TURKEY NEAR MARDIN

The ground shook with the now familiar boom of missile strikes.

Sofia Papandréou bent over the ancient vellum piece, attempting to prevent damage from flying debris. The lights flickered, the portable air conditioners clicked off and on, and the walls, high windows, and ceiling once more remained intact.

Still, the Syrian war was getting too close.

With a thrum of excitement, Sofia checked her precious vellum piece. Her first discovery of Deacon Olympias' letters.

> "...I am appalled at the behavior of the Imperial court during their so-called Synod of the Oaks. As a senior member of that family, I had expected my voice to carry weight. But I'm afraid, dear friend, your years

of telling the raw truth about their sinful behavior, have hardened their hearts. They prefer their comforts and debauchery while calling themselves Christian. Followers of Satan are more accurate..."

...my beloved John, we implore [undecipherable] daily for your rightful return to your See. Your flock needs your encouragement and protection. Corruption grows daily and my own family betrays the gospel. Some days I despair ... [torn fragment]. Your joy is my joy...[faded] ... -ympias

"Everyone all right?" Sofia gripped the edge of her table, trying to steady her hands, and took a deep breath, dust particles irritating her nose and throat. Her heart felt like it had taken another beating. If war was hell, then she was starting to feel its heat. Trying to distract herself, she checked her workstation for any newly accumulated detritus. Why was Assad so bent on the destruction of his country? What did the people of Syria do to deserve this?

"Brilliant. Soon I'll qualify for war pay from Her Majesty, serving off here in the far reaches of the Empire." Brother Makarios Addicott's flecks of debris had showered on his black habit.

Sofia smiled. In the years they had known each other, her colleague seemed to have an innate ability to absorb local nuances of the English language. "Sorry, Mac, you're about a half-century too late and standing on the wrong piece of real estate."

"Ah, you don't need to remind me of those minor technicalities."

Sofia surveyed the six stations containing laptops, digital cameras attached to frames, and drafting lamps. Several workers had thrown large pieces of cloth over the expensive cameras to protect them. She observed them removing the cloths and gently shaking off the debris without disturbing the manuscripts, vellum, and parchment pieces the workers were photographing and digitizing. Each re-laid the cloth over the cameras and resumed their meticulous tasks.

The adrenaline rush of unearthing the first clear evidence of Deacon Olympias' writings directly competed with her anxiety over these intermittent bombing episodes. She was determined to remain and search for more possible evidence of early women's writings.

Sofia clipped a small thread from the vellum sheaf and, using tweezers, placed the sample on a glass slide and fastened it with a cover slip. Taking a sharp knife, she scraped a tiny bit of the black ink and placed it on another glass slide, again fastening it tight. She labeled each with a code number, recorded the numbers with descriptions in their logbook, and then set the samples into the padded pouch nearby. All the slides would be delivered to the labs at İstanbul Üniversitesi for testing.

"Can you imagine? After all these centuries, and she finally emerges?" Sofia had been hunting the letters of fourth-century deacon Olympias since she began her graduate studies ten years ago. The woman was too prominent and powerful to remain relegated to obscurity. "This may be just a small piece, but it gives me hope that there is more out there."

The lambskin was distorted, yet the letters were easy to read. The frayed edges and lack of creasing indicated it had been informally rolled for transport.

"Your thoughts?" Brother Makarios adjusted his bifocals that had slid down his nose.

Sofia answered, "I agree it's a portion of a letter, not some document or text. The Greek is correct. This is the voice of a well-educated person." Or was she projecting her hopes onto this?

She repeated the process with the red ink sample on another piece of loose vellum. The manuscripts were intriguing. She would have time to study them when she returned to Thessaloníki, but with the war threatening to encroach on the monastery complex, they needed to photograph these loose pieces and take samples right away.

Brother Makarios held a scalpel in his ungloved hands, attempting to pull sheaves apart on a moldy mess of old vellum. She donned a pair of gloves and went over to assist him.

"Mac, let me help. Four hands are more useful than two." Sofia's long fingers gently held the underside of the vellum that was glued together with their blackened edges curled into a bowl shape, presumably from moisture in years past. Unfortunately, some of the vellum looked as if termites had eaten it.

"Bloody bastard, where's a decent surgeon when you need one," Brother Makarios cursed as he struggled to separate one of the sheaves from the rest.

Another series of booms echoed from the distant bombing. Talking ceased, a collective sigh was heard, and work resumed. For how much longer would they be safe?

Sofia touched the tabletop with her fingertips, trying to steady her hands. She took three deep breaths. "Maybe that's exactly what we need."

She was eager to find out what this mess might contain. This monastery held manuscripts well over 1,000 years old. Given the stunning vellum piece found in an old leather satchel that brought her to rural Turkey, locating a surgeon took on new importance.

"I was joshing you, luv." Brother Makarios leaned toward the magnifying glass as he separated another pair of glued sheaves.

With a scalpel in her free hand, Sofia helped him separate the sheaf. "I'm serious, Mac. If those bombs get any closer, they might damage this irreparably. I wish I could take this and the other manuscript," she nodded in the direction of a gray archival storage box at the further end of the table, "back with me to Thessaloníki so that I could oversee the surgeons and get this properly scanned."

"A Greek taking a precious manuscript out of Turkey? That should start another bloody uproar."

"My Greek passport evoked enough scowling as it was. Carrying this cargo would land me in prison." Why couldn't their two governments get along? Too much ugly history on both sides. Sofia picked up a magnifying glass and drew close to examine the sheaf they just removed. "Mac, did you have any history on this manuscript?"

"Thought it might catch your curiosity."

Sofia gazed across at him. "I had assumed that all the manuscripts housed here were in Greek or Classic Latin."

"Most are, as we'd expect, but several are in Armenian. I assume they found their way here in the early twentieth century."

Sofia picked up her scalpel and began teasing the edge of another sheaf that was proving stubborn. "During the genocide? Glad at least someone valued Armenian culture if not their lives."

Brother Makarios grunted. "That's what's concerning me. If I take this to Istanbul, will it disappear? I cannot imagine this current political regime would appreciate any reminder of Turkey's ugly past."

"Might a university northeast of here have the resources? But would the monastery even allow you to take it to Armenia?"

"*Bey*, Makarios." "*Hanim*, Sofia."

They both turned toward the door where a young monk, with a groomed beard, beckoned to them to follow him. Curious, she made eye contact with Brother Makarios, who also seemed surprised at the interruption.

"Is there a problem?"

"My abbot sent me to bring you to his office."

Sofia's stomach gripped. When she accepted Brother Makarios' invitation, she knew her presence was tenuous. The neighboring war had brought a significant military presence throughout the village and the nearby city of Mardin.

They each removed their gloves and set them on the table. Passing through the doorway, Sofia squinted and shaded her eyes. The sun's rays were intense, and the air remained piercingly dry, making breathing difficult. Walking alongside Brother Makarios across a broad courtyard, she heard the quavering echoes from the muezzin's call to early afternoon prayers. So tragic, the call to prayers met by missile strikes. Muslim against Muslim, just who will win? Certainly not God.

"Mac, I want to work on that manuscript. I can still access better computers at the university." Her situation at the University of Thessaloníki was precarious as the economy continued deteriorating and teaching positions disappeared. However, she knew enough people with access to the best technology to help her create the slides needed to begin her investigation of the damaged manuscript's history and what it said. "I'd like to take small samples of the remnants of cording and detritus in the binding to see if we can figure out where it's been all these centuries."

"Certainly, luv. We can trust the labs in Istanbul with our samples, but I'll see what I can do about getting both Armenian manuscripts."

"Both?"

"Yes, there's another in the vault."

Sofia was both pleasantly surprised and irritated with Brother Makarios. He constantly left chunks of information out of their conversations in his absent-mindedness. But she had great hope that voices of women from early Christianity be found in these Armenian codices.

The Olympias fragment might prove nearly impossible to trace until this damned war was over. Why so many hurdles? Why, when she again finds herself so close to finding the voices of women from the past, does the door slam shut on her?

The two were escorted through a series of doorways into a larger parlor. Sofia's stomach gripped when she saw that several military officers stood, hands behind their backs, and holstered guns on their hips.

The abbot standing nearby made introductions.

Sofia glanced toward the abbot and noticed that he had pulled their passports from the safe.

"Officers, here are their passports. They are our guests and are doing important work alongside some of our young people."

Brother Makarios turned toward their host. "Abbot, what's going on?"

The officer examined the first passport. Hers, Sofia noted.

"Papandréou. Greek. What brings you to this hellhole? And, only recently, I see from your visa." His statement was a challenge, not a question.

Sofia brushed dust from her lab coat and took a deep breath. Relations between Greece and Turkey were strained, but he did not have to take it out on her.

"Your people are working to preserve and save the older manuscripts in the monastery's library, and I was invited here to assist." Why did she need to explain this?

"Planning on taking some of them with you?"

Her cheeks grew warm. Brother Makarios inhaled sharply.

The abbot shot back, "Do not insult my guests. I trust them implicitly."

She slipped her hands into the pockets of her lab coat and dug her nails into the palms of her hands. "Is the basis for your accusation merely my nationality, sir?"

"A simple question," he asked as his eyes bore into her.

Sofia kept her gaze steady. "I have studied manuscripts at the Vatican, the National Library of France in Paris, and the Institute for Papyrology in Heidelberg as well as the Austrian National Library." Exactly how long does her list of credentials need to be to justify her presence to some people? She took a deep breath. "None of these renowned institutions have accused me of theft."

The officer tossed her passport back on the table and flipped Brother Makarios' travel document open. "British, and it seems you've been with us for some time now."

The Abbot interjected. "You insult our guests. Their work here is important to the preservation of our culture. They've been of great assistance to us."

The abbot's jaw clenched.

Brother Makarios adjusted his glasses, indicating he was preparing for battle. "Look here, why are you interrupting our work? You've never questioned my presence in the months that I've been here."

"We've been put on alert. The library at an Islamic Center in Mardin was stripped of all its old books. People looking to make money on the black market."

Sofia flinched. "That's terrible. Tragic." Did this officer consider her a threat to their national treasures? She sighed. More destruction of ancient cultures. The madness.

"We make no such claim here," the abbot said.

The insults she endured here paled in comparison to insults women bore in other parts of the world where she'd worked. She responded, "You may search my room if it will ease your mind."

The boom of another series of missile strikes silenced the room. The crucifix on the wall shuddered. Sofia felt her heart pounding, much like the bombs. One military officer strode over to the window and looked out.

Brother Makarios spoke. "You'd best look to Daesh for all the looting. We already know that—."

The officer continued to stare at her. "We cannot guarantee your safety. My men will be escorting both of you to the airport. Your time here ends."

Sofia's anxiety erupted. "But I'm willing to stay. I understand the risk."

The officer's voice grew louder and deeper. "No, you don't. I won't have your blood on my hands."

Sofia clenched her jaw, struggling to resist a shot back at the stiff-necked Turk.

Brother Makarios gently squeezed her shoulder. "Dottore Papandréou and I mean no harm to Turkish antiquities. Quite the opposite. We're struggling to preserve the monastery's library against our warring neighbors."

A door opened, scraping against the floor. They all turned in its direction. Mother Abbess entered; her black robes billowed with grey dust along the hems. She'd been outside, most likely with the children in the school the nuns still managed to operate. Sofia felt relief.

The military officer gazed at the two of them. "I cannot waste manpower protecting you. I am removing all foreigners immediately."

Sofia wanted to ask if the Kurds living in the area were among the "foreigners" being removed but held her tongue. "We'll stay, and we don't expect any protection."

The abbess touched Sofia's shoulder. "I must agree with the officer. I do not fear so much for Brother Makarios or the young men working in our library, but you must depart right away. The Syrian conflict expands daily. You see for yourself the flood of refugees and how traumatized they are. Daesh grows stronger."

"Mother Abbess, if I'm not safe here, then none of the women are."

"Sofia, dear, you've heard the same reports I have. Daesh doesn't merely kill women. You are in danger of being taken to one of their insidious camps. What they do to women is unspeakable. I cannot allow you to be placed in danger—.

"And the nuns? Yourself? Daesh will treat you no better. There may be protection in numbers."

"No, Sofia. You and your work are too dear to me. Your research and writing aren't just for yourself. You must go and take what you've learned. Publish and tell the world of our heritage."

Sofia was stunned by the abbess' words.

"You are a woman of faith, Mother Abbess. Why must women endure so much tragedy? Where is God? Why is God deaf to the cries of women and children?"

"Sofia, God is with all those who are suffering. God is with those who confront the lies of evil. One day, you will give voice to all you've seen and heard. You will give voice to all the women who've been silenced throughout history. You, Sofia, will give them a voice again."

The walls and floors shook. A window shattered. Vibrations echoed then silence settled in once again.

Two

The military police escorted Sofia from Mor Gabriel to the military base near Kayseri Erkilet, where she learned that the Turkish government had shut down Mardin's airport due to the growing conflict both with the Turkish Kurds and Daesh in Syria a few miles away.

She was ordered to remain in the secure area until her bus to Diyarbakir Airport arrived. Anxious about her colleague, Adélie, who had been working in Aleppo, she dialed her cell phone. A pre-recorded message: *The party you are trying to call cannot be reached*. They'd spoken a week ago, so this left her deeply concerned.

Sofia grabbed her laptop and quickly searched Al-Jazeera and other news sites before she lost her Wi-Fi connection. However, she did not find much news about Aleppo. Thus far, Assad's forces had spared that ancient city, but who knows? It might be days before she knew what was going on. She closed her eyes and sent a prayer of protection to her colleague.

The paging system crackled announcements in Turkish, but there was no sign that her bus would be boarding anytime soon. Glancing around, she noticed military personnel, guns slung over their shoulders, standing around. *Observing us? Or just me?* The harsh treatment of her escort, knowing that Turks do not like Greeks, left her feeling somewhat paranoid.

Finally, she was escorted to an old bus spewing ash black smoke out the back. The bus was crowded with bags, pets, and noisy people. She sat next to a teen wearing a headset, his head bouncing to his music. Setting her rucksack and laptop between her feet, she pulled out her e-reader as the bus pulled out to begin their two-hour ride north, settled in, and started reading one of her professional journals.

The bus swayed, managing to hit every pothole on the road, making reading more difficult. She gripped the bar on the seat ahead of her with her left and held her e-reader in her right. An hour in, and sweat bathed her body.

The bus took a hard left and up an incline, nearly knocking her into the aisle. She breathed deeply. Her phone buzzed. Setting her e-reader in her rucksack, she picked up the call.

Hearing Adélie's voice, Sofia nearly shouted, "Are you alright?" She breathed a sigh of relief.

"Yes, but we're working at a frantic pace. The civil war has moved near Aleppo. So many people had hoped that Assad and the rebel forces might stay away from here. But Daesh is pushing their war our way."

Sofia winced as she shifted in her seat. "That's awful."

"Civil wars are brutal. All because Assad wouldn't heed warnings about the devastating drought, Sofia. Nothing more."

The connection died.

Sofia stared at the cell screen, willing the connection to resume. She felt so helpless. People killed. Cultures destroyed. The cycle of violence never ceased.

Sofia redialed several times to no avail. She rested her head on the back seat in front of her. The noise, the dust, the smells, the frustration. The swaying bus and the exhaust fumes were beginning to make her nauseous.

Her head felt like it was caught in a vise. Then the bus slowed and turned. They'd finally arrived at the airport. The teen next to her stood shot up. She grasped the bar in front to keep from falling onto the floor. She grabbed her bags, clambered out, and entered the airport. Passing through security, whose lines moved like a turtle slugging through a dense marsh, she walked to her assigned gate. Her flight home to Thessaloníki would take her through Istanbul.

Her phone buzzed. Her headache lightened at the sound of Adélie's voice. "So sorry. Assad's people have been trying to cut internet and phone service, but our tech wizards have so far been successful in reconnecting us. The patriarch has ordered us out of Aleppo within the week."

Sofia sighed. "I'm so sorry, but you need to be safe. I don't know how your nerves have handled the past year. I was near Mardin for three weeks, and the shelling was twisting my nerves into a ball. Fortunately, the monastery has been transporting their precious library into some caves in the mountains as the staff finishes their preservation work. Turns out Mor Gabriel holds some damaged but fascinating Armenian texts. I think you'll be interested in helping us study these."

"Any in Syriac?"

"Mor Gabriel has many Syriac texts, but I've been looking at some early classical Armenian texts. I'll let you know when they're available online." Sofia shifted her position and took a deep breath. "Mac had insisted I travel to Mor Gabriel because of something he found there. It's just a portion of vellum, really in good shape given its age, but it seems I've located my first piece of Deacon Olympias' letters to John Chrysostom."

Sofia smiled as her friend screeched with excitement. Adélie knew how determined Sofia had been to find Deacon Olympias and was the only one of their colleagues who encouraged her obsession.

"I just don't know how or where to proceed. Nothing else in their collection hinted at Olympias. It was like she was one odd sheet in a mixture of other remnants."

Sofia's hand jolted when she heard a now too-familiar sound coming from her colleagues' end. Then, the connection died. Her throat constricted. She tried calling again, but it wouldn't go through. Aleppo? Her heart sank. Her mind raced. Too many of her colleagues were working in war zones, defending old manuscripts from greedy black marketers. And civil wars were the most ruthless and virulent.

She stood and stretched, breathing slowly, trying one of the mantras a friend taught her to slow down her racing mind.

Her phone rang. Sofia jumped.

Adélie was on the line again, her voice sounded strained. "Sofia, more bombs exploding. We have just a few days, so we're packing up the collection and remnants to move everything. My boss is searching for flights for us, but I don't know when or where that'll be."

Sofia sighed. "I'm glad to hear you're okay. You may need to drive out. I'd be surprised if planes are still taking off. You're always welcome at my family's home if you need a place to stay."

"That's sweet. So, tell me more about your discovery."

Sofia briefly explained what little she knew thus far. "My gut keeps telling me that the logical location for her letters would've been Pontus in Northeastern Turkey." Sofia glanced up at the screen to see if a new departure time for her flight had been posted. "The few universities in that area continue to deny that they hold older manuscripts. The Ottoman Empire might've destroyed anything Christian, or let them disappear into private collections."

Adélie coughed then said. "Dust is becoming a problem here, especially in private collections, which is why we work so hard to fill in all the gaps."

"But let's talk more once you're out of Aleppo."

The two said their goodbyes.

Sofia sent another prayer for safety and a miracle for herself. She smiled. Her grandmother would be impressed with all the praying she'd done today.

Her hunt for Olympias' letters had been maddening. Figure out where the Sultans of the past few centuries might've hidden a private library. Which cronies would've accepted old manuscripts as political bribes? And where would she find the money for travel, even if she did stumble into a lead? She was already strapped without a job. Discouragement rose like bile.

Sofia's flight finally announced readiness for boarding. Standing in line, her phone rang. Brother Makarios was on the other end.

"Hi, Mac. Just heard from Adélie. They're evacuating Aleppo."

She listened as he sighed. "If this weren't so tragic, I'd crack one of my famous jokes about we are the real 'Indiana Jones's.'"

"No kidding. No joke. Just endless tragedy." Sofia could hear her grandmother now chastising her for her negative attitude. "How long do you think you'll be allowed to stay?"

"We'll wrap matters up within the week. I'm negotiating with the abbot about moving the Armenian manuscripts to a university. He won't commit until we know where."

Sofia sighed. "I don't blame him, but at least the abbot is open."

"Alright, luv, I know that voice of yours. We're both concerned about Adélie and her team. So, what's bothering you?"

"How do I proceed? My funds have dried up, and universities aren't hiring. Greece's biggest export is still people like me leaving in search of work. "

"So now you will do the brilliant thing. Publish something breathtaking and knock 'em dead, as the Americans say." Brother Makarios held more confidence in her than she did in herself. "Let the universities come after you."

"I wish." Sofia cringed at the bitterness in her voice. "At this point, I'd need to find another Dead Sea Scrolls deposit and offer to bring it to my new teaching position."

She settled within her quiet thoughts. "If not eastern Turkey, I'd bet my money on Mount Athos. People have been talking about this for years. We both know the rumors—."

"—and the deafening denial," he finished.

Those rumors had long haunted Sofia. Agio Óros, the ancient libraries of Mount Athos. "We both know I'm not welcome there. Would you be willing to give it a shot?"

"Those cantankerous old monks don't trust anyone. Despite my illustrious title and credentials, I've never successfully gotten a visitors' pass. Even The Hill couldn't get me in."

The Hill Museum and Manuscript Library funded Brother Makarios' time in Mardin in central Minnesota in America. Rather pathetic, Sofia thought, if even The Hill couldn't get a renowned scholar like Mac onto Agio Óros. At least he's the correct gender.

"You belong to the wrong church." Sofia laughed. "Convert, and they just might let you in."

"But not out." Makarios' dry wit crept toward anger. "Maybe you're taking the wrong tack. You're a brilliant and tenacious detective. You don't give up the hunt. Fight back."

Sofia sighed. "Fight who? Every university on the planet?"

"Maybe you don't belong in teaching, as gifted as you are, but rather somewhere like The Hill—a major archive, no tenure, minimal politics, or a Research Fellowship. Americans favor those."

"I assume The Hill doesn't have an opening?" Wouldn't Mac have said something already?

"No, luv. Even my funding is temporary. Maybe the Greek Patriarch could open doors for you."

"For a mediocre believer like me?" Sofia sighed. "But I've no doubt he's the poorest patriarch on the planet. Most of his churches are in war zones with a flood of refugees. Greek Orthodox money is sitting on Agio Óros, and they don't share. Never mind, funding a search for early Christian women is essentially non-existent. If I just knew a millionaire feminist."

"Maybe you do. Think. Fight back. Now is the time to get feisty and even brash. Do something brilliant and unexpected. What could you lose?"

Sofia groaned, "Maybe you're right."

"You know I am. Follow the money, Sofia. Donors love to see their names on important projects. And universities, always hungry for funding sources, open doors to people like you to help build their reputation and bring in scarce funds."

"Thanks, Mac. You'll hear from me very soon. *Avtío*."

She hung up the phone as she approached the plane's door. Makarios. *Blessed indeed*.

§

Sofia's flight touched down in Thessaloníki at 8:40 AM the following morning. She waited until most of her fellow passengers departed before exiting.

Entering the concourse, she smiled at the familiar sound of music—that odd combination of soulful, sorrowful strings mixed with disco issued from the loudspeakers. The guys in military garb serving as security seemed more concerned with sizing up the young women than any smuggling operations that might be unfolding before their eyes. She hated being gawked at like some prized catch soon to be someone's dinner.

Sofia claimed her suitcase and passed through the glass doorways into the softening sun. The dry, warm air smelled of pollution mixed with sea salt. Exhaustion from the exhilarating but strange, long weeks was taking its toll on her. She crossed toward the front of a long line of taxis whose drivers appeared busy chatting with one another.

Approaching the queue of taxis, she was surprised to see her cousin Takis, hands waiving at her. What was he doing here? She approached with nerves on alert, and before she could ask, he encircled her in a bear hug. She barely succeeded in maintaining a firm grip on her luggage.

"Ah, *mou oraios*. My favorite cousin, my beautiful cousin." Takis kissed both her cheeks, his trim beard soft.

Sofia loved his capacity to laugh and flirt simultaneously. "Don't misunderstand me, but what are you doing here? Is someone sick? Is there an emergency?" Exhaustion from the adrenaline rush of the past few weeks was beginning to wear her down.

Takis swung her suitcase into the trunk of a battered Mercedes. Sofia helped him place her rucksack and camera bag in the back seat. Sofia climbed into the passenger seat. "So, *mou oraios*, I take it that our beloved Aunt Christina hasn't spoken to you yet."

"No. Is something wrong?" She reached for the seatbelt and remembered that Takis' car didn't have one.

Her cousin glanced her way, his expression awash with consternation. "No fretting, Sof. But she's called a family gathering. Just about everyone will be there." He started the car and backed out. "How did your adventure in Turkey go? Find Noah's boat yet?"

Smiling, "Takis, you've always been one of my greatest fans. Even if you don't understand what I do."

"What's to understand? The women in my family specialize in dusty old stuff I don't get. Not a useful politician among you!"

Takis had maneuvered the old car onto the four-lane roadway that curved along the Gulf of Thessaloníki, heading northwesterly into the city. To Greeks, driving was a sport. The Mercedes whipped in and out of lanes, accelerator to the floor.

"So true. Or, better yet, banking."

They both moaned, chuckled, and then sat in silence, each savoring their thoughts. Sofia couldn't stop thinking about Adélie. Theirs was supposed to be a dusty, boring profession, but civil wars and greedy, powerful people have turned them into daring adventurers trying to salvage the memory of ancient cultures.

"So, Takis, will everyone be at this family meeting?"

"Wouldn't be a valid family meeting if we weren't all there to fight and bicker in proper Greek fashion."

Sofia wished she'd inherited one of her cousin's "laid back" genes. "Important enough to entice you from Ouranoúpoli?"

"Apparently. But then you know how I love being in the company of beautiful women."

Sofia nearly fell into an exhausted sleep until she felt the pull of the car as Takis whipped into the roundabout and shot off to their right toward the hills above the city. The air had become dense with pollution, so she rolled her window up again. They were passing by the Kalamariá district. The university lay just beyond. Traffic was heavy. Horns blared. Takis expertly avoided hitting anyone while rarely slowing down. They started the ascent, the road curving sharply in a series of switchbacks. The homes grew larger with abundant gardens.

Finally, the car crested the hill on a curve, bearing right. Slowing, they turned into the driveway. Fatigue from harried last-minute preparations and enduring the bombing had caught up with her. Sighing, she wondered if she could pull herself out of the car and walk into the house.

Sofia sat and looked—hewed stone, three stories high, with terra-cotta tiles on the roof. Stone chimneys graced each end of the house. On each level were porches that maximized the view of the distant waters and mountains. Meticulously kept gardens wrapped around the house. Queen Alexandra, the charcoal cat that ruled the roost, stretched out on this moment's throne—an elevated hump in the stone fence. This had been home since her parents were killed in a car bombing in Beirut, Lebanon, where her father served as ambassador.

Sofia slowly climbed out of the car, eyes blurred from exhaustion and dehydration. Her cousin was already carrying her suitcase into the entryway. His footsteps echoed on the wood floors.

Trailing him, gripping her carry-on, and overwhelmed with exhaustion, Sofia trudged up the stairs, uncertain if she could reach her bedroom above.

Three

THESSALONÍKI, GREECE

Sofia awoke with a shudder and caught her breath. Her legs were tangled in her sheets, her skin clammy. Her heart pounded. Another nightmare that left her exhausted, as if she'd been pulling an all-nighter. She had been mostly free of the nightmares. Until Mor Gabriel. She had never told Mac or their colleagues what she'd been enduring there. She knew the bombing might stir up her past. The possibility of unearthing more of Deacon Olympias' letters was worth bearing the nightmares.

The sun's rays washed her bedroom with vibrant crimson and tangerine light. Stretching like Queen Alexandra and breathing deep to calm her nerves, she listened to the melodies of the choir of birds. What will she do now? She wasn't surprised at the content of the letter. It just made her situation more real. She heard the voice of her aunt speaking to someone. The phone? A neighbor? Turning onto her side, she looked out the window. The sun's rays cast long shadows through the trees. She rolled out of bed, threw on her cotton wrap, and looked for her aunt.

She found Christina on the veranda, taking advantage of the cool morning to tend to her flowerpots. Sofia was always amazed at her aunt's ability to entice her flowers into overflowing abundance. Vibrant red and yellow geraniums and nasturtiums, violet fuchsias, and red dahlias burst forth with life and color, a talent Sofia didn't share. She gazed at Mount Olympus with its dusting of snow on its peak. The mountain of the gods stood in the distance, south and slightly west.

"*Kaliméra*. Join me for some coffee?"

Christina glanced her way and then turned fully toward her. "Sofia, dear, you don't look well. Did you pick up a bug in Turkey?"

"No, I was careful as usual."

"Your face is clammy."

Sofia grimaced. "My nightmares have returned. The bombing we endured at Mor Gabriel stirred up bad memories. A colleague, Adélie, has been in Aleppo, and the bombing has begun. I cannot get through to her on the phone. I don't know what's happening."

Her aunt brushed her cheek the way she did whenever Sofia's nightmares returned. "Was going there a mistake?"

Sofia sighed. "No. I finally found my first piece of Olympias' letters."

Christina grinned. "Tell me all about it, but first, get us each some coffee."

Before turning toward the kitchen, Sofia asked, "So you're not going to tell me what this family meeting is about?" The last family gathering was after her uncle's cancer diagnosis.

Christina turned to answer. "As I said last night, I want all the family present."

Sofia's gut clenched. "Your health?"

"Sofia, dear, you worry too much. I'm in perfect health," her aunt returned to her gardening, "for a woman of my years."

Sofia felt the familiar twisty feeling in her chest. So much hitting her all at once. Entering the kitchen, she ground coffee beans with cardamom and set up the coffee maker on the gas stove. For a woman of her years? What was that supposed to mean? Finding pastries, she set them on the tray alongside porcelain cups and plates. Adding fresh fruit and thick homemade *yaourti*, she brought the tray out and put it carefully on the table. Returning, she poured two steaming cups of coffee.

Christina returned and settled down at the table.

Sofia savored her first sip of the ebony coffee and began. "Brother Makarios has been overseeing the digitizing of Mor Gabriel's library when he noticed some odd, unbound sheaves among the manuscripts. He called me when he began examining them. That's why I flew out right away. He was able to offer me an airline ticket." Broke, Sofia knew she couldn't have gone otherwise. "I believe this is a portion of one of Olympias' letters. And I know the rest are out there somewhere. Maybe no one recognizes what they have in their collection. Maybe these letters are being intentionally hidden away."

"I'm excited for you, dear," Christina said. "But why ever would an institution intentionally hide Olympias' letters? She's venerated."

Sofia broke open a fig. "I know. Maybe they're sitting in a basement somewhere, long forgotten as unwanted junk. More likely, an illicit collector has them, which means someone knew what they were selling on the black market."

"I'm afraid this is a real possibility. Our heritage has been disappearing into private collections. And now, I'm afraid you're facing some major challenges with all this political turmoil."

Sofia watched Queen Alexandra perform her morning ablutions as she took another deep sip of the coffee. She wondered if this region would ever know peace. "I was able to bring home scrapings of ink and vellum fibers. Any chance you know a lab that would test these for me? For free?"

Sofia thought she saw her aunt cringe. Or was it just the piercing sun in her eyes?

"I'll do what I can, dear. The Abbot is wise to move his library into the mountains. I've spent most of my working life dealing with politicians and defending antiquities from wealthy, powerful people."

Sofia shifted in her chair, trying to keep the sun's rays out of her eyes. "I'll be calling Mac tonight. I don't know how much longer he'll be allowed to remain at Mor Gabriel."

"He needs to be safe. Encourage him to leave." Queen Alexandra leaped onto her aunt's lap. "What's happening here is tragic. Greece cannot afford to properly care for the swarm of migrants arriving daily. Yet, we cannot ignore them. I'll contact the Foreign Ministry to see what they can tell me about Aleppo and where your friend, Adélie, may be."

Sofia smiled. "That would be wonderful. She's with the Hill Museum and Manuscript Library in America."

"Oh, they're quite well known in this region. It should be easy to get accurate information."

Sofia's mind wandered. Mor Gabriel. Finding evidence of Deacon Olympias' letters. Her friend Adélie's precarious situation. She looks forward to seeing the slides Adélie's team created. But now what?

"Dear, where are you?"

Sofia was jolted back to the present. "Oh, I'm sorry Christina. Just thinking." Queen Alexandra swatted at some imaginary enemy. "You probably saw that I received a letter from the university. I have no classes for the fall. Lower student enrollment and all." For too long now, she has battled against discouragement.

Christina stroked the Queen's fur. "I'm so sorry, but I'm not surprised. Unfortunately, our biggest export right now is our young people. They're leaving in droves seeking employment wherever they can find it." Her aunt's voice grew stronger, revealing a depth of passion. "A tragic loss for us. Italy and Spain are in the same situation."

"I hate all this." Sofia refilled their coffee cups. "I need to figure out what I'm going to do now." Sofia sighed again. "There are no teaching positions anywhere. Literally nothing posted on the websites." She'd followed the job postings for university teaching positions in her field since she was awarded her doctorate. "Since I graduated, there've been few openings anywhere. Professors aren't retiring or, when they do, their positions aren't being filled."

"Well, then, you're going to create your own path."

Sofia shuddered. "That's exactly what Brother Makarios told me, but I don't know how to proceed."

"Be bold, Sofia. Think outside the box." Her aunt stood, and an indignant Queen Alexandra jumped off and searched for a new throne. "I'd better clean up. I'm heading to the museum. I've got another finance meeting to endure." Christina sighed, draining her coffee cup. "We face brutal cuts. I don't know why we don't shutter all the museums and post ruthless guards. I fear our government is sinking so low, with all these austerity measures they're inflicting on us, that they're planning to sell our heritage to resolve their debt problems."

"Oh, Christina. I didn't realize."

"No reason you should. But don't you dare let Greek insanity discourage you. You listen to that British friend of yours and do something bold."

§

How might she trace where the Deacon Olympias piece came from? Where might the rest of her letters be hiding? Ink and vellum fiber testing will only give her limited data. Her old haunt at the university's rare book collection and archives would be her first destination, where she would develop a concise plan of attack.

Donning jeans and a loose knit top, Sofia slipped out the front door, rucksack in hand, and departed in the old Mercedes. She enjoyed the feel of its powerful engine, the smooth drive, and the gears shifting. Cousin Takis was a genius with engines. Sofia attacked the curves downhill as she headed into town.

She parked at a creative angle near the stadium and, remembering the archivist's penchant for sweets, swung by a bakery and picked up some Melomakarona, his favorite honey cookie, and Skopelitiki tiropita, a cheese-filled pastry. Paying, she started into the bright sun, crossed the street, and walked across the green toward the library complex.

Sofia approached security. The guard was napping, feet on the table and a monitor screen ignored. "I have an appointment with Dottore Hatzidakis."

The guard grunted and snorted. Apparently, he was still more asleep than awake. Sofia reached through the window and shook his calf. Why did universities and museums always manage to hire lazy idiots for security? No wonder the black market was thriving.

He stood, stretched, and rubbed the sleep from his eyes. "Your student identity card?"

Lazy guards again? "I'm no longer a student here." A knot dug into the back of her throat. She struggled to keep her anger at bay. "As I said, I have an appointment. Call down."

"Who was that?" Confusion strangled his voice.

"Dottore Hatzidakis."

"Your university identification," he demanded again. He gazed at her as he took a slow drag on his cigarette.

"I don't have any. Call down." Sofia felt her neck warm.

The guard began massaging his fingers with his thumb, the Mediterranean signal for an expected bribe.

Sofia shook her head, rejecting his silent demand.

The guard shrugged, sat back in his chair, plopped his feet on the table, and resumed his morning nap. Setting her pastry box down, Sofia pulled out her digital camera and began shooting pictures of the guard slumped in his chair with a cigarette dangling from his mouth. He shot back up out of his chair and reached for her camera. Sofia caught his wrist in a vise grip. Shock registered across his face.

Smiling as if it was all a joke, he called down to the archivist's office, then quickly unbolted the door and waived Sofia through.

Bless Takis. Bless his tender heart for insisting she learn self-defense. One floor down was the office of the head archivist, known fondly as "the Master of the Dungeon." Her gift of pastries was met by a smile.

"Dottore Papandréou, our illustrious scholar!" Georgios Hatzidakis was blessed with wisps of curly hair and a well-endowed mustache. His ample girth contained a history of fine food and good wine. She knew he was a talented chef as she had enjoyed some of his culinary explorations during her graduate school years. The archivist enjoyed the company of women. And intelligent women posed no threat to him.

Hatzidakis kissed her on each cheek. "You are ravishingly beautiful as always."

Laughing, she responded. "Liar. But I like your lies." They briefly caught up on their lives, including her lack of employment. She sat across from his ancient, battered desk piled with books, papers, and what looked like ledgers. His bookcases, as always, were overflowing with more books and stacks of documents.

Hatzidakis said. "Mor Gabriel? Deacon Olympias? Sounds intriguing. And to think your obsession is showing promise."

She described to him the Armenian and Syriac manuscripts found at Mor Gabriel. "I need to access some databases to identify where this piece of her letter might've come from and where more might be located." The archivist let out a sigh. He knew as well as Sofia that John Chrysostom's letters survived, although not the originals, but not Olympias's.

Sofia shifted in her chair and moved her rucksack away from the door. "How is the digitizing project going on Agio Óros?

"Moving at glacial speed. You know these matters can't be rushed. And yet we anticipate a funding cut soon."

Sofia was surprised to hear this. "But I thought you had big money behind this? Major donors like the Getty in Los Angeles and the Gates Foundation."

"Yes, but we're in such politically charged times. Donors are proving nervous."

"Why? They're not the ones digitizing with bullets flying overhead. We are." Sofia took a deep breath when she realized she was nearly shouting. Her gut twisted in angry knots at all the doors closing in her life. "I'm sorry, Hatzidakis. We both know with *Daesh* and the growing civil war in Syria that this work is more important than ever." She crossed her legs, trying to calm herself. She hadn't quite shaken off the nightmare yet. "Which monasteries are your people working in right now?"

His chair whined as he shifted forward. "We've focused primarily on Megístis Lávras and Simonópetra." The archivist smiled. "We've been enjoying down-right warm relations with many of the monks.

My men, sorry, Sofia, but you know their policy, are allowed entry to their libraries and photograph whatever we want."

"I suppose you would've told me if they uncovered a huge cache of ancient scrolls." Sofia was both mildly sarcastic and hopeful.

"None that they've reported. But we're funded to digitize the illuminated manuscripts only." Hatzidakis seemed to be studying her, but she recognized the look. He was thinking. "There's one monk on the Holy Mountain who might be able to help you. A Father Theodor. One of the more open-minded and better-educated monks there." His chair creaked as he shifted his weight. "An Oxford man. Lives in a monastery called Hagia Theotokos. Now his is a library you'd be interested in. He specializes in older liturgical texts but complains about a backlog of uncatalogued items."

Sofia's heart thumped. "That's exactly what makes me crazy about Agio Óros. Maybe this Father Theodor is an exception, but I've long heard they disdain university education. So how many precious manuscripts are shoved into corners and closets?" She needed to catch her breath.

"That's been shifting in the last few years. New monks are arriving there with advanced degrees and shaking things up on our holy mountain." The archivist had turned and rifled through a stack of papers. "Yes, here it is." He looked up at Sofia, holding what appeared to be a letter in his hand. "Father Theodor had written asking about resources for handling odds and ends in the cave below his library. Doesn't say what kinds of odds and ends. I hadn't gotten around to asking any of our graduate students. Frankly, I expect budget cuts to be announced any day, so I cannot be of assistance. Too bad. He's too frail to be clambering down there. Let me write Father Theodor and see if he recalls seeing these letters among his odds and ends."

"This is crazy." Sofia held back tears of frustration. "You know I'm one of the most qualified scholars that could work in those libraries. To assist Father Theodor. I'd die for the opportunity to go there."

"Don't even think of it!" His gaze was stern.

Four

UNIVERSITY OF THESSALONÍKI, GREECE

Sofia slammed the door behind her. Should she? Wouldn't that rock Hatzidakis's stuffy demeanor?

Heading toward the basement where the archives and rare book collection were located, she was to meet a graduate student who would get her in. Turned out to be one of her former students. "Mariam?" The two women hugged and briefly caught up on their lives as they descended into the basement. Sofia noticed that Mariam was still favoring the brightly colored sandals her mother sent from Addis Ababa, the medallions tinkling as Mariam descended the stairs. And her dusty rose tunic set off her dark caramel skin.

"You've kept up on your study of Ge'ez?" Sofia asked.

"Yes, and thanks for connecting me with Doctor Gessesse. He's been a great teacher.

After you, that is." Her laugh was a lilt. "And as you insisted, I've been scouring around for texts written by women in Ge'ez. Gessesse has been a sounding board for me."

"He's been a great help to me as well. Those damnable verb tenses hide whether the scribe or the author was male or female."

The two women passed through a door, down another set of stairs, and through a hefty steel-barred door, which Mariam closed and re-bolted after the pair passed through.

"Fortunately, Doctor Gessesse is open to the possibility of women as authors or scribes,"

Mariam said.

"I would've warned you if he wasn't."

The two women laughed.

"I hope to travel to The Hill to work with him in person. I've applied for a Fellowship there," Mariam said.

Sofia smiled at the news. The women entered a practical room with four workstations and a deep cavern filled with stacks of cranking shelving units, all heat and moisture-controlled. The lights emitted a soft buzz.

Mariam turned toward Sofia. "So, what brings you here today?"

"I'm following up on what we found at Mor Gabriel. We found a piece of a letter written by Deacon Olympias to John Chrysostom."

"Wow. Olympias. All the power to you. You're really tearing down walls for us women."

Sofia blushed.

Mariam pointed to another table. "I'm working here if you need anything. Or help with a search."

Setting up her laptop, Sofia logged in with the password Hatzidakis had provided. She adjusted the lamp and searched for recent entries in the archival database. Her screen flooded with files from the work on Agio Óros. Curious, she clicked on several entries from Megístis Lávras and Hagia Theotokos. The images were stunning. Many still bore vibrant colors—blues from Lapis Lazuli, reds from Vermillion, deep royal purples from a blend of Lapis Lazuli, Vermillion, and red wine, with delicate gold leafing. The manuscripts were from Ethiopia, Coptic Egypt, Syria, and Armenia. Like many illuminations from the Middle East, these were dense with imagery. Her friends from the West would have referred to them as more like folk art. Not the stiff and formal lines of manuscripts in the West. These tell complete stories. She focused the computer screen on one image from an Armenian manuscript—the left page portrayed the Annunciation, where the Archangel tells Mary that she will bear the Son of God. On the right, it speaks of the Nativity, the birth of Jesus.

Mostly she gazed upon assorted liturgical texts used for church services that dated much more recently, twelfth-century onward. Her doctoral dissertation had focused on women as liturgical leaders in the early Christian Church, so none of these, while lovely to gaze upon, would ever have aided her research. But Sofia made a mental note that one day she'd study these to see if the echo of a woman's voice might be contained here. One of her colleagues scrutinized early medieval liturgical texts, some of which she had established as being from women's monasteries in England, unpacking the liturgical leadership abbesses exercised. Maybe here as well.

"If you have time, I'd love your help."

Mariam looked her way.

"I'm looking for any recently digitized tomes or listings in their catalog. But especially individual sheaves. Anything Armenian or early Syriac."

"Sounds grand. How should we split this?"

Sofia smiled. "Thanks. Maybe you take the Balkan Peninsula and Bulgaria. I'll pursue Armenia, Azerbaijan, Eastern Turkey, and Syria. I won't be surprised if some libraries don't understand what they're holding.

Keys pounded away for nearly an hour when Mariam piped up. "I see some newly digitized tomes in Bosnia-Herzegovina and Albania. Some entries from Belarus in Cyrillic. But it appears to be all local stuff."

Sofia turned toward Mariam. "I'm only finding entries for the second millennium. None of the eastern Turkish or Armenian libraries list older or rare manuscripts. But then most of the universities were founded in the last few decades."

How would we tell if they're written by women?"

Let me know if you find anything in the first millennium. As I've taught you, we'd have to examine the text in person, or a very clear digitized image, to look for clues."

Yes, I remember. You showed us many examples of texts assumed to be written by men but were recently proven to be written by women."

"And with Ge'ez—when you are awarded that research fellowship with Gessesse—study the verbs and look for evidence of tampering."

"Like scraping off the earlier lettering and replacing it with newer ink." Mariam smiled and turned back to her computer.

Sofia stretched to ease the knot between her shoulders and resumed her search. She entered the sites for the Armenian Patriarch, His Holiness Torkom Manoogian, and the Gulbenkian Library in Jerusalem.

Sofia let out a soft cheer. "Seems the Gulbenkian holds some unidentified early sheaves." She sighed. "Well, another letter I'll need to write to make my requests. And more pastries for the Master of the Dungeon." The two women chuckled. Maybe Christina knew someone at the Greek Patriarch's office who might write a letter on her behalf besides Hatzidakis. Another delay. She made notations in her notebook of where to send letters of request.

Sofia took a deep breath. A low-grade headache was emerging. She knew from experience to never leave a stone unturned, especially with the abundance of rocks they enjoyed here in drought-stricken Greece. But, given the Armenian genocide and Kaiser Wilhelm's penchant for theft (never mind that the Soviet Union would have stolen anything that Germany hadn't already taken), she wasn't hopeful that the Gulbenkian held much that predated the Twentieth century.

Berlin.

Where would Kaiser Wilhelm's people have stashed the contents of any libraries they had looted? She shifted her focus to the databases in and near Berlin—universities, museums, and private research institutes. She clicked on the site for the Königliche Museen zu Berlin and the Royal Museums and searched for manuscripts. She knew this was a long shot, as too much had disappeared during and shortly after World War II. Most had never resurfaced. She sent an introductory email to the Kultural Direcktor seeking information on any manuscript holdings of the first millennium, especially parchment pieces.

But how to find the companion pieces to what Mac uncovered in Mardin? She knew the answer. Despite all the great ways archeologists and papyrologists utilized computers, she would need to contact every lab and talk to its director. But first, she needed the lab results from Istanbul. This meant more waiting, and Sofia was less patient with waiting, especially given her status as "unemployed" in a market allegedly saturated with wannabe professors.

Sofia asked Mariam, "Do you know any men digitizing manuscripts on Mount Athos?"

"One or two of my classmates are spending the summer break working there, but I hear most of the grad students are from Athens. We're ignored here in the north."

"And you and I cannot enter despite impeccable credentials." Words that curdled in her throat.

Mariam frowned. "Because we're women. There must be some way to get around that stumbling block."

"This is so frustrating, Mariam. I cannot enter Mount Athos, but first-year graduate students of the male persuasion can. They don't know what to look for, so my asking for their help is useless."

Mariam grimaced. "I hear this may be the last summer of funding anyway."

Leaning back in her chair, Sofia envisioned herself slipping—with an invisibility cloak—onto Agio Óros. That made her smile. The question was whether she was gutsy enough to counter her resentment and do something about it. Her aunt was right. Sofia spent too much time being angry. Better to channel that energy into something constructive.

Reaching for the phone, Sofia called Hatzidakis and asked if she might have Father Theodor's address. Certainly, this librarian would be willing to receive a letter from a woman, wouldn't he? Hatzidakis countered, after a deep and dramatic sigh, with an offer to include her letter with his.

Sofia entered her password into The Hill's site and explored their Armenian manuscript collection. She was surprised at how many they had managed to digitize, along with helpful information on where the manuscripts had been found. Also, she noted some sixth-century gospels in Syriac. Their earliest Armenian manuscripts date to the thirteenth century. However, the site reminded her that there was an Armenian Patriarchate in Istanbul. She googled and wrote his contact information in her notebook of growing contacts she would need to make. More signatures from the Master meant more pastries to keep him signing away.

Sofia sent an email to the director of The Hill, one Father Simon, asking about the status and welfare of Adélie and her team working in

Aleppo. Her friend's welfare weighed on her. And again, she had to wait for a response.

How might she access records at The Vatican Libraries? Rumor was that they had hordes of uncatalogued materials. Anything of Olympias they might not be aware of?

Closing her eyes and taking deep breaths, she tried a free-floating meditation exercise to de-cramp her brain. Then she remembered. Her doctoral dissertation advisor was one of her toughest and most liberating professors at the Louvain in Belgium. Despite being an American, she had heard that Sister Meg had become abbess of an old monastery in Rome. She stood and began packing her gear. What was the name of the monastery?

"Mariam, I need to leave now. Let me know if you have time to continue your search and if you find anything. And please, join my family for dinner on Sunday. We're rather rambunctious. I think you'd enjoy them."

When she got home, she would locate Sister Meg and place a call to her, who might be able to help her access the Vatican Library. Tomorrow morning, she would enter her account at the British Library and the Bodleian at Oxford, when her brain was fresh, and begin exploring any recent additions the British might be holding.

She climbed the stairs to the archivist's office. "Hatzidakis?"

The archivist looked up from a large book with fine handwriting, glasses askew. "Find anything useful?"

"Yes and no. I'll bring that letter for Father Theodor tomorrow. I cannot fathom that this might be the last summer the digitizing will continue on Agio Óros."

He sighed. "We'll certainly be one of the first programs shut down once austerity measures are agreed upon."

Doors slamming again.

"Surely the universities will stay open."

Stress and concern swept across his face.

"I expect salaries to be slashed for those not outright dismissed. And tuition will double and triple. The inevitable riots have begun with a quarter or more of our young people underemployed. These precious manuscripts are now more vulnerable to the black market than ever."

Her gut wrenched.

FIVE

THESSALONÍKI

Sofia thought about one of the tenets preached in her early graduate school days by her first Patristics professor, Sister Meg. *When searching original sources, if you presume women are present, you will begin to see them.* Remove the cataracts of patriarchy. Her professor's specialty had been fourth-century Makrina the Younger from Asia Minor, establishing once and for all that this Makrina founded Eastern Orthodox monasticism and not her younger brothers, Basil and Gregory, who got all the credit. Even the leadership of the Orthodox world now acknowledged this truth.

The Abbey's website gave the schedule for prayers and Mass, so 9 am seemed an excellent time to reach her former professor. Sofia dialed the number she'd been given for the Abbey of Santa Cecilia in Rome, which appeared on the map close to Vatican City. She gazed out over Thessaloníki while listening to the ringtone. A woman answered, and Sofia asked for Sister Meg.

"Mother Abbess?"

Oops, she hoped she hadn't already offended someone. "Yes, Grazie. Abbess Meg."

"*Un momento*."

Soon, she heard a familiar voice, strong as ever. How old was Sister Meg anyway? Sofia greeted her professor and reminded the nun who she was.

"Sofia Papandréou? Rock star of the Patristics world?"

Sofia chuckled and felt a warmth sweep across her heart. "I wasn't sure you'd remember me, given all your students over the years."

"Forget? You were one of the few who took my exhortations seriously. I've enjoyed your publications and heard rumors of your adventures. Quite the risk you took in the Balkans. Kruševac, wasn't it?"

"Yes, but I'm surprised that you know about that."

The two women caught up on colleagues and acquaintances. Sofia learned that Sister Meg had been marked for assassination by gangs in Chiapas, Mexico, for her advocacy work on behalf of the indigenous whose land was being stolen from them. Community leaders and bishops urged her to save her life and leave. Not wanting to be a further flashpoint in the conflict, Sister Meg agreed. Soon, she found herself in Rome and in the shadow of the Vatican. Not what she had expected.

A conflicting mixture of pride and anger emerged. Good for Sister Meg. Leaving the classroom to work with the poor. Where did she find the courage to stand up to powerful corporations like that? And face down guns? How do corporations justify stealing land from ancient peoples anyway? She shifted and refocused her attention.

"So, enough of me. I'm delighted to hear from you, Sofia, but what's happening?"

"A colleague called me to Mor Gabriel in southern Turkey. He found a parchment piece that he thought might be part of one of

Deacon Olympias' letters." Her foot tapped the floor, dissipating her excess energy.

"Really?" the nun interrupted with clear excitement. "Any possibility that this will prove true?"

Sofia laughed. "Well, I'm on the hunt now. My first examination says 'yes', but you know how it goes. We must wait for testing in Istanbul and begin a new search of parchment pieces with similar ink and vellum. Unfortunately, the most likely places where the rest of her letters might be are now caught in a civil war or on Mount Athos."

The nun sighed. "The news from Syria and Iraq is tragic for the people and the libraries. News around here is that the Antiquities Authorities are overwhelmed and underfunded. Ugly times, Sofia."

"I'm awaiting news on a friend working in Aleppo. I'm concerned for her."

"Oh, my."

"I know. Anyway, I hope to get into the Vatican Libraries. Consult with one of the curators. Might you help me get the proper papers to get in?"

"Yes, Sofia. And you'll stay here with us. But I must warn you. Despite the best efforts of the Library of Congress and the British Library, the Vatican Libraries are still about eight years behind on cataloging. I suspect they don't know what is down in the deepest part of the dungeons. And now the staff is battling mold."

"And that's exactly what I want to look at." Sofia's pulse quickened. "Any chance they'd let me into the deepest dungeons there?"

Sister Meg chuckled. "I'll put in the request, but first, I'll need to educate you on Roman ways. Once you know when you'll arrive, I'll plan for you to take the proper personnel out for a very long and expensive dinner where you'll discuss your interests and how they support the mission of the Vatican Libraries. Plan on doing this several times, depending on how deep into the dungeon you hope to go and how long your research will keep you here. I'll coach you in advance and join you to ensure you're successful in establishing the proper relationships that will get you what you seek."

She thought this a strange requirement. Beer at a local pub usually opened doors wherever Sofia had worked. "How expensive?" *How is she supposed to afford all this?*

"Expensive. But it's your best chance at getting into the uncatalogued dungeons. It's the Roman way. All about relationships. Certainly contradicts my American practicality."

Sister Meg promised to get back to Sofia as soon as she made plans with a certain Cardinal.

Sofia stared into the distance, absently petting Queen Alexandria. *Doors open as money dries up. How does she fund all this?*

§

Sofia had been soaking in a steaming bath, bubbles to her chin, in a clawed foot bathtub, when she heard voices echoing in the hallway. "Takis? Is that you?"

Takis poked his head through the doorway, a foolish grin awash his face. "Ah, is this our very own Indiana Jones?"

Sofia threw a bar of soap his way, missing his ducking head. "Thanks for coming you rascal. I'll be downstairs shortly."

Takis laughed and departed.

Sofia dried off, threw on some clothes, and descended the staircase as she ran her fingers through her hair. She found her cousin sitting at a laptop, scouring news headlines.

Takis looked at her with an expression of consternation mixed with humor. "Cousin, I haven't seen you this excitable since we got caught exploring our grandfather's office. What gives?"

Sofia grimaced. How were they to know that their grandfather's safe, too attractive for a pair of 10-year-olds to resist, contained politically explosive material? "It's that favor I need to ask of you."

"So, you need another office broken into? I'm not sure my safe-cracking skills have improved since our grandfather nailed us but good."

"Mine, neither." Laughing, Sofia slipped out of the room and returned with two chilled beers, handing one to her cousin. They clinked bottles.

She took a long pull. "Agio Óros." There, she said it. "I need your help slipping onto Mount Athos." She gazed at her cousin, trying to anticipate his reaction. His eyebrows raised, and a slow grin emerged.

"Agio Óros. The Holy Mountain, where few are permitted to enter? Not your popular vacation spot. I understand the Greek Isles are lovely this time of year," Takis dead-panned.

"I'm serious. Everyone keeps telling me to do something bold and original, to strike out on my own. Well, this is it. My way forward is on Mount Athos."

"Just what do you expect us to do there?"

She looked at her cousin in disbelief and then remembered that he never attended university, claiming a deathly allergy to books. "I'm sorry, Takis. I get so wrapped up in my work that I forget that most people don't know what I'm talking about."

The old clock tolled 8 pm. They both turned when they heard the thud of the Queen jumping down from some high perch. She continued. "Every monastery on Agio Óros has a library; most are seven hundred to a thousand years old. My colleagues want to gawk at medieval books, which are mostly illuminated. Gorgeous pictures. These I'm not interested in."

"No? They must be worth piles of euros."

Why, she wondered, would money decide what books a scholar wanted to examine? Except that her cousin doesn't share her passion for manuscripts. "Monetary value has nothing to do with scholarship. I hear the black market can be ruthless. But what I want, what I need, is to look at their oldest stuff, which most scholars either don't realize is stashed somewhere in the libraries or aren't permitted to see."

"Huh?"

Sofia heard her aunt speaking with someone out in her backyard. Sofia didn't want their aunt to know of her plans, at least until her return from Agio Óros. She motioned for Takis to join her in her workspace in the basement. She noticed his goofy grin as they took the steep, winding stairs.

Settled again, she resumed. "The oldest stuff is what I specialize in. Parchments and early codices. Most men who've been able to get into their libraries want to see the newer books. I believe, no, I know that some of those old parchments that the monks don't care about are the works of women important in early Christianity. They're hiding them, or they just don't care."

"Okay?" He obviously was trying to track what she was saying.

"I did my doctoral dissertation on women as liturgical leaders in the early Christian church. But one eluded me. Her name was Olympias, a member of the Imperial family. In fact, her monastery is located underneath Hagia Sophia, the famous church in Istanbul. She was good friends with a famous bishop named John Chrysostom—."

Takis grinned. "*Golden Tongue*?"

She laughed. "Yes, you're right. Chrysostom meant Golden Tongue. Just like you, he could sell old cars to a used car dealer."

Takis smiled, shifting in his chair. He took a swig from the bottle.

"He was a famous preacher who got into trouble with the emperor and was sent into exile around 404 CE."

"In trouble with an emperor. I like him already."

"Try this one: *Do you pay such honor to your excrements as to receive them into a silver chamber pot when another man made in the image of God is perishing in the cold?*"

Takis whistled.

Sofia smiled. "Chrysostom tended to be blunt. He had publicly denounced their corruption. Apparently, the Emperor and his family didn't appreciate the exposure of their financial irregularities, sexual promiscuity, political assassinations, and other intrigues being brought out into the public realm and condemned. We still have copies of John's letters to Olympias, but no one has ever been able to locate her letters to John. I'm convinced they're sitting on Mount Athos."

"Your friends told you this?"

He seemed perplexed. She didn't want to lose his attention. Or his interest. She really needed his help.

"No. Well, yes. But no." Why was she stumbling around for words? "I've got good descriptions of what my colleagues have seen there and what they were allowed to handle. But mostly, they tell me what they weren't allowed to see. Doors to rooms closed to them. I think they're vast rooms of rolled parchments."

"And you want me to steal them?"

"No, Takis." She laughed then remembered that was the second time someone had thought this of her this week. "I need to slip onto Agio Óros and enter a couple of monasteries. Two, maybe three at most. I already have some idea of who is holding what. We'd go in, and I'd take digital photos of what I needed. Just a couple of monasteries."

They gazed at each other in silence. She had always been able to read Takis' expressions, and he had hers. But this time, the silence dipped deeper than ever before. Then she watched as his body shook with silent laughter. She waited him out.

"*Mou oraios*. You are a beautiful, sensual woman. Greek Goddess doesn't do you justice. Has no one reminded you of this lately?"

She knew he meant this as a compliment, but her back stiffened anyway. Reminders of her alleged beauty infuriated her because her looks were often used to marginalize her. Apparently, no serious scholar was supposed to be pretty.

Takis' voice softened. "Sofia, I am thinking of the monks on Agio Óros. Even the old ones will notice that you're a woman. And beautiful."

Sofia felt her face warm. She blushed easily, she knew. She stood, paced the room, and then impulsively kicked a floor pillow. "Damn it, Takis. It's hard being a woman in a world that treats us like playthings. Objects. I'm every bit the scholar as any guy who has a better chance to visit those libraries. Better than most. Sometimes I feel cursed."

The silence deepened between them. Takis shifted in his chair. "Sofia, has someone hurt you? You seem upset."

"I'm rarely taken seriously here in Greece. Men's eyes roaming where I don't want them to. Few women are given permanent positions. Look at what happened to Aunt Christina. My friends are right. I must forge my own path and forget the universities. And my path leads through Agio Óros. I'm only asking you to go with me. I'll figure out how to get into those libraries and do my work. Just a few days. A week at the most."

Takis remained silent. She knew he was thinking.

"Why don't these guys help you? Seems as if they could photograph whatever you wanted."

She felt the flush of anger on her cheeks. "I'm the one who knows what to look for. Besides, if they found something, they'd publish it themselves and take all the credit."

"Sounds selfish."

"Scholars are no better than other people. Lots of competition for very few jobs. And it's only getting worse."

"Sorry to hear that. I'm not sure that I want to help you. I'd hate to see you disappointed when we're arrested our first day there. The monks are protective of their privacy. Few get onto Agio Óros. It's a fortress. Visitor passes take months to obtain, and those passes aren't necessarily honored. And how would you get into the libraries? Break in?"

"If I need to. I figure I'd dress like a guy, cut my hair, wear a cap, do whatever. Mostly, I'd avoid everyone and let you deal with the monks."

Takis' eyes gleamed with humor. "I can only do so much praying. And I'm not ready to make a good confession yet."

"I'll lend you a few of my sins. Just change the names to protect the innocent."

"Well, that's generous of you. Give me your list, and I'll pick the ones I want to use."

Sofia elbowed him. "Just tell them you're on pilgrimage and want to pray in their chapel. I'd think they'd have stunning icons."

"We have beautiful icons right here."

She was getting frustrated with him. "Oh, Takis. Mostly, you'd divert their attention if necessary. Talk to them or something. It would just be for a few days." Was he teasing her or resisting her? "If you don't feel up to the task, I'll go alone."

Six

T HESSALONÍKI

Sofia sat on the veranda cursing softly as she read the newspaper. Considering the recent financial meltdown and Greece's precarious relationship with the European Union, local politicians finally took an acute interest in the suspicious real estate acquisitions by some monks of Mount Athos. Greeks had known for a decade that someone on Agio Óros had managed to swap relatively worthless real estate in the countryside for prime holdings in downtown Athens, most likely with the assistance of senior officials in the very conservative government.

So, it's true after all. Hell, throw the entire lot of bastards in prison. How dare they steal Greece blind while most pensioners were losing what little they had in retirement? Is Greece finding her spine? Or just fearing the loss of EU membership more than the wrath of greedy monks? Send them all to prison. For a very long stay.

Sofia pulled out her cell phone and punched the number for her cousin. She couldn't deny feeling relieved at the idea of the house staying in the family. That, and where would she move? And what would she do with all the books in her study, especially now that she's hopefully on the cusp of a significant discovery?

Her cousin finally answered. "*Kaliméra*."

"*Mou oraios*, how is my favorite archeologist?"

Was he teasing, or did Takis not know the difference? Did it matter? "Ready to surrender to my wishes?"

"Naw, but I've got some exciting news from Agio Óros. Made all the newspapers."

She could tell he was crunching on something. "So, you've read about the arrests? Will that interfere with our plans?"

Definitely an apple he was eating.

"Arrests?"

Sofia brought him up to date.

"Well, that's interesting. I thought my news was important."

"What's that?"

"I'm reading our local, small-town newspaper that proudly announced that the monks have allowed their first females onto Mount Athos in 800 years."

"What?" Jolted, Sofia began flipping hurriedly through her newspaper, nearly knocking her expresso over.

"Yes, indeed. Right there in bold newsprint." She heard a teasing edge to her cousin's voice.

"What happened? I heard nothing about this," she said, incredulous. She thought she heard her cousin taking a long draw of something. A cigarette? Finally, he replied, "Hens."

"Hens?"

"Yes. News services have announced that our progressive monks now allow hens." He sighed. "For the sake of eggs. Any other females are still barred."

Hens. How insulting. All this pigheadedness did not seem possible in this day and age. And whatever was she getting into? "Hens but not women. All the more reason you're going to help me get onto Mount Athos."

Takis chewed but otherwise was silent. Sofia stretched her hands to counteract her tendency to ball her fingers into fists.

He spoke while chewing. "I hadn't considered what the arrests might mean. Maybe more police presence on Agio Óros." She could hear him breathing. "Could be good. Could be bad. But Sof, I was serious about my concerns."

How would her cousin know about what a "normal" police presence on the Holy Mountain was? "Takis, do you know someone there?"

He finally answered. "*Mou oraios*, let's meet this evening to talk. You need to hear what I have to say, and if you still want to do something truly insane, even by our family's standards, then yes, I'll help."

She flipped off her phone, feeling exhilarated and hopeful yet guilty for keeping her cousin away from his auto repair business.

§

Sofia sat in her basement office, searching the university library and archive website. Fortunately, Hatzidakis had given her extended access. With the digitizing project on Agio Óros, someone had downloaded a detailed map of the Holy Mountain, including maps of the few monastic libraries in which the digitizing project was permitted to work. But no others. She sighed. While the files were downloading onto her laptop, she heard the side door close and the familiar footsteps of her cousin.

"Hi, Takis. Thanks for coming." He had crossed the room and sat next to her. She watched him study her large computer screen; his expression serious. Seeing his hair, with curls like hers, reminded her that she'd need a haircut, maybe in a way like the monks.

"*Mou oraios*, I hope you weren't planning on using that map."

"Well, ..."

"Trust me on this. The monks only let people see what they want them to see." He returned his gaze her way. "Sof, there isn't much that happens on Agio Óros that we don't hear about in Ouranoúpoli. Even my pious neighbors chatter away. Things are changing up there, and not all for the good. Some monks are getting mean and nasty, wantin' little to do with the rest of us."

Her stomach clenched. "I won't let them stop me."

"More is happening than what makes the newspapers. I hear that the number of military police has been increasing, and the monks are headed toward a civil war of their own. It's crazy." He shifted in his chair and gazed at her. "If we head up there, be prepared for failure. Plan on being discovered and turned over to the military police, who'll escort you back to Ouranoúpoli. Probably you won't be arrested." He chuckled. "You don't look like a criminal, just a nuisance."

He shifted again. "For reasons I'm not explaining, I won't deal with the military police there."

What an odd thing for her cousin to say. "What happened, Takis?"

"Never mind that. I do business with a few of the saner monks, rebuilding their truck's engines and all. Some monasteries seem determined to take over Agio Óros and throw all the other monks out. We could get caught in this."

Sofia rubbed her temples. "Weird, none of the grad students there have said anything."

"Did you ask them?"

Sofia caught her breath. No, she hadn't thought to talk to any of them. Then she admitted to herself that it was probably because she'd been so angry and envious of what the young men were allowed to do, and she could not. She'll make some contacts.

He continued. "But you seem determined in that Papandréou way. You wouldn't last a day on your own. If I take you, then you'll follow my instructions."

"Well, of course, Takis. Get me there, and I'll take over. I've narrowed my list to two monasteries, Hagia Theotokos and Magístris Lávras. I'll use Google Earth to study the layout."

Her cousin leaned back in his chair, looked up at Queen Alexandra, and settled on the top shelf of one of her bookcases. The clock was gonging upstairs, announcing it was 9 pm.

"I've heard of them. I've done some work for one of the young monks at that first one you mentioned. An innocent kid named Brother Vassilis." He crossed his arms, shifted in his chair, and returned his gaze in her direction. "Your appearance is your biggest problem. Going into their libraries means somebody would see you, right?"

"I'd assume so, although I'd make every effort to disappear."

He visibly sighed. "Sof, remember? Hormones? Curves? No Adam's apple? Your dimples? Again, those hormones?"

She ran through possible options like the chess moves their grandfather taught them. "What if I wore a monk's sostikon and skouphos? That would hide plenty."

"Mostly, they only wear that stuff during church services. Otherwise, the monks wear simple woolen caps and work pants. And you're missing the mandatory beard."

"Well, I don't know what to do about that."

"Never mind that." Was she seeing him blush? "I think you're a hiker-like pilgrim. Some guys enter Agio Óros without seeking proper papers. I'm going to get you some anyway, just in case."

"How?" She again wondered how he did all this, except that Takis only has friends, no strangers.

"Never mind that. Most hikers don't have beards. You'll need some guy's turtlenecks and probably a hooded top. Guys boots and long pants. Can't let them see your legs, *mou oraios*."

Sofia felt her cheeks warm. She was uncomfortable with reminders of her alleged beauty. "All this seems sensible. My big feet and contralto voice should help."

He smiled and gazed down at her feet. "When we were kids, I was jealous of your feet until I started sprouting myself. Talk little, but if you must, lower your voice even more. We'll practice some guy things before we leave Ouranoúpoli." He paused, and then said, "We'll sleep in one of the caves nearby, putting out hermit's flags. That'll keep people away." Queen Alexandra dropped down, circled the two of them, and decided Takis' lap would do for now. He absentmindedly began petting her. "Are you planning on getting into those libraries unannounced or what?"

Sofia felt her anger dissipating and hope emerging. The walls were crumbling. "I thought I'd be Brother Pachomius from Meteora. I'd send letters on plain stationary and post them from some small town in that region. My abbot is giving me permission to do some research."

"That could work if you bump into someone. But that means your papers will need to say this. Just how are you going to find the libraries? I hear the bigger monasteries are insanely confusing, and we can't exactly go around knocking on doors."

Sofia noticed her cousin tapping his feet, which meant his mind was in high gear.

She spoke. "I noticed on Google Earth that some of the monasteries are undergoing renovations. They must've filed paperwork with some government agency in Athens."

Takis crossed his legs, one sandal dropping to the ground, and Queen Alexandra adjusted to the change in her throne. "Probably not. The monks don't answer to anyone."

Sofia gazed around her office, thinking. Might their aunt know someone in the government who would be sympathetic? A not-too-religious woman who would check for any filings? Unfortunately, her cousin was probably right on this.

Takis dislodged the Queen from his lap and turned toward her computer, pulling up Google Earth. They waited for the program to settle on Agio Óros, and then they both leaned in to study the screen.

"Takis? Christina told me you want to buy this house. I love seeing it stay in the family, but what would you do with all this space?"

He glanced her way, eyebrows raising. "Besides keeping two of my favorite women?"

"Yeah, like anyone I need to be checking out?" Her cousin had had several girlfriends over the years. Still, he was a more independent soul, and the clinging type never worked for him.

"Hmmm." Her cousin had turned his attention back to the screen and scrolled until he found Hagia Theotokos. "When did you expect us to commit this crime?"

"As soon as possible. If I wait, I'll lose my courage." Hearing footsteps from above, Sofia added. "Takis, we can't tell Christina what we're doing. At least not until we get back."

A crooked grin spread across his face. "I've never divulged my criminal activities to our aunt. But I may need to do an advanced scouting for you to find the correct doors to these libraries you lust after."

Sofia smiled broadly.

Seven

SOME DAYS LATER

Sister Meg once asked Sofia, *how does a woman fight the barriers that seem to grow by the hour? By doing precisely what no one would expect!*

In her office, Sofia sat at the long wood-hewn table her great-grandfather had crafted nearly a century ago, a large glass of white wine nearby. She had sold her beloved shell to fund her continued research. Odd editing and writing jobs barely brought in enough to cover her basic expenses. All this traveling left her with credit card debt that she detested.

The floor above creaked. Christina was on a long call, pacing slowly across the living room above. Sofia had studied correspondence from the monks on Agio Óros regarding the digitizing project to craft her letter from Brother Pachomius' abbot in Meteora to the abbots of Hagia Theotokos and Magístris Lávras, introducing the youngish monk and giving permission to spend some days there in their libraries conducting research. She wrote and rewrote until she felt her letter had the ring of authenticity. Their writing style was simple and to the point. She had located some onionskin paper that would provide an element of authenticity. Fortunately, her aunt never got rid of her grandfather's old typewriter. She would make two copies and mail one to each monastery from the Meteora region, probably the village of Trikkala.

Next, she set up an email account for Brother Pachomius, wondering how long it would take a tech-savvy monk, if there was such a guy on Agio Óros, to trace the account back to her. Did any of the monks in Meteora have email accounts? She hoped not.

She had called Brother Makarios, where she left a voice mail message, and Adélie, which did not go through. Why wasn't her friend calling her? When she had a free moment, she would look up The Hill's phone number and track down the director since no one had responded to her earlier email. Surely someone there had the means to get through to Adélie's team or, at least, to let her know what was happening. During her graduate school days, she never imagined that her colleagues would be risking their lives, and even dying, to save ancient cultures.

The next morning, Sofia headed into the downtown area with her list of purchases. She swung by the shop where she had ordered a heavy black pair of men's glasses with her prescription. She won that debate with the sales clerk when she explained they were for a play she would be in. And that was what her adventure on Agio Óros felt like.

Even if her plans failed, she could live with the satisfaction of knowing she tried. Small satisfaction, she fumed, given all the dead ends she had encountered in the past several years. Realizing she was grinding her teeth, so she stretched her jaw and rolled her shoulders. She may need to run a couple of miles tonight. That usually cleared her mind when she couldn't get out sculling.

In the crowded open market, some young musicians played an interesting mix of jazz and traditional Greek instruments. Sofia placed a few euros in their donations bucket (the poor supporting the poor, she mused) and then dug through bails of used clothing (what did Adélie call these? Pre-loved? Pre-owned?) while mentally reviewing everything that could go wrong in the weeks ahead. She located a pair of men's cargo work pants with worn but intact pockets. With no place to try clothing on, she guessed they were loose enough to not accentuate her hips. Takis would certainly correct her if not. The looser waistband might work to her advantage as well.

Bending over yet another bin, she felt several people jostling her, and that sickening feeling overcame her. She grabbed her belted pack and pinched small hands, trying to undo the fastener. She turned suddenly and shouted at a woman swathed in colorful clothing accompanying the apparent thieves-in-training. Mother? Grandmother? Older sister? She yelled louder, so others turned in their direction, and the group shuffled off.

Sofia breathed deeply to calm herself when she felt her phone vibrate. "Hello?" She smiled at the sound of Brother Makarios' voice as she searched for a quieter place, her eyes searching for any further trouble. "Mac, it's good to hear your voice. Where are you?"

He updated her on the final deliveries to the secured caves in the mountains north of Mor Gabriel and his successful delivery of their specimens to the university's lab in Istanbul. "I'm heading home to England to work on our discoveries."

"Mac, have you heard anything about Aleppo? I need help getting through to Adélie and her team."

"Nothing but reports of bombings. Turkey's military is getting more involved, and their president's paranoia grows daily. Luv, my return to the heart of the Empire isn't voluntary. It's getting ugly and dangerous. Have you tried The Hill?"

A stab of guilt swept through her. "I'll call them tonight, which would be morning in Minnesota."

"Keep me posted. If you're unsuccessful, I'll see what I can find out in London. So, what are your next steps, Sof?"

Sofia's mind raced. She trusted Mac, but something warned her against involving him before the crime. She'd tell him later. "I no longer have a teaching post, so I'll keep pushing the Olympias angle. I've been searching databases, but nothing is coming together yet."

"Grants and post-doctoral fellowships, my girl. Just keep pecking away at the institutions. Frankly, I'm of a mind to write that Patriarch of yours and demand he put you on his staff."

Sofia smiled while her gut soured. "Thanks, Mac. He'd probably prefer a believer. Besides, he's poorer than I am." She laughed.

"You're a believer, luv. You just forget. Keep the fighting fires blazing."

Saying their goodbyes, Sofia snapped her phone shut, gazed over the jungle of clothing bins, and resumed her search.

In her fourth bin, she squealed with delight when she located a hand-sewn hooded top that looked like the ones she saw in the pictures of the monks on Agio Óros. She also grabbed an ugly-looking turtleneck to cover her lack of an Adam's apple, something Takis was concerned about. Failing to find a pair of used men's hiking boots in her size, she paid the clerk and walked four blocks to a store that sold new and used camping and hiking gear.

Making her last purchases, Sofia squirmed into her new old pants, donned a pair of her new old socks, and put her big feet into her new hiking boots. Walking back to her old car, she stopped to adjust her boots; in some places, they were too loose, and in some areas, they pinched. She'd need to break these in.

§

Sofia sat on the veranda with her laptop and a mug of mint tea that evening. The sunset displayed a stunning array of reds to blues swept with magenta. She called The Hill and was put through to the Director's Assistant.

"Good morning, I'm Dottore Sofia Papandréou calling from Thessaloniki. I'm trying to locate a friend who is part of your team working in Aleppo. Adélie—."

The woman cut her off. "May I ask your connection?"

"Besides a friend? We're colleagues, and I've lost phone contact over the past few weeks, and I'm worried sick." Sofia was placed on hold, anxiety gnawing at her stomach and growing increasingly impatient. She studied the photos of the monasteries on Mount Athos, downloaded from Google Earth and from the graduate students working on the digitizing project. She had managed to contact most of them, who graciously shared what they had. She noted that some were grainy from cell phones, and some caught unexpected angles of doorways and shelving. Her lurking fear was that any old manuscripts she could shoot would be in places so dark that no images would come out with clarity.

"Dottore?" A man's voice, tenor with, she guessed, a Texan accent. "This is Father Simon."

"I'm inquiring about my friend, Adélie." Sofia explained their connections to appease his apparent reluctance to say much.

"Our policy is to say little for the protection of our teams. Adélie and the remainder of her team evacuated Aleppo days before the recent bombing began. They've arrived in Turkey, and we expect to hear word soon that she and the others have arrived in the States."

Sofia felt such relief she almost laughed. "Thank you, and please tell her to call me right away. She has my number. Father, the Syrians working with Adélie?"

He sighed. "We haven't been able to find out the status of some of our Syrian colleagues. We know at least one car trying to leave at the same time as your friend was hit by a mortar shell. Regarding the others, we don't have any reliable information. Nor what's happened with Bishop Ibrahim. But I doubt he was willing to leave Aleppo."

"I'm so sorry to hear this. All this fighting makes me sick." Flipping off her phone, Sofia felt a sense of pride that the Patriarch stayed with his people.

Sofia moved to the dining room for better lighting. She turned back to her laptop when she heard Christina's voice. "In here."

"What are you studying so intently?" Her aunt gestured with a bottle of wine and a glass, which her aunt filled and set by Sofia. "Just studying some of the photos from the digitizing project on Agio Óros."

Christina sat down near her. "Any chance someone would hire you? I cannot imagine anyone more qualified."

Sofia took a long sip while stretching her shoulder muscles. "Thanks, Christina, but I'm no medievalist, and those are the only books they're digitizing. Hatzidakis made the same suggestion but with no offer of a job."

"Sofia, dear. You may need to leave Greece. I don't want to see you losing hope. It saddens me."

Sofia sighed. "Me, too. I'm scouring the job postings, but there isn't much out there. Universities want sports coaches, bureaucrats, and grant writers, not scholars. I'm beginning to look at ways to offer my skills in the business world."

"Oh, dear."

"A professional scout suggested she contact several of the computer companies in Silicon Valley on my behalf, near San Francisco, as my language skills might transfer to whatever it is that they do there."

"Really?" Christina shifted in her chair.

"Yeah, but I'm heading out in the morning for a week to ten days to research."

"Anything to do with your trip to Turkey?"

"Some of it." Sofia squirmed. "I'll probably be out of phone's reach for most of the time, so don't worry when you don't hear from me."

Sofia headed upstairs to finalize her work out of the sight of her aunt. She hoped to avoid any need to lie to her aunt about her upcoming adventure.

Early the following day, she tightly packed the rucksack she'd take onto Agio Óros, including woolen socks, no-rinse shampoo, other toiletries, and an extra spandex breast binding to minimize her curves. That might hurt after a long day, but it's well worth it if she succeeds. Energy bars went into outer compartments, including a pack of memory cards, euros, her passport, and a credit card. Those last two items made her uneasy, but leaving them behind felt worse.

Sofia acknowledged to herself that she had also packed sufficient guilt for the trip. She strapped her sleeping bag on top. She placed the clothing she'd don at Takis' apartment in a separate bag. Slipping on her sandals, swinging the rucksack on her back, and grabbing her camera bag, she headed out the door. Miriam had given Sofia directions to her preferred hair artist.

EIGHT

Sofia's old car rumbled to the far end of the University campus to the hair salon that Miriam recommended. Said they were hair artists. Sofia's only contact from Takis in the past ten days was a message to meet him at his apartment above his shop in Ouranoúpoli. What did he learn?

She passing through the dark door into a room lit with bright fluorescent lighting useful for the creative work done here and waited to be called back. Miriam's braids were updated here. Sofia smiled.

A young woman approached, her hair an intricate dance of braids and locks. Her lilt suggested East Africa like Miriam. Sofia sat in the chair as she undid her braid, and her hair cascaded toward her waist. This would hurt, but she reminded herself that hair grows back.

Thinking of her adventure as Greek theater—a tragedy? A comedy—she said in the local Greek dialect, "I need my hair cut like a monk." She handed the young woman a photo of a couple of monks on Mount Athos, downloaded from the computer.

"Cool. Sort of windblown and shaggy. In the theater?" The young woman was pulling and feeling her hair as Sofia nodded in the affirmative. It was, after all, a play of sorts with a very small audience.

"Some curl. It might get curlier when it's shorter. This can work nicely. Cap or skouphos?"

"Cap or hood, depending on the scene." And how far she needs to go to succeed in slipping in and left undisturbed.

With her hair washed, Sofia returned to the chair. She closed her eyes as the young woman reached for an electric razor. Gripping the armrest as she felt pulls and tugs, the razor buzzing sounded like a mosquito on caffeine. The weight of her hair lessened, and she finally found the courage to open her eyes. Her hair hugged her face in a new way, layered toward the ends. She smiled in a cringing sort of way. The young woman sheared her hair just like in the photos of the monks.

Sofia paid and departed, pulling at her damp hair to create the "windblown" effect. She would need to stop staring at herself and begin to feel "monkish."

Hopping into her car, Sofia sat with eyes closed and hands gripping the steering wheel. This was it. Now, or let go of her obsession forever. Touching the icon of the Theotokos, the Mother of God, taped to her ratty dashboard in a gesture of petition—surely the Blessed Virgin would go to battle on behalf of a desperate woman—she turned on the ignition and whipped out into traffic.

Sofia drove across the Chalkidiki peninsula, heading southeast toward Ouranoúpoli, and with little traffic to inhibit her bad habit, she pressed the accelerator to the floor. Once out of Thessaloníki, she had opened all the windows to let the breeze caress her skin. Before her lay a heavily forested valley. The scent of pine after the uninhibited exhaust of the city was refreshing.

She thought about her recent discovery that a few of the monasteries on Agio Óros had websites, which meant a few monks could check on her character. Fortunately, Ipapandi, her alleged monastery, didn't even have electricity. But this realization disconcerted her even further. Like many Greek children, she studied picture books on the mysterious monasteries full of holy men and many miracles. Peasant women claimed that the Blessed Virgin Mary herself walked the gardens of Agio Óros. She could not deny a particular fascination with such an ancient yet forbidden place.

Approaching her destination, the road curved gently to the right and downhill. She slowed on approach to Ouranoúpoli, a fishing village and popular tourist destination. Smoke nestled toward the side of the mountains to her left and in the distance. Drought brought endless fires to Greece. The sun's rays glanced off the deep blue water of the bay ahead.

Slowing, her car rolled forward with all the congested traffic. The mixture of car exhaust and dry smoke from the fire made breathing uncomfortable. She rolled up her windows and fiddled with the radio, which only offered hissing and squawking.

An unusual number of police cars were parked at odd angles. In typical Greek fashion, the officers were busy socializing. Her palms were sweaty. This was getting more real. She was anxious and excited. And worried that the bank fraud investigation might bring more police onto the Holy Mountain. Would the government dare take the books to sell it for unpaid taxes? What a mess. And exactly why she couldn't wait any longer to find out what was sitting in their libraries.

Winding her way in low gear through the narrow, cobbled streets, she passed stone buildings with shops on the ground level and old men sitting in wicker chairs on the sidewalk. Above the shops on the upper floors were the homes of the proprietors and their families, many of them displaying window boxes of brightly colored flowers.

Will their plan work? At least she will have tried. If she succeeded in finding publishable material, a truly unique discovery, opportunities for permanent teaching positions might come her way. If caught, she would be world-famous for a day or two. And only gutsy universities would consider hiring a notorious patristics scholar. As Sister Meg said, *desperate actions for desperate times*.

Sofia could hear music, the haunting sounds of rembétika, the blues of Greece. She remembered her childhood, playing with her cousins along the shoreline. Hers was a warm and loving family that also carried a dense cloud that no amount of laughter could entirely dissipate. Hushed conversations only heightened the pain of her parents' suspicious death. Civil war had birthed the military junta. Now, Greece was in danger of being thrust from the European Union. Greeks could be so bloody self-destructive.

Sofia heard fire trucks. The smoke had grown thicker. Had the fire spread into town? Traffic came to a halt. Sofia, noting several elderly gentlemen walking nearby, rolled down her window. The smoke was pungent. She asked in Greek, "News of the fire?"

They stopped and turned. "Aye, been raging for several hours. The hills beyond."

"So, no homes or resorts are involved?" Why all the trucks in town?

The men moved by her window and leaned in. "Naw, Hilander is burning again." Hilander was the nearby Serbian monastery, uphill and inland several kilometers.

"That sounds terrible. But what do you mean, 'again'?"

Several answered at the same time. She learned that long-neglected buildings had caught fire, torched the nearby forest, and scorched some of the old walls of the main monastery. More forest land today, vineyards too, but possibly more of the old monastery was also burning. Opinions varied. Hopefully, her cousin had better information.

Sofia grew alarmed. "Had the library burnt?"

A helicopter passed overhead. Her car shook.

After the noise subsided, the old men returned their gaze toward her. They shrugged in a manner suggesting libraries were not important to them. "Who knows? Not that I heard. A couple of holy icons were lost, though. Terrible."

"That's too bad." She waved goodbye as her car rolled forward.

Sofia hit the steering wheel in frustration. The old gentlemen had said "again." Why didn't those monks take better care of their monastery?

Passing left through a turnabout, she caught the blaring sound of fire trucks with the sound of more helicopters, which proved deafening. A next left down an unpaved side road, and Sofia arrived at her cousin's auto repair shop on the right. Several old trucks were parked in his gravel driveway. One Mercedes, hood up and parts on a workbench, stood to her left. She backed into a corner next to Takis' truck. Climbing out, looking about, and not spotting her cousin, she grabbed her gear and began the ascent to his home.

His door was unlocked, and she found Takis at his messy desk. She was greeted with raised eyebrows and a slow smile creeping across his face. With his typical humor, he carried on about how "cutting edge" she looked.

Cringing, she tugged at her cropped hair. "Looks that bad?"

He smiled. "It's a shocking change, I admit. But *mou oraios*, you'll need to get used to your new look. And fast."

Sofia dropped her gear in his spare bedroom and returned. "Calling someone?"

"Sof, would you try your phone?" He gazed back at his phone, one of those newest ones not often seen with Greece's depressed economy.

She located her phone and hit the power button. Nothing. She checked her battery. Functioning. "No reception, I think. The fire?"

"We'd better find out how bad this is. We may need to change our plan of action."

"Change?" Just what she feared. She couldn't face returning home without trying. Only brick walls waited for her there. "How do we get on to the Holy Mountain with all these police and fire crews?"

"I've been thinking about that. Fire could hurt us but could help our cause. They're not looking for women slipping onto Agio Óros. It's fire lines that concern them, that and not getting killed."

A squall of questions ran through her mind.

"Fire trucks. Police everywhere. Never mind the tourists. I want to talk with a couple of contacts of mine. I'm headin' out, but I should be back within the hour."

Sofia's heart sank as she watched her cousin walk away. Would Takis abandon her? After using the water closet, she checked for a beer, finding only ouzo. With shaking hands, she poured herself a shot and slumped into one of his distinctly ugly and uncomfortable chairs. A second shot of ouzo invited a nap. She could never hold her liquor like her cousins. Even his sister, Kassandra, had been able to drink her under the table. Easily.

Sofia awoke with a start and realized Takis had not returned. She stood, and the room began to reel. She grabbed the side of the chair to steady herself. Where was he? Panicking, she wrote Takis a note in case they missed each other, grabbed her wallet, and searched some of Takis' favorite haunts. Surely, he would turn up somewhere.

Tourists were everywhere, greeting her with full-body slams with ne'er a glance in recognition of her presence. Live music wafted through the noise of trucks and helicopters and rude tourists. Picking up a thread of live jazz, she headed toward an alley and followed the sound, which grew louder. She found herself picking up speed, nearly into a run. Deep breathing helped calm her nerves.

What was going on with him? Takis was always so fun-loving and easy-going. Was he bailing out? Or just finalizing their ascent? Diving through strung beads into a darkened room, she had located the jazz band. And Takis. He was seated at a bar at the far end of the room, cigarette dangling from his fingers and listening intently.

Sofia was nearly out of breath. "Takis."

He looked surprised. "Sof? What is it?"

"You never came back. I thought ..."

Takis looked at her quizzically. "What? That I'd abandoned our project? I don't think so. You know I've always enjoyed a challenge. Niko here," her cousin gesturing toward a bald, bearded, bespeckled, cigar-smoking guy around their age, "has a brother on the fire crew. He's just updating me."

Sofia sighed. Why couldn't she relax?

"Niko, have you met my beautiful, talented, athletic cousin? She graces us with her presence on occasion."

Sofia punched her cousin's arm.

"Oh, did I mention she's brilliant too? A university—"

"You might have noticed Takis' exuberance?"

Niko smiled. "You mean he boasts too much. In your case, an accurate assessment."

Sofia nodded at the compliment. Her eyes began to water from the heavy pall of cigarette smoke. Outside and now indoors. One of the many things she liked about America was its intolerance for smokers.

"So, Niko, how bad is the fire?" Sofia feared her voice sounded shaky.

"Bad. Worse than any in recent memory." Her cousin's friend groomed his scraggly beard with his fingers. "Callin' in another crew from the north."

"Niko says no hiking."

Sofia froze in horror. Had Takis revealed their plans?

Takis dug his cigarette into a nearby plate. "No camping. No hiking. Nothing for the time being."

Nikos looked at her. "Too dangerous. But worse, tourists get underfoot with the fire crew. Taking pictures and filming while the guys are working. Had to throw the dumb shits out."

Takis stood from his bar stool. "I'm starving. Let's go find a meal worthy of your visit."

Takis took Sofia by the shoulder, and they left through another door. They headed toward the waterfront in the direction of the Byzantine tower.

The beaches in Ouranoúpoli catered to tourists who live on the sand, swimming, snorkeling, and building sandcastles. They walked along the shore, passing one creative endeavor that might have been an attempt at the Castle at Hogwarts School for Wizardry.

Takis glanced across at her and chuckled. "My dear cousin, if you're embarking on a career in espionage and general all-around crime, you must learn to trust your partner. And never begin a caper with outdated information."

"I know, but—" Sofia sighed, her nerves frazzling and her head aching.

"No 'buts,'" Takis waived to a couple he apparently knew and continued, "fire, wind, police, helicopters, all undermine our plans."

The two turned in at a taverna that sat alongside a pier, choosing a high table with stools on the outdoor patio. The bright sun was edging toward the bay. Sofia pulled out her new glasses to read the menu and heard a sharp intake and chuckle from her cousin. She glanced his way, "I couldn't bring my contacts, and I need to look like a guy. Remember?"

She ordered squid and her cousin Cod with Garlic Sauce with frizzante water.

"Sofia, you are still ready to do this. When we begin, we begin. No turning around. Yes?"

She stopped pulling at her hair, pushing it back with her glasses. "Yes, Takis. I'm nervous as hell, but once we begin, I won't look back."

She reminded herself that she had nothing to go back to anyway. If she wanted a university job, she must stun the patristics world. Otherwise, she'd be joining the mass exodus out of Greece.

Switching to English, Takis said. "Good. You need to make a choice. Hiking isn't an option right now. So, as I figure it, we can sail to one of several coves near Megístís Lávras and hike up. Then, hike on to this second monastery. I can arrange for someone to retrieve the boat. Or we can take my old truck and drive in. Your choice."

Nine

T HE HOLY MOUNTAIN

Sofia stepped through the doorway of her cousin's apartment and locked it. Another helicopter lunged low, hovered, and began its ascent into the mountains, its lights swooping through the haze of smoke. Dawn had yet to arrive. Sofia clambered down the wooden stairs of Takis' apartment, her men's hiking boots still feeling awkward. Her woolen monk's cap was firmly in place, and the early morning air bore the warmish stench of smoke.

Takis placed her rucksack into the bed of his old pickup truck alongside his own gear.

Hands shaking, Sofia opened the passenger side door. She climbed in, setting her camera bag with one lens, borrowed from a friend, between her feet. She yawned. In all honesty, she hadn't slept all night. She had kept running through the scenarios of their plans, especially everything that could go wrong. As Takis climbed in and turned on the ignition, she said. "Thanks again, Takis. I cannot imagine anyone else willing to try something this insane."

He smiled. "I like adventures. And you're my adventurous cousin."

Takis handed her an old leather portfolio, elegant and masculine looking. "Precious cargo in there. Some of the best work my source has ever produced."

Sofia slid out the papers. Bless her cousin, her pilgrim's pass—necessary if anyone stops and questions her. Anyone blind enough not to notice the odd-looking monk.

As she felt the pull of the truck, she asked. "So, you've decided where we'll enter Agio Óros?"

Takis laughed. "Relax, *mou oraios*. This is my neighborhood. Which road we take will be decided by this fire. Trust me. We will watch the sunrise on forbidden territory."

"I trust you. I'm just worrying."

"I know every rut and crevice and cave this side of Karyés."

Karyés was the administrative center of Mount Athos, the closest thing to a town found there.

Her cousin confused her sometimes.

He pulled a crumpled paper from his pocket and handed it to Sofia. "I've got a map for the other side of Karyés. We'll arrive at our destination this afternoon. Not to worry."

She looked at her cousin with a grimace that sought to suppress a smile. "Okay."

"My dear cousin, remember you belong on Mount Athos. Don't let those old monks smell fear. Exude stubborn confidence. You belong on Agio Óros. It's your home, Brother—what name are you using during our little adventure?"

"Pachomius. A common monk's name. I've decided I'm from Meteora, a monastery there named Ipapandi that's quite isolated. I'm one of their rare scholars doing some research with my abbot's blessing."

"Well, you should know, cousin."

Sofia smiled. "Brother Pachomius, please. And as far as I can tell, they have no cell phones or internet at Ipapandi. Should be hard to verify my story."

They cleared old Ouranoúpoli quickly as the saner residents and guests were fast asleep. Takis maneuvered his way around parked trucks and police cars with the confidence of one who knew he belonged there. The ascent began.

"So, more adventure or more business?" Sofia's curiosity and suspicion lingered. Takis had always been comfortable playing the edges of legality.

"I haven't changed so much. I always make my business my adventure and, whenever feasible, make my adventures profitable."

"You actually conduct business with these monks?" She still found this news surprising.

"Some. They're the reason my auto shop stays open."

"You repair their trucks."

"Yes, and other odd jobs." Was his silence avoidance? Or concentration?

Takis —."

"If it bothers you, don't ask."

Sofia glanced toward Takis. He appeared to be studying the horizon. Sofia realized the dark had become darker. The lights of Ouranoúpoli were behind and below them now. The truck's engine rumbled, its power taking on the challenge of rough terrain.

"When you publish your world-renowned book and win the Nobel prize, just be sure to give credit to your talented cousin. He glanced in his mirrors. "Just omit explaining some of my "'talents," please."

Sofia chuckled. "I don't think the Nobel committee gives awards to patristic scholars. We're too boring."

Takis looked her way, a smirk on his face. "Scholars, yes. You? Never."

Sofia gazed out, straining to see the outlines of a monastery. She had studied pictures of these older labyrinthine monasteries, but finally, seeing one up close felt exhilarating. She breathed deeply.

Takis' foot tapped something, and the headlights brightened, revealing the rough road ahead.

"Does Nikos do business with the monks as well?"

Takis smiled at her. "You're nervous. All these questions. Yes, Nikos shares my keen nose for profit."

Takis was aiming the truck through a narrow grove of cypress trees and occasional billows of smoke. The dirt road was barely visible. He shifted into high gear and lurched forward. Sofia came close to saying a prayer, reminding herself that her cousin did not harbor suicidal tendencies. Approaching the crest and rounding a corner, they encountered lights from a military jeep ahead.

Oh, great. Already. Sofia pulled her men's glasses out of her pocket and put them on. As Takis slowed, she pulled her turtleneck up to hide her lack of an Adam's apple. A military police officer approached the driver's window. As her cousin lowered it, the stench of smoke filled their cab.

"Who are you? Part of the fire crew?" The officer flashed his flashlight in their direction, its beam dancing around the inner cab. The light bounced off Sofia's glasses, temporarily blinding her. She squinted, careful to keep her hands in her pockets.

"No, we —."

Pointing in the direction they had just traversed, the officer commanded, "Then get back to town. We don't need curiosity seekers getting underfoot and stirring up trouble. Now."

"Troublemakers? *Gia ónoma tou Theoú*. Brother Pachomius," pointing in her direction, "needs to get back to his monastery."

"Another day." The officer turned and walked away.

Sofia sat, somewhat aghast, watching Takis climb out of the cab and follow the officer. The two men spoke with their hands as much as the words she could barely make out. Sensing something, she looked to her right to see an ash-smeared face under a black helmet, light on, looking at her through the cab window. He wore the heavy suit of a firefighter. He kept staring at her. She turned back ahead, ignoring his stare and reminding herself that Brother Pachomius had every right to be here. Besides, they really hadn't entered Mount Athos. She hadn't seen even one monastery yet. Damned if she was going to be evicted before she got the chance to do something wrong.

Takis returned, climbed in, and cursed under his breath. Sofia still had an audience. The guy was still standing and staring. Her cousin turned the truck around.

Sofia grumbled. "We're returning."

Takis looked at her with a surprised expression on his face. Then, a smile emerged. "*Mou oraios*, have more faith in me, but he'll have my ass if he sees us again."

She felt a dark pressure in her chest like a bad case of heartburn.

Takis put the truck in reverse, backed partway down the hill, and turned right into what appeared to be a ravine bordered by smoking trees. He shifted into second gear, gunned the engine, and continued the ascent. Barely breathing, her shoulder slamming against the door several times, and holding on tight to the door handle. Her cousin seemed to find invisible tracks.

"You really do know your way around here."

"Hmmm. I've spent lots of time here. Our destination, no."

As the morning sun crested the horizon, their truck emerged through a cypress grove and onto a more established packed dirt road. With no signs of smoke, Sofia rolled her window down.

"Well, Brother Pachomius," Takis chuckled. "You might want to pull out your fancy camera and get ready. A couple of monasteries ahead."

Sofia gazed at the horizon like a child peering through a candy shop window. "Zographou?"

"You'd know better than me. I see rooftops and mind my own business."

Sofia reached into her bag and pulled out her camera. Rounding a corner and approaching a grove of olive trees, Takis parked the truck. Sofia gasped. They sat on a ridge above the clear rooftops of Zographou, the lone Bulgarian monastery. She walked to the grove's edge and began shooting photos, knelt, and studied the panorama before her. To her surprise, the complex looked much like the Google Earth images. The quiet was pleasant with just the sound of birds—fan-tailed warblers, she guessed—and the ocean washing up on the cliffs below.

She returned to the truck. Takis had finished his cigarette and offered her coffee out of his thermos. They continued down the road.

"Do we have to stop in Karyés for some reason?"

"I'd prefer to register as a visitor so they'll leave my truck alone. You'll be fine. Just lie low."

Sofia gripped the dashboard and door handle, breathing deeply and sending a silent prayer to the Blessed Mother in case She was listening. Sometimes, her cousin was a bit too relaxed for her. One truck approached, Takis waved, and each continued. An onion dome appeared on the horizon, then evidence of vineyards, and then buildings.

Cresting the dusty horizon, their truck rounded a corner and entered the rustic village of Karyés. She saw the burnt red and white bell tower, the oldest building on Mount Athos. This tower's pointed roof predated the first monastery built in 963 CE.

Near the bell tower stood the peninsula's only basilica, the Church of the Protaton.

Takis parked in the town square. Looking out her window, Sofia was stunned to see military police standing near several parked jeeps. A lump of raw fear formed in her throat. She and Takis hadn't noticed any evidence of fire for miles. Did someone think the fire would spread this far? The police appeared to be gazing in her direction. Or was that her paranoia?

Takis climbed out to register their presence. Sofia needed to use the bathroom. Dare she? Her cousin kept telling her to chill out. She pulled on her knitted cap, pulled up her turtleneck, assured herself that her hooded top covered her ass, and adjusted her glasses. Then she climbed out and scanned the stone buildings.

Seeing the sign for the bathrooms, Brother Pachomius strode toward the entrance with the longer stride that Takis had suggested. Men's voices and laughter greeted her as she entered the dark, dank room. To her left was a bank of urinals. To her right lay several toilets with walls but no doors. Takis had warned her that the shelter provided by stalls was considered unnecessary and frivolous on Agio Óros. Entering the last stall, she noticed that there was no toilet inside, but rather a hole, just like she had seen and used in the countryside of northern Italy and France. At least she was experienced at negotiating this particular rustic simplicity.

After finishing her business, she left and noticed her cousin standing by his truck, sharing a cigarette with a young military police officer. As she approached, he called her name.

Brother Pachomius."

She responded using the lower range of her contralto voice, trying to sound distant and gruff, barely glancing at the young man standing next to her cousin.

"Why are the military police on the Holy Mountain?"

Unfortunate situation. We're required to check everyone's identification and limit access," the young officer responded. "Papers, please."

Brother Pachomius reached into her rucksack on the seat. With a pounding heart and shaking hands, she pulled out her papers and handed them to the officer.

"Meteora? Don't get many from there. What brings you here?" The officer was looking over her papers.

"Research," she replied. Sofia struggled to act like it was her right as an Orthodox monk to be on Mount Athos.

"Hmmm, your monks are rather isolated from the rest."

Now you've met one." Brother Pachomius reached out and took back her papers. Turning, she climbed into the truck. For her, the matter of her presence on Mount Athos was settled. At least, she hoped she had left the officer with that impression.

Takis glanced her way with a grin painted across his face.

Sofia thought her heart would stop. Would she make it through the first day without being exposed? Her mind raced as Takis gunned the engine.

"Seems a monastery called Esfigmenou is under scrutiny by the military." Takis swung the truck out, accelerating on approach to a curve. She knew this would not be a smooth trip with the rough roadway and his Greek propensity for speed.

Esfigmenou was one of the older monasteries on Mount Athos. Their collection of illuminated manuscripts was extensive. The monks were conservative with a primitive observance, the archivist had told her.

"Did the military say why? Something to do with the financial meltdown?"

"No. The monks hated the Patriarch and broke off all relations with the Church. Even with the other monasteries here."

Too bad. That was one of the monasteries she considered entering, except for the reality that they're ultra-conservative.

Before them lay a long, windy road past orchards, vineyards, and lots of rocks and then a deep downward slope. To their left was a deep gorge. She could hear a waterfall, but the angle did not allow her to see much. Sooner than she had expected, the Byzantine rooftops of Magístris Lávras appeared. They were at the southernmost tip of the peninsula. The pinnacle of Mount Athos lay to their left. They both scanned the hillside. They wanted to locate a cave before the sunset.

"There's one."

Takis glanced in Sofia's direction and veered the truck off the dirt road. Their ascent was bumpy, but the engine remained powerful. He pulled up and maneuvered the truck in between two cypress trees. Above them was the entrance to a cave, partially walled-in and known as a skiti. Dusk was setting. After placing the hermit's flag, staking out this cave as "occupied," and setting their gear within, the two sat on the ledge and gazed toward the ocean.

Sofia savored the view and her reality. She was sitting on Agio Óros, the ocean toward her left and Mount Athos, even more, majestic from this angle, to her right. She felt a tear escape her eye. A tear of joy. Her dream realized.

After another cigarette, Takis climbed down to his truck, rummaged within, and returned with something in his hands. Closer, Sofia realized Takis had brought beer with him. She chuckled. Her nerves could use calming. She couldn't believe she was here—in forbidden territory.

"*Mou oraios*, a proper toast to your new career in crime."

Sofia laughed then stopped herself. Her voice carried. Even a contralto could too easily be mistaken for a woman. Tapping bottles, she took a swig. "Just what is your business here?"

Takis chuckled. "Lovely cousin, I am a renowned horticulturalist."

"Huh?"

"A very select product for an exclusive clientele." He took another swig. "Very select."

TEN

ESFIGMENOU MONASTERY, AGIO ÓROS

Father Yeorgi was passionate about rare books and parchments. He was equally passionate about his life in the monastery with its ancient traditions and beauty. Possibly his abbot was the only person more determined to protect their way of life from the encroachment of modernity with its hedonism and contempt for God.

In his mid-forties, Father Yeorgi wore the thick glasses of one who had dedicated years to voracious reading and working with the fine, nearly illegible script found in ancient books. His unusually thick beard reached mid-chest, his hair black, and coarse black habit cloaked his agile strength.

Father Yeorgi had just received several newly acquired early medieval manuscripts for their library collection. The thousand-year-old library at Esfigmenou had one of the more ancient collections on Agio Óros, containing illuminated manuscripts, rolled parchments, old books called codices, and other oddities given to the monastery over the centuries. Being nearly illiterate and uninterested in all the bothersome debris, past librarians piled the donations in odd corners, crammed into already overstuffed shelving and whatever spare space could be found.

After Father Yeorgi returned from doctoral studies in Jerusalem, where he had spent years working with delicate, old texts, including the Dead Sea Scrolls, the newly elected Abbot Methodius had assigned him responsibility for the library. He discovered a mess, a dense and unaccounted-for accumulation from decades, if not centuries, of neglect. He delighted in his work and could not have been happier.

The space for the library that Father Yeorgi had inherited needed to be more adequate, and his priority was to create more space for the collection. Esfigmenou was a mishmash of brick and stone, evidence of its labyrinthine growth over the last eight centuries. The odd structure of the building complex gave him several possibilities for creating larger areas without drawing attention from outsiders to his activities. He located an unused cavernous space underground, and with the assistance of several of their monk carpenters, he installed a simple but effective climate control system, dim lighting to protect the books from light exposure, and special, acid-free shelving.

Over the years, Father Yeorgi had painstakingly repaired and cataloged the collection, assigning an archival number and marking the back corner of each book, codex, or parchment in pencil. Then, he meticulously described each book in his personal ledger before deciding which area of the stacks would store his newest addition. Acquisitions were not stored by topic or subject; instead, the librarian designed a system of record groups for his personal use. The researcher needed to understand the librarian's mind to locate anything in the collection.

Certain manuscripts were dangerous for simple monks to read. He and his abbot had agreed that these volatile texts would not be made available except with their express permission. So, he ordered the work crew to dig further into the mountain, seeking a secure space with a hidden entrance.

Father Yeorgi stood in his office on one of the upper floors of the monastery at a long wooden table topped with a thick cloth that protected the old paper and parchment from the oils, stains, and acid from the wood. Several nearby tables were stacked with papers and books. 0 Long-armed or engineer's lamps were clamped to the tables, allowing him to focus light where needed.

Glaring sunlight was just as dangerous for his work. Father Yeorgi kept this table at the far end of the room, away from the large window with its easterly view. He was examining the outcome of his talented cousin's latest efforts, taken from a Viennese collector of antiquities.

Convinced of the value of expanding the scope of their collection, Father Yeorgi and his abbot were constantly alert for leads on significant manuscripts that they felt should be housed here rather than in a private collection elsewhere. Once Father Yeorgi ascertained the location of certain codices or parchments that he wanted, his cousin Kostas took care of the arrangements quietly and efficiently.

"Father. Busy at your treasures again, I see," Abbot Methodius said.

Father Yeorgi had made a few notes in his private journal while examining an exquisite eleventh-century prayer book. The illuminations in the psalter made sweeping use of reds, yellows, greens, and blues, still vibrant after centuries. The full-page miniatures contained delicate gold leafing in excellent condition whose personifications of Night and Dawn in the Prayer of Isaiah were unique, common to the work done in Byzantium during the Macedonian Renaissance.

"Yes. Kostas served us well. This will make a fine addition to our collection." Pushing his glasses back onto the bridge of his misshapen nose, the monk stepped aside to give his abbot a better view of the illuminations. "Just look at this workmanship. How vibrantly the colors have endured."

Father Yeorgi had learned a deep appreciation for miniatures and illuminated manuscripts in Jerusalem. He could not deny the excellent education the papists provided. They were demanding and exacting.

"Exquisite. This is an art we need to resurrect. God forbid these traditions ever die out," the abbot said.

I agree. Hopefully, the Holy One will see fit to send us some monks with an aptitude for art. We need someone with a better hand and eye than mine," the librarian replied, smiling.

Abbot Methodius stepped away from the worktable and began pacing the large room. Metal bookcases lined the walls, overflowing with the jars, brushes, styles, bottles, and other equipment used to restore and preserve manuscripts.

"What utter arrogance!" Abbot Methodius took long strides that belied his short stature. He appeared more like a lumbering bear in his flowing black habit, shoulder-length gray hair, and thin, untrimmed beard. But anyone in his presence would not doubt his power or commitment to God's call.

"Only such outrageous arrogance could explain the Apostate's behavior." The apostate, one accused of abandoning the faith, was Ecumenical Patriarch Bartholomaios I, leader of the Orthodox Church. He held ultimate legal and pastoral authority over the monasteries of Mount Athos.

"Military police indeed!" the abbot growled. The patriarch ordered the civil authorities on Mount Athos to surround their monastery and place them under house arrest.

"As you requested, I met with our solicitors in Athens. All our petitions before the secular courts have been rejected. The courts side with Patriarch Bartholomaios and refuse to defend us," Father Yeorgi replied, watching his abbot move about the room.

The abbot punctuated his words with intensity. "Weak and useless. I had placed little trust in solicitors and their courts. They've proven my judgment accurate."

The patriarch requested that the Greek military remove them from their home and be barred from the Holy Mountain.

"Yes, Father Abbot."

"We must never forget what we lived through during our brutal civil war. Never forget."

The monk librarian had heard the stories over the years of the military junta's ostracizing the monks for refusing to support the military dictatorship. Imprisonments and numerous attempts to take away the autonomy of Mount Athos had all been vain attempts to coerce the monks into recognizing the legitimacy of an illegitimate government.

"I fear I gave validity to the legal system by seeking resolution in the courts. Our authority is elsewhere, and we must not be reluctant to exercise it."

"Yes, Father Abbot. You know that your monks fully support you. The most recent expression of cowardice on the part of the monastic council unfortunately demonstrates how alone we are."

"A useless band of old women who will not listen to the clear path of truth before us," the abbot raged.

The monastic council of Mount Athos consisted of the abbots from the twenty major monasteries on the peninsula, where all decisions were made regarding governance, finances, and policies, subject only to Patriarch Bartholomaios in Constantinople. Some monasteries wanted to relax visitors' restrictions and expand contacts with Western monasteries. Abbot Methodius had argued against allowing hens onto the Holy Mountain for eggs, so now Father Yeorgi listened as his abbot raged about women being next.

"Always preaching ecumenism. Openness and ecumenism. There is only one, true Christianity. Orthodoxy. All else is pure heresy. In bed with a whore and they want to call it 'openness to the world.' We come to the Holy Mountain to seek God and leave behind this 'world' they so love," the abbot seethed.

Father Yeorgi remained quiet and let his abbot talk. Once Abbot Methodius decided he was a pillar of granite. But until then, the abbot needed to talk his way toward that decision. Father Yeorgi admired the strength and convictions of this visionary. Sometimes he struggled with impatience when his abbot seemed too slow to act, too tolerant of the lax monasteries nearby.

"Except for a few faithful, the council backs the apostate without question. They speak of a new reality. Of new possibilities. They're treading dangerous ground, blind to the seductive evils around us. What makes me angriest of all is that the council supports the apostate's openness to reconciliation with the heretic of Rome! Those damn papists have been seeking to seduce Bartholomaios for years."

Patriarch Bartholomaios and Pope John Paul II had been committed to healing and restoring full relations between the Churches of the East and the West. Increasingly, they had issued joint statements condemning militarism, the sex slave trade, and rampant greed. With building frequency, the two religious leaders had presided at prayer together. All this pious activity looked acceptable to the world, Father Yeorgi mused, but apostasy and compromise of truth was its harsh reality.

"Why the military police?" Never had Mount Athos witnessed the military interfering in internal matters, one monastery against another. "What do you think the apostate will gain from all this insanity?" Father Yeorgi asked.

"Silence. Compliance. He should know better. We will not be beaten into submission. We will not leave the Holy Mountain. We will prevail."

Abbot Methodius stopped his intense pacing and stood, looking out the window. The blue-green waters of the Aegean Sea were softening with the afternoon sun, a subtle shadow washing over the land.

The abbot continued. "We will not bend. Ours will remain a true and pure observance. We will prevail, showing those of wavering commitment the one authentic path. We are blessed with an abundance of courage. And courage can defeat any tyrant."

Abbot Methodius ran one of the most demanding regimes on Mount Athos. Liturgical prayer was meticulously chanted. The observance of silence was absolute. Fasts and austerities abounded. His monks were trained to spread the Orthodox faith with zeal and devotion. Unlike the practices of other monasteries on the Holy Mountain, visitors received a cool reception. Guests were kept separate from the monks, who were strictly forbidden to speak to them and confined to the chapel's rear during worship. The abbot sent his monks to other monasteries to reform them according to his vision. A few trusted monks recently assumed leadership in some of the more influential parishes in Athens and elsewhere.

Father Yeorgi knew his abbot envisioned nothing less than the complete and uncompromising restoration of the Orthodox faith to its preeminent position. No more of the concessions for which the heretic of Rome and his minions were famous. Politicians will respect the Orthodox Church, seeking her guidance and even taking orders when necessary.

"Father Yeorgi, I trust you have given this matter thought?" The abbot turned to face him. "Your counsel?"

"We face treachery from every side, Father Abbot." The monk pulled at his beard as he often did when deep in thought. "We must always remember the broad support of faithful followers worldwide. They long for restoration. Unfortunately, our finances may be compromised."

A thick wall of silence embraced them.

The abbot sighed. "Abbot Ephraim remains in the custody of the police. Satan is afoot."

"Money laundering. How could any court accuse one of our abbots of this? Legitimate donations. Kostas and I haven't figured out who would enter such an accusation."

His abbot remained quiet, an expression of intense thought awash his countenance. Father Yeorgi waited in silence. A soft wind graced the windows.

"Abbot Ephraim may have been played an innocent. Sometimes, men of prayer are too trusting of others. Putin's greedy bankers were most likely behind this. Dirty Russian bankers."

His heart sank. What will this do for their own case before the courts?

"Greece doesn't lack greedy bankers either. Any word on whether other monasteries might have been involved?" He remained standing, watching his abbot.

"Have your cousin check into that possibility. The information might prove useful." Abbot Methodius had long been estranged from his fellow abbots on Agio Óros.

Abbot Methodius resumed his pacing but with a quieter step. "I find it beyond comprehension that this Greek government would dare arrest one of our abbots. First, they invade us with their accursed military. Now they arrest one of our most faithful abbots. Satan indeed, Agio Óros is off limits to this decadent world."

Talking ceased when they heard the semantron, a large wooden beam beaten with a mallet, summoning them to prayer

Eleven

Thump. A loud "meow" echoed off the cave walls, startling Sofia from a light sleep. Settling back down, grunting with surprise, the lump of cat didn't move off her stomach. She had just begun an extraordinary adventure, hardly believing she was here. Looking over, she noticed Takis was still snoring quietly. She stroked the warrior cat, absorbing the calm of its purring that countered her excitement and anxiety. She ran through the day's details – slip into the library, discover hidden treasures, take clear pictures, and leave. Simple. Will this be the library where Olympias had been hidden all these centuries? The newest expedition member enjoyed a decidedly bent tail, a blind eye, and a shorn ear. Sofia had obviously inherited one of the grizzled feline combatants roaming Mount Athos. Had this creature ever won a single battle?

"Takis? You awake yet?" she asked, stretching. "Takis?" She heard a moan, the one that betrayed that he was awake but inhabiting a world of deep denial.

She crawled out of her sleeping bag, disturbing the mangled prince, and dressed. Groping for her guy's glasses and binoculars, she peeked out of the hermit's cave. An owl hooted. Before her lay Mount Athos, dawn barely cresting the horizon. So close, as if she could reach out and touch it. The peak was breathtaking with its steep, rocky incline and a dusting of rose-hued snow at its pinnacle. Sweeping the horizon with the binoculars, she spotted an eagle soaring in a long arc above her. She saw no human activity around them. As Takis suggested, maybe the firefighters have successfully kept hikers out. This could work to her advantage.

She reviewed the challenge, steadying her breathing to contain the adrenaline rush. Takis was right. She must trust her intuition to avoid the monks and blend with the graduate students.

With the briskness of the early morning air, Sofia dragged her sleeping bag near the cave's entrance. She covered herself, struggling to stay warm until it was time to depart. She enjoyed the silence, processing everything thrust her way ever since Brother Mac's call and the news about Adélie. Sofia sent a prayer for safety toward Mar Musa, where Adélie's group had been hiding.

As daylight emerged, Sofia picked up her binoculars and again swept the horizon. An orchard, well-tended gardens, and several structures appeared to serve as barns and workrooms. Megístis Lávras, meaning the *Great Cave*, was located on a rocky crag at the foot of Mount Athos and overlooking the ocean. Established by Saint Athanasius in 963, it was the oldest and most powerful monastery on the peninsula. Its buildings, a progression of stone and brick construction over the past millennia, had never been disturbed by fire.

She heard rustling, and soon, Takis appeared.

"What ungodly time of the day is it?" Takis yawned as he spoke.

"8:15. I'd forgotten that you're a late sleeper. When did you go to bed?"

"Too early for my taste. I listened to music and watched the stars. Tame stuff."

"Our monks get up quite early, but the students won't arrive at the library until 9 am. I don't want to get there before them. The crowd should provide cover for me." She glanced his way. "And I hope you don't veer far from me."

"*Mou oraios*, my eyes will always be on you unless I need to run interference. Just remember what I taught you. You belong here. Stay aloof and project a healthy dose of arrogance. Then they'll believe you're one of them."

She hoped he was right. She ate a protein bar while packing her rucksack for the day, bringing a blank book with pencils and her camera with lenses. And in one side pocket, her letters of introduction from her alleged abbot, and in the other, several protein bars. Soon, she smelled the coffee that her cousin had brewed. She gladly accepted a cup of the thick mahogany liquid gold whose caffeine should keep her blood pumping for the day. As if her excitement and anxiety weren't enough.

With the tolling of the bell—nine solemn times—Takis stood, slung a daypack over his shoulder, and headed downhill a kilometer or so toward the monastery. Sofia took a deep breath to calm her nerves, grabbed her gear, and pushed her old, knitted cap over her hair. She made sure the turtleneck of her sweater covered her throat, flipped her hood over her head, and followed. She tried to imitate her cousin's sauntering gait. She caught up with him, and he signaled her to go ahead. He had insisted that she mimic the monks in striding ahead of a mere commoner. Brother Pachomius' humble cousin would follow in deference to the holy monk.

Hands in her hoodie's front pocket, Sofia kept her eyes on the open gates and took long, purposeful strides. She barely glanced at the working monks, returning the identical hand signal, one of greeting, given to Brother Pachomius. Anxiety heightened her awareness of her surroundings. She heard sparrows chirping nearby and noticed several bird feeders hanging on posts nearby. She slowed and deepened her breathing as Brother Pachomius passed through the gates. To her left were parked several university-owned rigs. Ahead and to her right stood some graduate students and staff lingering after breakfast, smoking and talking to a group of monks. Smoking? The monks permitted this, with fires raging down the road? With old manuscripts stored here?

She kept her eyes focused ahead despite the temptation to look about. In her peripheral vision, she saw curious eyes glance her way. She hoped her steady gaze would send the proper signal. Leave this monk alone. She could hear Takis' footsteps behind her. He greeted someone, pouring out his charm.

Rounding a stone and brick building, most likely the monks' living quarters, Sofia crossed an empty courtyard to the katholikón and entered. This would be expected of her as a visiting monk. The vestibule contained bright stained-glass windows and a pair of magnificent baroque doors carved with the eagles of the Orthodox Church. The frescoes were only about 200 years old, painted with muted colors and depicting basic themes of Heaven and Hell with a dragon consuming the wayward. She opened one of the heavy doors and entered the nave of the Church. She stepped to the side and gazed around her, absorbing the powerful imagery. For an old chapel, the place was surprisingly clean and well-tended.

Hearing footsteps and chatter outside, Sofia strode forward. She knelt before the iconostasis, a screen of mounted icons that separated the altar from the main body of the Church, one hand touching the ground in reverence. She remained kneeling as the door thudded closed and footsteps around the outer perimeter accompanied by whispers filled the air. She offered a quick but ardent prayer for the success of her mission, particularly eyeing the icon of the *Theotokos*, the Blessed Virgin. Another woman would hopefully understand. She stood, turned away from the whispers, and exited.

With head bent, she walked the perimeter of the katholikón toward the smaller chapel of Saint Athanasius, wondering where Takis was. Sofia kept her gaze on her goal. Constructed of burnt red brick with multiple domes, the chapel housed the remains of the saint who died when the original katholikón dome crashed down upon him. To its left stood the two-story treasury, which now housed the monastery library. Following the outer wall, she reached the entrance.

Several students were standing about, debating the coming season's football. They glanced at her; their conversation idled and then resumed. She strode through the doorway as one who had a right to be there, wondering if today would be her first time to be arrested. The building was constructed of brick, stone, and old wood with windows, the lower ones currently covered with black cloth. The interior was of stone flooring with modern shelving and dimmed lighting. Nearby was a panel that controlled humidity. Across from her was a metal circular staircase leading to the floor above.

She gazed around the room, looking for any familiar faces that might cause her trouble. Young men dressed in blue jeans and T-shirts with unshaven faces and thick glasses whispered among themselves as they worked.

Sofia walked around the perimeter to get a sense of the librarian's shelving system. The university staff had placed special lamps on movable stands and photographic equipment set on frames about the room. They were photographing each book page, creating the same computer files she produced for her own use. As the archivist said, the university employees only digitized the illuminated manuscripts made during the medieval times, a far later period than her specialty.

She glanced around, looking for Takis. Where was he?

Taking the stairs up, Sofia discovered that the upper floor stored many newer books, from the eleventh century to contemporary theology. Where were their oldest manuscripts stored? Dare she ask one of the monks? Gazing out the upper floor window, her stomach fluttered with excitement. Monks walked in pairs, going about their business. She was actually standing on Agio Óros.

Shifting her rucksack, Sofia returned to the main floor and climbed clumsily around cords, boxes, and lamps. She strode across to the far end of the floor, quickly locating a librarian's workspace. Scanning his open shelves, she could not find any of the index books. Seeing a monk nearby glancing her way, she nodded in acknowledgment and headed toward what appeared to be a corridor. She shot a quick prayer that he would not follow her. Turning a corner, she noticed a hallway leading to another long, narrow room. Here, the librarian had installed shelving on tracks, allowing for density in storing books, which was safe because the library rested on stone. Setting her rucksack down, she slowly walked the length of the shelving, cranked the lever, and scanned the shelves.

"*Dóxa to Theó.*" Glory be to God. "I am Father Theóphilos."

Sofia froze. Her heart started pounding. She turned with feet apart as her cousin had drilled in her. She stood before a monk with thick glasses and eyebrows raised. His face registered more curiosity than suspicion.

"*Dóxa to Theó.* Brother Pachomius," she responded from her lowest vocal range.

"Brother, I apologize. My abbot hadn't advised me that one of our own would be here. I thought you might be a graduate student." Nodding to the main library room, he continued. "No point in maintaining silence here with all the filming activity. You are from?"

"Ipapandi." Reaching into her rucksack, she pulled out her letter of introduction and handed it to the monk librarian.

"Ipapandi. I haven't met a monk from Meteora in years." He read her letter and glanced her way several times. He studied her. Too polite to say anything about her minimal facial hair?

"Early Patristics? You're in the right area, but our Patristics collection isn't large. We've mostly medieval texts, specializing in the Divine Liturgy." His eyes continued to gaze at her. "I didn't see you this morning."

Her chest tightened. The monk meant the long early morning prayers called Orthros. "Just arrived."

The monk studied her letter again. "I was under the impression that my brother monks in Meteora disapproved of our observance. And especially of our welcoming the university to digitize some of our collection."

She put on her "I belong here" attitude and responded. "I haven't heard my abbot dismiss your monastic community. As you see, I was given permission. Might you have an index to the collection?"

"I'll bring that to you." His eyes remained fixed on her as he explained how the collection was put together.

Sofia felt sweat dribble down her back.

"Brother Pachomius, I must go. I'll talk further with you and my abbot in the trapeze this noon. I want to assist your research, but I must also monitor our graduate students."

She nodded as she mentally scrambled, trying to figure out how to get away from this monk. His abbot? Stay or leave? Forget food.

Brother Pachomius was now on a private fast. Knowing she'll never have this opportunity again, she walked to the far corner of the room, cranked the levers, and began an intense search for Deacon Olympias.

TWELVE

LIBRARY, MEGÍSTIS LÁVRAS

Sofia scanned the shelving, tipping back book after book that was not a recently published tome on patristics. She did not see anything like flat archival boxes that might hold unbound parchments flat and away from the glare of light. Yet she'd been told that they held an impressive early Patristics collection. So where was it?

What might Olympias' letters look like? Probably later copies like Brother Mac found at Mor Gabriel. Most likely nothing older than the last millennium. She pushed on, hoping that a librarian may have rebound early texts despite their fragility. Sofia knew that many medieval book owners took parchments, cut them up, and sewed them into quasi-books.

She reached for another tome, bound in softer leather than most books she'd handled, and sneezed. Damn, did she sound like a woman? She listened, a throat cleared, but when she didn't hear anyone coming, she sat down on the ground and began delicately turning pages.

This book was a collection of seemingly unrelated papyri held together by silk fabric strips. Scanning while barely touching the papyri, it seemed apparent that these were pieces from different scrolls. She noted different scripting styles, evident even though these were centuries old. One of its former owners had made meticulous notes in the margins of each page. She pulled out her pen flashlight and studied the pages. The writing was Greek, formal, and typical of early Christian writings. The vellum appeared in good shape, probably dating from the turn of the last millennia.

The line of thought in the text was like the early and original Saint Paul, not the later pseudo-Paul. Later, followers changed some of his radical teachings, writing some letters in Paul's name. He had been blamed for their conservative and rigid bent ever since.

A glance at one of the pages brought her browsing to a halt. The notes in the margin in early Greek said, Susanna. The other pages were an unrelated assortment of sermons and letters. But this page was different. Someone before her had been convinced that the author was a woman. Straining to see, she began to read the text, translating as she went:

> ...do not be snared in the battles ... who is a Jew ... what is a Jew. We are all called to the Word. We are all people of the Word. The Temple has passed. The Holy Spirit will not be silenced. As Christ called the Establishment to reform, so we must refuse to cooperate with the attempts of the scoundrels to return us to oppression. The Holy Spirit calls leaders, not that caste of powerful priests of the Temple. Temple priests are disappearing, and the fool and the disdained of this Empire make the power of the Holy Spirit manifest.

Some grieve the destruction of the Temple and look
heavenward for Christ's return. But I tell you that
the new Temple is in our hearts and homes. The new
sacrifice is the breaking of the Bread. This is why the
Lord is called the Healing Physician and the Bread of
Life, the new Tabernacle...

Wow. Sofia's mind began to expand around possibilities. This was
the voice of an early Church leader and not private correspondence.
Whoever scribbled the notes in the margins seemed to think the author
was *Susanna*.

But which Susanna? Susanna the Martyr? This was not the typical
martyr's testimony. The desert ascetic? Possibly, since such were forever calling for society to reform. Susanna, the Deacon of a church near
Pontus in Asia Minor? Susanna was a common name, like Maryam or
Mary. The writing itself was in the mode of preaching or teaching, not
prophetic utterance.

Somehow, what she was reading didn't seem to make sense. Sofia
hadn't encountered works like these in all her reading and research.
The content didn't fit what she'd expect Olympias to say to Chrysostom, and some words seemed confusing: *Establishment*, *Scoundrel*,
and *Empire*. Sofia made a note to check comparable sources when she
returned home. Tracing the use of single words revealed much about
the history of a piece of writing. While not Olympias, these pieces
intrigued her.

Sofia moved to a table farthest from the hallway entrance and pulled
out her camera. She positioned each page and began shooting from
several angles, zooming in and out. Why hadn't anyone made this dis-

covery public? Certainly nothing earth-shattering about these pieces, even if it is a woman's voice. She noted the archival number in her blank book and then remembered to shoot the inside cover. Then she clipped a small thread from a vellum sheaf and, using tweezers, placed the sample on a glass slide and fastened it with a cover slip. Taking a sharp knife, she scraped a tiny bit of the black ink, placed it on another glass slide, and again fastened it tight. She labeled each and made notations in her book.

Sofia stretched her stiff back. The soft rumble of the crews working in the main library remained consistent, and no one seemed interested in heading her way. She resumed her search.

Cranking another shelving unit, Sofia spotted something unusual. She pulled out what appeared to be more a leather file with ties rather than a bound book. She returned to her table when she heard the bell announce midday. She could hear the students breaking to eat. Her own stomach growled.

"Brother Pachomius, unfortunately our abbot is unable to join us for our mid-day meal." Startled by the voice of the monk librarian, Father Theóphilos, Sofia nearly spilled the loose pages from the file. "But please follow me to our trapeze. We can discuss your research needs there."

Her hands went cold with sweat. Now what? Refuse his hospitality and risk getting into trouble? Join him and risk exposure?

Looking at her gear, he said, "Don't worry about your belongings. Security is tight here," nodding to the main room, "especially with all the university's expensive equipment out there."

Feeling like a trapped animal, Sofia set her pencil down, thankful she had already stored her slides in her rucksack and out of his sight, adjusted her cap and hood, and followed him out. She listened and nodded as he gave her a verbal tour of the monastery. Students greeted them. With her big feet and bulky hiking boots, she struggled to climb the steep, rough-hewn steps without tripping. Their dining room had quite a view, given that it was on the floor above.

Exposed to the curious glances her way, sweaty hands gripped tightly within her front pocket, Sofia was escorted to a long wooden table. Her breath released at the sound of her cousin greeting Father Theóphilos and joining their table.

"So, Father, you've met my cousin, Brother Pachomius?"

Sofia breathed deeply, trying to release the headache that came upon her as a deep rumble. This librarian, because of his keen eyes, frightened her.

The librarian poured wine into several glass jars. "Cousins? I hadn't realized the connection."

Takis chatted away as dishes of white fish and grilled vegetables were passed around and wine poured. Dare she drink wine? Might it cause her to let down her guard? The monk librarian ate heartily and glanced her way more than once.

"Brother Pachomius," the monk librarian spoke and ate all at once, "what area of patristics are you studying."

Sofia tried to mimic the librarian's way of eating. In her deepest contralto, she responded, "Early Syria and Armenia."

"Father Theóphilos, may I join you?" A distinguished gentleman with the stocky build of a northern Greek grabbed a plate from the stack and filled it from the serving bowls resting on the tabletop.

Sofia gulped some wine, bowed her head, and gave diligent attention to her fish, pita, and vegetables. Why bother asking if they may join a group after staking out a space?

"Hello there." He extended his hands her way, enlarged with arthritic joints. "Professor Drosinis, Medieval Studies." His voice is soft and raspy.

Sofia responded with a slight bow of her head. "Brother Pachomius." Drosinis? Her mind scrounged for names of scholars she might have met.

"I don't believe you're one of the monks here. Visiting from another monastery?"

"Ipapandi," Sofia responded with a low voice and without looking his way.

"So, Meteora. Where did you study?"

She could see him examining her.

Turning away, she answered. "Louvain."

"Louvain. Isn't that unusual for an Orthodox monk, especially one from Meteora? A Roman university? No offense intended, Brother, but your monasteries are not renowned for openness to us, let alone Westerners." Like Father Theóphilos, this guy could eat and talk simultaneously.

Takis came to her rescue. "My cousin is the family scholar, and I've escorted him to several famous libraries. Me? Just an auto mechanic and a simple farmer."

This Drosinis is too curious and might even blow her cover innocently. "Not always so true. Several of my brother monks are language scholars. We work anonymously." Realizing her hands had gripped so tight that her palms hurt, she stretched her fingers, still hidden under the table.

"We are concentrating on those beautiful medieval texts. Your area of research?" His noisy chewing gnawed at her nerves.

She responded by turning toward her cousin and praying he could read her thoughts. "Early patristics. I doubt we will bother each other."

"Yes, of course." The professor tried to get a clear look at her face. "Have we met before?"

Drosinis. Was this guy also in the Patristics society? The name didn't sound familiar to her. "No, I don't think so."

Takis spoke up. "Professore Drosinis, my cousin's a hermit. I was happy to get him here since I don't see him much anymore."

She still felt the gaze. "Hermit? No, I've seen Brother Pachomius before. At the university, I think," he persisted. "Yes, you're from Thessaloníki. I never forget a face. Your family is from Thessaloníki. Of that, I'm certain. I know the old families."

If he only knew. Seféris and Papandréou were among Greece's old families and became more famous since the civil war of the 1960s. But, damn, she just couldn't figure out his connection to her.

"Brother Pachomius, what is your family name?"

Her jaw clenched. Sofia turned toward Takis, raising her eyebrows, hoping he'd intervene.

Takis nodded his head. "Professor, why this interest?"

"The old families are a hobby of mine." Drosinis appeared upset at Takis' interruption. "And you are?"

"Since he usually eats silently, all your questions exhaust Brother Pachomius."

Sofia could cry; she was so wound tight by this interrogation. She nodded in dismissal toward the professor.

"Well, yes." The professor's frustration grew. "Brother, your family name?"

"We leave our family ties behind when we enter the monastery." Sofia bit into her vegetable-filled pita.

Takis responded a twinge of playfulness in his voice. "Hmmm, Seféris, I'd say."

"Now that you mention it, there's quite a resemblance," the professor responded.

What was Takis up to?

"Yes, George Séféris. Definitely." The professor finally seemed satisfied.

George Séféris, Greece's Nobel poet laureate, was their great uncle. Would Drosinis make the connection to Christina Séféris? Or worse, her parents? Why did Takis always have to play with fire?

With her face down, monkish style, she heard Takis say. "Well, let's give Brother Pachomius the space he expects." Takis had placed his hand on the professor's shoulder, escorting him toward the door.

When the monk librarian turned and answered some questions from one of the graduate students, Sofia stood, polished off the last of her wine, and departed. She was anxious to get back to her search. Her hands shook, and her mind raced. She carefully clambered down the steep wooden steps, nearly tripping several times. She landed on solid ground and noticed an older monk fingering his prayer cord. She cursed herself for not bringing one herself. It might've helped with her shaking hands, sweaty palms, or both.

She entered the library again and passed by the monk librarian's desk. She noticed that he had placed several bound books that contained the archival entries. She grabbed them and took them to her table. She heard the scraping of a chair. She turned to see Takis sit down, lean the chair against one wall of the hallway entrance, and put his feet up on the other. He was blocking anyone from entering without his permission. He grinned at her and opened a book.

She scanned the archival records, found what she was looking for, and copied the information into her notebook. Then, she decided to photograph all the pertinent pages in case she might send requests to the librarian from Brother Pachomius in the future. Especially since she hasn't located anything related to Olympias.

The first find was like a scrapbook whose only connection from the pieces was that an earlier librarian identified them as coming from northeastern Asia Minor, now Turkey. These were apparently copied in the 800s CE from earlier rotting texts. The leather file contained as yet unidentified vellum pieces that were only given the archival number. Space was left for future identification. Sofia again photographed each sheet from several angles. Then, she took samples of each and returned the leather file to the shelf.

Sofia gathered her gear. Pulling her hood over her head, she approached Takis and signaled her need to leave. And fast.

As they approached the library entrance, a student looked at her quizzically. With a lowered head, she passed around him.

"Dottore Papandréou?"

Thirteen

HAGIA THEOTOKOS

Sofia gripped her rucksack and lengthened her stride as she passed through the library entrance. She heard a male voice ask, "Wasn't that Papandréou from the Patristics department?" She bore right and headed back toward the exit of the complex. Her hands shook. Her heart pounded. She breathed deep, eyes focused straight ahead. She nodded in response to a group of monks who looked her way and heard Takis give a verbal reply while still covering her backside. This was the fastest departure and the longest journey Sofia could recall making.

Damn, why didn't she ask Hatzidakis to see the list of graduate students working here? She assumed most of them were from Athens. Sofia passed through the gates, praying that no one would look her way and that no word would be sent to her next destination. Should she still go to Hagia Theotokos? Or leave without trying?

Finally, Takis broke the silence. "Sof, you're safe. No one is follow-ing us. You fooled them all."

"Not all. You heard him."

"Yeah, you must've made an impression on your students." He chuckled. "I told you that hormones might cause you trouble. But I suspect he's still standing there confused."

"But if he says anything –."

"So what? The monks won't believe such ideas."

Discouraged that she didn't have more time to explore that library, Sofia remained quiet as they packed up their cave and returned to his truck.

"This next monastery or home? Your call."

Sofia sighed. "I can't leave without trying. No grad students at Hagia Theotokos, so maybe I'm safe."

Takis turned on the engine and shifted into gear. "Were you happy with the stuff you found?"

"Yes, but no letters of Olympias. I wish I had more time to ex-plore their holdings. Thanks, Takis." The road was rougher, and Sofia grunted as her shoulder slammed into the door. She gazed out across the water and obsessed over what had happened and what she might do differently at Hagia Theotokos.

Forty-five minutes later, Takis pulled beside a grove of trees above the monastery complex. They climbed out of his truck, and Takis pointed.

"The library is at this end and away from their chapel. Just straight downhill."

Sofia studied the layout below as Takis explained again what he had seen on his visit here.

"Maybe we don't unpack until we see if I can make it in. Save us time if I'm caught."

"Remember what I said. Act as if you belong. It got you through that last place, even if that kid remembered you."

Sofia slung her rucksack over her shoulder and took a deep breath as they climbed down the rough path and crossed through a grove of olive trees. Sofia pulled her cap down and hood over her head. Ahead lay a low stone wall with a dozen stone steps worn with age led onto a terrace. The staircase wrapped around the outer wall of the library. If the door was locked, a key would be hanging nearby. She could hear the waves crashing against the rocks below. Glancing over the wall, she saw the sea shimmering blue-green with whitecaps. The seagulls squawked.

She rounded a corner and spotted the staircase ahead.

"Guests. Welcome, brothers."

Sofia halted and caught her breath. An elderly monk, each hand grasping a wooden cane, gazed in her direction.

Shaking hands gripped within her front pocket, Sofia bowed and greeted the monk in her lowest voice. "*Evlogíte*. Brother Pachomius."

"*O Kýrios*. Brother Isaák. Welcome." The old monk hobbled closer, his bent spine slowing his gait. "And you're from?"

Sofia gazed down at the amiable, weathered face. His yellowed and blackened teeth suggested poverty. His eyes seemed to speak of this peninsula's centuries of quiet history.

"Ipapandi." She kept her voice low and soft.

The old monk smiled. Or was it a grimace of pain? "Indeed. It's been years since I've spoken with any of your monks. I did visit several of your monasteries in my youth. When I was still agile enough to climb those precarious rope ladders." The old monk laughed. "I could never make it up now."

Brother Isaák extended a gnarled hand, balancing his cane on his wrist. "What brings you to us?"

Sofia gently grasped the old monk's hand. "A few days of research."

He gazed at her hands. "Scholars hands. Mine bear witness to my years in the vineyard."

She noticed the smile on his face. Sofia shifted her rucksack. The weight of the straps cut into her shoulder. How long would it be before someone mentioned her presence to the abbot here?

"Father Theodor. Old, like me, but gifted with a stellar mind. I'm sure he'll be of great assistance."

Theodor was the name of the monk with whom Hatzidakis corresponded. She nodded in assent, but it seemed that Brother Isaak could not see that well.

The old monk walked over to the stone ledge and rested against it. "Your monastery is renowned for your observance. But in all my years here, you are the first scholar from Meteora I've ever heard of. I find this a pleasant change. We certainly have been negligent in sharing the endeavors of our life. We need more young monks like you. Prayer, practices, and studies. They constitute a monastic trinity with a long history."

"Indeed." Did she make a mistake in choosing Ipapandi as her alleged monastery? Sofia had assumed no one here ever had contact with Meteora. She bowed for a blessing from the old monk and then slipped away, trusting her talkative cousin to continue the diversion. She silently said a heartfelt prayer that she might be left alone this time.

She could hear her cousin asking the old monk how long he had been on Mount Athos. God have mercy on Brother Isaák; Takis will fill every ounce of silence.

After walking the length of the monastery, Sofia saw a group of monks ahead, huddled in conversation. One glanced her way. She made a quick left around a corner, head down.

Descending, she nearly slipped. Her boots still felt awkward. The stone steps wrapped around the exterior of the monastery. About halfway down the staircase, she spied a heavy crucifix hanging from the stone wall, and behind it hung an old key on a nail. She grabbed it and continued. No one was following.

Inserting the bulky key into the large lock, Sofia opened the door, pushing the heavy oak with her shoulder. With bare light through narrow windows, she closed the door and descended yet more spiraling stairs into darkness.

Reaching the bottom, she turned toward the soft light ahead. A deep blue, red, and gold Persian rug covered some stone floors. At the far end of the long room, an elderly monk bent over a book at his desk. Father Theodor?

Not ready to be seen, she quickly turned and entered one of the long aisles. As with the library at Megístis Lávras, before her were aisles of metal shelving stuffed with volumes and volumes of books. She began to roam, familiarizing herself with the library's layout. She noticed that the library had stone walls with no windows and ancient wooden beams that served as pillars supporting its ceiling. Set in corners were simple climate and moisture control devices to protect the books.

She set her rucksack on the floor in a discreet corner and pulled out her pen light. Wandering up and down the aisles, she was tempted to stop and pull a volume for a closer look. Instead, she disciplined herself to keep exploring and see if she could discern a pattern to the arrangement. She had to move quickly, and the Olympias letters had to be somewhere here. She could not see any old scrolls or parchments. Hatzidakis, not easily impressed, was impressed with the holdings. So where were they?

She continued exploring. The musty smell of aged leather lingered in the air. Sofia's excitement grew. The spine labels, primarily tags hanging from the top rim of the spine, were in Greek. The library holdings covered Biblical topics, early Christian writers, some philosophy, theology, the lives of the saints, and Church history. Surprised, she noted an extensive collection of rabbinical texts as well. She stopped and looked closer every so often when the tag had a series of numbers rather than a title. This library appeared to hold a vast collection of Orthodox liturgical books: hymns, rituals, sacramentals, chant mode studies, prayerbooks, and more.

Sofia was bothered more by what she was not seeing, namely rolled parchments and vellum scrolls. One of her dissertation advisors mentioned the sheer number of scrolls he had seen on Mount Athos. So why didn't either of these monasteries have some?

The challenge was bigger than she had anticipated. This library collection made sense to the librarians, but she didn't have time to learn someone's system. How could she think like the librarians here? So would the sermons of her women prophets be in early Church history, called Patristics? In Liturgy? Philosophy? They could even be in Biblical Studies since many of her women died before the Bible was put together in its present form.

Deciding that anything appearing to be less than 700 years old would not help her, Sofia found a crate to stand on and resumed reading tags from the uppermost shelving. The lighting was dim enough to protect the old books yet gave enough illumination for her to make out the titles. She began pulling an oversized volume off the shelf when she heard a deadening thud and a second echoing off the walls. She ran down the aisle toward the old monk by instinct, concerned that he might have fallen and hurt himself. Apparently, he had dropped a thick, leather-bound portfolio. The librarian waved her away. So, he didn't consider her presence unusual? She ached to have a serious conversation with him, to grill him on everything he knows about the libraries on Agio Óros.

She felt an urgency to speed up. Continuing to read tags and pulling anything that might prove useful, she was both excited and anxious. Breathe deep, and keep an even momentum. Stay calm. Stay focused. The prophets were here somewhere; just maintain a steady pace. Sofia struggled to keep her apprehension and excitement in check. She scanned, removed, and returned countless books.

She stopped where she could observe the old monk, but he could not see her. He returned to his desk and examined some papers with a magnifying glass. His hands gently shook, and he wore no hearing aids. His power of concentration was impressive. Dare she talk to him? Her gut told her that Olympias' letters would have been in parchment or codex form, not modern binding. So where should she put her energies?

Despite what happened earlier today, she decided to risk the encounter. She might not have more than one or two days here. She approached the frail monk sitting at the desk, carefully set her rucksack down, and bowed respectfully. His desk was covered with books in need of repair. To the side, a table stood where a press held a codex being restored. Behind his work area was a staircase that presumably led to the private living space for the monks of this monastery. The old monk appeared unaware of his visitor's presence. After a moment's wait, she finally said, "*Evlogíte*. Brother?"

Surprised, the old monk looked up, and a smile crossed his face. "*O Kýrios*. So, a visitor. I wasn't told I'd have company." His voice was soft and raspy. Sparse white hair and a long, thin beard graced his rough face.

She wondered if the librarian used formal Greek because he was addressing a stranger or was an unusually well-educated monk? "Brother

Pachomius. I have a brief opportunity to do some research. My brother monks spoke highly of your collection."

"Indeed. I hope we don't disappoint you. You are from...?"

"Ipapandi. In Meteora –."

"Yes, yes, I know where that is. We're not that isolated down here." The old monk growled through his talking.

This one reminded Sofia of her grandfather. A bear with no teeth.

"Pardon my presumption, Brother. I –."

"Father Theodor. Now, what are you looking for."

Sofia kept her head tilted down while answering. "The early Christian prophetic movement, especially in the eastern part of the old Roman Empire."

The old monk sat quietly for a moment, but his eyes struck Sofia as alert and searching. Could he already tell she wasn't a monk? Finally, he responded. "Any one person in particular?"

Sofia wasn't sure how to respond. Would naming a woman make him suspicious? His eyes were studying her. Or did he have bad sight?

"Well, yes. The early deacon Olympias. She was a friend—"

"—of John Chrysostom. Yes, Brother Pachomius, I know my church history. Interesting choice. I recall seeing something related to her. But where?"

Sofia was thrilled, at least an acknowledgment of Olympias' existence. She gripped her hands. The library remained quiet. Deep in thought? Then he stood and wandered off. Should she follow him? Wait here? She didn't want to get into more trouble with him than necessary. She decided to stay put until he told her otherwise. She inspected the codex under repair. It was an old copy of the *Didache*, the Teachings of the Apostles, written in the mid-first century. She guessed this was a sixth-century copy.

Father Theodor returned. "I have no record, but I know I've seen something." He lowered himself into his chair and began digging through the top drawer of his desk. "The best sources are imprisoned at Esfigmenou. Those monks won't let either of us anywhere near their collection. Tragic. Their behavior shames Orthodoxy." He slammed his cane against his desk. "Unfortunately, I'm years behind in my work with no one to assist me. This younger generation just isn't interested in old books."

Sofia gulped. God, what would she give to stay and help him! How could the other monks not care? "I understand. If I were free to help you, I would."

Father Theodor waved his hand in dismissal. Devastated, Sofia picked up her rucksack and turned. Where else could she look?

"Brother Pachomius, where are you going?"

Sofia turned back to see Father Theodor hobbling off in the opposite direction. Not knowing what he wanted of her, she followed. He slowly led her around a corner and to the end of the stacks.

"Yes, indeed." Father Theodor appeared to be talking to himself, but Sofia wasn't sure.

The semantron sounded. Father Theodor sighed. The call to prayer.

As Father Theodor slowly turned to leave, he looked at Brother Pachomius. "When you return in the morning, explore the rooms beyond. If my memory serves me correctly, and mostly it doesn't anymore," he said, chuckling, "you may find what you want." His shaking hand pointed at an old wood-hewn door.

Fourteen

H AGIA THEOTOKOS

The following morning, Sofia entered the library while the monks were still attending Orthros, one of the primary services prayed at dawn. She passed by Father Theodor's desk and down the long aisle. She reached for the door to the cavern below and pulled. Much to her chagrin, the old oak door resisted any cooperation to opening easily. Pulling on it created a cacophony of noise that seemed loud enough to echo throughout the monastery. She had been working hard to avoid bringing attention to herself, and now she feared that she had managed to announce her presence to the entire complex.

"Many apologies, Brother Pachomius. I'm afraid I'm somewhat slow this morning," Father Theodor said from behind.

Sofia jumped at the unexpected voice. Why wasn't he with the other monks at services? The fragile librarian appeared to be shrinking, much like her grandmother, shorter on one side than the other.

"Let me help you there. I'm afraid our home has its stubborn quirks. Need to outthink it somedays."

With a strength that surprised her, Father Theodor, with a cane propped on each forearm, grabbed the door and pulled. The badly worn panel of wood yielded to the master's resolute will. The librarian waved her onward, turned, and shuffled to his work area.

"Brother Pachomius."

She turned and looked his way.

"You mentioned the prophets? I expect you're particularly interested in the women prophets. I'd start at the far wall, I think." Turning, he continued on his way.

Sofia stood in stunned alarm. Did he know? If so, why was he letting her stay? She was finding Father Theodor a dear heart. She decided to head down before he changed his mind. Or maybe he did not know?

As she passed through the doorway, dry, dusty air accosted her. How long since someone had been in there? Sofia turned on her flashlight. With its low ceiling, the stone passageway sloped downward and soon gave in to unevenly packed dirt. Navigating the space felt disturbing, like an optical illusion. She resisted the onset of vertigo.

The flashlight was of limited use. She kept one hand on the stone wall to her left and tread carefully. Soon, the smooth stone turned jagged to the touch—the rock was hewn rough and jagged. The beams of her flashlight illuminated a change in the wall's surface. She had arrived at another door, excitement centered in her chest. This one opened quickly. After several more steps downward, she entered a large, cavernous room whose rock appeared chiseled somewhat smooth. Flashing her light around the room, she saw boxes stashed everywhere and crates filled with rolled vellum. Tables were filled with books in various stages of disrepair and stacks of parchment and vellum. On closer examination, she detected several battery-operated lamps.

Sofia turned on the lamps and gazed about. What she saw was both a nightmare and a dream. A treasure lay before her. What she would give to spend months down here exploring. But she reminded herself that this would never happen. Some hours, and if her nerves could handle it, one more day, and then she must leave.

This space certainly was smaller than above, yet she could not see the far wall. Deeper possibly? She set her rucksack down. Father Theodor clearly said the far wall. But she could barely see the far wall, just a long tumble of crates. Climbing around these, she made her way toward the far wall. Since her first conversation with him, she sensed that Father Theodor's memory was far better than might be otherwise apparent. His absentmindedness seemed to be more about concentrating on his projects than some form of dementia.

All she could do was begin her exploration with the crates and boxes. Some books were held together with string. Single sheets of vellum, as well as parchment pieces, were all jumbled together.

Correspondence between people whose names she did not recognize. Copies of land deeds. Copies of known texts, even copies of some old Greek plays. Some pieces of oddities that she was not interested in deciphering. She would stay on task. Anything after 1000 C.E. would only interest her if the voice was clearly that of a woman. She had begun the now familiar rhythm of research, which mainly consisted of sweat, dust, and luck. Before her was a scattered mess of ancient vellum and codices. She was having fun.

Sofia began unpacking and repacking each crate. As she progressed, she knew Brother Makarios must see this. He'd be hooked. She was confident he could commandeer several young male scholars to assist him and Father Theodor. Conversion or no conversion, she chuckled. She was having a blast sitting among all this history. And she felt hope rise, something she hadn't experienced in a long time. Mor Gabriel was no fluke.

When her stomach growled, she made a spot to rest and ate a couple of protein bars with juice from her canteen. What would Makarios make of her adventure? He would cheer her on *go, old gal*. She shot some photos of the general mess to send Brother Mac.

By late afternoon, she had dug her way into a corner collection of codices that had attracted her attention. Crates of rolled vellum tucked behind more crates of odds and ends. Her head hurt. Her back ached even more. She resisted discouragement and was afraid she was beginning to make mistakes. Dare she spend another night on Mount Athos? Surely, word would spread that Dottore Papandréou had been seen at Megístis Lávras.

Cobwebs suggested it had been some time since anyone had looked through these crates. The rough thickness of the vellum rolls began to indicate to her that there might be something special there. She had been digging around tenaciously, long enough now that she was starting to recognize the paper as suggestive of the region or era in which the document was produced.

More copies of known texts and assorted correspondence with kings of several nations, the Ottoman Empire, and abbots she'd never heard of. What she had learned in graduate school had undoubtedly become more real for her now, namely that Mount Athos had been a major political force in its day. She noticed what appeared to be several goatskin scrolls, unusually thick. That's where she will begin in the morning. She was willing to risk one more day here.

The hour was growing late. From years of experience, Sofia knew that she did not do her best work when exhausted. Even if she failed to locate Olympias, she wanted to shoot something as proof she had been there. She pulled her hood over her hair, swung her rucksack onto her back, and put her boots back on. Taking the stairs and through the doorway, Sofia noticed Father Theodor bent over a press, working on an old book.

Hiding her hands in her front pocket and bowing her head, Sofia said goodnight with her low-range contralto voice.

He glanced up. "Found something useful?"

"An interesting assortment you have down there, but nothing to help me."

"Patience, Brother. They are there. I don't recall where. Chrysostom and Olympias.

Such a friendship."

"So few are aware of them, especially Olympias," she said.

"True, but one doesn't need a distinguished university education to appreciate the great spiritual masters of Christianity. Oxford, myself. Read Biblical Hebrew and Aramaic." His shaky hands were moving an old volume with delicate skill.

Sofia felt stupid. He obviously had spent years among old codices and scrolls, and she had failed to notice. She had never shown him the courtesy of asking about his background. Apparently, Father Theodor felt like he had been put out to pasture long before he was ready.

Father Theodor began to speak of the steadfast friendship between John Chrysostom and Deacon Olympias, one that cost her greatly. During his exile, she financially supported Chrysostom. She continually petitioned the imperial court and the other bishops for his return to Constantinople. Chrysostom never relented in his condemnation of corruption and compromise with the world's more questionable values. Most scholars agreed he would have failed without Olympias' friendship and support.

Father Theodor emphasized his belief that today's world needed a new Chrysostom and Olympias to challenge modern misbehaviors.

He was surprisingly well informed on politics, both Church and secular, and was opinionated about it. The monk spoke of the wars in Afghanistan and Iraq, the growing civil war in Syria, Turkey's disputes with Kurdish refugees, the so-called Arab Spring, the Palestinians, and especially terrorism – the terrorism so acknowledged and the terrorism we failed to see.

"So much violence and harm. So much violence." The old monk shook his head.

"Father Theodor—"

"The souls of our children have been irreparably harmed."

Sofia stood silent out of respect and shock. She had not expected a monk on Mount Athos to be politically aware and certainly not so passionate about world events. Somehow, she had expected them to be otherworldly and unconcerned. Before arriving on Agio Óros, she would have added cold-heartedly.

"Yes, Father. We should pray daily for the children. May we live to see the day when Christ's peace reigns," she said softly.

"I'm sorry, Brother Pachomius. Sad news sometimes overwhelms me."

"What happened?"

"Suicide bombing in Jerusalem. Another village in Gaza bulldozed into oblivion. The children, the children." He appeared near tears.

After a moment of silence, Father Theodor resumed. "Excuse this doddering, old monk, Brother Pachomius. I rarely have anyone to talk to and—"

"I understand," she replied.

Clearing his throat, he continued. "Olympias. Yes, you will find her."

"I'm afraid this has all taken me by surprise. I hadn't expected anyone here to be familiar with early women leaders," she said.

"Why?" Father Theodor again looked at her with something like surprise, sliding into hurt.

"I don't know. I had assumed—" How might she explain? Most men were entirely ignorant of women's contributions to early Christianity. And now this.

"Brother Pachomius." The old monk shifted, punching the floor with one of his canes. "Excuse my familiarity, but I have found you frankly odd. You say you're from Ipapandi, a monastery with a long history of suspicion toward anything even remotely intellectual. Yet you come to us assuming that we lack any scholarly perspective."

He was getting mad again. How did she keep provoking him? A few days on the Holy Mountain, and she, the only flaming feminist here, might well find herself evicted for being narrow-minded and conservative.

"You're right, Father." How could she argue with him, especially without giving herself away?

"Forgive me, Brother Pachomius. I have no right to talk to you this way. I've had an irritating week. Seems one of our errant monks from Esfigmenou drove his truck off a cliff, and their abbot is accusing the military police of killing him. Stirring up trouble all over the Holy Mountain."

Sofia bowed and crossed the foyer toward the doorway.

FIFTEEN

C AVERN UNDER HAGIA THEOTOKOS

Sofia returned at dawn with Takis in tow. Today would be their last day on Mount Athos. Her nerves would not last much longer. Passing by Father Theodor's desk, she set her gear down, and together, they managed to open the old door.

Then she went and pulled several illuminated manuscripts from their shelves and set them on a table near the entrance to the cave.

"Takis, sit here and pretend to be interested in these. Keep anyone from coming down below."

He grinned. "Now I'm a spy? Or just pest control?"

She picked up her rucksack. "Just be your warm, affable self. And if necessary, talk them to death."

Returning to the cave below, she was satisfied that everything was as she had left it. She pulled off her awkward boots again, setting them by the doorway. She placed her camera equipment at one end of the table. Settling on the stool, she gently removed the goat skin scroll from its crate. As she unfolded it, she realized several pieces were rolled together. She separated what turned out to be four vellum sheaves. She started her examination with the innermost pieces, which appeared to be liturgical texts in Syriac Armenian. She would shoot these and take samples for study.

She found it interesting that these had yet to be bound in book form, which she had often encountered, including in the collection upstairs. The goatskin was in excellent shape for its apparent age. She saw no Imperial notations or the formal script used for declaration documents, such as Imperial letters or Christian texts. She noted some frayed edges, small tears, and expected fading of the ink. Shifting her penlight, she examined the script, a form of Greek that she was comfortable reading. Some lettering had faded, but faint lines remained visible.

Then, she unrolled a heavier piece. She examined the text; again, some letters were faded and barely readable. She stopped. A name leaped out at her. *Chrysostom*. She stared in a mixture of delight and disbelief. Had she finally found Olympias?

Her heart hammering, she removed her glasses, cleaned, and adjusted the lenses on the bridge of her nose to ensure she clearly saw what she thought she had read. The word was definitely *Chrysostom*.

As she did while crewing, Sofia disciplined her breathing. Breathe deep, hold, and release slowly.

Had she found more of Olympias after all these years of searching? The goatskin was sturdy despite some tears. Portions of the text were missing. Moving her flashlight to the best possible angle, she continued reading.

> I have been questioned on my ministry, which some
> hold as fit only for a man. I must reply: when the
> flock is hungry, and there is no shepherd, are the sheep

> to starve? Haven't women been shepherds since time
> began? Is the faith of Christ so weak that only a man
> can administer it? Are Hannah's words empty? Is this
> truly what the Risen One came for? God forbid that
> I allow the passing opinions of others to silence my
> tongue. Indeed, every occasion for preaching libera-
> tion from this life and the freedom to come...

Sofia caught her breath. She had stopped breathing while reading, a bad habit of hers. The scroll had been written in early Greek. This writer must be her Deacon Olympias, Chrysostom's closest friend and staunch ally. Who else? And who is Hannah? The text ended and was missing a piece. She wondered what that portion might have said. She continued reading with the next sheaf.

> While I and other more worthy saints of my
> monastery have been ordained and proclaimed dea-
> con, I seek to preach the Good News through service
> to the holiest of saints, the poorest of God's children.
> Some hold me in contempt for giving my wealth away,
> but I know I draw nearer to the heavenly realm when
> I serve these most precious of God's children. I bear
> contempt...

The text fit what was known of Olympias's life as hers was one of the better-documented lives of a woman leader in the early Christian movement. One of the wealthiest members of the Imperial family, she had built a monastery near where the Cathedral of Hagia Sophia,

meaning Holy Wisdom, is now located. Sofia shifted the scroll and
continued reading,

> Publicly, I am condemned for my support of the em-
> inent John, called Chrysostom. He is a dear friend
> in the faith who rightly calls his flock to holiness.
> He is just attacking the corruption and greed seeping
> into the Church. Followers of the Way must purify
> themselves of the evil ways of this world. Alas, wolves
> in sheep's clothing have entered our midst with a
> viciousness of intent. In God's name, they steal the
> worldly wealth of Holy Mother Church intended for
> her good works and support of the widows and chil-
> dren.

Sofia stopped to think. This was not addressed to John Chrysostom, so to whom might it be addressed? Why would someone beloved
by the Orthodox Church be hidden away like this? Where has this
scroll been all these years? She returned her gaze to the scroll and
resumed reading.

> Truly, I proclaim: our home, refuge to so many lost
> and hungry for the Living Wisdom of God, is rightly
> called The Church of Heavenly Peace, for Wisdom is
> birthed and nurtured and proclaimed within her holy
> walls. As Hannah taught, Wisdom must...

Some sections of the text were faded. Holes appeared in the vellum. Multispectral imaging would pull some of these words up like she recently used in Mor Gabriel. Again, Hannah?

> I am familiar with the easy deception following those trained in the skills of rhetoric for which Athens is so famous. Holy Makrina worked diligently to convert her brothers Gregory and Basil after their sojourn to Athens, returning wise in the eyes of the world but fools indeed. Greek philosophy and those who consider themselves the new Gnostics will deny the Incarnation of God and the humanity of the Teacher. Remember that the Teacher is fully present, fully Resurrected, and One with Abba...

Sofia sat on a nearby crate, focusing her breathing to help her think. This sheaf included a mention of Makrina the Younger, another early leader. She was known to scholars and Orthodox believers and not erased from history. However, this was still a scarce mention of the holy woman. It is rarer to find anything near that era connecting Deacon Olympias with Makrina the Younger.

All the evidence of Olympias' life was in the form of biographies. Her letters to John were lost. John's letters to Olympias, however, remained intact. His letters often chastised Olympias for her discouragement in the face of his exile and for failing to take care of her health. This was different, but the voice sounded right for her milieu. Yet this doesn't appear addressed to John. Sofia would enjoy the challenge of figuring out what this scroll is and how it fits in with the early Christian movement.

Looking closely at the document, she could not find an archivist's number. She would need to ask Father Theodor to enter it into his collection and assign an archival number to the document so that she would have verifiable proof of the scrolls' existence.

She couldn't believe her luck. These sheaves were fascinating, whatever they were, plus what she found at Megístis Lávras. She pulled out and examined another sheaf from the crate. This one was not goatskin. Others in the crate were not in Greek, and one was an early Slavic language. Each was intriguing. Where had the contents of the crate been? Would Father Theodor know?

With shaking hands, Sofia finished searching the remaining crates, hoping for more of Olympias. Then she pulled out her digital camera and lens. Setting the first sheaf on the table and using two old books to hold it open, she examined it through the camera's viewfinder. Wanting a better angle, she carefully emptied several crates. She climbed onto them ~ for height to shoot each sheaf from above. The crates wobbled under her big feet. Carefully moving to the crates' corner, she could steady herself. Bending over the parchment, she obtained a good angle on the text. The flash around her lens created perfect, even lighting.

Sofia began to shoot. After taking a dozen shots of the entire scroll, she concentrated on photographing small blocks of the text. Trusting her instinct, she photographed the back side of each sheaf in case some ink from the faded letters seeped through. She'd gotten clear shots without shadowing. She'd seen the amazing analyses that computer imaging could do. She would ask Father Theodor to provide a name for these sheaves. All scrolls and parchment pieces worldwide were named and codified so libraries and scholars could keep track.

While photographing the other scrolls in the crate, barely looking at what they were, she kept thinking. Father Theodor mentioned women prophets in the Early Christian Movement. What was he recalling?

Maybe "Brother Pachomius" should send a letter of request to Father Theodor: please, where are those early women prophets? If Brother Mac won't come here, maybe she could arrange, through Hatzidakis, to send a graduate student here to assist Father Theodor in straightening this mess. If only she knew a billionaire or two to fund her dreams.

She again took minuscule examples of fiber and ink, just enough to run tests. Sofia felt guilty but kept rebutting herself that this process was all in the interest of scholarly investigation.

§

Exhausted and satisfied, Sofia condemned her sore feet to her boots, restored her hoodie, packed up her gear, and returned to Father Theodor's desk, goatskin sheaves in hand. She found him stooped over an old chant book. She glanced around. Where was Takis? Why would he leave?

She bent over the book to examine it herself: large and obviously crafted for some monk's use in choir. Latin, not Greek or Slavic or Russian.

Sofia asked. "Carthusian?" These were monks who lived lives of absolute silence and solitude.

Father Theodor looked up at her, a smile awash with an expression of surprise. "Brother Pachomius, you continue to astound me. A monk of Ipapandi recognizing a Western text?"

Sofia could feel her cheeks warm to a blush. How does she explain her knowledge of Western texts, even monastic ones, when she was supposed to be from a narrow-minded and bigoted monastery? By mainly telling the truth. "I spent some time in Belgium, learning to care for old texts."

Father Theodor smiled. "Refreshing to hear."

"I was fortunate to spend some days at the Grand Chartreuse in the Alps. They were gracious hosts if silent ones."

The librarian laughed. "Silent, indeed. Their dedication to silence puts us to shame. I see you found something."

"Yes," she responded as she set the sheaves carefully on his desk. "But I noticed there is no number on them." Sofia kept her voice soft and low.

He waved his gnarled hand. "Oh, nothing below has been recorded yet."

"Is it possible for you to assign a number for me? Maybe a title as well? In case I need to reference this later."

Father Theodor stared at her, apparently surprised. "Brother Pachomius, I know the content of my library. I hardly need a number to assist you in the future."

Sofia was taken aback. "It's my need, not yours, Father."

"Indeed. Some may assume that my memory has already gone before me to the heavenly realm —"

Not this again. "Never, Father. If I publish, the editor will insist on an archive number to identify materials. I mean no disrespect."

"Oh, I suppose you're right." Father Theodor picked up the sheaves and laid them on his desk. She cringed at the offhand way he handled such treasures. "Let me get you your number. No title for today." He shuffled over and picked up an old ledger. Returning, he opened it and recorded the information.

"Father, how are you describing these?"

"Describing it?"

"Is this a letter?"

He looked at her quizzically. "Letter? No, it's a sermon. There are several more. Unfortunately, they're held in Esfigmenou." He sighed. "Our very own terrorist organization."

She caught her breath. More? More sermons of Olympias? Letters? She'd only hoped to find a couple of her letters to Chrysostom. Will anyone believe her discovery? Damn, she cannot leave Agio Óros until she finds her way into Esfigmenou.

Sixteen

HAGIA THEOTOKOS

Father Theodor leaned back in his chair as he considered Brother Pachomius. A scholar with his determination and skill with languages, a monk of Meteora? He sighed. What he'd give to have Brother Pachomius working with him for a year. Maybe he should talk to his abbot about a request. Those hands. That awkward gait. And couldn't grow a beard if the brother's life depended on it. He leaned forward again, chuckling and shaking his head, when he heard footsteps behind him. He glanced up to see Brother Vassilis arriving.

"Who was that?"

Father Theodor shuffled papers to clear the oak slab. "Brother Pachomius. Surely you saw him at meals?"

"No, I haven't seen him in the trapezda or the katholikón." Brother Vassilis sat on a nearby stool. "How long has he been here?"

"Oh, just a couple of days, I think. Maybe our brother chose to spend the few days given him by his abbot to complete his work here."

"Not often we get monks coming here for our library." The young monk gazed at him in a way that irritated Father Theodor. "But where is he staying? The only guest I've seen has been that noisy, talkative one named Takis. But then," Brother Vassilis sat on a stool, "he said something about camping outdoors. Maybe they're together."

"Maybe. Brother Pachomius seemed rather determined in his search. He reminds me of some of my colleagues at Oxford. Always pining to discover something new. Earth-shatteringly new."

"Which monastery is he from?"

"That's the odd part." The librarian took a deep breath and finally turned toward him. "Apparently from Meteora."

"Meteora? I didn't think there were many monks left there."

"Not many."

"Why is he here? I mean, what's he looking for?" Brother Vassilis was clearly agitated, his face wrinkled in thought.

"Women. Brother Pachomius is searching for women. Spent several days examining my mess of uncatalogued old texts down below."

"Women? Do you mean our *Theotókos*? Really? What more is there to discover about our Lord's mother?"

"No, not the Blessed Virgin." Father Theodor began rummaging on his desk. Women. The Deacon Olympias, for sure. But others as well."

"Who?"

This was again one of those irritating attempts at conversation with a monk who does not read much. He would have enjoyed a long conversation with Brother Pachomius, discussing their areas of interest. He looked at Brother Vassilis. "Unfortunately, that's most people's response. Friend to John Chrysostom and a leader in the early Christian movement. Are you aware of why we chant the names of some women in our Divine Offices?"

Brother Vassilis raised his eyebrows in surprise. "Well, because they're holy."

"Women were leaders in the early church and then were suppressed," Father Theodor responded, his voice taking on volume. "Power. All about power. And then we silence their message. We are blind to women, Brother. Blind."

Brother Vassilis let out a breath and stood. "I don't think so. Let women take care of women. We are here to seek God."

The librarian pulled out a logbook from a stack. "Unfortunately, yours is a common reaction. I'm afraid we monks are part of the problem. Just think of the families ruined by the financial misdeeds of our brother monks at Vatopedi. All because of our greed."

"Father, how can you speak of one of our own this way? Besides, the Monastic Council will clear the abbot's name."

"Not if he's guilty. And I hope the auditors find every stolen euro, but God have mercy on us all if we give it back to the government." He crossed himself three times for the Trinity. "Our economy is in ruins, and it's the families, and especially the women with children, who suffer."

"Father —"

"Yes, I go too far, but we're harsh with women."

"I don't think so. I'm glad we don't bother with them here on Agio Óros."

Father Theodor grabbed his canes as Brother Vassilis picked up the heavy oak slab. He was torn. Was this Brother Pachomius who he said he was? Just a monk with a few physical oddities? Certainly, he'd met some graduate students who appeared somewhat feminine.

Father Theodor adjusted his wire glasses and looked at him. "Why would a monk from Ipapandi care about women?" The old monk sighed. "But then what do we care? Maybe it's just my long years, but I find myself getting angrier every day with the way we men treat women. I saw too much disrespect toward women during my years at Oxford."

"But Father —"

"You're right. Brother Pachomius is an unlikely candidate for caring about women, let alone researching them. But his abbot permitted him to conduct his research here, and I'm happy to assist." The old monk sighed, that expression of consternation returning. "Olympias. I don't understand why he didn't find her in the library at Megístis Lávras."

"Where people are filming old books?"

"Yes." Father Theodor began shuffling around his desk.

"Father? Is it possible that this Brother Pachomius is not who or what he claims? Should we alert Father Abbot? He isn't staying in our guest house, he doesn't join us for meals, and worse, he's not joining us for prayers. We might have a thief among us."

Father Theodor looked up at him, alarmed. He had long known the reports of theft from libraries. But here?

Brother Vassilis moved toward the doorway. "I don't know. Something's wrong. Maybe I'll talk to Takis and see what he knows."

Father Theodor passed through the doorway. A gay monk? A woman? Certainly preferable to a thief. He'd write the abbot at Ipapandi to find out.

§

Sofia slammed the door hard as the latch had been getting troublesome. She pulled off her knit cap and, looking at the rearview mirror, saw that her hair had become especially curly from sweat. She left her window open, hoping to catch some breeze. Her spandex breast binding was soaking in sweat again.

Takis started the truck's engine, coffee mug perched between their seats.

She held the rim of his mug as the truck lurched forward over rough terrain and away from their *skiti*. "Thanks, Takis. I owe you for life." She gazed over the patchwork of rooftops below. "Did any of the monks suspect me being a woman?" She flipped her hoodie back in place.

He gave her his crooked grin. "You mean the rude and distant monk of Ipapandi?"

Sofia felt insulted and then remembered. "You told me to act arrogant and rude. So, nothing more?"

"Your acting skills are impressive but not that good. I heard a few comments about your lack of a beard and unnatural gait. But with this last group, your arrogance only increased their curiosity."

"Curiosity? They didn't suspect anything." Her words dripped with hope.

Her cousin slowly blew cigarette smoke out the window. Classic Takis maneuver when he wanted his audience to wait. "Suspect? Yes. Why doesn't anyone know who this strange guest is? Doesn't appear for meals or prayers and doesn't venerate the saints. Was he even an Orthodox monk? Why wouldn't he stay in our guest house? It seems the abbot did tell his curious monks that he'd received a letter from an abbot in Meteora giving permission for your visit. Still, there was no word about where you'd be staying. Many rounds of wine and ouzo to keep them at bay."

"Quite the sacrifice on your part," Sofia said. "So, they didn't guess my gender?"

Takis chuckled. "One or two of the younger ones were disturbed by your presence. I hope they decided you were gay, particularly camp."

Sofia playfully punched Takis.

He continued, "And some guessed you might've been a spy sent from that schismatic monastery."

Sofia felt a phantom fist drive into her stomach. "Esfigmenou?"

Takis shrugged his shoulders. "Yeah, they're quite nasty. Their abbot is trying to take over Agio Óros. Strange sort of beast, I'd say."

"Did they say anything more about Esfigmenou?"

Sofia noticed that her cousin was gripping the steering wheel unusually tight. "No. Nor did I ask. I can do without that sort." He glanced her way. "Why do you ask?"

His disgust was evident. Since he left home, Takis had had little to do with the Church. Neither one liked the arrogance nor aloofness of the monks they'd encountered as adults. Both had loved their parish priest as children.

"Oh, just wondering. That name appeared several times while I worked in the libraries since we arrived."

They rode in silence for a while.

Her shoulders relaxed, and she smiled broadly. "I found some of Olympias' letters."

Takis grinned. "Gonna write a famous book?"

"Some articles for sure, but if I get around to that book, I'm dedicating it to you with a big glossy picture of your handsome face." She chuckled. "First, I need to arrange some tests and figure out how I let people know what I found."

Her cousin glanced her way. "Tests? What kind of tests? And besides, you tell people."

Smiling, she said. "It's a bit more complicated than just telling people. And I need to arrange to test my samples in a lab." And that's going to cost her money. Might Brother Makarios be able to help her with this?

The truck rocked over the rough terrain. Last night's light rain left the dirt slippery and more challenging to navigate. They were heading back uphill toward the main dirt road, the truck's engine working hard. All these ruts and potholes seemed a deliberate attempt to discourage visitors.

Takis grabbed his coffee cup before it went flying. "I know some labs that might be able to help you. Get you a good deal."

What kind of labs would her cousin know about? "Thanks, Takis. I can only use labs associated with research universities and libraries."

As they approached the crest of the hill and bore toward the right, Sofia gazed down the cliff back at the monastery. She could no longer contain her joy and let out an exuberant hoot.

"Oh, really?" Takis asked.

"Really. I can never thank you enough for doing this for me."

"An expensive dinner. That dedication in your book. Besides, I haven't gotten you off forbidden territory yet. You may still get caught."

Sofia was quiet. She needed to get into Esfigmenou. Would her cousin help her? An idea had been niggling its way into her consciousness, and she wasn't ready to discuss it with Takis. "If I'm caught, forget the dinner and the dedication. But you can visit me in jail as much as you'd like."

"Visit you in jail? No way." Takis chuckled. "So, you're happy with your finds? Another gospel or a letter from Jesus?"

She grinned with delight. "Wouldn't that be something? If I could find some 2000-year-old clean parchment and ink, I might compose one myself. But yes, I'm happy."

"Good. You seemed frightened last night. You never interrupted me once the whole evening. Normally, only Aristotle is so patient with my chattering." Takis maneuvered another curve, hitting a deep rut that sent the back of their truck fishtailing. "Are you okay? Did the monks frighten you?"

Sofia gripped the window frame to steady herself. "I'm astonished your dog, Aristotle, is still alive. But yes, I was frightened of getting caught before I could find anything."

Sofia thought about his last statement. Adrenaline had been driving her since she'd decided to pursue Mount Athos. She dreaded every moment that she might be discovered.

"Takis, I've been surprised at how normal and even nice the monks here have been. Although I've only met a few, they didn't fit my image of what we'd experience here." She told herself to write a letter to Father Theodor when she arrived home.

Her shoulder hit the door a few more times before they crested the hill and the road leveled. She gazed at the grove of cypress trees. The birds' chatter was particularly lively this morning. "Takis, thanks for diverting the attention of the monks."

The truck lurched. Sofia grabbed the dashboard to steady herself.

Takis' grin reappeared. "You want to know if the monks suspected you of being a woman? I think their hormone alarms were on high alert, especially a couple of the younger monks. Kept gazing your way. I'm afraid, *mou oraios*, that the way your hips swayed left them concerned. Besides," he threw his cigarette butt out the window, "learned that women have been here before."

Sofia shifted in her seat and nearly shouted. "What?"

"Yup, got an interesting history lesson from Brother Isaák. Seems that during and after the Second World War, refugees fled here, including women and children. Same during our stupid civil war a few decades ago."

"I've never heard any of this. Why—"

"A great cover-up, I'd guess. Didn't want any women like you," he grinned, "getting any crazy ideas. And maybe the monks didn't want the world to know they had a heart."

Seventeen

Sofia glanced back toward Hagia Theotokos off in the distance as Takis shifted gears and his truck ascended the last switchback from the coast. They passed an orchard of lemon and lime trees and headed toward Karyés. Sofia noticed the air shifting from salt from the sea to sweet from the orchards to dusty and dry. The sun bore down on them.

Rounding a sharp bend, Sofia cried out as their truck hit an oncoming jeep. She was thrown against the door, and her glasses flew off her face. The truck's engine ground to a halt.

The wind knocked out of her. Sofia breathed long and deep, trying to calm herself. "Takis, are you okay?"

Looking across, she saw Takis chuckling, wiping cigarette ash off his clothing, and rubbing his side. She was going to take up the issue of his smoking when they returned home.

"Yes." Then he looked at her with concern. "Sof, you?"

"I don't know. I hope so." He kept chuckling as he climbed out, the door squeaking. She pushed her door open, clambered out, and turned to reach for her fallen glasses. "Takis, we can't let the police get involved, or I'm in trouble."

She heard a man's voice, shoved her cap back in place, and pulled her hood forward, covering as much of her neck as possible. The frame of her glasses was bent. Glancing across, she could see that they had met an old jeep, driver's front to driver's front. Reaching for her rucksack, she noticed Takis and the driver laughing and talking while examining the two rigs. Her cousin was so strange sometimes.

Afraid this guy might ask her questions, she stepped away from their truck and walked toward some rocks and privacy. She twisted her frames mostly back in shape. They sat crooked on her face. She stretched her back and hamstrings in the hopes of minimizing any muscle pain as a result of the accident. She checked the contents of her rucksack. Her camera seemed okay, and, fortunately, she had put her precious wallet of memory cards in a zipper pocket. Nothing lost.

She gazed across. Her cousin seemed fine. But whiplash might compromise her attempts to get into Esfigmenou. The only person she could blame would be herself for chickening out.

She stretched her right side and shoulder, noticing her cousin climbing back into his truck. The other rig took off, fender flapping precariously.

"Can we still drive? How bad is the damage?"

"Drivable. I'll fix it when I return. Let's go. I'd hate for you to miss the last boat out."

Sofia returned to the truck. "Boat? I thought we'd be driving out. Or will you fix this rig while we're in Karyés?"

"No, it can wait. I've some work I need to get done while I'm here. You don't want to wait around."

"Work?" What was Takis up to?

He shrugged his shoulders. "Our unfortunate victim was one of my colleagues." Takis lit up another cigarette, hands steady.

Sofia was amazed at how calm her cousin remained, no matter what was going on, just like when they were kids. "A colleague in what, exactly?"

"Horticulture. Gifted, that one is."

Sofia felt her gut sink. "Horticulture?" Why did Takis, who considered himself a man of the earth, suddenly use such fancy words?

"Specialized only." Again, he slowly blew out smoke.

Sofia sniffed. The truck lurched. "Takis. Exactly what do you grow? What is this 'specialty' of yours?"

Her cousin smiled. "Καλαμάτα. The finest in the region, I'd say."

"*Kalamata*? Olives?"

Takis laughed. The truck veered to the left. Sofia grabbed the frame of the window. Her cousin straightened the truck out. "No, *mou oraios*. Marijuana. Ice, too."

Her mind scrambled to comprehend all this. "Ice? That's a marijuana?"

He chuckled. "Yes, the good stuff. And both thrive here on Agio Óros."

Sofia felt her face warm up. "Your plants are here? Won't the monks find out?"

He looked her way, eyebrows raised. "My fields are in assorted locations around the peninsula's northern end. Like you, I'd doubt they'd recognize what they were looking at."

"But why?" Her voice sounded strained.

He shrugged his shoulders. "Money. How else could I survive or even consider buying Aunt Christina's house? Not much demand for auto repair nowadays. And if I cultivate my crop on private lands, the federal authorities will confiscate the land along with my crop. They won't bother the monks if they find my crops here."

Anger surged, but she really couldn't say why. A violation, yes. But that's what she had done. Who did he harm? "Takis, have you ever been arrested?"

He looked her way. "No, Sof. I'm careful."

"None of the monks use this, do they?"

Her cousin laughed so hard that he nearly lost control of the truck again. He stopped and continued laughing. "No, *mou oraios*. At least not that I'm aware of. I mean no harm to the monks. I repair their trucks and some of their equipment. I provide them needed tools. I don't charge them for my costs or time." He put out his cigarette. "But I stay away from the nasty ones." He was eyeing her in his quizzical way.

Did he know what she was thinking? He could read her mind at times. And if she missed the boat, she would have an excuse to visit one more library.

"Maybe I should've taken some of this Kalamata with me on this insane adventure." She felt her skin continue to flush. "I might've been more relaxed."

"*Okhi*, no. You have the finest mind in the family. We're all proud of you. Don't ever waste your gift on weed."

They drove on in silence. She studied rooftops in the distance, her mind calculating the "how" of her next stop.

Sofia popped some ibuprofen to stave off stiff muscles. The sun glared, and the dust increased. She shifted in her seat to ease the discomfort of her full bladder. Cresting the horizon on approaching Karyés, they saw some parked military vehicles. Her cousin's eyebrows furrowed as he slowed on approach. Sofia tried to glance away, but military personnel approached them from both sides. She placed her knees apart in the stance Takis grilled her on, pulled her hood over her cap, and tried her best to look otherworldly and uninvolved.

"Pull over there and park. No entry right now," the officer near Takis barked.

Sofia could feel the guy's gaze outside her door, but she refused to look his way. Then he leaned on the door frame, and she could feel his sour cigarette breath.

"What's going on, Officer?"

"Karyés is closed. Another hour or two." The officer pointed toward their left.

"Are the boats departing from Dafni still running?"

"No buses down to the boats until our vans leave."

Takis offered a new pack of American cigarettes and asked. "I see pedestrians ahead. May we get out and stretch our legs?"

The pack disappeared. "Stay away from police vans. Don't question the men working. Otherwise, you're welcome."

Takis pulled forward and parked under a tree. Sofia grasped her rucksack and camera, following Takis out of the truck. She wouldn't take any risks with these two precious items. She was frightened she might be exposed, but desperation meant a bathroom. They headed toward the pointed roof of the burnt red and white bell tower. Rounding an old building, she spotted the Church of the Protaton.

Takis perched on a bench in the little shade available in the scorching heat. A few of the military police constantly scanned the area. Looking for someone? Sofia squirmed as sweat trickled down her back. She spotted the WC sign for the water closet, an entryway with no door.

Sofia nudged Takis. "I don't want unexpected company. Keep 'em away?"

"So, add bodyguard to my list of accomplishments?"

Sofia smiled. "Of course."

"*Mou oraios*, if I had known of your need, I would've located a grove of trees. Water closets are rustic here. Stalls are considered unnecessary and frivolous."

"I think I've already noticed. I've managed to avoid detection thus far, and I'd like to leave with my reputation intact."

Takis laughed and led the way. Taking her gear, Sofia followed with the longer stride that Takis had taught her, hands ensconced in the pocket of her hoodie and eyes cast downward. Takis waived her in, then perched against the door frame and folded his arms.

"Primitive but should suffice."

Sofia looked at him. "Find a way to keep company out, please." She smiled at his mock look of surprise.

Sofia entered the dark, dank room. Takis had teased her. Stalls with walls and a door. How nice of the local authorities to provide such decadent luxury to their soft visitors. She slipped into a stall. No toilet inside, but rather a hole, just like she had seen and used in the countryside of northern Italy and France. At least she was experienced at navigating this particular rustic simplicity.

Too soon, she heard footsteps accompanied by men's voices and laughter. She almost stopped breathing. Where was Takis? One tried her door and then moved on. She listened to their respective doors close. Talking. They had witnessed the military police hauling boxes out of some administrative building but saw no one arrested.

A smoker's voice said, "One of the guys told me that his group is being sent over to Esfigmenou. Seems things are getting hot there. Those crazy monks have supporters coming in from the mainland to protest the military presence."

A deep voice responded. "Insane behavior. Agio Óros is a sacred place. I've been coming here for years. Those crazy monks are ruining this place. I wish the military would bring all this to an end and evict them. Just what we don't need, a protest on sacred ground."

Sofia awaited their departure. A protest? More arrests? She had to agree with those guys. Agio Óros was no place for vicious politics. She laughed at herself. Isn't it all politics, including their exclusion of women?

Passing through the doorway, she looked around for Takis. Did something happen? Why did he abandon his post? She discreetly scanned the area for her cousin but couldn't see him anywhere. Sighing, she decided to visit the old basilica and escape this relentless heat. With the dust, she labored to breathe. The bell tower cast a shadow across the dirt. Rounding the corner of the stone basilica, she found the old carved doors and used her shoulder to push one open.

Entering, she relished the cool air and the sweet, soft smell of beeswax candles. Her eyes followed the flickering light cast off the two rows of pillars toward the iconostasis, the screen hung with icons that separated the nave from the sanctuary. She slowly approached, knelt, and touched three fingers to the floor. A bank of flickering candles caught her attention to her left. She walked over and bowed in reverence for the *Theotokos*, the Mother of God, and lit a candle before the icon, offering a short prayer for her deceased parents.

Turning slowly, she took in the full beauty and history of the basilica. Sofia gazed across to a fresco of the Dormition of the Virgin, a classic scene of the death of Mary. Each other wall held a fresco of one of the four Evangelists. Sofia smiled and crossed over to a fresco she remembered from her childhood. Curved sword, a bow slung over his shoulder, a silver helmet on his head, and a gold-rimmed shield in his hand. Saint Mercurius was a warrior saint from Cappadocia.

Finally, Sofia sat in a chair and studied the ceiling. She wondered if the interior had been repaired or repainted since the fourteenth century. The colors were faded, and repairs to the plaster were needed. But she savored the antiquity, a power that emanated from the past.

The silence was interrupted by the heavy door opening and then footsteps. She pulled her hood forward and lowered her head in a posture of prayer.

The footsteps stopped. Her gut twisted. Should she leave? Stay seated? Walk out with her now-infamous arrogance, and head turned away?

EIGHTEEN

KARYES, MOUNT ATHOS

The footsteps drew closer, their echo muted. Sofia felt a warm presence. "*Mou oraios*, do I interrupt your prayer or remain standing?"

Takis. She stood and turned. Her goofy cousin held the tops of two beers tucked discreetly into his shoulder bag, mostly hidden from view. Sofia laughed. Grabbing her rucksack and adjusting her hood, she followed him out. She squinted as her eyes adjusted to the bright light, nearly tripping over the uneven cobblestones. Settling on a low stone wall under a tree, the two enjoyed their cold beers and watched all the activity. A few monks milled about but kept their distance from the military police. Taking a deep gulp, she watched the police talking on their phones and gesturing with their hands.

Nodding toward the military police, she asked. "Why do you think the police are carrying guns strapped over their shoulders? Are they expecting trouble?"

Takis turned her way. "Probably just to send a message that they're in charge."

Doors swung open. A policeman exited, turned, and watched as another guy hauled several large boxes from a nondescript building. Several monks stood nearby, speaking in low, intense whispers. Sofia wondered if this investigation might make her attempt at Esfigmenou easier or harder. More military presence but with attention focused away from the library and on the crazy monks.

Sofia set her nearly drained beer bottle beside her and gazed toward her cousin. "I'm surprised at how many boxes are being taken over one monastery's misdeeds."

From behind, a guy responded. "Not just one. All of the monasteries are being audited."

Shocked at the unexpected presence, Sofia bumped the bottle beside her. It clambered away, spilling the last of its contents. She pulled her hood forward to cover more of her head and shoved her glasses back into place. Steadying her nervous breathing, she reached for the bottle. Now what?

Her cousin turned, gazing up at the officer, then stood and extended his hand. "Takis. And you are?"

Sofia could feel the guy's gaze as he answered her cousin. "Gounaris. We're heading south to more of the monasteries. Damned dirty assignment. Hate disturbing the honest houses, but we've got our orders."

Sofia reached into her rucksack and pulled out the only book she had brought, a collection of Chrysostom's letters. She pretended to be engrossed in its contents.

Takis' offer of a beer was rejected. "All the monasteries?"

"Yeah, in case more dirty money might be found."

Sofia could see Gounaris' shadow shift around, but he kept standing.

"Dirty money? Someone thinks there's more out there?" Takis asked.

"Possibly. I think they've got the main crooks, though. My parents' pensions disappeared because the government claims the coffers are empty. Maybe the government really is broke."

The officer looked her way. "And this is?"

Sofia struggled to know what to do next. Her heart pounded.

Takis answered. "My cousin, Brother Pachomius."

She surrendered to her fate, whatever that might be. Sofia stood and turned toward the officer. She extended her hand and aimed for the firmest grip she could muster. "*Yassas*." She hoped her fear was not all that obvious.

Gounaris was slow to release her hand. Instead, he studied her fingers. She felt her cheeks warm as he scrutinized her face, one eyebrow raised. She pulled her hand free, sat, and opened her book again.

"My cousin is leaving today. We've spent the last week in a couple of monasteries where he's been researching."

"Brother Pachomius?" Sarcasm edged his words. "Not Mother Pachomius?" The officer laughed.

Sofia's jaw clenched, and her gut gripped.

Her cousin asked, "Why the insult, Officer Gounaris?"

Sofia glanced sideways, and she could see her cousin's spine straighten.

"And we're leaving, so why bother?"

"Just what kind of monk is he?" Disbelief oozed around Gounaris' words.

Sofia shot out in her lowest voice. "From Meteora. I'd give you my abbot's phone number, but we don't tolerate much technology."

Sofia wondered when the guy would arrest her. Hopefully, she can keep her rucksack with her precious cargo inside. Or maybe she'll insist it belonged to Takis.

"I'm no fool, and your cousin's no monk. Don't know how she's been able to elude detection, but that's their problem, not mine. We take all the boxes to Athens, and then I'm done." He barked another laugh.

Takis offered the military officer a pack of American cigarettes. He continued, "Don't understand what my cousin does in those libraries, but we were able to do a bit of hiking as well. Hadn't seen any trouble other than those graduate students while we've been here."

Takis slipped a second beer her way. She took it but then changed her mind. She wanted her brain to be clear in the hours ahead. Sofia pulled out her prayer rope and fingered it.

"Yeah, whatever. Just be sure she's out of here. Today. Me, I don't care if women want to come here. But the monks say 'no women,' so that's the way it needs to be." She felt his gaze. "You're both crazy."

All three turned their attention to the commotion in the plaza. Several more vans had arrived and opened their back doors, orders were being barked, and more loaded-down carts were being delivered. Gounaris headed over to the vans.

"Sof, the gods must be smiling on you. Normally these guys are hard asses, like to throw their weight around."

Sofia's back muscles began cramping. "Must be my sudden outburst of prayer since we've arrived here." She stood and turned toward Takis. "Does he know you? Know what you grow here?"

"No, I've never seen him here before. And I steer clear of the police anyway."

"I'm nosy but worried. Do you pay taxes on your illicit business?" She noticed her cousin cringe. "I'm just worried the government might go after you. Being desperate and all."

"Yes, *mou oraios*, I do. I'm actually a registered business, not particularly specific about what I grow and sell, and have a solicitor as well."

"Really? But—"

Takis tossed their bottles into a glass recycling container. "I wouldn't want to burden you with visiting me in prison."

Sofia watched Gounaris saunter back toward them, and then he turned to Takis. "They ought to pay more attention to the Russians and Esfigmenou and leave the rest of the monasteries alone."

Sofia was not insulted that Gounaris ignored her. Maybe the guy was soothing his conscience by not exposing her to the monks.

"I've heard some rumors about them," Takis said.

"I bet. The government should wonder how they support themselves while under siege by the military." Gounaris tipped his hat to block the sun from his face. "I had expected my assignment here to be so quiet that I'd go stir crazy, but my time has been anything but. I had no idea things would be so busy." Gounaris laughed. "Japanese Zen Masters, Bulgarian businessmen, a Hindu priest, and now criminal activity." He turned toward her, "Now I can add women posing as monks." He laughed again. "Can't wait to tell my wife when I get home."

Sofia reminded herself she would be off Mount Athos before too many rumors took root. Then she would be safe.

Takis put out his cigarette. "How can one small monastery cause so much trouble?"

"Their crazy abbot attracts trouble-makers from other monasteries, especially from Meteora. They move here and then stir up trouble."

Turning toward Sofia, "I hope you didn't tell some crazy story about being from there."

Sofia felt her cheeks warm. What might Gounaris mean by that?

They heard doors slam and engines start up. Was the military finally done? Several monks walked over to the building and entered, closing the door behind them. Gounaris returned to his rig.

Sofia felt a nudge.

"Looks like we can head out now."

She scooped up her rucksack, and the two cousins began returning to their truck. Sofia matched Takis's long stride with her head down, perplexed at Gounaris's reaction to her. Would he tell anyone about her? Apparently, no one at Megistris Lavras had reported her. Or didn't believe the graduate students.

§

Takis maneuvered his old truck through Karyés and entered the roadway in a northwesterly direction. They took the same road they'd arrived on. The sun's rays remained intense as it moved toward the western horizon.

Sofia sighed with visible relief, her body's shaking lessening. "I can't believe that I survived that. I'd expected to be arrested."

Takis popped in a CD, *rembétika*, Greek blues.

"Won't someone hear us?" Sofia asked.

Her cousin looked at her. "And do what, *Mou oraios*? One sinner driving a holy monk of Agio Óros," he hesitated, "somewhere?" He laughed again. "Sofia, relax. You've pulled off one of the greatest heists of the last half-century.

"I didn't steal. I mean—" She blushed. But she had, in a sense.

Takis smiled at her. "Relax and enjoy your victory."

"Why didn't he arrest me? Gounaris, I mean."

"Maybe he thought you were a transvestite or transgender." Takis laughed so hard the truck veered.

Sofia elbowed his arm and joined in his laughter.

"Thanks again, Takis. You're the best."

They drove on in silence. An occasional military rig approached and passed them by.

Sofia ruminated on her next steps. She couldn't leave without trying to enter Esfigmenou, yet it was surrounded by the police. Was she insane enough to give it a shot? Father Theodor had mentioned how rich their library was, full of ancient texts. And the collection continued to grow, the old librarian had claimed, despite being watched by the police. Why were the weird monks of Esfigmenou even tolerated? Father Theodor had wondered why Patriarch Bartholomaios hadn't ordered the monastery evacuated by the military. What little was known of Esfigmenou seemed hopeful. Their library was away from the main entrance and chapel. The military could provide a diversion. And Gounaris didn't seem interested in arresting her. She would need to leave her precious memory cards behind and only take the unused ones.

They rounded a familiar corner past a grove of lemon and lime trees. The smell was sharp and sweet.

Sofia took a deep breath. "Takis, I'm going to do it."

Her cousin glanced her way. "Do what?"

"Esfigmenou."

Takis moaned. "*Mou oraios*, you're crazy."

"Crazier than you?"

Takis let out an angry sigh. "I'm driving you back to Ouranoúpoli, and then you're on your own."

"If I must, I'll hike back to Esfigmenou. But either way, I need to try. If I don't, I'll regret it for the rest of my life. Besides, I'm just too stoked."

Two stubborn Greeks.

"Don't you have enough 'whatever' to make you sufficiently famous?"

"This isn't about fame. I need to know what these crazy monks have got and why they're hiding it from everyone else. Even Father Theodore was convinced that some of the libraries from Meteora were brought there."

He hit the steering wheel with the palm of his hand.

"I'm not involving you in this. You're not allowed to come along. Drop me off alongside the road, and I'll hike down."

"They aren't civilized. Those monks could hurt you. Seriously harm you."

"The military police won't let them. I'd just be arrested if I'm caught. They'll escort me to Ouranoúpoli and drop me there."

"You'd be under military arrest."

"Okay, maybe Thessaloníki or Athens."

"Sofia. You don't understand. This is serious."

"Yes, it is. And I know it doesn't make sense to you—"

Sofia heard a thud and a hissing sound. She lurched forward and to her right as the truck veered sharply to the left. The steering wheel shook violently. Bringing the truck to a halt, Takis got out, cursing under his breath.

Sofia caught her breath. But now was the time for her to act. She pulled her used memory cards from her rucksack, put them into a sealable plastic bag, and left them on Takis' seat. Swinging her rucksack securely onto her shoulders, she looked at Takis.

"Takis, please don't worry about me, but protect my bag of memory cards." She took a deep breath and crossed through a grove of trees and toward the ocean.

Nineteen

ESFIGMENOU MONASTERY

Abbot Methodius sat in his presider's chair, deep in thought, elbows on the armrest, his large hands massaging the sides of his head. Candles flickered around the myriad icons alongside the ancient frescoes. Soft light glowed in the dark, cavernous katholikón. The comforting presence of sweet musk incense, intense and smoky, enveloped him, reminding him of the holiness of God, Ever Present. Agripnia, the prayer services that included Great Vespers, Orthros, and the Divine Liturgy, had concluded, and his monks had left for their meal. He needed to be alone with his thoughts. Brother Iákovos, one of their newest members, had died while returning to the monastery with supplies from Ouranoúpoli. His shattered body had been found at the bottom of a cliff; the jeep jammed on the cliff wall. Clearly, Brother Iákovos had been forced off the road by the military police. As expected, the police denied any involvement.

Since his arrival as a young man on the Holy Mountain, Heaven on Earth, this katholikón had provided the sanctuary for the peace and contemplation he craved. Here, his heart was strengthened for the unending battles, spiritual and earthly, that had been his reality. He had never wanted to assume leadership for this monastery. Being ensnared in the petty politics that cursed Greece was his hell on earth. Why the Lord, Blessed Be His Name, chose to torment him so became his Agony in the Garden of Gethsemane. Borne with patience, he hoped. The only changes he supported for Mount Athos were those that tightened the observances and further restricted outside influences. His ardent prayers went out on behalf of the few monasteries on the Holy Mountain that held out against the onslaught of modernity.

The Holy One, Blessed Be His Name, was to be served and obeyed, especially during these most challenging times. The abbot stood and left the katholikón, his eyes squinted at the rising sun. His black skouphos swept about him, and he massaged the crucifix that hung from his neck, a comforting habit when in turmoil. Crossing the courtyard and passing through a stone archway toward the hated van with its radio antenna on top, he eyed the police gathered in clusters. His neck felt so stiff it resisted movement. He could see military jeeps parked up on the first crest of the hill above, effectively barring his monks from returning to the monastery. Something had changed. Whereas the police should have left the Holy Mountain entirely, their presence had increased overnight.

The military police stopped talking when they saw him coming. Appropriate reaction for the spiritual leader here. Respect was to be demanded.

Abbot Methodius strode through a group of milling policemen toward a more official presence standing at the van's rear. He observed a man with disheveled, graying black hair and mustachioed, deep olive skin ripened by decades in the burning sun. He had the build of one whose ancestors had seen hard labor.

Abbot Methodius faced the officer, demanding, "You are in charge of this disgrace?"

"Commander Leontis," his gravelly voice was soft in pitch, even-toned, and respectful.

"Get off this mountain. You defile our way of life with your presence."

"No, abbot. I have my orders. Your monks are permitted to leave but will not be allowed to return. I'm told that one day soon, I will be ordered to clear this place out. Using force if necessary. I suggest you go now and in peace."

A ripple of anger swept through his body.

The invader looked at the abbot without expression, his gaze penetrating. Steel knew its strength and did not need to flex it. A worthy opponent, the abbot admitted to himself.

"You will leave now," the abbot repeated, his voice cold and firm.

Leontis pulled out a linen envelope bearing the official seal of Bartholomaios, the Ecumenical Patriarch of Constantinople. Something in the Commander's eyes shifted. A gentleness, maybe.

"Father Abbot. It's over."

"Over? Yes. Leave immediately."

"You are called *zealot. Son of Thunder.* I've come to understand you've earned that title."

"Yes," the abbot replied, his hand grasping his prayer cord. "Zealous for our pure monastic observance. Thundering on behalf of an uncompromised gospel."

The abbot watched Leontis grimace.

"The Jesus I heard about cared more for mercy and compassion than the hard rule of law," Leontis said.

The abbot stared at the officer in disbelief. "That very mercy and compassion drives us to lead you to the truth. My monks are faithful witnesses to the Eternal Reign of the Father. We will not depart."

Leontis stood silent, gazing at the abbot. The silence stretched between them.

"Leave," the abbot said.

"No. It's over." Leontis' voice remained dispassionate.

No softness in those eyes, the abbot decided, rather a quiet sense of victory emanating from one who thought his job was straightforward. They stood looking at one another.

Leontis handed the abbot the letter.

Slapping it out of Leontis' hand, Abbot Methodius turned and stormed away. Encountering a young monk, he ordered the bell to sound and the monks to gather within the half hour in the synodikon, their meeting room. Then the music resumed, loud, pounding, and screeching.

Soon, Abbot Methodius walked down a stone alleyway to the synodikon. He encountered their eldest monk and assisted 102-year-old Brother Anthony to a seat within. Silent monks, hands within their sostikons or holding their prayer cords, shuffled in and took seats. Sitting, he gazed at a fresco of Saint George, the Dragon Slayer. He felt comforted at the saint's presence. So many dragons needed slaying to restore the true observances.

He noticed sweat on the bowed heads. Nervous anticipation permeated the room. As springs wound tight, they were all ready for release. The years of defiant standoff against lax observers of Orthodoxy had been painful for many of them. God knew the monks stormed heaven day and night for Divine Justice, but the Blessed Trinity could undoubtedly be slow to respond on their behalf. But now, a window was opening.

Abbot Methodius stood and began the meeting with the usual lighting of the candle and chanted an invocation of prayer for God's blessing on this meeting. "*Kyrie eleison. Christe eleison. Kyrie eleison.* May the Merciful One hear our prayer," the abbot's bass voice echoed off the frescoed walls.

"The heretic has moved against us. He is beyond mercy now," the abbot began. "The crimes he and his parasites have committed against the faithful few will be punished. God's justice will prevail. Vindication will be ours."

"The call to awake was given us in 1965. We failed to heed God's command. Our slumber turned into our living hell. Orthodoxy betrayed. Perversion of the worst sort. Lifting the anathemas of condemnation against Rome without requiring their conversion." His fist punched the air. "Appeasing the West."

"I repeat. We failed in our response to God when the Almighty's voice thundered upon our holy mountain. Rather than listening faithfully to the Master's beckoning, we rolled over and returned to sleep. And in our stupor, Lucifer moved in."

Some of the monks cringed at the pounding noise, the bass thumping, that the military police were inflicting on them, invading their sacred monastery.

The abbot countered by speaking even louder. "Evil is never satisfied with small victories when larger ones are possible. Benevolence from a distance grew into a politician's friendship of the worst sort. And so we, among the faithful few, took our historic stand in 1983. Acknowledging Istanbul's break with Orthodoxy, we lamented their heresy by draping our monastery with the black flags of mourning."

"I had warned our fellow monks. So many poor and uneducated. Their observances had softened. They became undisciplined. Dumb sheep so easily led to the slaughter. Promises of wealth and comfort, of prestige restored. Compromise everything, and this too will be yours, they were told. Fools."

He stopped, out of breath, gazing around at his faithful monks, their eyes attentive. He continued, "We instructed our fellow monks. We urged them to return to the one true monastic observance. We know our fellow monasteries that have returned to the faith. I praise God for our monks from Meteora who have reformed degenerate monasteries. These monks remain firm in their resolve. But we have also witnessed how Megistris Lavras has defied us, opening their monasteries to Catholics and their Protestants, to tourists and heathen from the east."

"Then the soft ones began arriving, coddled at the universities. No discipline. No understanding of our ways. These vacuous imbeciles came to reform us." The abbot took a deep breath. "Yes. Reform. Us. Look around you. Notice your brothers. We have some of the finest minds on the Holy Mountain. We do not compromise with the soft ways of the world. Rigor in prayer. Rigor in scholarship. I will not compromise my resolve. We will expand true Orthodoxy, not merely protect the few monasteries true to the primitive observances."

The abbot breathed deeply. His head continued to pound. Nausea roiled his stomach. His monks remained attentive. Even Brother Anthony remained alert, leaning on his canes.

"But no. The other abbots kept drifting from the true path of Orthodoxy. I used every tool God gave me to call them home. Begging, persuading, reasoning, commanding, even tender mercy. I struggled to clean up all our monasteries that lacked discipline. Instead, they found new ways to soften the observances. We have slid into a war. Lucifer is rampant on the Holy Mountain. Few monks remain faithful to our ancient ways."

The abbot stopped, looking around the synodikon. He loved and respected his monks. They were 117 strong, some reforming major parishes in Athens. He knew each soul's struggles, talents, and joys placed in his care. Transparency was the goal on the Holy Mountain, and he demanded nothing of his monks that he did not require of himself.

"Ecumenism. Dialogue, they say. Learn from others. Indeed, do monks have anything, anything to learn from a world rotten with sin? Some thought it a small matter to recognize the West's calendar. No, the Julian calendar is our time, not their Gregorian calendar. It is God's time, given to us on earth, to glorify God alone. To grow into his image. Not the world's image."

The abbot continued. "They think us weak and defenseless. Remove us from the Holy Mountain? I see hope on the horizon. What appeared to be a disgusting violation may well prove a gift. After the government examines our heretical monasteries for deception and theft, we will move in and take over. Not faithful Abbot Ephraim. Rather, every other wolf in sheep's skin will find themselves in exile from the Holy Mountain." The abbot felt the blood in his head pounding, and stars began to invade his vision. An aura not of God.

"We will remain firm. Our path is clear. *Orthodoxy or death!* I would rather die than deny our faith. I would rather die than live in sin. Or worse, compromise with Satan himself. We on Mount Athos are here to be the living embodiment of truth. Our ways are not the world's ways. Blessed Saint John tells us that everyone who does not abide by the teaching of Christ but goes beyond it does not know God.

"And when we grew comfortable with the presence of evil in our bed, the ultimate betrayal occurred. The gullible and mindless, seeking approval in the eyes of the world, elected this Bartholomaios to the one true Church. Bastard, indeed."

Since Patriarch Bartholomaios' election as leader of the Orthodox Church in 1991, he had been unrelenting in pursuing powerful relationships with all the world's religious leaders, including the heretical Patriarch in Rome. He doggedly pursued peace negotiations in his troubled part of the world. He had been outspoken in defense of the environment. The rejection of his leadership by the monastic community at Esfigmenou began their travails with the courts. The law expressly prohibited schismatic monks and communities from living on Mount Athos. Schismatic, indeed, he fumed. Better to break with the heretic of Istanbul than to break with the one true Lord, Jesus. And so, their access to the funds controlled by the monastic council had been cut.

"The courts have abandoned our just cause. We are alone. We will not heed an unjust order against God's faithful. We will not leave our home." Every word was pronounced with the fierce precision of a swordsman's sharp, rapier-like thrust.

From a slit in his habit, he pulled out his prayer cord of worn knotted rope and held it up to his monks. "These 300 knots are our 300 bullets. We wage a spiritual war. We will continue our fight with our prayer. Prayer is our weapon. And we will not leave."

The accursed music shot up louder.

TWENTY

ESFIGMENOU MONASTERY

Sofia cleared the grove of cypresses, set down her gear, and crouched. Her heart pounded, and she took deep breaths, trying to calm her excitement and anxiety. She pulled out her binoculars and did a slow sweep of the terrain. Was Takis right? Was she crazy to try and enter a monastery under siege? She pulled out her map and tried to figure out where she was. Before her lay a steep incline with the ocean beyond but no sign of a monastery. Her intuition told her to head in a northerly direction.

Scooping up her gear, Sofia made her way downhill toward the shore, then turned toward her right and followed the shoreline from above the hill. The dirt was dry from the scorching heat, and dust swirled about. Making her way carefully over the rough ground, searching for hikers or campers, she tried to imagine the reaction of her family and friends to her adventure.

She was delighted at how successful she and Takis had been thus far. She had hoped beyond all hope that threads of women's history would be found here. And now she had the evidence. How long before Takis stopped being mad at her? Probably when she arrived safely home, or he bailed her out at the police station.

The uneven terrain proved hard on her legs and hips as no path or trail existed. North seemed to be all downhill or uphill. Sofia remained on high alert as she treaded odd angles, maneuvering around knolls and tromping through small ravines. Deciding she had gone too close to the shoreline, she began an ascent, using remnants of a scraggly bush to pull herself uphill. Her leg muscles stiffened and ached from negotiating several miles of this rough and uneven terrain, especially since she was still sore from their accident.

Reaching a boulder, she set her gear down and sat. Her hands shook from hunger, a tell-tale sign that her sugar levels were dropping. Pulling out two energy bars and her water canteen, she ate while stretching her legs as her calves cramped. The ocean had picked up some energy, and the waves crashed against the rocks. The breeze was refreshing. The sun had moved across the peninsula. How long till sunset? How long till her final act of insanity?

Her breathing calmed. Maybe insanity, but the only way forward was to go forward. And she knew beyond all knowing that Esfigmenou was the key. Why else would those bastards hunker down and take on the Greek government as well as the Patriarch? There was something inside that place. Sofia chuckled. Who knows?

Sofia gathered her gear and began walking again. The exertion had calmed some of her nervousness. She had missed her regular heavy exercise these past weeks. Ahead, she spotted twin fawns. Mother would be nearby. She heard a faint sound, more like a thumping. So did the deer, whose ears perked into alert. Sofia stumbled and landed on her knees. She caught her rucksack before the contents could be damaged. The noise was not like anything she had heard here on Mount Athos.

The ground reverberated like some heavy equipment being used. She was getting tired. This had been a long day. Resting briefly, she hoped her knee and ankle would hold up. She crawled up, shifted her gear, and continued, alert for hikers and for signs of a *skíti* where she could park her gear and spend the night.

Rounding another hill, she stopped and knelt. That thumping grew louder. The sound was jarring amidst all the quiet she had experienced. Takis had told her that hikers didn't play music while on the Holy Mountain. She scanned for the source of the music and saw no one. So strange. A definite thumping sound like bass speakers emit. She had not heard music, besides the monk's chanting, anywhere on Mount Athos, neither at Megístis Lávras nor Hagia Theotokos.

Sofia trudged on. Sharp pains emanated from her hips. She just wasn't used to lopsided hiking. Her stomach growled. The sunlight softened toward dusk. The music became clearer. Would the military police come and make the fools shut it off? Cresting another hill, she saw the first signs of Esfigmenou. Numerous small and large onion-domed towers set amongst the orange-gold tiles of the roof. The music, which had grown louder as she approached, seemed to emanate from the monastery. Odd.

Locating a knoll above a grove of olive trees, Sofia knelt and swept the horizon with her binoculars. Esfigmenou lay parallel with the coastline, and she was at its southernmost end. The library was at the northernmost end of the complex. She would need to find her way across the entire length of the monastery, round the northeast corner, and then look for the door. Her heart thumped with excitement, almost to the beat of the music. She stopped and knelt behind an olive tree. Below her lay the tower and main entrance to the monastery.

Zooming in with her binoculars, Sofia saw vans. Military police vans, just as they had seen in Karyés. On top of one van rested two large wooden boxes with loudspeakers emitting music near earsplitting levels. Rempètiki dominated by bouzouki, the Greek mandolin. Giorgos Zampetas? The music echoed off the hillside. She chuckled. Were the military police merely entertaining themselves? Or were they driving the monks crazy?

The tower that served as the formal entrance was draped with something black and long, with words on something white. Adjusting her binoculars and straining her eyes, she could barely distinguish the words: *Orthodoxy or death!* Good God, were they serious?

Military police cars were parked outside, with uniformed men sitting in their meager shade. She watched as one of the vans pulled away and ascended the hill in her direction. Her heart slammed in her chest. The van passed on without stopping.

Strategy. Terrified and excited, Sofia pondered what to do next. The sun was setting. Dusk could help hide her presence. She sat and studied the monastery complex. An idea was forming.

§

"Commander Leontis here." Communication from headquarters increased daily. Too many politicians and news media hovered over them like hungry vultures. This long call would be another rant from someone who did not know what he was talking about trying to tell him how to handle the situation.

"No, sir. We have seen no unusual activity here." He strained to hear his caller over the blasting music. At least the music was of his choosing. He hoped this earsplitting music would be effective in disrupting the monks.

More screeching came from the other end of the phone.

"You ordered me and my men to maintain a firm blockade. No entrance allowed. Are you telling me my orders have been changed?" He was shouting into the phone.

Commander Leontis wondered why he bothered trying to listen. Headquarters wanted him to solve this situation without doing anything. Damn bureaucrats, more interested in their careers and reputations than doing a day's honorable work.

"Press? Don't those media guys have more important things to report on?" Leontis hated this assignment. While the caterwauling continued on the other end, he covered the phone with his hand and nudged one of his sleeping officers.

"Sergeant, wake up." The intense heat and sheer boredom of this assignment wreaked havoc with discipline.

"Oh, sorry, sir." No sooner had his subordinate apologized than he was back to snoring again.

"No, sir. I was talking to one of my men. Sir, give me the authority to storm the monastery and arrest these monks. Otherwise, my only option is to maintain the stranglehold. Headquarters has given me no other options, press or no press."

The commander nudged his sleeping sergeant again while listening to more tirades about the situation. He would have to do something to break the monotony for his men.

"Frankly, I agree with the Patriarch. I'm growing to hate the intolerance of these monks. Fanatics, every one of them." Commander Leontis could feel his voice harden with anger. Faith was faith to him, so why all the fighting? He was embarrassed to be here, arresting every monk who dared to return to the compound, escorting each to Athens. "Let me place them all in custody. We've arrested two abbots. Why not a third? Otherwise, let us all go home."

More noise. The commander pulled out his worry beads as he listened to plans for a contingency of media, religious leaders, and government bureaucrats to arrive and conduct negotiations with this stubborn abbot. Just who were they fooling? This might be the only time he might side with the abbot. Having heard enough, he concluded the call. "Sir, I've got to check on one of my men." Commander Leontis decided his men would not endure another idle evening.

"Arrange for some of our men to begin another sweep of the hillside. These damn campers are a nuisance. Keep 'em away. And be sure none of them are monks trying to get back in." The commander's deep, firm voice shook his men to attention.

"Yes, commander." The sergeant hesitated, then added. "What about the shore? And that garden the monks keep? Let's haul 'em all in."

"Yes, maybe it's time. We've been slacking."

Commander Leontis leaned against the van and wiped the sweat from his forehead. This had been a scorcher of a day, and the breeze only arose later in the afternoon. He decided he would put one of his guys in charge and go for a swim before dark.

The commander tried to think of new ways to make life intolerable for the monks and leave. Smiling, he decided his younger officers were right. He walked over to the back of the van, opened the doors, rummaged through the selection of music, and pulled out The Rolling Stones. Surely, the monks will not appreciate being entertained by the British. He popped in the CD and hit play. '*I can't get no satisfaction....*' Leontis laughed. Those Brits have that one right.

Smiling at the dreadful music, he considered some new way to convince headquarters they should give up this harassment of the monks since they don't have the spine to shut the place down. So what if these monks were hard-asses? Nothing new for Greece.

Something shook him out of his train of thought, but he was uncertain what he had seen. Shaking his head, deciding that it was the sun, he started to turn away when he noticed it again. Picking through his gear, he found a pair of binoculars. What he could be seeing was one of his men who wandered off to find a comfortable piece of shade with which to sleep. They certainly never bothered with any form of discipline and order. His men acted more like they were out on a damn family excursion.

Commander Leontis removed his glasses and focused his binoculars, scanning the hillside in sweeping motions. Something had shifted.

TWENTY-ONE

ESFIGMENOU MONASTERY

Dusk was approaching. Sofia hoped to slip inside as evening set and depart before sunrise when the monks would return to the katholikón for prayers. A night and her flashlight should suffice and be the most incredible adventure of her life. Daytime was too risky.

Sofia squatted between the trunk of a cypress tree and several scraggly bushes surrounding it. The music, still blasting, had changed. Mick Jagger now sang,

"I've been around for a long, long year
Stole many a man's soul to waste
And I was 'round when Jesus Christ
Had his moment of doubt and pain
Made damn sure that Pilate
Washed his hands and sealed his fate."

She smiled. The song blasting was "Sympathy for the Devil." Great choice to bug hard-nosed monks. They must be going crazy. She continued studying activity near the monastery with her binoculars. Some military police appeared to be branching out and walking the grounds. Two headed uphill to her right, not in her direction. Another pair, adjusting their gear, seemed to be looking her way. Looking for what suddenly? Had she done something to garner their attention? Her shoulders tensed. Fear wormed through her stomach.

Light reflected off the ground near her position, momentarily blinding her. Where was the light coming from? Sofia focused her binoculars again near the tower gate. An older military officer was scanning the hillside with his own binoculars. She realized the sun's rays were refracted off his binoculars. Would the same happen with hers and draw unwanted attention her way?

The military police standing around the vans and jeeps were now gone. She swept the hillside and saw several more police hiking the grounds. Where were the rest? Focusing again on the tower area, she noticed the older officer had climbed onto the back of the jeep and scrutinized the hillside. What was he looking for? Her gut gripped.

Quietly shifting onto her stomach behind the cypress tree, she observed his actions. Ten minutes later, the older officer climbed off the jeep and began walking toward the hillside. Time to move forward. If she was going to be arrested, it would not be here, so close to her goal. Sofia scrambled across the surface of the hillside to the other end of the monastery, crawling behind lime trees, bushes, and anything else that provided cover. Her rucksack proved cumbersome as she tried to keep her balance and remain quiet. She stopped behind a large bush and looked again. The older military officer had crossed the monastery gardens and begun hiking up. What had caught his attention? Had she set a bush trembling?

Hiding behind another knoll, she again scanned her target. The olive trees were older, which meant they were dense with branches and leaves, providing good coverage. Within the olive trees were waist-high brick walls with vegetable gardens and grape vines. Her challenge would be an open space of grass, fifteen steps long.

Sofia rolled onto her butt and checked her gear. Too bad there wasn't a beer inside to help calm her nerves. What she was about to do was just plain crazy. *An act of desperation* would be her plea to the authorities. She studied her descent to the library door.

A soft, dry wind carried the smell of sage. A yellow and black butterfly perched on a shrub nearby. This is it. One more insane adventure and then home. This had been one hell of an undertaking she had been dreaming of for years, and finally, she had made it.

The two military police officers walking near the library door strolled back toward the vans, and she saw no monks nearby. With sweaty palms, Sofia shoved her cap more securely on her head and pulled her hood over her cap, pushing her glasses back in place. She scurried through the lime grove, down onto her aching knees, scampered along the brick garden wall, crawled up a buttressed embankment that supported the high stone walls of the monastery, and then stopped. Two curved walls ahead. She heard no noise but her own anxious breathing.

Rounding a corner, Sofia saw her goal, the original entrance to the library. She dashed toward the door in the wall, hands gripping the straps on her rucksack. When she reached the door, she was surprised to see that it was solid metal and appeared to be a recent addition. The handle would not budge. Her pulling and pushing yielded nothing. Sofia patted the upper frame and then scanned around the doorway for a key. Nothing. She touched the bricks with her shaking hands. Solid. While searching around the nearby bushes, she became aware of footsteps approaching.

"We're both missing Apodeipnon. Deplorable, but then these are unfortunate times."

Startled, Sofia whirled. The monk standing before her, wearing a coarse canvas work apron, appeared older and weathered. Without glasses, he seemed to be straining to see. Evening prayers. Why isn't this monk with all the others?

"You're not one of us." The tenor of his voice was matter-of-fact. "Police?"

Bowing, she responded with her deepest contralto, "Brother Pachomius."

"Police?" He demanded an answer. His cheeks flushed a fierce red. "How dare you —" He moved toward her.

"From Ipapandi. Meteora." She kept her hands in her front pocket. She gazed at him, trying mightily to maintain her composure and give him the impression that she was home in the monasteries.

"Meteora?" He appeared honestly confused. "So, you're not the police? How did you get through the blockade?" He scrunched up his eyes. "Why aren't you in the katholikón with the other monks? Your clothing —"

"I simply entered, never asking their permission. They have no right to be here." Nodding toward the door, she continued. "I had assumed this entrance to the library would be open."

"The police have barred our own monks from returning. No one has been getting through." He seemed to be pressing for an understanding.

"I did." Bold confidence was her best cover.

He gazed intently, confusion written on his face. "But our monks have been arrested and taken away. Down on the beaches just now and following close behind me." His mind appeared caught in conflict. "Why are you out here in the open? Dangerous, so dangerous."

She heard noises in the distance, muffled by the booming music. "My abbot gave me permission to do research here on Agio Óros. Your library is one of the finest."

The monk moved closer, eyes squinting. "Yes, I'm sure it is. Father Yeorgi is dedicated to his work. An excellent scholar. Yet he and our abbot allow few in to use the collection. I must ask —"

She stood tall and erect as her mind raced. What to do next? She steadied her breathing. "May I wait inside?"

"I need to speak with my abbot. We rarely accept visitors, even monks." He turned away, muttering. "This is not making any sense."

"I've come a long way. I do not accept the presence of your tormentors. In holy obedience, do as you must. As must I. My presence proves that I am one of you." She was desperate for that key, and he seemed uninterested in revealing its location.

"Wait here. Someone will come with word."

Her heart sank. He turned and walked toward the other end of the building, leaving her standing there. After he rounded the corner, she began frantically searching again. She heard thuds on rocks. Someone climbing up from the ocean? Then she saw it. A reflection at the base of an old drainpipe. Kneeling, she pulled out a clear case with a modern key inside. With clammy and shaking hands, she tried inserting the key into the lock. Finally succeeding, she turned the key and pushed the door with her shoulder. She heard a loud call from a distance. Glancing back over one shoulder, she saw two military police running toward her.

Grabbing her rucksack, Sofia slipped inside the door to the library, bolting it shut. She was standing in a spacious reading room filled with tables, chairs, and racks of journals. A large Icon of the Transfiguration was perched on an easel, a candle hung next to the icon as a sign of the presence of the Divine Holy.

Sofia's heart raced at the sound of pounding on the door, like the butt of a rifle hitting the lock. She would have to work fast. She spotted a staircase to her left. In most of the libraries she had worked, the upper levels held the most modern books while the lower levels held the older books. Putting the key in her pocket, she descended the circular stairs, the rhythmic thumping of the music outside and the pounding on the door fading.

At the first landing, she entered the open space, looking for any monks using the library. Deciding to keep her rucksack with her, she slipped into the aisles. She scrutinized the shelves containing illuminated manuscripts and older monastic texts too recent for her interest. She walked up and down the aisles, listening for trouble while examining spines to discover the librarian's pattern of cataloging and shelving.

Several titles caught her by surprise. She thought the only known copies were in private collections. One, known as *The Istanbul Antiphonal*, a collection of prayers and antiphons for the liturgical year, had been produced in Hungary. Written on parchment in Gothic characters and illuminated with what appeared to be colored tempera, this codex was a unique piece that she thought was located near Vienna. How did it get here from the library at Saint Gall? This librarian must have access to lots of money and political contacts to get his hands on these. She reshelved the codex, wondering if Brother Makarios knew the codex was now here and chastising herself for being so easily tempted away from the task at hand.

Her stomach churned with acid, but she moved on and explored the floor below. Halfway down the stairs and finding no light switch, she stopped and pulled out her flashlight. Reaching the landing, she turned the knob. She entered and was impressed that the monks had installed blue lighting, effectively protecting the old books from harmful light, and controlled temperature and humidity. Neat, tidy, all in order. This librarian loved his books.

Stiff, sore, and needing to scan more quickly, Sofia set her rucksack down in a discreet corner and concentrated on her task. This level proved more interesting. Codices, hand-sewn leaf books, and some old Coptic tomes that came from Egypt and the Sudan. She pulled out a stool and sat low next to the shelving. She lifted each piece carefully to see if it was from her era and mainly about women. She discovered more homilies, sermons, and letters, especially during the Arian debates when the early Christian movement was nearly destroyed. She found some musical and liturgical texts.

She felt torn, wanting to scan everything carefully and knowing she had little time to work. With only the thud of the music outside, she pulled out her camera and photographed the spines of these books. She would send these photographs to Father Theodor, as Brother Pachomius, and ask him about them. He might be very interested.

Sofia needed to find evidence of where the librarian's office might be containing his precious records. She wondered, as was the case with Father Theodor, if an off-the-path room for odds and ends and works not valued by these monks might exist? Impossible to think like a librarian she had never met.

Assuming she had little time, she quickly scouted the whole facility. Where would this obviously neat and meticulous librarian hold the oldest parchments? Thank God these monks spent most of their day in prayer. Maybe the police would be a helpful distraction, buying her precious time.

The place remained quiet. She trusted her instincts. She found several more staircases. This library appeared to go down and around and down again. How far down could she go and still find her way out again? Hell, how would she get out without being discovered? Taking another set of stairs down and reaching the end of the labyrinthine hallway filled with shelving and with no time to search every shelf, she pulled out only codices, carefully opened them to avoid damaging the fragile pages with hand-sewn bindings, and began reading. She found codices written in Ethiopic Ge'ez, Copt, Aramaic, Greek, and Latin. Why so much from Ethiopia and Egypt?

Sitting on a stool and reading an intriguing codex, an early prophetic text from the Church at Ephesus in Asia Minor, Sofia was shocked back into reality by the muted sound of a male voice barking orders and the steady thud of boots descending the stairs.

TWENTY-TWO

ESFIGMENOU MONASTERY

Commander Leontis stood in the shade with a radio receiver, obtaining status reports and shouting orders. He enjoyed the noise the Rolling Stones created, so he slipped in another of their CDs and blasted *It's All Over Now*. His foot thumped to the beat of the music.

After having endured the interference of several politicians and his boss, he had decided to fill the van with any monks found outside the immediate perimeter of the monastery and send them to headquarters. His men had caught two so far.

"Orthodox flag? I don't care that there might be occupied caves. Send the hikers away, and if any of them are hermits, warn them off. I need to know where these damned monks are lurking about out there. Our security screen is a broken sieve. Go back and check on it. I want every cave, shack, and shanty searched. Thoroughly."

The commander clicked the off button. How in the hell was he or his men supposed to figure out which monks belonged here and which were from other monasteries? Babysitter, that's what he was like separating sheep from goats. He was muttering about what his men had for brains when another call came in.

"Leontis here."

He listened as one of his men reported finding footprints, apparently no more than a few hours old. Every so often, his guys surprised him by doing something correctly.

"Follow them. We need to know whether these footprints were left by our bull-headed monks or pilgrims." Leontis fought to keep sarcasm out of his voice.

His man continued his report. The footprints led through the grove toward the monastery, off the dirt road leading away.

Someone traversing the grove headed toward them? "Sweep the grove, the forest, along the hillside. Everywhere. You have all afternoon. I don't want you back here till you've covered the entire area."

His frustration mounted. Despite the arrests they had made, he had allowed his men to become lax. Their stranglehold was more like a fishing net in dire need of repair. Sharks could pass through. Had passed through, he swore to himself.

Leontis next called his men sweeping further to the north when he heard familiar footsteps. He clicked off his headphones and turned to face the abbot.

"Abbot Methodius." Leontis kept his voice firm and steady. What he'd give to arrest this royal pain, but he'd been ordered to leave the abbot alone. Seems the abbot enjoyed diplomatic immunity. Hell, why was he here then if he couldn't remove the source of the problem?

"Shut off that demonic noise," the abbot demanded.

"No."

"This is an outrage. Your presence here is an abomination before God."

"Orders. I'm just following orders. It is time for us to bring this to an end. Peacefully."

"Peacefully? You shame yourself and your uniform." The abbot's face flushed crimson.

"You knew my men would detain any monk who left your compound," Leontis began.

"You had one of your people disguise himself as a monk and break into our monastery, violating our sacred space. How dare you!" The abbot's voice strained with rage. "The insolence!"

"I don't know what you're talking about," Leontis began. Was the intense sun affecting the abbot?

"You think us fools? My monks are searching the complex now, and we'll find the devil ourselves. I demand you order him out." The abbot moved closer. "Now."

Leontis maintained steady eye contact. "I have no one –." He wondered if one of his men had taken matters into his own hands and done something daft.

The abbot interrupted him again. "Get your man out of my monastery and leave our grounds immediately."

"I have no one in there," Leontis responded. He would not let this man control the situation. "It's over, Father Abbot. You and your men will be leaving."

"We'll see who departs!" The abbot shook his fist. A prayer rope woven around his fingers.

"You know as well as I that this is over. You'll be leaving soon."

The two men locked stares, then the Abbot turned and stormed away, his robes swishing and his feet stomping. After Leontis saw the abbot's black robes disappear behind the stone wall, he returned to the van's rear to deal with the situation awaiting him there.

"Sergeant, bring the detainee here. He might know something about the abbot's claim," Leontis ordered.

Since his arrival on Mount Athos, Commander Leontis had lived with a slow sinking dread. Headaches and a burning stomach came to haunt him. He had loved the simple, orderly life of the military. Skirmishes with Turks, Cretans, and Cypriots, the occasional overzealous demonstrators, and protecting politicians never bothered him. He did not even mind the occasional tour with the United Nations. But in recent years, nothing was simple. Department politics drove him to contemplate early retirement—this assignment was the worst. He now found himself caught between church and government, all over a few insubordinate monks that the authorities refused to ignore.

Hearing his men approach, Leontis turned to face the recalcitrant monk, a man closer in age to himself than most of his troops. Handcuffed and resisting arrest, the monk appeared disheveled with graying hair matted from sweat, his coarse canvas work apron askew over frayed work clothes. His scowl bespoke defiance and anger. Understandable, Leontis thought. He became angry every time politicians and senior military commanders screwed things up for him. Why shouldn't these monks be as frustrated as he was?

"Commander Leontis. And you are?"

The monk remained silent, struggling to break free.

"As you wish. Before you're escorted to Athens, your abbot and I have a few questions for you." As he suspected, that earned a reaction. "Abbot Methodius believes that he has an intruder in his monastery."

"Why are you disturbing us? Why won't you leave us in peace?" The monk growled. Leontis noticed the monk was grinding his teeth.

"Ask your abbot. I didn't ask for this assignment." Leontis wiped his forehead with a cloth. "I never ordered my men to enter your monastery. I don't think this intruder is one of us."

"I saw him with my own eyes," the monk said.

"What did he look like?" Leontis pressed.

The monk's brow knit together; his thick glasses shifted on his face. "Tall, slender, black hair. No beard, little possibility of one."

"I don't understand," Leontis said, bewildered.

"Appeared to me that your man couldn't grow one even if he tried," the monk responded.

"Not my man." Leontis found these monks increasingly strange. If he had remembered to pack his sense of humor, he might find this assignment hilarious. "Any reason that someone else would want to break in?"

The monk peered at him, perplexed.

"Holding something you shouldn't," Leontis asked.

"This is a monastery—"

"So I'm told. Tell me why someone would break in," Leontis asked, wondering what he might have stumbled into. Is he now dealing with the attempted theft of icons or old books? Traffickers in antiquities?

"One of your damned military police. Disrupting our lives, spreading dissent—" the monk began.

"Dissent?" Leontis asked.

"Damn you, don't put words in my mouth," the monk sputtered.

Leontis studied this old monk. Surly and distrusting, but why not? His home had been surrounded for over a year, disrupting his life. Leontis studied the monk's hands. "You work in the gardens?"

The old monk's countenance slowly relaxed, and he took a deep breath as he studied Leontis.

"You remind me of my grandfather. Master viticulturist. Could make grapes thrive in the rockiest places, even higher altitudes." Leontis offered a cigarette to the old monk, who refused and then lit one for himself. "Your name, Father?"

Standing upright, he replied. "Brother Petros."

"Like the apostle? Appropriate, since most of Agio Óros is rock anyway." Leontis laughed at his own joke. "Brother Petros, why in heaven's name would anyone want to break into a monastery that's under siege?"

The two men studied each other in silence.

"Not one of yours?"

"No," Leontis observed the old monk while pulling on his cigarette.

Brother Petros cleared his throat. "Guy claimed to be from Ipapandi. Something very odd about him. Eyes of a scholar but," he seemed to search for words, "more like a woman.""

"A woman?" Leontis bit back laughter. He hoped so, just what these monks deserve. "Strange, indeed. Could this be one of those grad students working at Megístis Lávras? Or a pilgrim?"

Brother Petros remained quiet and in thought and yet appeared confused and agitated. "Possibly, but they don't belong here."

"Maybe someone forgot to tell them. Maybe a comrade challenged him to a dare." Hiding a smile, Leontis escorted the monk back to the van. He hoped the kid wouldn't get hurt if that's what was happening.

The sun inched toward the horizon. His men needed to deliver these monks to Karyés before sunset. The monk's claim of an intruder made no sense. Any thief with common sense would avoid a monastery under military siege. Young people too often lacked common sense, especially the brainy ones. He had not sent any of his men into the monastery, so who was the mystery intruder? Was the Greek government spying? The patriarch's people? All possibilities seemed ludicrous except the possibility of a young person's hoax. Maybe he needed to contact the antiquities authorities in case someone was after whatever valuables were sitting inside the monastery.

And those footprints corroborated Brother Petros's claim.

No matter what he did or which way he turned, he landed deeper in the convoluted maze. Time to bring this to an end.

§

At the express orders of Abbot Methodius, Brother Stefanos organized a search of their monastery. His abbot accused the military police of disguising one of their own as a monk and entering their sacred home. And Brother Stefanos was to find this intruder. He was as confused as Brother Petros, their master gardener, who first reported the appearance of a strange monk to the abbot. The military police had never acted so daring or disrespectful of them before.

Struggling to be heard over the satanic music blaring outside, Brother Stefanos sent two monks to their katholikón with strict orders to guard all entrances and another two with keys to check the sacristy where their sacred vessels were kept.

Brother Stefanos took three other monks with him and headed north toward the library. Entering the reading room from the corridor, he stopped short. Confused, he scanned the room but saw no evidence of Brother Petros. Odd. Father Abbot told him Brother Petros was waiting for him in the library reading room to describe the intruder and help with the search. Brother Stefanos crossed the reading room and checked that the outside door was locked.

"I don't want to wait for Brother Petros to arrive. Brother Iannis, remain here. We'll begin searching," Brother Stefanos commanded. He pointed for one monk to take the stairs to the floor above and took the stairs down. How would anyone get through a bolted door?

Brother Stephanos followed the other monk down the winding stairs. Did Father Yeorgi's questionable cousin cross someone he shouldn't have? He disapproved of Father Yeorgi's hunger for old manuscripts. Greed was a vice that needed to be rooted out to finally secure a truly primitive observance pleasing to God. Unfortunately, his abbot disagreed.

As his monk companion swept to the left, Brother Stefanos veered right. Each made as little noise as possible as they checked the stacks. Not hard to do, given the vibrations from the damnable music outside. Their intruder must be a trafficker in rare books. Otherwise, the finance office made more sense with its banking records and confidential correspondence, especially with their solicitors. That's what the military had done with several of their brother monasteries. But the library? Did they know something about Father Yeorgi's activities that he did not? *O Kýrios*!

After making a clean sweep, the two monks proceeded to the lower floor.

TWENTY-THREE

FEAST OF THE TRANSFIGURATION

Sofia dimmed the lights, gathered her gear, and slipped through the only other doorway out of the room. Gently closing the door, she switched on her flashlight. With her ear to the door, she couldn't hear anything and hoped the monks hadn't heard her. Steadying her breathing, she wondered if there was another way out other than the way she just entered.

Pulling out her pen light, she scanned this space. Before her lay sturdy wooden steps that looked several years old. With remaining where she was not much of an option, she began her descent. About 20 steps down, she was met with uneven stone steps. Her face smacked directly into a giant spider web, and she jerked back, nearly screaming in surprise. With one hand on the wall, she carefully picked her way downward as the depth of the steps grew deeper. As the rugged stairway dropped, it curved toward her left and became a hallway under the floor above. The air remained dry and cool.

The beam of Sofia's flashlight reflected against a shiny surface ahead of her. Drawing closer, she faced a metal door with a large heavy handle. When she pressed the latch down, it opened. Why wasn't it locked? She opened it a crack and peered around. Total darkness.

Passing through, she found herself in a long, narrow room. She listened for any indication that she had been followed, closed the door, and scanned the room with her flashlight. No other outlet. She set her gear down. The room held two-meter-tall bookcases in front of rough-hewn wood paneling, the cases holding thick leather-bound books.

Sofia rested her aching back against the wall, gulping air. She had a bad habit of holding her breath when thrust into an anxious situation. She found the light switch and turned it on; its light soft and diffused. With shaking hands, she pulled out her water bottle and a couple of protein bars, ate, and drank, pondering her few remaining options. Her insane side trip here had gotten her little besides a few rare or curious books. And any moment now, she expected those monks searching for an intruder to come down here. Not much she could do about that.

Scanning the shelves while thinking, she pulled out several tomes, revealing that each was an illuminated choir book only several centuries old. The monks stored their most important books for major feast days in this room. Why clear down here and not near the katholikón?

Reaching the far wall, Sofia noticed that the corners did not match correctly. She continued her exploration of the book spines, but something nagged at her. She glanced at the ceiling and saw a thick electrical cord behind the bookcase. Then she realized what was bothering her. She retraced her steps and reexamined the first corner.

Sofia reached a hand in and behind a row of books and pushed the wall. When nothing happened, she began pulling on the vertical bars of the bookcase. The wall seemed to move a crack. Who would believe this? Just like in the movies—a hidden "something." What though? After pulling a second time, she returned to her original position and studied the wall again. With one foot on the stone wall as leverage, she dragged the end of the bookcase away toward herself. The bookcase felt like it was on wheels, and, as was soon revealed, a false wall had been attached to the rear of the bookcase and moved with it.

Picking up her flashlight, Sofia peered into the room beyond. She entered and flicked her flashlight around a cavernous space full of metal shelving brimming with rolled tubes covered in cloth. As she grabbed her gear, she heard footsteps from beyond the door. Turning off the entrance light, she slipped in, closing the wall unit behind her. She was sweating from the exertion.

Sofia set her gear in the corner and crouched with her back to the wall that contained the moveable bookcase. She forced her breathing to a slow, minimal pace as she prayed fervently to the *Theotokos* to blind the monks to her presence.

She listened to the muffled sound of a gruff voice.

"Anything?" the gruff voice asked.

"No," a soft voice replied.

"Check the wall. Father Yeorgi has been excavating the hillside in recent years."

"What?"

"The wall," the gruff voice commanded. "Here, help me."

Sofia heard the wall react to apparent pulling, opening several inches. A hand reached in and turned on the light. A hooded head peered in and then grunted dismissively.

The wall closed again as she heard, "I still think it's the finance office the military police are after." This voice seemed to move away as quickly as they arrived.

Sweat rolled down her back. Sofia held her tilting head, breathing deeply. Now what? She glanced at her watch and decided to remain here for several hours and try leaving when the monks were at prayer.

After resting briefly, she used her penlight to scan the room again, rough-hewn with stone walls and sophisticated lighting above. Metal shelving with rows of cloth-covered cylinders, so familiar to Sofia, rolled vellum but with no tags or labels. Why were these stored differently? She found the light switch, turning the dimmer switch to a low setting.

Sofia pulled one tube off the shelf and untied the strings. The fabric was fine, unbleached cotton. Squatting on the floor, she pulled out and unrolled the vellum scroll on her lap, angling her flashlight to better examine the lettering. She recognized the early Armenian with its feathery script. She could make out a few words but would need time and her reference books to make sense of this. She guessed that she was holding a series of letters from the formatting. Why hidden away down here? Since she had time to kill and her curiosity heightened, she set the sheaves on the floor, pulled out her camera, and began shooting copies of each sheaf. She would figure out later what these were.

Sofia moved to different shelves, wondering if these were stored by century or region, and pulled out another tube. Pulling the darkened vellum out and unrolling it, she smiled at the beautiful, colorful, boxy script of Ge'ez. She recognized some of the words. This appeared to be an epistle defending Christianity against one of the early heresies. Several of the neighboring parchment tubes were also in Ge'ez. Her hands shook with anger. Ethiopia had been robbed of so much of its heritage in the past century. She took photos, clipped a piece of the vellum, and scraped a discreet bit of the ink. She would ask Brother Mac to help her get these tested. And try to establish from which monastery in Ethiopia these really belonged.

Might Deacon Olympias's letters be here? Sofia began to move more quickly, pulling tubes.

Two bundles caught her attention. Reaching across, she pulled each of them out. Heavier and bulkier than most of the rolls in this room, she set one beside her and the other on her lap and untied the strings. The contents appeared more fragile than most scrolls she had seen on Mount Athos. She gently opened the delicate lambskin vellum and examined it closely.

In the center were several smaller pieces of vellum stored, much of the text barely legible and the edges frayed. Scanning the clear Greek lettering, Sofia's hands began shaking. She read such familiar words—*Chrysostom*, *dear brother in Christ*, and *Cucusus*, one of the towns to which Olympias' friend had been exiled. Not trusting the time, she photographed each sheaf in this tube and took samples.

Returning the scrolls to its sack, Sofia opened the other bulky tube. This one was written in Ge'ez, its scripting more faded than the other scroll. Sofia took her time examining the text, unrolling, and rerolling. Several times, she had to set it on her lap, and her hands were cramping from excitement and the odd angle she was working. Some of the words eluded her. While seeming to be part of a letter, the document appeared formal. Sofia paused and breathed deeply. Certain names kept emerging: Maryam, Hannah, Joanna, and Salome were unmistakable. Each was common enough in the early Jesus Movement. The same Hannah from the other fragments she unearthed?

Unrolling the scroll further, she continued reading what she was able to. Second-born, what did that mean? Hannah was *chokmah*? She needed help and time to make sense of this. Surely, rumors of its existence would have persisted over the years, but she had heard nothing. None of her professors had ever mentioned the possibility of something like this. How could these be hidden for so many centuries? Were the Ethiopian monks hiding this? Afraid of it being found?

Unrolling and rerolling, she continued reading. Several times, she stopped and reviewed some of the text. Words eluded her. She would need her reference texts to figure them out. She would need to investigate. Was the writer Miryam? Or Hannah? Painstakingly lifting the roll, she glanced at the layers of vellum below.

Sofia sat there and agonized. This might be the discovery of the century, just like the Dead Sea Scrolls or Nag Hammadi. Even a fraud, if centuries old, was significant. What she held was more volatile than anything she ever had expected to find. The inevitable controversy required carbon dating of the vellum and ink.

More importantly, this scroll was so potentially explosive that she would need to prove its existence. My God, her students would have loved to see this. Too bad she didn't have students right now. Maybe soon. Her detractors would undoubtedly want to paint her as another cheat, trying to advance her career by fraud. These mean-spirited monks might seal this room off and deny its existence. Or worse, the librarian or even the police could remove the library's contents, and she would never be able to retrace this discovery.

Sofia sat, anguished. What would Brother Mac think? What would her family say? The act of stealing abhorred her. Her family had been passionate about the theft of their Greek heritage. She would be behaving just like these monks. When the testing for authentication had been completed, she could arrange for its return to the Greek government. Or, better yet, Patriarch Bartholomaios as head of the Orthodox world. She would figure out a way to ensure that, during its return, the scroll's existence was revealed to the whole world. Her driving need was for proof – not to possess something that was not rightfully hers. Her hunch was that this document, if authenticated, would fill some considerable gaps in Christian history.

Carefully laying out the scroll, one sheaf at a time, Sofia photographed each. Taking several of the cloth tubes, she gently rolled the parchments around the cotton and then returned it to its original tube. She popped out the memory card and put it with the others. These she slipped deep within her breast binding, hoping that, if caught, the men would be too embarrassed to do a strip search of her. She would hand-carry the rolled tubes to ensure their protection.

Needing to wait until the depth of night before venturing out of this room, she returned to the corner, resting her eyes and thought. If she gets out of the monastery, does she run into the hillside and aim for the hiking path above? She recalled hearing that each monastery had its own boat launch. Surely these monks did. How else have they kept supplied? They've smuggled stuff in. Was Takis helping them? Is that why he didn't want her to come here? She almost laughed.

Time passed like a funeral dirge. She had glanced at a few other tubes, but her mind was glued to the precious document perched in her lap. Could this date to the time of Jesus? Or within a century?

Sofia glanced at her watch. It was almost one in the morning. Gathering her thoughts, wits, and what little was left of her battered courage, she secured her rucksack on her back, picked up the scroll, scrunched down her knit cap, and flipped her hood over her hair, moving toward the entrance. With an ear to the opening in the wall, she heard nothing. She peeked through the crack into the darkness. She began pushing the door. Nothing moved. Did the monks lock something she had not noticed? Trying to calm her rising panic, she pushed again, sustaining her efforts. Finally, she felt the wall move and continued straining until there was enough room for her to slip through. Pushing the wall entrance back into place, Sofia crept out, sliding her hand along the shelving to guide herself across the dark room.

She kept thinking about one of Takis' favorite American movies, *The Great Escape*. The room was dark and cool enough to feel like she crawled through one of those underground tunnels. After what felt like an eternity, she reached the end of the hallway and began her ascent up the uneven stairs, stumbling several times.

Reaching the top of the stairs, she pushed the door open slightly and peeked through the crack. She could see and hear nothing in the darkness. Had they really given up? Opening the door, she slipped into the dark hall, felt her way across, grasped the stairs' handrail, and continued upward. Now or never. Climbing, she made as little noise as possible.

Reaching the top of the stairs, Sofia stepped out into the deserted reading room. The moonlight glancing into the room through the window provided the illumination for her to find her way to the door leading outside. She pulled the key from her inner pocket. The lock released, and she yanked the door open.

At that moment, she heard footsteps behind her. A harsh voice declared, "As I suspected."

Taken aback, she nearly dropped the scroll. Whirling around, she came face to face with a monk shorter than herself.

"So, our intruder finally reveals himself," his words triumphant.

TWENTY-FOUR

SOMEWHERE ON THE AEGEAN SEA

Sofia bolted through the doorway, out along the path, and bore left. Her only hope of escape was to reach the shore. Too soon, the level path began a deep and winding descent. She carefully cradled the scroll while her left arm brushed branches away. She strained her eyes, trying to find the holes and rocks in the footpath. As it bore right, her foot slipped on a rock; she regained her balance and dove over a hole in the path. She lengthened her stride whenever she could, desperate to put distance between herself and her pursuer.

Her thigh muscles ached from the strain of avoiding holes and underbrush. The path curved a hard right, and the moon's beams revealed a steep cliff to her left. She could see the water ahead, giving her hope.

She heard the monk yell at her but did not look back. The path grew steeper. She struggled to stay upright. Her foot slipped on gravel. She extended her free hand to keep upright, scraping her palm. The monk cursed. Fabric tore. His robes caught in something?

Sofia's foot skidded. She went down, still holding the scroll up. Clambering back up, her knee burning, she sped headlong down the hill toward the shore. She felt exhilarated despite raging terror. Racing past the arsenas, the fort-like storehouse where supplies were received, she careened out onto the wood planking of the dock and toward the only boat moored there. She unwound the line securing the boat to the pier, shoved the bow away, and jumped in, the weight of her rucksack nearly causing her to stumble. She hefted one strap off her shoulder and used her heel to push the stern away.

The boat rocked. Sofia released the strap off her other shoulder, letting her rucksack drop to the floor. She lowered the outboard motor and turned the key. With one hand holding the scroll, she steered the bow away from shore as she heard her pursuer's feet hit the dock. But then she heard another voice yelling as well.

To be safe, she set her precious tube between her legs. *Merciful Mary, let me succeed. Keep me safe*, she cried out.

Sofia pushed the throttle forward, causing the engine to roar to life. The boat rocked as she steered away from shore and toward the sea. She increased the throttle as waves slapped against the bow. Both the monk and some military guy stood there, yelling. Her thigh muscles shook, her knee ached, and her breathing came hard. She headed straight out to sea and shoved the throttle forward, 10 knots, 20 knots, scrambling to figure out her next steps.

Sofia kept one hand on the scroll as she struggled to steer. The boat slammed into the waves, hitting her with a salty spray. She breathed deeply, trying to calm her spasming stomach as she gripped the handle. She scanned the waters ahead, straining to see through her salty lenses.

Rounding the first bend toward the north, Sofia leaned forward, scanning for possible rocks. Glancing around, she realized she had just stolen a boat from the military police. She could expect company soon. But maybe not too soon. Greek police were not renowned for efficiency. That crazy monk would pursue her if he could get his hands on another boat. Her gut twisted.

Would the military police care that something was taken from the monks? Maybe the standoff between the monks and the military police would buy her time and safe deliverance. *Kyrie Eleison*, please send interference. She had to succeed. Someone besides herself must see these scrolls. Just one eyewitness would do it. She strained, listening for signs of any other boats in the area.

Sofia steered further from shore, not trusting her ability to see rocks or shallow waters in darkness.

Brother Mac and Adélie would be thrilled with her discovery. They'd anything to help her with the translations and the testing, but she could not take this to Turkey with its current political unrest.

Above the sound of the boat's engine, she could hear the distant sound of monastery bells tolling. What were the monks and police doing? Out in this vast sea, she felt like she was sitting still as the coast moved slowly.

Sofia scanned the waters ahead, struggling to figure out how far from shore was safe without getting too far away. Where to go from here? She could not leave this scroll in Greece as the chances of theft were too great. She laughed. Who is the thief here?

She searched the water for boats and the shore for any weird activity. She maintained speed although the boat slapped hard into the water, the hull dropping into the valley of the next wave. She used her body to shield the tube from ocean spray. Fortunately, she had sea legs from years of sculling.

Sofia needed to find a safe place to get this scroll properly scanned and arrange to test the lambskin vellum and ink. She smiled. Dare she? A great location, but would she be putting Sister Meg at risk?

The boat shook as it broke waves. Sofia kept alert for sounds of pursuit, but all she heard was the boat's engine and the pounding in her head. The wind felt good on her skin. The full moon provided decent visibility, allowing her to steer clear of the rocky shore. Sofia followed the coastline north at a decent distance. She had just passed Ákra Arápis, and a large bay opened to her left.

Straining to hear, she shifted and checked her tube. The drone of a boat's engine was somewhere out there. Her mind, exhausted, scrambled to think. Was it after her? Oh hell! *Mary in heaven, I need a miracle now.* Turning, Sofia saw a faint light dancing across the surface. The noise grew. She was not giving up and wouldn't risk trying to reach Stratonian.

Sofia turned toward the west and the small town of Ierissos. All she had were the lights along the coast to guide her there.

She spotted a sandy stretch of beach with the town's lights to her left. Heading toward the darkened shore, which hopefully would provide cover, she pulled the throttle back, beached the boat, and then killed the engine. Inland was her only option now.

Unlacing her boots, she stuffed her socks inside, tied her boots together, and clipped them on her rucksack to pin them, hoping she wouldn't mind hiking barefoot tonight. Shouldering her bag and holding the tube by its excess cotton covering, she carefully lifted her foot out in search of solid ground. The sea was cold, and her foot sunk somewhat into the sandy bottom. As her other foot touched the surface, she saw the sweeping lights from the police boat. She ducked, holding the tube safely away from the waves. The police boat slowed and shifted into reverse.

Before her lay sand and a hill with scrubby brush and sea salt-weathered trees. Sofia slogged to shore, headed across the short sandy beach to the hillside, and began climbing the narrow, rugged path. A searchlight brushed her backside. She tucked her arm, holding her discovery inward toward the hillside. The strobe light repeated its sweep.

She pulled deep breaths to stay calm, especially to steady her hands. Sweat stains on the vellum could be damaging.

Sofia heard a high-pitched squeal and a harsh voice ordering her to stop. The police already? Well, she was as stubborn and as determined as they were. Seagulls were squawking, maybe cheering her on.

She continued her long strides up and across the hillside, passing through shrub-like trees. What would they do? Her breath grew labored. Climb out and swim? She would need to move quickly. They would locate a dock and begin their own pursuit. She smiled at the thought through a grimace. She easily had a five-mile hike to Ouranoúpoli. Would her cousin be there?

§

Commander Leontis was in a deep sleep when the phone's shrill lunged him into hazy consciousness. Reaching out, he knocked the phone to the floor, nearly falling out of the sagging narrow bed. Retrieving the receiver, he answered.

"Leontis here." His voice sounded as if someone were choking him.

"Emergency, sir," the night duty officer said. With the increasing media curiosity and politicians interfering, Leontis had left orders that no action would be taken against the monks without his permission.

"Emergency? What now?" the commander bellowed. His days had grown exasperating.

"A "break-in, sir." He hesitated. "Or, rather, a breakout. The monks claim they saw someone running from the monastery and stealing one of our boats. The monks are demanding that we go in pursuit. I didn't want to do that without clearance."

"A "breakout?" Leontis could not believe what he was hearing. Who in the hell would break out of a monastery when they could leave at any time? "For God's sake, we want these hard asses to leave!"

"Sir?"

"Are you pious or something?"

"Well, sir." the field officer's voice sounded dismayed, holding just the fear of hell Leontis wanted to deliver.

"Listen. We want these monks out, not in. Let'm all escape."

"But sir, the monks claim that it wasn't their own. In fact, they claim it was one of us."

"Not that again." Leontis was groggy. All he wanted to do was go back to sleep.

"Seems this intruder fled from the library. The monks claim something was taken." The caller's voice was cut off by interference. Then, "but they couldn't say what."

"*Βλάκας*. Fool. The commander grew convinced this was connected to the black market. But wouldn't it be easier to steal from one of the other monasteries? "So something was allegedly stolen, but they don't know what."

"Yes, sir," the officer answered.

"Too bad their thief didn't take a few monks with him." The commander swung his legs off the bed, his feet landing on the cold floor, surrendering to the inevitable.

"Uh, sir. Officer Dalaras just reported that one of the monks chased a hiker or someone who stole our boat. Sir. Believes it was a woman. Sir."

"Leontis burst out laughing. "I hope so. Do nothing till I get there. Nothing. Got it?"

"Yes, sir. Do nothing, sir."

The commander reluctantly dressed, wondering why he could so effectively put the fear of hell into his men but not into those damn monks.

TWENTY-FIVE

S ANTA CECILIA IN TRASTEVERE, ROME

Sofia arrived at Leonardo da Vinci airport outside Rome exhausted, stiff, and sore. Her head heavy like some horrific hang-over. She could hardly believe what she had done. She had driven Takis' car from Ouranoúpoli to Thessaloníki, by-passing a return home for fear of uncomfortable questions or, worse, the police. Buying a cylindrical leather tube with a handle, used by archivists and architects, and repackaging the parchments within, she passed through airport security with her discovery as a carry-on. Her heightened awareness of any police interest added to her already frantic nerves.

Since the trains and metro would not take her anywhere near Trastevere, Sofia walked through the glass doors, glanced around to see if anyone was following her, and hailed a taxi. She slipped into the backseat and, as the black Mercedes peeled away from the curb, she swung her rucksack on the floor near her, holding the tube securely on her lap.

In true Roman fashion, the driver attacked the freeway with skilled speed, weaving in and around slower-moving vehicles. Sofia watched as the countryside changed from farm and field to office buildings, hotels, towering apartment complexes, and the city. Within thirty minutes, the taxi ripped off the freeway and headed into the heart of old Rome. Like Greece, the Roman concept of lanes and right-of-way was merely suggestive. Heading down a congested main arterial, they crossed the Tiber River into the Trastevere district. The dome of Saint Peter's glimmered between old buildings to her right.

Slowing to a crawl, her taxi wove around pedestrians, scooters, produce carts, and groups of determined tourists. Sofia scanned around her to see if they were being followed. But then, would the police know where she was? The monk who chased her? The Mercedes stopped, and the driver gestured to his left. Paying the agreed fifty euros, she climbed into the humidity and acidic air pollution, standing before the gated inner courtyard of the Church of Santa Cecilia in Trastevere.

Sofia was accosted by a cackle of brightly colored, wrinkled old Romany women. She shoved her way through, using her rucksack as a battering ram and gripping the tube. Pushing her way through the gate, she heaved it closed behind her and then checked her pockets for any evidence of theft. She cursed herself for not remembering to have a euro or two available to bribe her safe passage. To her left was the only door she could see that was clearly not a church entrance. The door's handle refused to turn. A cursory glance revealed no doorbell or other means of attracting attention.

Crossing the courtyard, she pulled open the heavy church door and entered. The cool air was a welcomed blessing. The interior was classic Italian Carrera marble in bright yellow, black, and ivory. A few candles flickered on the high altar across from where she stood. Fronting the altar was an ivory marble statue of a woman lying in a prone position, apparently in passionate, mystical ecstasy. Saint Cecilia, she figured. This twelfth-century Church was built on top of the martyr's home.

Sofia sat on a bench along one wall of the Church, trying to figure out how to let the nuns know that they had a guest. She set her rucksack under the bench, out of sight, while grasping her precious tube. So tired and sore that she struggled to think, she decided to stay put, figuring someone would offer to assist. These nuns must pray the Divine Office or Mass or something eventually.

Sofia nodded off several times, cursing herself each time she awoke since someone could have stolen her precious cargo. Exhaustion bested her, and she nodded off.

"*Kuamsha. Svegliati.*"

Sofia awoke with a startle, instinctively grasping the tube, and caught her breath. "Oh, excuse me. Uh, *mi scusì.*"

"May I assist you?" The nun sounded East African, with her clipped consonants and musical voice.

"*Sì.* Is Sister Meg home?"

"*Aai-*, Mother Meg, she knows you?"

"*Sì.* May I see her?"

"I am Sister Redemptrix. You are?"

"Sofia. Doctor Sofia Papandréou from Thessaloníki."

Sister Redemptrix responded with a clicking noise. "Dottore, come."

The nun gripped Sofia by the elbow and led her toward the rear of the Church. Pulling out a ring of keys, she inserted one into a lock in the frescoed wall. A portion of the wall opened to reveal the inside of the monastery. After climbing some of the steepest stairs she had ever encountered and walking down a long corridor, they reached a frosted glass door left ajar.

Tapping softly on the glass, Sister Redemptrix inquired, "Mother?"

"Come in," a familiar voice responded.

Sofia slipped through the doorway into a large room with high windows. Books overflowed every available space, and piles of paper and other odds and ends were stacked on the tables. She searched the room for several seconds before finding Sister Meg half-hidden behind a stack of books on one of the tables.

"Sister Meg," Sofia began.

"Oh, my goodness!" The nun smiled as she rose from her chair.

"I apologize for this sudden intrusion. I had no time to call." Sofia, feeling overwhelmed with paranoia, avoided using her cell phone for fear a cell tower would find her.

The women hugged. "Please, have a seat," her host said as she cleared a chair. "Thank you, Sister Redemptrix. Dottore Papandréou is a former student of mine. Would you arrange a guest room for Sofia?"

After the nun departed, Sister Meg continued. "I'm delighted to see you but haven't finished arrangements with the Vatican Library staff. And the Director hasn't returned from summer holidays for us to take him out to dinner. I'm afraid you've wasted your time coming here."

Sofia looked across and down at the petite scholar, glasses propped on her salt and pepper hair, and immediately knew she had made the right choice.

"I've been through a rather harrowing week. We need to talk before I change my mind," Sofia said. "As you Americans say, I'm scared shitless."

"Shitless? Well, I'm certainly curious."

"This." Sofia pointed to the tube on her lap. "I've just spent the last week on Mount Athos."

"What?" Astonishment swept across Sister Meg's face. "How?"

Sofia blushed, as much with excitement as with guilt. "Until last night, I've been passing myself off as from Meteora or as a graduate student." She felt another wave of piercing guilt.

"How? A lovely woman like you?"

"With the help of a rather creative and talented cousin of mine." Her nerves were fraying.

The nun's countenance was an open book of curiosity and confusion. "Is that why you cut your lovely hair?"

Sofia touched her hair and gazed at her dirty clothes. "I just had to do it. I knew Olympias had to be hidden there."

"And you found her letters?"

"Some, yes. And more."

Sofia told her tale, from her loss of employment and encouragement to interview with the big tech firms in California, to the silent wall she encountered by Hatzidakis, to Brother Makarios' reluctance to "convert" to access their libraries, to the graduate student's being limited to scanning illuminated books. And finally, to her desperate actions.

The two women sat in silence, gazing at one another. Then, a smile swept across Sister Meg's face.

"A gutsy move on your part, Sofia. And you did them no harm."

Guilt stung her gut. Sofia continued. "I was thrilled with what I had unearthed, but I kept hearing about this schismatic monastery called Esfigmenou and Father Theodor's belief that they held the greatest riches on Mount Athos. I couldn't resist."

Sister Meg leaned back in her chair. "Obviously. And you knew the risks you were taking. I'd expect nothing less of you." She chuckled. "Really, Sofia, the smartest move the Vatican Libraries and Archives could ever make would be to hire you. You'd revolutionize the place."

"Put in a word for me? I'm desperately poor right now."

"I'll see what I can do about getting you a bit of cash, and yes, I'll speak to the right people at the libraries. Maybe your discovery of these texts, especially of Deacon Olympias, and your work in Turkey will loosen some funds." Nodding her head toward the tube in Sofia's lap, she continued. "So, if you've spent the week photographing old parchments, what is in that tube?"

Sofia was unaware that she had been grasping the tube so tautly. "Two finds. One in Ge'ez, something wholly unexpected. It's either an extraordinary fraud or a treasure the Ethiopians had kept from the world. As I've thought about this, it makes perfect sense. And yet, it doesn't." She looked at her friend. "I'm hoping you'll allow me to store this here and begin my work on it. I need to keep this safe. And I'd appreciate your professional help."

"You took something?" Sister Meg leaned forward. "You? I've only known you as a professional with deep integrity." Her voice was sharp. "Why would you do such a thing?"

Sofia felt her face blush. "Because someone besides me needs to see this and verify its existence. Once that happens, I'd want to return this to Greece or Patriarch Bartholomaios."

The nun sat back, gazing at Sofia. "Obviously not the monks. I'd expect them to be angry. Not just your presence there but also taking something from them. So just what did you find?"

"It might be better if I showed you. Is there a secure place where I can unroll this and show you? Do your archives have a long table?"

§

The two women headed down several corridors and began their descent down deep stairs, soft lights allowing them to negotiate the steep stairs. The underground reminded her of Mount Athos. Sometimes, the stairs veered to their left, and then they took another set of stone stairs to their right. The air carried an essence of dry sweetness.

Sister Meg broke the silence between them. You'll find that our convoluted monastery complex will serve your needs. Few people understand the layout. Few outside my community even know we have an archive."

"Reminds me of Mount Athos."

"Italians are the ultimate recyclers. Over the centuries and whenever more rooms were needed, people simply built upward."

"I can never tell you how much I appreciate your help. I hope I haven't put you in danger."

Sister Meg glanced toward Sofia. "Danger? You're really worried, aren't you?"

"I've made some monks angry. And I won't be surprised if the police get involved."

"You know as well as I that antiquities theft is taken seriously."

The two women walked down a long hallway with sconces giving off soft light. Sofia noticed it had a downward slant. They were still going deeper underground.

She noticed intricately carved archways, suggesting old buildings. "What is this space, Meg?"

"The stairs took us down below the monastery, built in the thirteenth century. This passageway connects us to Saint Cecilia's first-century family home. Now we're moving into the original eighth-century Church I've turned into our archives. A bomb would not do much damage to the space.

Sofia nearly tripped, trying to see everything. Old frescoes of family members and of exotic animals. Carved pillars with recessed lighting. And a sweet, musty smell.

Sister Meg pulled out keys, opened yet another heavy door, and turned on the lights. "We have several settings, so when we begin work on whatever you've got there, we can utilize blue lighting to protect it."

Sofia passed through the entryway to a large, cavernous space with rows and rows of metal shelving on tracks filled with gray archival boxes.

Sofia smiled. "I hadn't realized you might be holding so much history."

Sister Meg looked her way. "Most people don't. Santa Cecilia, as a monastery, is around twelve centuries old. And when other communities of women either shut down or were suppressed, their archives came here. We want to keep the history together as much as possible."

Her host set the rucksack near a desktop computer and disappeared around the corner to their left. Sofia followed. Before her lay a long table nearly as wide, covered with a padded tabletop. Sister Meg grabbed a bolt of very fine silk cloth and unrolled it along the entire length of the table. "This should protect the vellum nicely."

"We need to shoot the scroll and download the digitals. And I need you as my eyewitness that this thing exists." Sofia unloaded her thumb drives, samples, and camera onto a nearby surface. "And maybe someone else as well, just to be safe."

"Well, I'm certainly curious to see this. And the Olympias pieces." Sister Meg switched the light to blue lighting as Sofia set the roll down on the worktable.

Sofia untied the package with quivering hands and gently slid the contents onto the table. "I found this with some pieces tucked inside, and I haven't looked closely at them to see if they're connected."

"You're assuming the monk librarian stored it this way?" Her host bent over the table to look closely at the vellum. "Or something else?"

Sofia put on her glasses. "I don't know. I need to begin solving the mystery of this. What is it? Why store it deep into the hillside under the old monastery if it's fake?"

"Were the monks trying to hide this from someone? That would make sense if the document were about women."

Sofia sighed. "When will we all grow up enough to stop considering women as a disease or as the enemy?"

"Maybe that's why the Holy Spirit led you to this."

Sofia glanced up to see Sister Meg's smile.

After locating some delicate T-pins, Sister Meg moved to the other side of the table. Sofia began unrolling the scroll, and her host secured the top of the vellum with a pin. Each separate piece was moved toward Sister Meg and again secured with pins. They were creating a tier to confirm the order in which the pieces were originally found, just in case the means of storage proved critical.

"This is in excellent shape, Sofia. Wherever this has been, its owners have taken good care of it."

"Yes. I suspect it's remained in a dry, warm climate. Rarely seen or used."

Sister Meg grasped a cloth and helped hold down the vellum as Sofia pinned her edge. "Dry is good. The Vatican deals with serious bacterial deterioration in several da Vinci and Michelangelo letters. Those are only 500 years old."

Sofia's hands started shaking as they unrolled the next section. "The vellum is relatively soft. Not dry and brittle as I'd expect." More than once, Sister Meg stretched across and placed her hand on Sofia's in a calming gesture.

Sister Meg walked around the table and stood by Sofia, then gazed at the several tiers of vellum with several odd pieces that Sofia had pinned off to the side. "This is stunning, Sofia. Three different scripts. I recognize the lower sections as Ge'ez, but I don't know the others."

"This is Armenian. It's old enough that it's closer to Syriac Aramaic. I don't know why Olympias' letters are not in Greek." Somewhat absent-mindedly, Sofia pointed to the lowest tier of velum. "This is the most stunning piece in the earliest form of Ge'ez."

The two women studied the bold, curly script in unusually good shape.

The nun responded. "In Ethiopia. Makes sense."

Sofia began pointing at certain words in the script. "*Maryam. Hannah. Salome.*"

Her host moved closer to look at the words Sofia had pointed out. "Who is Hannah?"

TWENTY-SIX

ARCHIVES, SANTA CECILIA IN TRASTEVERE, ROME

The following day, the two friends returned to the cavern to study their work and proceed with the next steps. Sofia had slept little, chimpanzees chattering in her brain and sometimes gorillas taking her down, reminding her of all the disasters that could unfold in the weeks ahead.

They stood before the long table, studying the layout of the parchments. Only a few broken fragments needed to be set apart as the remainder of the vellum had survived its sudden exodus from Mount Athos intact.

"I don't think we need to do much shuffling. We can photograph it as is," Sofia said.

"I'll assist. Then I'll need to make some calls to locate the thin sheets of acrylic we'll need."

"Discreetly. I don't want to draw attention to what we're doing here," Sofia responded.

"In Rome? Whoever pays attention to anything around here?"

"I'm terrified that word of my theft will get out before I'm ready. I don't want this to disappear, never to be seen again. And its existence denied."

"We can be careful. But, Sofia, this trip to Mount Athos was good for you. Your spirit has changed somehow—for the better. I see excitement in your eyes."

Sofia knew Sister Meg was right. Excitement outweighed her terror.

"I know, but so many things can go wrong. Probably will."

"And?" the nun asked.

"I stole from my own country. My own Church. There is nothing more shameful in my family than anyone who steals our heritage," Sofia said.

"But we both know you didn't steal this to make money. It's not like you will sell the scroll at auction or something."

Sofia's heart stung with the possibility that people would think her a greedy thief. "No, never. But I also won't let it disappear again. That's why I need time to think."

"I've now seen this. We'll take snips for testing. That should protect you. But really, the fun will be in exploring what this is." They were setting up the lighting and bringing in some sturdier chairs to stand.

"Any idea how to get our hands on digital imaging equipment without raising curiosity?"

Spectral photography would clarify the fading of ink, which reflects differently from vellum. And show if there was any text underneath.

"The one person in Italy that I believe you can trust. Besides me, of course." Sister Meg chuckled. "Andrucci at the University of Bologna."

Sofia smiled. "Yes, and none of the scruples after what happened to him."

"Italians with scruples? The country of flamboyant politicians?"

"But tough investigators with the Antiquities Authorities. Normally, I cheer their work on, but not if they catch wind of this and go after me." Sofia adjusted her camera. "Before I'm ready, anyway."

Sofia climbed on the stool, bent over the scroll, and began shooting. "Andrucci was betrayed by the institution once. He won't let that happen again."

Sister Meg moved the lighting at Sofia's instructions. "The Vatican library has sent him some sensitive items. His work is very accurate and methodical."

Sofia nodded in agreement. "His work would be respected. But how would I fund this? His university would only go so far for him. Maybe I should also give him my samples from Mount Athos. But then I'd need to let him in on my secret." She sighed. "And then the circle would continue to grow."

"Who else do you trust with this?"

Sofia turned toward Sister Meg but gazed into the distance before responding. "Brother Makarios, but he's trying to find a lab to test Mor Gabriel's parchments. And we're both trying to find any similar holdings in Armenia." Sofia stepped back from the table, set her camera down, and stretched her back. "And I'm long overdue in calling him. Mac may think I've abandoned him." She looked across at her friend. "Meg, have you heard any news from Syria? About Aleppo?"

"More bombings. A flood of refugees from Syria. Why?" Sister Meg was returning lamps and chairs.

Sofia had moved to the desktop and began uploading her pictures to a file she created. "A friend with The Hill has been there digitizing a library. Maybe you've met her, Adélie. Anyway, they were to be evacuating, and I don't know if the group got out safely. She hadn't been picking up my calls. I'm worried about her."

"No, I don't know her. But Sofia, when we break, you'll call The Hill and Brother Makarios after you call someone in your family. People need to know you're okay. Just say we're working on a project together. They don't need more specifics than that right now. And I'll track down Andrucci.

Sofia clicked through images, surprised at how clear some of her files from Mount Athos were. She knew Sister Meg was right. Her friend pulled a chair alongside her and gazed at the images.

"These are stunning, Sofia."

"I'm surprised at how clear most of them are. I'll need to work on a few to get better clarity."

"What did you find?"

Sofia kept clicking through images and uploading more. "Some of Olympias' letters. Here, she says,

> "Do not worry, dear friend, for me. To Eudoxia's shame, her puppet Prefect Optatus accuses me of setting fire to the cathedral. The Temple of God? My past life ought to avert all suspicion from me, for I have devoted my large inheritance to the restoration of the temples of God. I consider this sham of a trial yet another opportunity to speak truth to corruption and to call my Imperial family to repentance. Let them howl like the wild animals they are..."

This fits in with what we know of her history. And this other is probably a letter whose author was "Susanna," but I don't know which one. I will need to investigate some pieces, but what they say I've never seen anywhere before."

"Olympias? That's wonderful." Pointing to one of the texts, Sister Meg asked, "What does this say?"

"That seems to be part of a letter." Sofia began to translate,

> "I have heard disturbing reports. Word has reached Rome that some Followers of the Way are being denied the Bread of Life and the Cup of the New Covenant. God forbid that this great evil proves true. Are only some worthy of the Lord's Supper? Does lowly birth in the eyes of this depraved world keep some from a place at the table? Are some denied a place for sins since repented, cleansed, and healed? Is this the Gospel you received?"

"Wow, this sounds both old and contemporary at the same time," Sister Meg drew closer to the screen to study the image.

"I know. We haven't changed much. But my best guess is that this fits in with some of the controversies of the fourth century."

Pointing to the scroll, the nun asked, "And this?"

"The big pieces seem to be an epistle."

Sister Meg gasped. "Of Mary?" Among the Nag Hammadi library was a partial gospel according to a "Mary." Some scholars believed this gnostic Gospel honored Mary, the *Theotokos*. Others said Mary of Magdala, one of Jesus' apostles.

"One might be from Mary of Magdala, but the other's subject is someone named Hannah."

"Who was Hannah?" Meg was standing to look at the scroll.

Sofia kept quiet about what much of the text said, at least for now. "That I'll investigate, but there are clues in the scroll."

"How fun!"

"Or a fraud." Sofia's heart sank. How could an epistle or a gospel, especially one attributed to a woman with its stunning message, be hidden from the world all these centuries?

"No matter, Sofia. I'm very proud of you."

§

The two women had returned from shopping for decent clothing for Sofia and CDs to burn the vellum's images as backup, along with all her uploaded images that she had digitized. All paid for by the nuns. Her friend seemed to be in overdrive, determined to not let Sofia back off on all this. Andrucci arrived the next day with equipment to preserve and safeguard the vellum. Sofia would return with him to Bologna with her samples.

"Sofia, I don't think you're just tired. More is going on in that mind of yours. What is worrying you?" The two women were off in a corner of the refectory enjoying a light dinner.

Sofia set her wine glass down. "I'm dirt broke and unemployed with no hope on the horizon. Other than maybe the Silicon Valley in America."

"You wouldn't be the first gifted linguist they hired. But that would detract from your work."

"I've stolen from some monks. My aunt might kill me when she finds out what I've done. The police, afraid of the monks, might arrest me when I return to Greece. And for some reason, the faith of my childhood is becoming more important to me now."

"Not bad work by the Holy Spirit. All in one month." Sister Meg laughed. "But seriously, Sofia, do you need to contact a solicitor before you return? Maybe you can contact Patriarch Bartholomaios's office and tell them you'd like to meet?"

Sofia refilled her glass of wine. "The Patriarch? But he doesn't know me."

"I think he will soon, don't you?"

"What if these crazy monks track me here?" Sofia hardly touched her food and knew the wine would go to her head soon.

"Sofia, you've got more ammunition in your court than you realize." Sofia asked Meg to explain what that phrase meant.

"Brother Mac, Andrucci, and I will all be in your defense. Let the Patriarch's office know you want to meet with them, and they'll recognize your honesty." Sister Meg took a bite of her fish. "Bringing this out into the open will silence any mean-spirited monks."

"I'm afraid someone will track me here. Especially the monk who chased me."

"Sofia, you're a published scholar who has worked with some important Orthodox texts. Of course, he can find out who you are. But here? Anyway, he'll never get his hands on your discoveries."

Sighing, Sofia said, "You're right. I'll go make some calls. May I use your office? I don't want to use my cell phone as someone might track me here."

"Of course. And call your family first."

Turning several corners and asking for directions, Sofia found her way to her mentor's office. She dug around piles of books and papers until she found Meg's landline. She smiled at realizing she wasn't the only one not fully entering the 21st century. She dialed Takis' number, figuring he was a good place to begin. He didn't pick up, so she left a message.

Sofia went onto her friend's computer to look up The Hill's number in America. She called the Director, still worried that she hadn't heard from Adélie. She learned her friend would land in the United

States the next day. Sofia sighed with relief. Hanging up, Sister Meg's phone rang, loud and obnoxious. Guessing it was Takis, she answered.

"Sofia, where are you, and whose number is this? And by the way, why did the police come visit me at my shop?"

TWENTY-SEVEN

E SFIGMENOU

Father Yeorgi passed through the monastery doorway, bag slung over his shoulder, and headed toward the main gate. More music blared. A raspy woman's voice screeched. American, he guessed. Satan's serenade.

He hated what he was about to do, but the damnable police had confiscated all their boats, leaving him little option. He had removed his beloved sostikon and skouphos, and donned the canvas work pants, shirt, and cap favored by the brothers working in the fields and orchards. Clearing the gate, he scanned their violated entrance area and spotted his monastery's chief tormentor talking to some of his minions. He strode over, stood before Leontis, and set his bag down. As he had expected, the commander stared at him, a surprised smile written across his face.

Father Yeorgi shouted over the music, "Are your minions enjoying themselves? Violating our sacred space? Stealing from us?"

The commander stood still, his countenance frozen, eyes examining him.

"I doubt your authorities know what you're doing here. Doing business on the black market?" Father Yeorgi's nails pierced the palms of his hands, hidden within his garment's front pockets.

The commander's face turned dark. He had hit a nerve. "Watch your words, monk."

"As a Greek, can't you at least honor our heritage?" Dry ice oozed with each word.

"As your abbot knows, our boat was found drifting off the shore near Stratonion. Nothing left onboard. Your thief could be anywhere by now. Unfortunately, your description of what was taken is rather brief and nondescript. But the Antiquities Authorities have been alerted. I'm surprised your abbot hasn't informed you of this."

Anger knotted Father Yeorgi's stomach. This is precisely why he was doing what must be done. "I'll deal with the authorities. Did the local police even bother to check for fingerprints?"

"Prints? I'd think so. The authorities do take the theft of antiquities seriously. More than you seem to give them credit for."

Father Yeorgi knew this, so he refused to let these "authorities" catalog his holdings. Provenance might prove problematic where some of his collection was concerned.

"Turn that accursed music off. I can hardly hear you."

Leontis smiled. "Don't care for Janis Joplin?" The commander signaled with his head, and two men moved toward him. "Just how are they to know what they are looking for if all you'll tell us is that this scroll is old? The black market is sophisticated. And vicious."

Father Yeorgi felt his face warm. He had bolted shut the violated space and ordered the monks to keep the library locked. No one, including their own monks, was to enter until his return. This tragic theft might alert these authorities to wonder what their collection held, and he was determined to keep them out.

The commander looked down at the monk's bag. "It seems you already expect to be escorted off Agio Óros. Curious. I had assumed I'd be dragging you out of the monastery, not that you'd voluntarily leave."

"I have some business matters in Athens. Our monastery staffs several parishes there."

"I know." The commander sighed. "I assume you're going to get involved in investigating this theft. I hope you don't do more harm than good."

Father Yeorgi nodded, acknowledging the sarcasm. He stood still, waiting. He loved Esfigmenou more than anyone realized, save his beloved abbot. His heart lay here. Always would. It hurt for him to leave, but necessity demanded this of him. He promised himself that not only would he return with his scroll, but he would return to a monastery free of oppression.

"Father Yeorgi, your passport, please." The commander's orders had been to take passports away from every monk they removed until the courts ordered otherwise. Investigators didn't want monks leaving the EU until all legal matters had been settled.

His passport? His shoulders tightened. "No."

As the commander's eyes glanced behind him, hands slammed down on his shoulders from behind, the fingers digging into his flesh with a painful grip. Agony shot through his muscles, leaving him unable to move his arms. He was thrown around, stumbling to keep his feet under him, and slammed into the side of the jeep. A handcuff was snapped onto his right wrist as hands patted his pockets and chest.

"Found it, Commander."

Father Yeorgi noticed his passport being handed to the commander. He struggled against his assailant as another arm grabbed his left wrist and forced it behind him. The other handcuff was slapped on. Why were they doing this to him? How dare they?

Without ceremony, his head was forced down, and he was pushed into the back seat of the jeep. Another of Satan's minions climbed in from the other side as a harness was snapped across his chest, bolting him in. His bag was dropped into the rear of the vehicle.

The commander, arm leaning on the side of the vehicle, looked at him with hard eyes. "My officers will be escorting you to headquarters in Athens. You won't return to Agio Óros without the Patriarch's express permission."

Father Yeorgi ground his teeth. The insolence. He'd return when his tasks were completed, and he'd ask no one's permission.

Kyrie eleison. Orthodoxy or death!

§

Father Yeorgi pushed the station door of the military authority open so hard that its handle crashed into the wall. He strode down the steps toward the waiting car, a silver convertible, with his cousin Kostas behind the wheel. Passing around to the passenger side, he began to lift his bag and realized there was no back seat. He climbed in, sinking down low, raised an eyebrow, and set his bag between his legs.

Kostas glanced at him, sunglasses hiding his eyes. "*Evlogíte*, Father. I trust our authorities were respectful and cooperative?" Kostas' humor was irritating, but his talents served the monastery well.

"*O Kýrios,*" Father Yeorgi responded, voice soft yet seething with anger. "I need another passport. Mine was confiscated. Charging me with apostasy. By an apostate heretic. I've been formally barred from returning to Agio Óros. Fools!"

The engine roared to life, an energy that surprised him.

"Not a problem. I'll go to the same source. To my condo?"

"No, our parish. Saint Panteleimon. We'll talk there."

How could his innocent find in Ethiopia during his graduate studies become such a nightmare? Once he learned what it said, he should have destroyed it. He had learned to respect antiquity from his brother monks and professors, but to protect innocent and naïve believers meant destroying it. His mistake.

The car swept away from the curb, heading toward the parish. "How do you like my new baby? Aston Martin Vanquish Volante. V-12 engine, all leather interior. Has a Bosch surround stereo system."

His cousin sounded like one of the monks proclaiming the Gospel during Divine Services, caressing each word.

The car whipped in and out of lanes. His knuckles, growing white, gripped the door handle. Why did his cousin take so many unnecessary risks?

"Took her through the mountain passes like a racing course, headin' to Vienna." Vienna was one of several locations where Kostas conducted some business for him.

They ran a red light, horns blaring, and then took the next left. Children playing soccer scrambled off the street as they approached. Several waved.

"Guess how much she cost me?" Kostas slowed and turned right into a narrow side road.

Father Yeorgi grunted.

"248,000 Euros. Doubt there's another one in Athens, or anywhere in Greece for that matter." His cousin was grinning like a new bridegroom.

They slowed, pulled into the parish church's rear parking lot, and parked. The two men disembarked and headed to a set of double doors.

"Did you get a good look at your thief, Father? I know most men with the talent to pull off something like this."

"Taller than me. Thinner. Athletic. Olive skin and dark hair. Little chance of a beard. I still think it was one of the military police."

Kostas frowned. "That's not good. If the wrong authorities hear of it, they might start digging into your business."

After pulling on a rope and an interior bell sounded, they were let in by one of the deacons.

The two men entered a large room, paneled in dark wood and with bookcases lining two walls. Father Yeorgi kissed the icon of the Theotokos, the Mother of God, in veneration. At the same time, his cousin plopped into an oversized chair.

Father Yeorgi turned to his cousin, his hand massaging his prayer rope. "We need to move on this right away. Nothing takes priority over finding that scroll. Utterly damaging if it gets into the wrong hands." Why hadn't he burned it when he unearthed it? Those seeking to destroy Christ's One, True Church on earth would find the scroll an effective weapon.

Confusion etched across his cousin's face. "Damaging, how? Just old books. People like to have what others can't."

Father Yeorgi worried that this had gotten more complicated. "No, this isn't about collecting. I doubt it's about making money. We're looking for an ancient parchment stored securely, so I'd thought, in a cave, we dug into the mountainside." He felt his anger flare again. "I don't know how anyone knew about the cavern, especially this scroll."

"So?" Hesitant curiosity colored his cousin's words. "What is this thing? What does it look like?"

"Vellum, in exceptionally good shape. About 120 centimeters long. I am aware of only a very few examples that compare." Father Yeorgi was pacing. "Dates to around 400 CE. The script is Ge'ez."

Kostas whistled. "That old? Really? Is it legit?"

"Yes, that old. I'd had it tested when I stumbled onto it."

"Why would this be taken and not the illuminated manuscripts? Big demand for beautiful books, not so much for simply old stuff."

"The value isn't in its beauty. It's what the document says that will draw attention and money." Its content couldn't possibly be God's holy word. He shook his head to clear his mind.

"What does it say?"

Father Yeorgi resumed pacing, hand massaging his prayer cord, ignoring his cousin. The thief had to be working for someone. But who? Who knew what he held down there? He had never cataloged that collection, at least not formally. He kept his acquisitions books in a discreet vault. But had he checked it recently? Probably not.

"We'll leave that for another time. Put word among your contacts that you have a client with clean money. Provenance not an issue, as usual. You're looking for any ancient vellum codices. Listen for words like Ge'ez or any Middle Eastern languages like Arabic or Armenian. The seller may not know what they've got." Hopefully, they do not know what they have other than the beautiful script and an antiquity.

"Maybe this is a private buyer and isn't for sale."

"You've handled cases like that. That's why you can blow so much money on a car. Get creative. Time is of the essence." Father Yeorgi stopped and turned. "Also, try to find out if we've got new rivals. This might be the work of seasoned players but might also be someone new in the game."

"Sure, but this strikes me as someone good. Talented. Your monastery is a thief's nightmare. And to know about the cave? You might have to think about an inside job. A monk with a habit to feed? Some money to strike out and start a new life, maybe?"

Father Yeorgi glared at his cousin. An inside job? No. One of the military men haunting them? Yes. He turned and moved toward the window, gazing out at the garden courtyard.

Or maybe one of those accursed graduate students who had been welcomed by the heretic monks polluting the Holy Mountain. Yes. He'd pursue the universities and discover who's been on the Holy Mountain. He'll secure every name and find out who each one is. Selling it to pay for school? A new car like his foolish cousin? He'd have this back. Fast. And then he'll burn it.

If his scroll is made public, he would be ready, through his contacts, faithful priest-monks, and scholars, to declare that this document is a fraud. He'd shame its contents. The work of an early heretical community. What sane person would ever believe its contents?

TWENTY-EIGHT

THESSALONÍKI, GREECE

The plane shuddered. Sofia gripped the armrests. Were the pilots finding every possible pocket of turbulence in the two-hour flight from Bologna? In a week's time, she would be on a plane again, headed to California for job interviews with a hi-tech firm. She hated to go that route, but she was dead broke and in debt with no hope on the horizon. She needed to consult with her family's solicitor, Melina Paspala, before then.

The plane began its descent into Thessaloníki, banking left. She shifted in her seat, attempting to relieve her cramped legs. Hopefully, her discovery was safe, as she needed time to determine her next steps. The plane hit the runway as Sofia's worry beads broke, splattering all over the floor. She sighed in frustration.

Takis met her at the airport. She noted he had trimmed his beard. Climbing into his old Mercedes, she placed her carry-on, which held her precious memory cards and CDs, between her feet. It took her two tries to get the door closed completely.

She turned toward him. "Takis, I'm sorry if I caused you much trouble. I hope you're not angry with me. Did the police suspect you of anything?"

He gave her a lopsided grin. "*Mou oraios*, let me give you a cousinly piece of advice. Once you've taken on a life of crime, you need to know when to be alert and when to relax."

She cringed at his use of the phrase, "life of crime." True. But that wasn't her intent. Her cousin took the first turn so swiftly she was pressed to the door.

"Has Christina asked about my absence?"

"Just got here yesterday, and while it took the best of my acting abilities, I played dumb. I only told Christina I was picking you up. She's smarter than us, so we need to coordinate our stories. I'll just keep playing dumb. What are you going to tell her?"

They passed a homeless camp on approach to the city. The sight saddened her. "The truth. I need to trust her on this." She had spent several restless nights obsessing over possible reactions her aunt might have when told Sofia stole two scrolls. Sofia knew how hard Christina worked on security at the museum she once directed.

Sofia shifted in her seat. "Takis, did you run into trouble after I left?"

"Nothing I couldn't handle. You ended up causing the biggest whopper of a fire on Agio Óros. And I don't mean the physical kind. I hung around discreetly, listening for word that you'd been arrested. More military arrived, including a Chinook chopper, and the radios were all ablaze, rumors flying everywhere about what might've happened to stir up such tight-assed monks. No news of your arrest, so you just left me in the dark. That part was cruel, *mou oraios*. You could've sent me a postcard or something."

"Oh, Takis." Sofia glanced his way, and seeing a grin, she gently punched him.

"Christina thinks you're heading to one of those big computer companies in America. True?"

"I'm dead broke. I'm desperate for money. If they accept me, I must be content as a weekend scholar." The idea pained her, but she felt backed into a corner.

Takis whistled. "What do computer companies do with dead language professors?"

"I'm not sure, but they hire a number of us 'dead language' types. They've sent me a ticket to California."

"Seems a shame for you to stop doing what you do. Even if I don't understand exactly what it is you do."

"Maybe I can save enough money from this job, if they even hire me, to return to full-time scholarship." She reminded herself that she might become an "untouchable" once her discovery was made public.

The two remained quiet for a while. Cresting the hill toward their aunt's house, he chuckled. "The biggest fright you gave me? One of the monks insisted their thief was a woman."

Sofia felt her face warm. Damn, they may just succeed in figuring out who she was. "So, your other business is safe?"

"Don't worry about that." Takis grinned. "So, Rome? Joining the Vatican or something?"

Sofia laughed. "I wish. Then I wouldn't be so poor. But Sister Meg, one of my former professors, said she'd put in a word on my behalf at the Vatican Libraries and maybe a few of the local universities."

Takis whistled. "The Vatican, eh? Big-time stuff. So that's what you've been up to since you abandoned me?"

As Takis braked, Sofia responded. "I'm sorry. But shortly, you'll have all your questions answered. And I promise not to make you escort me back on to Agio Óros."

Takis turned toward her. "Return? No, Sof. The next time you want to check out a book from there, you'll just give me the title, and I'll ask one of the monks to get it for me."

Sofia laughed as she climbed out of his car.

§

After dropping off her bags in her bedroom, Sofia searched for her aunt. She pulled long, deep breaths, trying to calm her nerves. She had to get this over with, or she might never find the courage again.

Heading down the stairs, she heard her aunt call from the veranda. "Is that you, Sofia? Your cousin and I are out in the garden. Do join us."

Passing through the open French doors, Sofia noticed her aunt pouring iced tea into glasses, holding one out for her. Then, a look of surprise crossed Christina's face. "Oh my, you cut your gorgeous hair. Whatever for?" she asked. The heat made the air smell like something burnt.

Taking the offered glass, Sofia answered. "Yes, it's kind of shocking even to me. Took me a while to get used to it."

As Christina took her seat, she said. "So, Takis tells me you have quite the story to tell us."

Sofia glanced at her cousin. Kill him? Or thank him for giving her the emotional shove she might have needed?

"Yes," Sofia's chair scraped on the stone as she pulled it out. "And your favorite nephew may need to get you some ouzo to add to our tea by the time I'm done. Or before then."

"Really?" Christina glanced at her with the look so familiar from her childhood, the *I'll reserve judgment until I've heard from your teachers look*.

Sofia began telling her story, taking responsibility for pushing Takis into helping her slip onto the Holy Mountain, which Christina's expression clearly meant her aunt didn't buy that one. She had passed herself off as a monk from Ipapandi. At the same time, Takis distracted any attention directed her way, and she used a hood over her monk's cap. "That's why I cropped my hair like the monks."

Sofia pressed on with her story. Christina expressed surprise when Sofia explained that she had uncovered some of Deacon Olympias' writings along with pieces of some other early women's writings—one Susanna among them.

"Dear, I know you're determined, but was this necessary? Couldn't the librarians simply send you copies of these texts?"

Sofia's anger grew. "Christina, haven't you heard me all these years? I'm the one with the expertise to know what to look for. A colleague like Brother Makarios cannot get into the libraries because he's Roman Catholic. I've tried every avenue, and all I get met with is a stone wall."

Her aunt blushed.

Hadn't her aunt heard her talk about all the dead ends? Didn't she understand? She breathed deeply and continued. "Then, as Takis and I were planning to leave Agio Óros, I decided to chance getting into Esfigmenou—."

"What? Sofia, you could've been seriously hurt," Christina said. Her aunt knew well the history of the schismatic monastery with its defiant abbot.

"But I wasn't, and to me, it was worth the risk. But what I found shocked even me. The monks have a room under the library to store beautiful liturgical texts and a separate room with vellum scrolls. I found a couple of scrolls. One especially shocked even me. One is in Ge'ez, and the other is Syriac Armenian." And then she took another deep breath. "I was under pressure. Several monks were nearby looking for me, and I knew that someone besides me needed to see these, and I needed to arrange for testing of the vellum and ink."

Christina and Takis looked at her expectantly. She swallowed. "And so, I took it."

Takis leaned toward her, "And?"

"And a monk chased me to their dock, and I stole a boat."

"Good for you," Takis shouted as he slapped his knee. "I knew we're related."

Christina nearly shouted, "You stole? How could you?" Christina looked her way. "We don't steal. Not our national heritage."

"Maybe we restore what had been stolen from other innocents."

Christina shot a look of reprimand to her nephew. "Young man, how could you let Sofia do something as crazy as this?"

Takis blushed. "Because it was so important to her. And I like a challenge." He grinned. "It's in your rucksack? Can we see it?"

"No, Takis." She glanced at her aunt and proceeded. "That's why I've been in Rome. I've placed the scrolls in a safe location."

Christina's voice sounded constricted. "How? What were you thinking? You could've been arrested or, worse, harmed."

"I know, but it was worth it to me. The scrolls are safe. Once the testing is completed, I'll figure out where to place them, but not back to that monastery." She felt her chest constrict with anxiety. She desperately wanted her aunt's support for what she had done.

"You most certainly will return them." She sighed as she shook her head. "I'll assist you in finding an appropriate home, a museum, or university here in Greece that could house them," Christina responded.

Sofia also hated the looting of Greek antiquities, but scholars had a right to see what the monks kept from them.

After a brief silence, Christina said, "Sofia, this just doesn't sound like you. Takis, maybe, but not you."

Her aunt's countenance was still, but Christina's cheeks glowed pink like what had happened to her when she had gotten angry or frightened. Takis grinned.

"I couldn't take all the closed doors anymore. I was desperate. And I was right about what was sitting on Agio Óros. The universities there are only scanning medieval texts, nothing older." She then recounted her journey to Santa Cecelia in Rome. "And so, these scrolls are two floors underground in climate-controlled space. And a colleague in Bologna has all my samples in his lab for testing." She took a big gulp of her tea.

§

Sofia took the stairs to the basement to her office and workspace, wondering how long before her aunt calmed down. She began downloading her data files and digital photos, alternating between combing her emails for word from her university on the possibility of teaching some classes this fall—only confirmation information from the California tech company—and checking on the progress of her file transfers. As she had expected, there were no teaching positions. She would call California late tonight to confirm arrangements. She opened the email account she had set up on behalf of Brother Pachomius, but it was empty. No word from Father Theodor. After meeting him, she questioned if he had ever touched a computer.

She called Brother Makarios next, and after brief updates on their work at Mor Gabriel, she told him about her saga on Mount Athos.

"Luv, you are one courageous, gutsy woman. I knew you were brilliant, but this?" He laughed again. "I'm delighted that you found more of Deacon Olympias. And these other women, too. When will you let me know what these scrolls are that drove you to theft?"

Her stomach clenched. Again, that word "theft."

"Soon. I'm working through some challenging passages. You'll be among the first. You will be thrilled when you see what I found. Some texts are in Syriac Armenian, but my stunning find is in early Ge'ez.

Brother Makarios whistled. "I know you'll be careful and approach your next steps thoughtfully. Let me know how I can assist you." After a moment of silence, he resumed. "Sofia, this may sound loony, but the Ecumenical Patriarch might be your best protection for these scrolls and your reputation. I think you need to find your way to Istanbul."

"I've considered the Patriarch. My aunt has some ideas of her own as well."

"There's a woman there, Aminah Taşbent, who teaches at the university. But her real passion is the archeological dig next to Hagia Sophia."

"The government hasn't shut that down yet?"

"She says the authorities have informed her that it will happen soon, so no time to waste in getting you there. Have you been following her work at all? She is convinced that she is unearthing Deacon Olympias' home and has made some interesting discoveries recently. Some might even corroborate your finding of some of the writings of Olympias on Agio Óros." Brother Makarios told her to look for his email in the next day or so.

How will she add Istanbul to her growing list of "must-do's." A headache slithered up her neck.

Queen Alexandra purred from above, tail swishing in contentment.

She called Georgios Hatzidakis, who answered immediately, unlike his regular routine. "Sofia here. I'm working on some translations and need access to your specialized dictionaries, especially the old ones. Any chance I can get in?"

He breathed heavily as his chair creaked. Finally, he answered, "I can give you space in the rare book collection for a few days. But first, I want to see you in my office." His voice sounded tense.

"What's going on?"

"Tomorrow at 10 am, and we talk." He hung up.

Her stomach gripped. Sofia stared at her phone, stunned. Yes, they'd parted on a strained note, but they'd known each other for years and had worked well together. Why is he so tense? She scanned her email for anything from the head archivist, but nothing.

After a restless night and strong coffee, Sofia grabbed her gear, glad to resume work on her translations but worried about the archivist's response. As she approached his office, she heard voices. Peeking through the window in his office door, she saw the archivist talking to Mariam, who held a clamshell box used to protect rare books.

When she came out, they nodded in acknowledgment. Then Sofia entered and set her gear on the chair before her. She stood.

He studied her for a moment. "I've been contacted by the librarian at Hagia Theotokos, one Father Theodor, who asked if I knew any grad students who'd help him in his library. His letter said that a monk from Ipapandi, who impressed him as quite a scholar, went rummaging around in his underground storage area looking for women in the early Church." His gaze sharpened.

She struggled to steady her breathing. Did Father Theodor make the connection?

"He commented how unusual it was for anyone on Agio Óros to have a guest from Ipapandi, especially a scholar who read numerous early languages." His face reddened. "Said this monk was looking for women in early Christianity, especially one Deacon Olympias. Unusual coincidence, don't you think?"

Sofia's mouth was dry, and her thoughts raced, searching for words.

Hatzidakis slammed his fist on his desk, rattling his pen holder. "What were you thinking, Papandréou? Or were you?"

They stared at each other.

"How dare you question me and what I do. You know every avenue I've attempted has failed." Sofia clenched her fists, feeling the sharp pain of her nails. The pressures of the past month were taking their toll on her.

"You know the proper channels for contacting the libraries on Agio Óros. Why couldn't you be patient and simply wait for an answer?"

She nearly shouted, "Haven't I already?"

"I could've sent a grad student there to look on your behalf. As you recall, I offered to make the arrangements."

"What grad student did you have in mind? With my language skills and education? You know damn well that I'm the best-qualified person to assist in any of those libraries, including Father Theodor's."

Well, she had done it. Her secret was out. Would he report her to the authorities? Anxiety constricted her lungs.

Silence is like a dense fog. Hatzidakis stood and began pacing his office, then turned toward her. "Your insane actions could cost us access to Agio Óros. We've spent years trying to earn their trust, and you may well have destroyed all our hard work."

Sofia gripped the chair in front of her. "Is that what the librarian threatened? Have you heard from other monasteries?"

He gasped. "Did you violate more than one? Could you be that—"

Sofia interrupted, her voice lowered. "Did you just say 'violate'? With the way this world treats women? We aren't the ones who 'violate'." She gestured with her hands to emphasize the quote on the insidious word.

He leaned in. "Whether you like it or not, Agio Óros is sacred space for many people, and we respect their traditions."

Sofia breathed deeply, knowing this was getting out of hand. "The content of those monasteries is the heritage of all Orthodox believers, and frankly of all Christians, not an elite few." She noticed her voice lowering, which happened when her anger was sliding out of control. "So really, I suggest no woman 'violates' Agio Óros but merely claims her rightful heritage."

"This university cannot protect you."

"I don't need your protection. And yes, I found Deacon Olympias. And more."

Hatzidakis' eyes widened, barely breathing. Silence ensued. Then he turned, "You found letters from Olympias? But that's nearly impossible."

"You've told me that for too many years." Sofia grabbed her gear and departed, slamming the door

TWENTY-NINE

A THENS

Father Yeorgi entered the office with its' stone floor and walls lined with reference books he had commandeered upon his arrival at Saint Panteleimon. He would need to forgo Great Vespers to make his phone appointment to America. Over the last ten days, his cousin Kostas had continually failed in his every attempt to find this dangerous scroll. Kostas reported that his contacts had heard no word of any kind of ancient parchment new to the black market. His contacts had pressed him for more details, competition being competition. Kostas suggested money would come their way if their leads led to its recovery. No new players that his cousin could identify. His cousin insisted this was an inside job, which ripped Yeorgi deep in his gut. Who?

Father Yeorgi was more successful with their solicitor, who had just sent him the names of the graduate students and their professors who had been granted access to Agio Óros. His cousin put his security contact to work to dig into each guy's background and to monitor their finances in case someone suddenly came into new-found wealth. But none of the professors ever worked in antiquities, their specializations being much more recent, which was why their interest was solely in the Holy Mountain's illuminated texts.

The phone rang. "Yes?" His voice was sharp and distant. His solicitor.

"I thought you should know. Your abbot called distressed. The military police show increased interest in entering your monastery to seize your library."

Father Yeorgi was silent, gripping the phone until his knuckles turned white. He clenched his jaw and felt his ears pounding. "They cannot be permitted in. Do whatever you can to stop this travesty."

"I'm trying, but you already know that the Monastic Council on Agio Óros holds the power to allow this. We may not be able to stop them. And there's more—"

Father Yeorgi heard his solicitor shuffle some papers.

"I've been unsuccessful in getting information on the military personnel surrounding Esfigmenou. One Commander Leontis was forthright about his identity and seems to have a clean and honorable record."

No matter, he will have Kostas monitor the Commander's finances. Just in case.

"Why would this information be private? Isn't this a matter of public record?" Father Yeorgi felt his throat tighten.

"Not on Agio Óros. Seems the military doesn't want to deal with retribution for holding your monastery hostage," his solicitor responded.

"I pay you big money to stop this insanity. Go and earn it!" Father Yeorgi slammed the phone down. His head began to pound as he tried to strategize his way out of this growing nightmare. They cannot have his library. And he knew the authorities would connect some of his precious books to their theft.

He began pacing. The specter of an inside job haunted him. His stomach had burned since Kostas first presented his take on the situation. So he had reluctantly put Kostas to work investigating each of his brother monks once the Abbot's secretary sent him their birth names and other information. A few he knew from memory, but not all of them. This thief knew too much. Or had the luck of Satan. He gripped his prayer cord. Satan indeed.

Father Yeorgi heard a knock at his door and turned as a young monk wearing full robes and skouphas entered. One of their recently ordained priests, he had a keen mind and good business sense.

The young monk strode up to Father Yeorgi. "Father, I've pondered what you shared about the stolen scroll. I have contacts within several monasteries on Agio Óros, monks who are secretly faithful to our cause."

"Faithful?" Heat rose up his neck. "Then they'd abandon their apostate monasteries and join us."

"Father," the young priest pressed him. "They've been useful to Father Abbot. And they tell me that word is spreading of an unusual monk from Ipapandi, a scholar comfortable with ancient languages. They say his name is Brother Pachomius."

Father Yeorgi absorbed this information. He would have known of any scholars in Meteora and had heard of no one from Ipapandi. An imposter? "Go on."

"Well, this monk, Brother Pachomius, was apparently researching the early Deacon Olympias. Unusual, don't you think?"

Father Yeorgi's gut clenched. He turned and gazed out the window into the darkness. His breathing grew more shallow and rapid. He prayed for guidance. *Ágio Pnévma, min me enkataleípete tóra. Holy*

Spirit, do not abandon me now. Turning, he asked, "Did anyone provide you with a description of this Brother Pachomius?"

"The monk I spoke with hadn't actually met Brother Pachomius, just heard about him."

"Press for a description or get the name of someone who did. And find out which monastery welcomed him. Time is of the utmost importance." Father Yeorgi headed toward his desk, then stopped and turned back. "Get someone trustworthy to Ipapandi tomorrow, someone young enough to climb those rope ladders, and speak directly with their Abbot. Find out whether they have a Brother Pachomius." His hands gripped his prayer cord. He doubted this. Ipapandi was a monastery faithful to their cause. Unless something changed recently. "And if they do, bring him back here. I will need to speak with him."

Father Yeorgi heard the door close as he walked to his desk and stood, thinking. He would certainly find this Brother Pachomius. He had spent prayerful hours trying to figure out a scenario where someone could have known of this scroll and its hiding place. A few of his own monks did the construction, and only one had been arrested thus far, and that faithful brother was now stationed at another of their parishes. He sighed. Unfortunately, he had found it necessary to order Kostas to screen this monk for unknown bank accounts.

But what really ate at him with his suspicion was that the thief was a woman. The person he chased to the dock did not run like a guy. The gait was feminine. He crossed himself.

§

Closing his eyes, he breathed and prayed to clear his mind. To *Ágio Pnévma, érchetai kai me kathodigeí, ton tapeinó sas ypiréti. Holy Spirit, come and guide me, your humble servant.* This next call was delicate and important. His research led him to an American monastery with a university and The Hill Museum and Manuscript Library with its growing collection of digitized manuscripts from around the world. The site proved quite impressive, with free access to anyone interested. And their collection of Ethiopian codices and fragments in Ge'ez was impressive.

The website identified the scholar in charge of this collection as one Ephrem Gessesse, originally from Ethiopia. Father Yeorgi had studied his face and was sure they hadn't met. Gessesse's biography stated he fled Ethiopia in the late 1970s when the military junta jailed all scholars, including this gentleman. Father Yeorgi suppressed a surge of guilt. He had used the chaos of that time when Ethiopian Orthodox monks needed help secreting their sacred texts into caves in the mountains to save them from destruction by the military. Father Yeorgi had offered to take several of the damaged scrolls and books back to Agio Óros for restoration. *Kyrie eleison.*

The monk massaged his prayer cord, prayers running through his mind. He was seduced by the language of this accursed scroll and the impossibility of its "message" and took it with him. He had yet to return anything to Ethiopia, allowing the passing of a generation—many of the monks died at the hands of the military junta—and no one demanded the ancient texts' return.

Father Yeorgi sat and clicked on the link to their video conference call, adjusting the screen. Soon, Gessesse's face appeared, ebony and unlined, yet crowned with curly pewter gray hair.

"*Iwi selami newi.* Thank you for giving me some of your time, Doctor Gessesse. I apologize for not remembering much of my Amharic. Few guest monks from Ethiopia on Agio Óros anymore." Amharic was the official language of Ethiopia.

"You knew Amharic? I'm impressed. I hear so little anymore. And please, call me Ephrem."

Gessesse's English was British and academic. His voice was soft, forcing Father Yeorgi to raise the volume on his computer. The two introduced their respective backgrounds and research interests, the conversation where scholars of shared expertise usually began.

The Ethiopian scholar pushed his glasses back up his nose. "How may I assist you?"

"I've scanned your catalog. Your earliest books seem to date back to the Fourteenth Century." Father Yeorgi continued. "I'm trying to trace the whereabouts of earlier texts in Ge'ez. As I mentioned, I did some research in the north of Ethiopia during graduate school. Still, with the tragic civil war in the late 1970s and when I was forced to leave, books were moved, burned, or lost. Possibly, what I seek is in loose parchment form. Might you be holding anything like this? Or have you heard about private collectors holding such books or parchments?"

Gessesse seemed honestly confused. "I assume you've checked with the National Archives in Addis Ababa? But they've been ineffective in locating looted libraries. And some libraries were bombed or burned during the war."

The pain in the man's face was evident, and Father Yeorgi knew he was a small part of inflicting this pain. "Yes, and we'll never know what they hold."

"That's the very purpose of our work here at The Hill. We go into regional religious centers, establish professional relationships, and hire local people to do the digitizing for us. We're clear that we're not there to steal. A few national treasures have even been returned to the Ethiopian Orthodox Church once the collector realized how sacred the texts were." Gessesse appeared to reach across his desk for something, then resumed speaking. "We have staff digitizing several very fine Tenth and Eleventh Century codices, but it will be several months before they're ready for scholars to access. If you'd like, I can let you know when these become available with a link to their description."

Father Yeorgi nodded an assent. "Dottore Gessesse, would you or your colleagues know of the existence of earlier Ge'ez scrolls or parchments not in your own collection?"

Gessesse appeared confused. "Not in our collection? Besides Germany and the Vatican Libraries, I don't have much contact with scholars in other collections. I mostly work with researchers who come to us because of our holdings. Most Ge'ez texts outside Ethiopia are in Europe, with your own monastic libraries, or Russia. Their librarians are first rate."

"Yes, of course." He fought back his weakness toward impatience. Of course, he knew what the major collections held. Father Yeorgi kept his facial expression neutral, countering Gessesse's animated expressions. He grudgingly admitted to himself that he had been impressed with the scope and success of their work. God forbid they ever see this damnable scroll. His chest tightened at the very possibility.

Gessesse was still explaining their procedures. "We pursue collections and rarely individual texts. On occasion, a private collector makes something available for our digitized collection. Is there something in particular that you're trying to locate?"

"I confess my interest is in the earliest Ge'ez texts, but your collection seems more recent."

"Yes, I work with what has survived an ugly period in my country's history. I'm grateful for each and every ancient text that was once part of my country's culture that we can locate and digitize. It's been a long process requiring depths of patience. Is there anyone or a monastic center that you're seeking?"

"Like many scholars, I follow numerous threads. Early monastic writings, even those translated from Syriac into Ge'ez. Writings of the followers of Fremnatos would be a stunning find for all of us." He heard a satisfying grunt from Gessesse.

"Those would be stunning discoveries, but I've seen no hint here. But I'll talk with our director about possible monastic writings as his specialty is Egyptian monasticism."

"I would appreciate that." Trusting his intuition, he asked. "Do you have much demand for texts related to early Christian women? Thecla or Olympias, for instance?"

"In Ge'ez?" An expression of surprise crossed Gessesse's face, his voice shifted. "Interesting, you should ask. I was contacted by a woman working on translating an early Ge'ez text; she didn't say which one. She had questions about how to best translate some words. As you know, translations are difficult in themselves, but she is struggling with some challenging passages. I'm afraid English is not a first language for either of us. Still, she is attempting to render it into academic English. But the concepts we've been playing with across our language limitations have been intriguing."

A sucker punch to his gut. His scroll? Father Yeorgi's heart sped up. "Curious. Her name?"

"Sofia 'something.' Lovely young woman. She contacts me the same way as you, on video conferencing. But her recent questions lead me to believe that this text she's working on relates to early Christian women." Gessesse searched through some papers on his desk as he continued. "As you know, some names in Hebrew, Greek, or Aramaic were rendered in the local vernacular of the early Ethiopian church." Gessesse shifted in his chair and adjusted his screen. "Like you, she seemed interested in identifying holdings around the world of early Ge'ez texts, which is beyond my scope of work here."

Father Yeorgi's chest tightened, and he sat upright in his chair. "Did this woman give you any indication of how far she's gotten in her search?"

"No, and I'm afraid I didn't think to ask."

Father Yeorgi's voice constricted, and his voice grew thin. "How might I contact her?"

"Here it is. She had questions about 'Hannah' and 'Johanna.' Also, expressions used for the Holy Sacrifice."

Father Yeorgi's mind raced. She had translated more of the codex than he'd thought possible. She must be quite bright. And how much might this smart librarian figure out? His voice was sharp and impatient. "Again, how might I contact her? Where does she work? Her surname?"

Father Yeorgi heard Gessesse take a deep breath, revealing his reaction to Father Yeorgi's rudeness. The librarian hesitated. "I'd feel more comfortable letting her know of your interest when she contacts me again. Let me know how she might contact you, and I'll pass that information on to her.

Father Yeorgi was grinding his teeth as Gessesse ended their conversation. Had Gessesse been alerted to something?

THIRTY

ATHENS, GREECE

Father Yeorgi spent the evening in their chapel, ruminating over all he had been learning. He felt like he was getting close to his quarry, yet every turn seemed to complicate his attempts to retrieve this damnable scroll. At least he had the first name of someone with the necessary credentials that allowed her access to Doctor Gessesse at The Hill Museum and Monastic Library. But what if she shared his scroll with that institution? He would never get it back and then be forced into a campaign to prove the scroll was fake. Even though he was deeply suspicious, it was not. He had found the content intriguing but too upsetting to all he had known and given his life. *Christus Eleison. All Merciful One, spare your children. This sin is mine alone.*

The following day, he arrived at the University of Athens and strode across the campus to the library. He requested access to their the-ological and patristic databases. He was escorted to a modern room with banks of computer stations. Students slumped in chairs occupied most of the desks, with strings dangling out of their ears. Nervous feet tapped. A few glanced his way, eyes rolled, then returned to their screens. One student stood in reverence and kissed his palm. He extended a blessing, grateful that there was still some respect and civilized behavior left in this ungodly world.

Father Yeorgi dropped his bag on the table next to the screen, gathered the veil of his skouphas and sat in the chair. The graduate student helped him get into a search engine and, once learning that the monk was computer savvy, left him to his work.

Father Yeorgi began searches with both spellings of "Sophia" and "Sofia" combined with "Olympias," then "Makrina the Younger," and then "Hannah/Johanna." Up came links to numerous articles and notifications in professional journals regarding Makrina, both the Elder and Younger, but nothing connected with the other two women's names. He scanned through each article and then downloaded each to his thumb drive. He pulled out a pad and wrote down the names of the women associated with the articles, then decided to add the men's names in case he had to search for them.

He next scoured the indices of several English, French, and Greek journals. He stretched, working out the kinks in his back. Computer screens were tedious to read. Eventually, he found a doctoral dissertation from a papist university on women leaders in the early Christian movement by one Sofia Papandréou, submitted in English. He googled this name and came up with several interesting items. She had helped save a library collection in Albania from the black market and received praise from leaders in the Orthodox world.

He scanned the article, which indicated she had some capacity to read early Slavonic. His gaze intensified as he whispered aloud one of her translations,

"Wisdom springs from right living. Some of our age
seek wisdom that is nothing more than pretty words
fed to vain ears. Wisdom springs from holiness and
leaps into holiness. Wisdom is birthed from humility,
a right knowing of ourselves before the Creator of
all..."

What was this? He was not familiar with any texts from Albania.
But she was?

His chest constricted. His thief? Another notice stated that she
had been working on preserving the library at Mor Gabriel with one
Brother Makarios Addicott, apparently another papist.

He cleaned his glasses as he thought about what he was finding and
not finding. Next, he entered the site for the *Journal of Early Christian
Studies* and searched their index. Numerous articles written by Sofia
Papandréou appeared. These he scanned as he downloaded them to
his thumb drive. He gazed at her biography. She had been identified as
connected with several impressive research libraries. This Papandréou
was convinced that the letters of Olympias had survived. How did she
know? Maybe they were short-sighted in not releasing the tamer ones.

He sat back to think. His chair creaked. A student chuckled at the
sound. This woman had the precise ability to understand what the
scroll contained. From the articles he scanned, she was adept with
Armenian and Aramaic. But nothing about Ge'ez. Unusually gifted
in languages. So why wasn't she teaching at a university? Or working
in one of the rare book collections around Europe or the Middle East?
No, Satan was destroying the Middle East.

Then he remembered. Returning to one of the articles she wrote, he
scoured the footnotes. And there it was. She thanked several scholars

at the University of Thessaloníki for their assistance. He went to their site, but she was not listed as faculty. Why?

He stepped away for private prayer, a light lunch, and a walk to clear his head and ponder all he had learned. His cell phone rang. It was one of their solicitors. "Geia Sas."

"Father Yeorgi, I apologize for interrupting you, but I thought it was important. One of our associates thought you should know that another of the professionals involved on Agio Óros has been identified. One Georgios Hatzidakis at the University of Thessaloníki. He oversees their archives and rare book collection."

His chest constricted. "*Katálava.*" He snapped his phone shut. Thessaloníki it is.

§

THESSALONÍKI, GREECE

Sofia leaned back in her chair, appreciating the coolness of her basement office. Her aunt was upstairs, pacing their living room and talking on her phone. In the last dizzying day, she had contacted this Āminah Taşbent, their only common language being English, who explained what she was finding and why Brother Makarios wanted Sofia to see what had been unearthed before she was forced to shut her dig down—pieces of parchment in clay jugs. Sofia smiled at the thought of what she might find there.

Next, Sofia went online and, after deft negotiations with an airline representative, downgraded her generous first-class flight to California, given to her by the tech company, to tourist class and then changed her return from Thessaloníki directly to Istanbul. She could get to Istanbul for free. She just needed to find a hostel there.

She had emailed Doctor Gessesse at The Hill with several translation questions. She was determined to aim for the best translation because what she read in Ge'ez was astounding. Critics would challenge the accuracy of her work. She was both excited and anxious about the ensuing debate among scholars.

Her phone rang. "*Chaírete*?"

"Ephrem Gessesse here." After catching up on pleasantries, they discussed her questions, and she made notes as he explained how he would approach her translation conundrums. "Like all languages, Ge'ez words shifted meaning over the years. Knowing the age of the vellum you're translating could pin down some of these words."

"I haven't received test results yet. My colleague is one of the best in the field and won't discuss his findings until satisfied with his work." Sofia's foot was tapping her chair. Her impatience with waiting on these test results was wearing on her.

He continued, "I remain intrigued by your work."

"Dottore Gessesse, you will be among the first to know. I hope you will be able to see this soon. Any chance The Hill would send you to Europe to see the scroll in person?" Ephrem Gessesse and Brother Mac were the first two people she wanted to see her discovery.

Gessesse cleared his throat. "I could make a case for such a trip. When might this happen?"

"Probably best after the test results are in. I'd hope you can be there when the person handling the tests could also be there. Then we can all discuss this."

"Sofia, I was contacted by a monk from Athens who asked me unusual questions about our conversations. He indicated that he'd appreciate speaking with you." She tried to still her dancing foot, driven by anxiety and excitement.

Her hands began to sweat, and her breathing became shallow. She heard rustling sounds at his end.

"Yes, here it is. One Father Yeorgi. Quite interested in texts in Ge'ez and any old manuscripts involving women in the early Church. He knew Amharic and said he'd worked in Ethiopia during his graduate school days. Unusual for me to have two requests about texts in early Ge'ez in one year, let alone the same month."

So, that was the name of the monk who chased her to the dock? Her voice was thin, barely audible. "Did you give him my number or email address?"

"Oh, no." His voice sounded surprised at her question. "I told him I'd give you his contact information, and it was up to you to reach out to him." With shaking hands, she wrote down his phone number, and they concluded their call.

Her eyes constricted with worry. If the monk admitted to being in Ethiopia, she guessed twenty years ago, that might be when and where he found this. What should she do? This damn librarian found his way to The Hill—how did he even know of this library, him perched and secluded on the Holy Mountain—and did Gessesse give enough information away in innocence that the librarian could find her? Feeling a headache coming on, she acknowledged that she had best assume he would find her with her published articles, if not the papers she had read at conferences. Was her family safe?

Sofia called Takis. "Are you back home or still here in Thessaloní-ki?" He mumbled something about picking up specialized parts. "I'm worried about Christina's safety. I'm leaving the day after tomorrow for California and then directly to Istanbul." She was irritated when he whistled, though he meant it teasingly. "I just learned that that angry monk from Esfigmenou may have identified me. If he comes here, he could get mean." Her hands shook as she listened to his breathing.

"Well, you can't exactly call the police 'cause then you'd need to explain how you managed to piss off some holy monks." She heard muffled sounds as her cousin was talking to someone nearby. "*Mou oraios*, I'll return this afternoon. And you will explain to our aunt why a couple of my friends and I will pay an extended visit with her."

She thanked him profusely and, with shaky legs, took the two flights of stairs up to her bedroom, grabbed her gear, and headed to the university. This would be her last conversation with Hatzidakis before she revealed what she had unearthed.

Approaching his office, Sofia heard a deep, angry voice yelling at Hatzidakis. No one else was nearby. She set her gear down and drew near, her heart racing. The voice sounded much like the monk who chased her out of Esfigmenou.

"Are you protecting this Sofia Papandréou? Where is she? Do you have what she stole from me?" accusation dripping from the deep voice.

Hatzidakis' voice sounded equally angry. "Who are you to come in here and accuse me or anyone associated with the archives of being a thief? And just what are you claiming was stolen?"

"Tell me where she is, and I'll deal with her directly."

"Even if someone had stolen something from you, how do you know it was Papandréou?" Hatzidakis asked.

His voice low and slow, "I know."

Sofia grabbed her gear, turned, and ran.

THIRTY-ONE

Sofia's legs cramped and her brain muddled. She had been placed in the back of the plane with lines of passengers standing in the aisle waiting to use the water closet, which left her with little space for her legs. Her journey had been a grueling 18 hours after an exhaustive series of interviews focused on her abilities to work with ancient languages. Her interviewers seemed impressed and promised an answer and, most likely, an offer within the week. She gazed out her window at the familiar terrain below. The deep turquoise waters of the Sea of Marmara shimmered, and ahead, she could make out the minarets and curved rooftops of several mosques. The plane circled around Atatürk Airport outside Istanbul and began its descent, the gravity pulling on her stomach.

Sofia's mind wouldn't stop racing. She had been shooting craps when she infiltrated Agio Óros. And now, her translations are coming together, and she has framed several articles on the letters of Deacon Olympias. Brother Mac suggested she wait to finalize these articles until she had met with Profesör Taşbent.

Exhausted, she needed a solid night of sleep to function well in the coming days. And "days" may be all she had before this Father Yeorgi finds her. Should she contact the office of Patriarch Bartholomaios while she was here?

Within an hour, Sofia arrived at her hostel in the Sultanahmet neighborhood. After settling in and stretching her taut muscles, she ran to work through her exhaustion. On her way back, she picked up some *mihaliç peyniri*, a salty white cheese made from goat's milk, figs, and pears. After eating and grateful that her bunkmates were out, she closed the curtains and fell into a deep sleep.

The next morning, she grabbed her briefcase and departed for İstanbul Üniversitesi. The morning sun was warm, and as she climbed uphill and away from the water, car exhaust mingled with the salt air. Horns blared, and tires screeched. Mothers were out with strollers, and she heard young children shrieking with laughter. She stopped at an outdoor stand, ordering a Turkish coffee. She slipped back into a quiet corner of the park to drink and observe. Her nemesis is after her, but does he know she's in Istanbul? She struggled to figure out if any monks from Esfigmenou had followed her here. They couldn't wear their monkish habits in Turkey—by law. She hoped their beards and simple homespun clothing would give them away. She scanned the noisy crowds, but no guy stood out.

Resuming her hike uphill, she noticed the polluted air dissipating. She passed among the ruins of the old hippodrome, the Blue Mosque, and the Museum of Turkish and Islamic Arts. And what would he do to her if he did find her here, especially since she didn't have the scroll with her? When she nearly crashed into Father Yeorgi at Hatzidakis's office, the vibes she sensed were cold and mean. Just like when he chased her down to the docks. Menacing, that monk. But then, she was a clear threat to his worldview.

Her cell phone rang. It was a number she didn't recognize. Should she answer it? Softly, she replied, "*Yeia sou*."

"Luv, your favorite Brit here."

Sofia sighed with relief. "Hi, Mac. I'm heading to the university now. Āminah Taşbent expects me within the half hour."

"Why are you speaking so softly? Something wrong?"

"The crazy librarian—by the way, his name is Father Yeorgi—is on my tail. He knows who I am. And he might be around here, and I wouldn't notice."

Brother Mac was quiet for a moment. "Of course, this Yeorgi does. Sofia, you've always struck me as unaware of your accomplishments and how many scholars of differing backgrounds you connect with and do so easily. You move comfortably through many worlds. But Taşbent will be an ally. Stay close to her. Maybe even stay with her family. I'll arrive in Istanbul within a few days. Are you able to hang around that long?"

"Well, I'm here on a day-by-day basis, but it would be good to connect and talk. I feel like I will burst soon if I don't get some resolution around all this."

"We certainly cannot have you doing that," he chuckled. "I hear big tech in California is trying to steal you from us Antiquities types."

"If they make me an offer, I have to go. I'm beyond broke, in debt, with no hope. And a huge discovery for which I have no funding to support and protect it."

Sofia felt her cheeks blush. She quickened her pace, heading toward Beyazit Square with its bazaar. She shouted over the vendors selling fresh produce. The spices were pungent. "Are you coming about our Mor Gabriel finds?"

"Yes, following up on the testing, but also trying to catch up with you. I'm concerned about Taşbent and her dig. I want to see it."

Turkish men dressed in traditional garb with a samovar, a large metal urn, slung over their shoulders, offered tea or fruit juices to shoppers and passersby. She heard the laughter of children.

Sofia told him where she was staying before they ended their call. Knowing Mac, he would arrive at the dig as soon as possible. She forgot to ask him why he was concerned. Her brain still felt a bit scattered.

She moved to the shade of a tent and scanned the area. Across the way, she spotted a man in simple attire glancing her way. A shiver danced up her spine. She moved deeper into the tented area. His beard was trimmed, something monks on Agio Óros don't do. Done to deceive her?

She moved on at a fast clip. Ahead and to her right stood the fortress-like entrance to the university. Glancing around, she did not see the guy. Passing through the stone arches, she walked along the pathway under cypress and evergreen trees. The hibiscus and bougainvillea were in bloom. Students were lying in the sun, reading, talking, and gesturing, often with a cigarette lodged precariously between fingers or lips.

She rounded a corner and saw a petite woman with stylish black hair waving to her. Āminah Taşbent was stunning, with large brown eyes and long black eyelashes. In her late forties or early fifties, Sofia guessed.

"*Hoş gildiniz,*" Taşbent greeted her. "Welcome."

"*Hoş bulduk,*" Sofia responded.

"It's so good to meet you. Thank you for coming." Taşbent took her by the elbow. Turkish women walked arm in arm. "We have much to talk about."

Out of the corner of her eye, she thought she saw him again. Her jitters metamorphosed into a flock of butterflies in her stomach.

Crossing another grassy courtyard, they entered a newer building and turned right. Taşbent's spacious office, which included several large rooms guarded by an elderly secretary, was near the entrance. The office was filled with fine leather furniture and a carved rosewood desk. Its walls were adorned with original artwork, carved masks, intricate calligraphy, and several sculptures displayed.

Sofia sat as Taşbent's secretary rolled a cart in with coffee, tea, and pastries.

"I'm so glad you came. Some things cannot be properly discussed by phone, especially complex matters."

"Profesör Taşbent—"

"Āminah," she corrected Sofia.

"You have some beautiful pieces of artwork here." Sofia bit into a butter cookie, realizing how famished she had become. Turkish coffee on an empty stomach hadn't been very smart of her.

"Thank you. My family is blessed with gifted artists. Some pieces came from my father, who spent years as a member of the Ambassador's staff to several countries."

"My aunt was a museum curator in Thessaloniki. I grew up around old treasures."

Taşbent looked up at her. "The names of Papandréou and Seferaides are known, even here in Istanbul."

Sofia felt her cheeks warm. She took a gulp of her tea.

"Brother Makarios Addicott encouraged me to invite you here to see certain items, including the archeological dig my students and I have been working on. The authorities intend to shut it down within two weeks. He thought you might have some ways of helping us."

Two weeks? Sofia was surprised to hear this. And what did Mac think she could do? "Āminah, I look forward to seeing your dig. But there has been no news in our journals about what you're discovering."

Taşbent shifted in her chair, gracefully maneuvering her cup of tea. "I was given strict parameters, to move in quickly and assess what construction workers might encounter and decide if there was anything worth preserving." She sighed from deep within and set her tea down. "We Turks are losing our sense of history, even pride in our heritage. But I'm afraid my government doesn't want another reminder of our Christian past."

Sofia cringed inwardly. "What is your government planning on doing near such an historic and sacred site?"

"Sewers to serve new buildings in the area. And ultimately, business dictates policy. The sewers must be completed, the developers must be happy, and I'll be heartbroken."

Is this why Brother Makarios insisted she come here? "Why wouldn't your government not value its history?"

Taşbent cringed.

Sofia chastised herself as she was a guest in this country. "I'm sorry. I didn't mean to offend you. Turkey hosts so much ancient history," Sofia set her cup down, "and not to protect it?"

"Money is power. History, in our modern Turkey, is powerless."

Sofia felt the surge of sadness and anger that had become so common these last few years. "Is there some way that I could help you keep your dig open?"

"That's what Brother Addicott thought. The Patriarch's influence is limited here in Istanbul but his is a sane voice in tumultuous times. In sensitive matters, we work together," Taşbent said. "We walk delicate roads in Turkey. Some would have us return to Sharia, a harsh and rigid religious law. Others want secularism. Neither befits Turkey's future."

Sofia gulped the tea and set her cup back on the cart. "I see." Was this another lead that will die?

"On this dig, the Patriarch has been most generous in sharing some of his staff and answering questions. And more important for me, helping to negotiate my crew's presence on ground holy to both Christians and Muslims," Taşbent said.

Sofia was intrigued. The Patriarch could help her? She and Brother Makarios experienced little cooperation between Muslim authorities and the small Christian presence in southeastern Turkey. "What exactly is going on?"

"The dig is on the grounds of Hagia Sophia, back in a discreet corner."

Sofia broke out with a wide grin. Thank you, Brother Makarios. Her pulse increased.

Taşbent led Sofia to the next room, where she had a long conference table covered with hand-drawn maps laid out in sequence. More maps, mainly geological, were on the walls.

"Our work makes some Muslims nervous that Christians may try to reclaim *Aya Sofya* or render the site an even bigger tourist attraction. We want to offend no one. Let me explain what I've done. My questions will then make more sense. These are the outer walls of *Aya Sofya*. We know that they are the originals. The Ottomans reinforced these old walls with buttresses and added the minarets."

Taşbent used a pencil to point out what she was referring to as she spoke. Indicating the outer wall of the northeast corner of the Basilica, she continued, "These date to the fifth century, all that remains of the original structure before Emperor Justinian tore the original two churches down to build the current one."

"And that's near where you're digging." Sofia gazed across at one of the maps, her mind racing with possibilities. Sofia's chest constricted, and she forced herself to breathe deeply. She grabbed the table's edge with both hands to steady herself against the table. "Olympias. You found Deacon Olympias' monastery, didn't you?"

Taşbent smiled and continued, "As you know, the early records testify that Deacon Olympias built and led a large monastery of women attached to the original church sometime between 390 and 410."

"*The Church of Heavenly Peace*. Have you found evidence of where the original church was located? Where the narthex was situated?" Sofia asked.

"We're still working with educated guesses, and one possibility is that it stood where the current Basilica now stands. We only know that her monastery was on the church's south side."

Sofia scanned her memory for what Olympias' biography, called a *Life*, said about the monastic community. "The monastery housed at least 250 women of prominent rank, so it had to be pretty big."

"Our first findings confirm this. As you can see, the site is a portion of a series of buildings. We've discovered some kitchen artifacts, oil lamps, cloth samples, the usual," Taşbent said, pointing to another section of the drawings.

"All evidence of living quarters," Sofia said.

"And no separate chapel," Taşbent added.

Sofia traced her finger along the lines of the church plans. "No need since they would gather in the church for prayer. We know that at least three others besides Olympias were ordained deacons, presiding at prayers, preparing the dead, visiting, and supporting prisoners and the sick."

"We know of John Chrysostom's letters to Deacon Olympias but little else."

Sofia smiled. "Now I understand why Brother Makarios wanted me to meet you. And why he's coming himself."

Thirty-Two

T HESSALONÍKI, GREECE

Kostas had driven his cousin to Thessaloniki and then went to meet one of his contacts, Stavros. Because he had put out word regarding a strange theft on Agio Óros, Stavros called requesting a meet. Curious, he suggested *Youkalis*, a traditional *kafeneio* near the White Tower and the bay. Public enough for the two men to be anonymous.

Sitting at an outdoor table under the trellis, Stavros approached him, a worn leather portfolio clutched under his left arm. Stavros waved to a waiter, ordered an expresso, and sat across from Kostas.

"I think I have something of interest to you. About that thing you're investigating on the Holy Mountain."

Kostas nodded to the portfolio. "That's it?"

"I was in Karyes. I saw one of my suppliers," Stavros laughed. "The guy has the guts to grow his specialized product right under the noses of those old monks. Well, he got out and escorted a woman across the plaza and away from the police. Hips swayed despite the cargo pants, and her rucksack swung over her shoulder. Cap and hood couldn't hide that face. Tall with soft skin that glowed like an early morning sunrise."

Gutsy indeed, Kostas thought.

"Anyway, I headed toward them and noticed she left this in the truck's bed. Papers inside, though I admit they don't make much sense to me. Think this might be worth 500 euros to you." Stavros swigged the remaining expresso, arm draped across the portfolio.

Kostas agreed, passing over five bills and taking the portfolio. It was of handcrafted fine burgundy leather, worn from many decades of use. Kostas had seen this sort of thing working security detail for corporate heads. Papers inside, including hand-sketched maps, notes on the libraries there, and outlines of what appeared to be Church history—an odd mixture of scholarly work like his cousin kept handing him and yet like someone planning a heist. Nothing inside indicated its owner and nothing about Esfigmenou. The hand-sketched maps were of several other monasteries. Why?

Stavros remained seated. Kostas looked across at him. "For another five bills, I'll give you the name and haunt of my contact. Just don't interrupt his specialized business," Stavros said.

Kostas considered this. His name and address might speed up his search, especially if he doesn't find Father Yeorgi's scroll at the dame's house.

Kostas slid another five across but kept his hand securely on his investment.

Stavros looked at it. "Seferaides. Takis Seferaides. Mostly lives in Ouranoúpoli. Owns the auto repair shop there. Rebuilds engines for the monks. That gives him free movement on Agio Óros."

Kostas released his hand. "This conversation never took place." He scooped up the portfolio and departed with answers and more questions.

§

Kostas had borrowed an old Mercedes from an equally old gardener for another wad of euros. As he approached the Seferaides residence, Kostas shifted and scanned the neighboring homes. The home was in an old neighborhood with its old oak trees, wood frame, and stone homes. The homes of professionals and politicians. He scanned for parked cars, gardeners working among the well-manicured lawns, and pedestrians as he listened to a soccer match, Olympiakos against Athletic Bilbao.

His cousin was adamant that this "Sofia Papandréou" was his thief. It took more work to tease out her whereabouts. While the name "Sofia Papandréou" only turned up the scholarly stuff his cousin loved, Kostas scoured the internet and made a few discreet calls, enabling him to connect Papandréou with Seferaides, two old and prominent families in northern Greece. Christina Seferaides had been a fancy museum curator who lived in this neighborhood. So, was this Takis a son? A nephew? So, the crappy economy drove even the old families into creative business opportunities. He chuckled at that bit of news.

A talkative employee at the university, who was grateful for the gift of 100 euros, told him that Sofia lived with her aunt. Hopefully, the scroll was somewhere in the house.

Stopping, he shifted into reverse and backed into the driveway of the next home, one whose occupant he had verified was still in Germany on business.

Shutting the engine off, he stepped out of his car. Glancing along the stone wall that separated the two homes, he saw the gate to the backyard. Within minutes, Kostas slipped over the wall and crossed the terrace to the Seferaides' home. He stopped before the first window and scanned inside. No shadows moving about.

Gloves on, Kostas picked the lock on the patio door and entered—easy as slicing fresh mozzarella. He had entered through the kitchen and dining area, clean and relatively modern, with a wall of windows looking out onto Mount Olympus in the distance. He passed into the living room, large and spacious. As he had expected, this was the home of a cultured family. He scanned shelves filled with museum-quality books, mostly about Greek antiquities, and a few small artifacts—clay and stone figurines. A few pieces of contemporary artwork, each an original, he determined after close examination. An icon of the Virgin Mary and Child, which appeared quite old, he guessed, hung near the doorway.

Off the living room and tucked under the staircase, he found a cluttered office. He searched the desk, carefully rifling through stacks of papers and drawers filled with files. A letter from a solicitor lay off to the side. Opening it and quickly scanning the content, it seemed this "Christina Seferaides" held significant land holdings. So this house was connected to the old Seferaides family after all. He had read some of Georgios Seferaides' poetry for which he had been awarded a Nobel Prize. Impressive. He kept the letter in case he might need it later.

Everything in this office told him that this occupant was connected with several museums. Did his cousin realize this? No way a museum curator was off stealing for her own museum, not with Greece suing the British Museum for the return of the stolen Parthenon Marbles, what the British refer to as the Elgin Marbles—aptly named after the thief. He glanced at the contents of a slide viewer on a table alongside the desk containing slides of finds from an archeological dig. No pictures of old books or scrolls. The bookcases were filled with more books and stacks of papers. He didn't see any connection to Esfigmenou or the missing scrolls. The phone rang, and Kostas knelt, alert to any movement in the house. A beep and a message left—Takis,

Stavros' supplier, calling to say he would be home within the hour. Kostas noted the time. If he's calling, then he expects someone to arrive home before him.

Kostas slipped upstairs and systematically searched closets, bureau drawers, and bookcases. In one room sat a steamer trunk secured with an old padlock, which proved immune to his lock picks. He'd need to cut it. Looking around, he noted maps of Mount Athos and a secretary opened with a small stack of papers. Return addresses from several European Universities and one "The Hill Museum and Manuscript Library" from Minnesota, USA. The name read "Sofia Papandréou." He grabbed the envelopes.

He pulled out his metal cutters and knelt. Outside, he heard some distant voices, male, and a car backfire. No sounds nearby, a reminder that he needed to get moving. He applied intense pressure, cutting through the rusted metal after a seemingly long minute. He twisted the ancient padlock and opened the trunk. Peering inside, he began to rifle through old newspapers, magazines, books, and family memorabilia. Names leaped off the pages. The contents of this trunk belonged to a "Seferaides," "Papandréou," and "Lambrakis." So, he was searching the home of one of Greece's oldest and most powerful families? Grigoris Lambrakis was assassinated in 1963. Kostas whistled softly.

But no scroll nor old book. And why would an old and powerful family stoop to stealing from monks? This case kept getting stranger.

Descending the staircase, he heard a car enter the driveway. A woman's voice calling to someone. Or was she speaking on the phone? He quickly got to the landing and scoured his options. Seeing what appeared to be the door leading out to the side of the house and stone fence, Kostas turned and passed through the doorway, losing his footing on a stair landing as the door closed behind him. He stumbled down some stairs, slamming his right shoulder against a wall. Sharp pain jarred him. He clamped his jaw shut to keep silent. He steadied his breath, listening for evidence that his fall had alerted anyone of his presence. A woman called out the name "Takis." Silently straightening himself, he quickly descended the remaining stairs and slipped under the staircase, waiting. The woman's voice grew distant, and the door never opened.

His Piaget read 1:21 PM. Kostas flipped on his small flashlight and swept the room, seeing bookcases filled with boxes, odd-shaped containers, cylinders, old books, computer equipment, and a long worktable. Another office? Limited daylight filtered through the dirty panes of two small basement windows, each opened from the top. His instinct convinced him that the scroll had to be here somewhere, and he needed to find it fast.

Keeping alert for the basement door above, Kostas began with the boxes on the shelves. About the tenth box opened revealed an old book, probably the one his cousin had said was taken along with his precious scrolls. The slip inside had all that fancy coding numbers those monks liked to use. Setting the gray box with the book on the table, he quickened his pace. His shoulder throbbed, and his frustration grew. He saw older books, stacks of papers, and journals but no scroll. He climbed on the desk and searched the upper shelving. Nothing.

The problem with this woman was that she was no professional thief. Father Yeorgi and his other clients typically sent him to well-organized places with vaults, safes, and discreet locked rooms, including numerous collectors' libraries. This woman was pure amateur where stealing was concerned.

Father Yeorgi's nemesis was every bit the scholar that Father Yeorgi was—and a woman. That certainly irritated his arrogant cousin. He smiled. Where would an intelligent woman keep old scrolls? Somewhere that she could do whatever scholars do with old scrolls. Nothing was making sense. He would expect that, like his cousin, this woman would give thought and care to preserve something she wanted so badly that she had resorted to stealing. Why wasn't it here? He heard the woman's muffled speech and footsteps in the room above. He needed to clear out.

He grabbed two USB drives left in her computer and more in a top drawer. He noticed several unmarked CDs and gathered those along with the thumb drives. Needing time to examine all this, he took letters stacked on the desk—letters that bore the letterhead of some distinguished universities from several continents and loads of bills. Telephone bills, he realized. Who had the professor been calling?

Wood scraped on wood as the door above pushed open—the sound was distinct and unmistakable.

"Sofia? Are you already home from Istanbul? Did everything go well?"

He placed everything in the storage box alongside the old book. Turning, he scrambled across the room toward the underside of the staircase. The overhead light came on.

"Sofia, take those headphones off."

As the woman stepped off the last wooden stair, Kostas came from behind and, with his right fist and with the entire thrust of his shoulder, punched the back of the woman's head, sending her hurling across toward the table as Kostas, clutching the box and his shoulder hurting more than ever, shot up the stairs.

THIRTY-THREE

SULTANAHMET DISTRICT, ISTANBUL

"Āminah, we need to fight to have the dig expanded."

Taşbent smiled. "That would be wonderful, but how?"

Sofia slipped on the lab coat she was handed, grabbed her oversized tote, and followed Taşbent out of the office. After retracing their steps, they were soon back on the street. Several young people greeted her host and gazed her way with curiosity.

"I've had some unusual success lately in locating a few of Olympias' letters to Chrysostom." Sofia was still piecing together which sections of these letters might fit in which order, much like attempting a puzzle without the box lid as a clue.

Taşbent stopped abruptly. "Really? I hadn't heard about this. No notices in our journals."

Sofia turned toward her host. "You're only the third person to know. And I ask that you keep this quiet until you and I figure out how to release this news in a way that will help us with your dig."

"This is stunning news, Sofia." Taşbent's face glowed. "Where did you locate these? Have the letters been independently verified yet?"

Sofia was delighted to see the astonished expression on her host's face. "Samples are being tested in Bologna. I'll explain more when we can talk privately."

Someone bumped Sofia from behind, startling her. She grabbed her bag tight as she scanned the area around them to see if anyone was watching them.

Taşbent grasped Sofia's elbow, "Why don't you keep your bag between us. Unfortunately, we have an abundance of pickpockets around here."

Sofia moved her bag to her other side as Taşbent released her elbow. The two kept moving at a good clip.

Taşbent waved to a friend. "Sofia, I am astonished at your news."

"If we word the announcement carefully and choose carefully how and where to make the announcement, I'd think Olympias' letters will help us keep your dig open." The din of noise in the marketplace grew. Breathing deeply, she noticed the scent of safran and cooking oil. "Just how big is the site?"

"Not large. I was given only ten laborers. I have a few graduate students assisting with identification. And when the developers grow impatient enough, it will all be filled in and disappear. I am under pressure to move as quickly as possible with little help. But now your presence might change all that."

Sofia's shoulders tensed. Why did developers need to destroy historic sites? "Have you located any entrances to the monastery complex?"

"Yes. It's a typical Imperial home, adjusted to house many adults and their activities," Taşbent said.

"The women should've had a library. Any evidence of parchments or codices?"

"Mostly fragments," Taşbent answered. "You can examine what we've unearthed thus far."

The two women walked in silence, Sofia gathering her thoughts. Might there be something at this dig that would support her stunning discovery at Esfigmenou? Corroborating evidence could only come from a woman's monastery and one with deacons. Did they have deacons in Ethiopia? Were the women known by another title? She would need to investigate that.

Shoppers at the marketplace and sellers hawking wares jostled them. She gripped her tote and picked up their pace. Sofia broke the silence. "Āminah, have you seen or heard of parchments, probably stolen, passing through Istanbul from Africa?"

Taşbent gazed at her as they rounded a corner. "Africa? Our collections are mostly Islamic texts. Maybe Persian, but very little that is Christian, which is why I asked you here."

"Did the Patriarch's staff ever mention anything about Armenian or Ethiopian parchments that shouldn't be in Istanbul?" She had been struggling to figure out how her stunning scroll came to be on Agio Óros and why it was in such good shape.

"No, but I can ask. Or introduce you to his archpriest, Father Andreas."

"Thank you. That might be helpful." She might get in trouble with the Patriarch, especially if he knew a thief who visited Esfigmenou.

Approaching the park surrounding Hagia Sophia, they turned left again onto *Caferiye Sok*. Spray from the fountain drifted across the grass. Traffic was less here, but the horns sounded anyway. As they walked along the pine-lined street, the burnt red brick exterior of the Basilica with its grayish cream minarets appeared through the grove of flowering Judas trees to their right. The dry air was filled with their scent. Sofia strained her neck, trying to get a clear look at its rooftop. In seeing this ancient and venerated site, Sofia wondered what the women who had lived after Deacon Olympias had witnessed here.

"Breathtaking, isn't she?" Taşbent said, looking toward the majestic old edifice. "In the early 1980s, there were several archeological sites around Istanbul—major digs associated with repairs to mosques and the old homes in and around Sultanahmet. Workers were not getting paid or were simply greedy. When some urns were found, the workers set them aside and sold them on the black market. We know what happened but have never found out who bought them or what the urns contained."

Sofia felt like a football slammed her gut. "How awful."

"A story we hear all too often."

"I wonder what could have been inside," Sofia said, groaning. Could this be where her discovery came from?

"Me, too. They're gone now. Old manuscripts disappeared, too. When I was given this project, I enticed some colleagues at Oxford and the British Museum to help me tighten security," Taşbent said.

"That's good to hear. It always pains me to learn of the theft of precious books." Sofia would ensure her stunning discoveries are placed in a safe research facility. But where? "They usually end up in private collections so scholars cannot study them."

Taşbent led her to the right across the grass toward a discreet wall of canvas attached at one end to the Basilica. One of the workers greeted Taşbent as he lifted the canvas, Sofia saw shovels, picks, and trowels with small orange flags attached to strings and sticks, marking the direction of different aspects of the excavation. The area of the dig closer to the basilica wall appeared well-cultivated, and as her gaze swept away from the wall, the team had barely begun to work. A mixture of young graduate students and day laborers in jeans with hard hats and gloves were kneeling, scraping away the dirt.

"As you see, it's not large. Our government has limited how broad a field we can open up unless I can give compelling evidence for expansion." Taşbent smiled, "And now you're here."

Sofia's heart fluttered. The dig's potential delighted her. Her discoveries about Deacon Olympias could build a strong case for the expansion of the dig. Why would governments want to minimize this anyway? Might she connect her strangest discovery on Agio Óros and this archeological dig?

Taşbent walked her through, pointing out what appeared to be ancient living quarters, the detached kitchen with six clearly separate fireplaces, and even a household garbage dump. Since no record existed for the original plans of Olympias' monastery, her host explained, she was not certain in which direction her team would need to dig, even if they had the authority, to find the remainder of the complex.

Pointing down into a long, narrow trench that appeared to have a brick or stone floor, Sofia asked, "This leads toward Hagia Sophia. Might this be the private entrance to the original church for the women living in the monastery?"

"That would be my guess," Taşbent responded.

"The nuns would have gathered in the church seven times daily for the Divine Office. Many Christians around Byzantium would have joined the women. I wonder if any of the parchment pieces you've unearthed might contain either their chant texts or even record of their preaching."

Sofia had long wondered if Olympias or any of her fellow nuns preached only in the church, or did they go out in the city and countryside to preach as well? Might some of the unearthed parchment pieces back up the letters she found on the Holy Mountain?

A cat brushed Sofia's calf. Taşbent bent and picked the cat up. "Meet *Gli Kizim*, senior staff of Hagia Sophia."

Sofia stroked her fur, the striated brown of a mackerel tabby, and noticed that her green eyes were cross-eyed.

"*Hoş gildiniz*, Profesör Taşbent."

The cat hissed and jumped away. The two women turned in the direction of the male voice. A swarthy man dressed in a silk suit tailored over his robust frame with French cuffs on his white shirt and crafted leather shoes approached. Then she noticed the unhappy expression on her host's face.

The man continued. "Soon you will be finished here? My employees are anxious to begin."

Sofia's back stiffened.

"Mr. Dağdelen

They shook hands. As Sofia had experienced too often with men in this part of the world, his handshake was diffident, and he began to turn away as if the presence of two professional women were of no importance to him. She gripped his hand firmly. "Mr. Dağdelen, I don't think you appreciate the international importance of this site. Deacon Olympias—"

"No, no." His smile grated on Sofia's nerves. "You academics think every piece of dirt holds significance—"

"Only when it does," Sofia interrupted. "I specialize in the writings of Deacon Olympias." She felt the heat rise on her neck. "This dig cannot be closed until our work is done."

Sofia turned toward Āminah. "Shall we continue?" She could use Takis about now.

"No, ladies, this will end. Progress must—"

Bristling again, Sofia hooked Taşbent's elbow and turned away. Something caught Sofia's attention. "And over there?"

"Ladies, it's over. The people of Istanbul want progress, not smothered by irrelevant history."

Sofia nearly choked.

Taşbent raised her voice. "That's the entrance to the Basilica cistern," her face awash with worry, "the original cisterns that Justinian built for his own Great Palace."

Sofia's ears piqued when she heard the developer speak on his phone. The two women turned in his direction. Taşbent stepped toward him, listening, then turned back toward Sofia.

"He's ordering his men to begin delivering heavy equipment." Taşbent's face was ashen.

Sofia felt the heat on the skin of her neck. "Place a call to the Patriarch's office. Insist they intervene with whichever appropriate department has the power to halt this." And maybe it was time for her to consult with the Patriarch's staff, perhaps this Father Andreas, about her discoveries on Agio Óros.

Sofia turned and marched toward the closest entrance to the Basilica. Rage pounded in her ears. Entering the cool, dark interior, she scanned for the all-familiar tour guides with flags or umbrellas to direct their charges. She swept the interior with her eyes and listened for a familiar language.

Soon, she heard English and moved in that direction, stepping around scaffolding. Approaching the tour guide, she listened to the distinct sounds of American English spoken among some silver-haired women. Sofia noticed that the thirty or so faces were well-dressed, some wearing caps with the embroidered initials UND.

Sofia, loud and clear, introduced herself to a young royal blue-suited tour guide while looking at the women in her group standing nearby. Smiling, she asked, "What does UND stand for?"

Several answered at once, "University of Notre Dame. Except we graduated from Saint Mary's next door."

"You have a wonderful opportunity to witness the unfolding of women's history outside these walls." Her voice echoed. The women quieted and turned their attention to her. "Might you be interested? I'd be happy to show you what we're accomplishing here."

The tour guide looked at her questioningly. "But, madam, the site is strictly forbidden to us."

A silver-haired woman with porcelain skin interrupted. "Women's history? Here?"

Sofia smiled. "As I am a consultant on the dig, and the head is just outside these walls, we'd love to show your group what we're discovering." She turned toward the women, "This holy place is full of women's history. Have any of you heard of the Deacon Olympias?"

A tall redhead interrupted. "A woman deacon?"

Sofia looked in her direction. "Yes, one of many. Or of the First Council of Constantinople that her community hosted in 381?"

Murmuring and questions echoed off the walls. "Deacon Olympias, a member of the Imperial family, established a monastery on these grounds long before Emperor Justinian thought to begin constructing this basilica."

Sofia hooked the elbow of the tour guide and led the group back the way she came. She pointed to her right, "And this is the Wall of the Council, a remnant from the earlier church attached to her monastery." She knew she might be pushing some edges here.

She turned and began walking backward to face her audience while loudly explaining about Deacon Olympias and her community. "Her earlier church was called The Church of Heavenly Peace."

Sofia heard the women chatting loudly with each other, echoes blending their voices, mostly saying, "Women?" and "Why doesn't the tour book tell us this?" She waved to other tourists to join them.

Passing through the doorway, Sofia shielded her eyes from the sun while guiding her growing audience around one of the massive buttresses toward Taşbent and the developer. They were clearly arguing.

"If you would all gather along the tarp, Profesőr Taşbent and I will explain what we're unearthing." Sofia noticed her host turning away from the developer with a look of surprise. The tour guide came up alongside her and turned toward the group. Tourists spread themselves along the inside of the tarp.

"Profesőr Taşbent is directing this highly valued archeological dig to help us understand the role of women in early Christianity. If you direct your gaze beyond the ropes, you'll notice that we've already unearthed portions of the living quarters, and over there are the remnants of six fireplaces." Sofia made eye contact with Taşbent, whose face was still red with rage, and nodded her to join in.

"Yes, and in this direction is the passageway to their chapel." The women continued explaining elements of the dig and what they expected to uncover when they expanded it.

"What's in the tent over there," one gentleman asked.

"We're unearthing the women's library."

The silver-haired American asked, "Library? Why don't the books tell us all this?"

Another said, "We took a class in preparation for our trip, and nothing was mentioned about women."

"Silence around this sacred site is shameful." Sofia stared at the developer. "The profesőr and I may need to write a corrected version of this site's guidebook. Women were an important presence here," she raised her voice a notch, "for the first millennium of Christianity. Long before Hagia Sophia was built."

Taşbent turned toward the group. "The women were highly literate with what appears to be an extensive library. Dottore Papandréou will continue piecing together the bits of parchment and provide translations."

Good, Taşbent was getting into this. And would Sofia ever enjoy working on any translations.

Another asked, "How many women lived here?"

Sofia responded. "250 to 350. We're still trying to figure it out. We will expand the excavation until we can ascertain the full size of the women's complex." She hoped so anyway. She led the group in the direction of the developer.

Mr. Dağdelen had snapped on his phone again and yelled at someone. A few tourists looked his way, annoyed with the interruption.

Taşbent glanced toward Sofia with a curious expression. "The cisterns that Emperor Justinian built," she pointed across the walkway, "known as the Basilica cisterns, were an expansion of what the women had for their fresh water source. Be sure to visit them for their stunning mosaics."

"Mosaics," commented one who was flipping through her guidebook.

The silver-haired American woman asked, "Who's that guy? He's rude."

Sofia smiled. "Yes. He's trying to shut the site down and fill it all in. He thinks no one cares about women's history."

Sofia noticed Mr. Dağdelen glaring at her, nostrils flaring.

"What?" Several people shot out with disbelief.

"We're working with the authorities," Sofia knew she was stretching things again. Still, the only worthwhile game of football was a strategic and aggressive one. "If you'll give me your emails or business cards, we'll keep you posted on our progress."

She went among the group, collecting scraps of paper and business cards while answering questions. Turning, she approached the tour guide, who gave Sofia her business card.

Taşbent handed her a generous tip and suggested she might bring more tourists out here, especially those who might support the project.

As the crowd thinned, Sofia noticed that the developer was gone. "Āminah, I hope I haven't caused you too much trouble."

Her host smiled. "That was brilliant. You may have just given us time to save the dig."

THIRTY-FOUR

NORTHERN GREECE

The woman posed a problem for Kostas. She could provide the police with an accurate sketch. He dumped the old gardener's car at the airport. He took the first flight out to the capital of Bulgaria and checked into a small pensione in the old city, where few questions would be asked of him. Before he had boarded the plane, he had mailed the old book to Father Yeorgi in Athens. He settled in to see what he could learn from the stuff he took from Papandréou's office. He scanned her mail while waiting for his laptop to power on.

The first letter was from a scholarly society accepting her proposal to deliver a paper at Oxford University on Deacon Olympias next year. Whoever that was. Setting that aside, the following letter was from the University of Bologna. More scholarly stuff? He started reading, and his pulse intensified. The letter referred to some tests on numerous fibers of vellum and ink, with lots of data and graphs that began to sound quite familiar. He used a lab in Vienna on behalf of several of his more discreet clients, including his irritating cousin. He whistled.

Father Yeorgi had been elusive about his stolen scroll, and this An-drucci indicated that it dated from the Fifth Century CE. Might his cousin's scroll be sitting in Bologna? Possibly, but if it was as important as Father Yeorgi insisted, she'd hide it.

While clicking open some of the files off the Papandréou's thumb drive, Kostas dialed the number and learned that he had reached the Paleo-Archeology Department at the University of Bologna. Which professor was he trying to contact? Glancing at the report, he asked after a Paolo Andrucci. He declined to leave a message for the "other-wise occupied" professor.

The next letter contained her phone bill. Utilizing a search engine, he confirmed that several of her calls were made to Turkey in Istanbul and near Mardín. Several calls were made to Oxford and Belgium, somewhere near Brussels. He confirmed several of these area codes were for Rome and Bologna, even the Silicon Valley in California. Was she seeking their help with this scroll? Did computer geeks do that kind of work? His shoulder tightened. He stretched his muscles, trying to release the cramp.

Next, he called the number in Rome. "Monasteria Santa Cecil-ia," a woman's voice answered, Italian-accented. He hung up. Why a monastery? What could Papandréou want with a Roman monastery of nuns? Father Yeorgi would steam over this one. Kostas pulled up the abbey's website and began to scan for a clue. It was located close to the Vatican. Had Papandréou taken the scroll to the university or this monastery? Getting it through airport security would be a nightmare for an amateur, so the woman must have driven as border crossings did not exist anymore. Bologna or Rome first?

His phone vibrated. Glancing at the screen, he took the call. "*Yeia sou.*"

"What did you find?" The brusque voice of his cousin greeted him.

"The old book your abbot wanted back was in the house, but no scroll."

"You're absolutely certain?" his cousin demanded.

His cousin's attitude pissed him off. When had he ever screwed up? Father Yeorgi might be a monk but would not last a week on the street. He probably would trip over his worn prayer cord.

"Yes. And the theft wasn't a professional job—strictly amateur. The scroll is sitting either in Bologna or Rome."

"What makes you think that?"

"Correspondence I found in her office. Papandréou had arranged for tests of fiber and ink. Lots of tests at the university in Bologna. I'm curious about what else she found."

"The university." His cousin's voice grew thoughtful.

"I'll head out tomorrow."

"No. I'll head there myself. I've learned a few things about universities dealing with Athens and Thessaloniki. You pursue your lead in Rome. We must get this back and fast," Father Yeorgi said.

"I still don't know why this has you worried."

Father Yeorgi sighed with exasperation, "She could ruin our plans."

"The woman doesn't care about your plans. Just wanted this scroll. Not much different than you."

Kostas listened to his cousin's fierce intake of breath. "I want that scroll back, no matter the cost. She's a risk to us."

"She's not much of a risk. My take is this is just someone who saw something old and grabbed it."

"From a hidden underground cavern? This scroll and none of the others? Somehow, she knew about it." Father Yeorgi hissed, "Did one of those workers you sent me sell out on us?"

Kostas swore under his breath. His cousin doubted him. But just how did she know where the cave was located? And about this scroll that has his cousin tied in knots? "What is the connection between this scroll you're so desperate to retrieve and any political plans? How can this help you now that you're evicted from Agio Óros?"

"Don't concern yourself," Father Yeorgi said.

"I've been flying in the dark without radar. If you'd give me specifics, I might've been able to move faster." His cousin seemed to be increasingly irrational. This situation could be dangerous for him. Better if the two of them split up.

"You don't need to know."

"Then focus on Bologna. Have any contacts there?"

"I don't see how anyone could get the scroll to a university without raising questions," Father Yeorgi said.

Kostas needed to be careful. Something about this case bothered him. Now, he was increasingly angry with his cousin. He could make mistakes if he did not get his anger under control.

"I've thought about that. She's Papandréou, Seféraides, and Lambrakis. Their influence among the old families is significant. Papandréou is a professor of some international reputation from a family still respected and honored." Kostas sipped his cognac and popped in another thumb drive. "I'd think she has some professional contacts in Bologna and would know how to present their lab with samples. Maybe the scroll is there, or maybe she only brought samples." He watched the screen as a series of files came up. He leaned forward and began scanning the file names. Some names were in Greek, some in English, and several in a language he thought he had seen before. But where?

His cousin sighed. "Too many unknowns. I don't like it."

"So you've said." Kostas realized his sarcasm was getting away from him.

"Are you still on this case?"

"As long as you continue to make it worth my while." Kostas heard a sharp intake of breath.

Father Yeorgi responded in a whispering hiss. "Damn you. Where's your loyalty to the one true faith?"

Kostas was dumbfounded. Didn't his cousin realize his "loyalty" was limited to money? If his assignments didn't harm the little guy?

"I haven't decided on that question yet." Kostas shut off his phone.

He copied all the files to his hard drive and stuffed the thumb drives into his attaché. No need to tell his cousin about them until he knew what Father Yeorgi was hiding from him. And if the scroll was as explosive as his cousin claimed, he may get bigger money elsewhere. He'd store these in his safety deposit box in Geneva.

Kostas spent several quiet hours reading the computer files he had lifted from the Seferaides home. The thumb drives and CDs contained a surprising amount of information. He examined photographs of pages from old codices, like those he had procured for his cousin and other clients over the years, except these mostly did not contain gorgeous illuminations. Papandréou seemed more interested in the words, just like his cousin. What he guessed to be the scroll his cousin was increasingly desperate to recover had also been photographed from multiple angles. It appeared to him that Papandréou had transcribed each section and each sheet of the vellum in its original language. Still, Kostas could find no translations into modern Greek or English. Why not? He kept searching. He recognized old Biblical Greek, something that might be Syriac, and one old language looked like something he had seen from Ethiopia years ago. The other script he did not recognize. Damn, still no translations that he could find. His curiosity deepened.

Some of the woman's files looked to be scholarly articles with the name *Olympias* appearing in titles. Others seemed to be about some monasteries, maybe in Turkey. He scanned some of those articles written in English, but they were still too technical for him to understand. Kostas' curiosity grew. He took another sip of his cognac and examined the old Greek, looking for words he might recognize. Another name—*Junia*—also showed up a couple of times. Who was she? And a *Hannah* appeared. Was she in the Old Testament? While all this might fascinate some people, why did his cousin need this thing? Why his desperation?

This Papandréou was as smart as his cousin, and she knew what she was doing. He was pleased to see a woman give these arrogant monks a run for their money. He liked intelligent women. Stupid ones irritated him.

His phone rang as he was getting ready to head out to dinner. He sighed at the number, Father Yeorgi again, but took the call anyway.

His cousin told him he would head to Bologna the following day. Did Kostas need an advancement against his expenses? Kostas gazed at his cognac but declined assistance. He had begun distancing himself from his cousin. He just didn't like all these unknowns that Father Yeorgi threw his way.

"I reviewed Papandréou's correspondence. Seems she's been in contact with Patriarch Bartholomaios." Kostas listened to a subtle shift in his cousin's breathing, then shut off his phone.

§

ROME

Trastevere was a comfortable neighborhood in old Rome filled with misfits, gypsies, pickpockets, and University students. The Abbey of Santa Cecilia was in an obscure corner of this colorful neighborhood. Kostas studied the abbey complex—the nuns had never upgraded their locks, and windows were without bars, but he did notice a few guards milling about.

Kostas blended with German tourists who had arrived near the Abbey gate. They were given a tour of the church and then descended to the site of the saint's house, located beneath the church's high altar. The lighting was soft and diffuse. Smooth stone floors led to compacted dirt where the ruins of the home lay.

The walls seemed to absorb the footsteps and soft voices of the others around him. Kostas noted doors, additions, and scaffolding near the original ruins and exits. He could locate the entry into the alleyway—opposite from where the group had entered the site from the church above.

The additions bothered Kostas. Did the fire code require a refit? Was there another reason? He noted a corridor opposite where they came down from above—did that lead to the monastery? He would need to study the architectural plans so he would not go in blind.

Returning to his pensione, Kostas turned on the radio and powered up his laptop to begin his search for the architectural plans for Santa Cecilia. These he located through the Italian government's Division for Antiquities. All requests for upgrades, repairs, and expansions had to be approved by a sea of bureaucrats, and, fortunately for him, he saw evidence of recent work within the complex.

The place had over 100 rooms. He sighed. The abbey was three stories above ground and two levels subterranean. He hadn't realized that there was another level. Above where he had just been? Or below? He kept studying.

The radio announcer clearly mentioned "Mount Athos." Kostas stopped and listened. The announcer stated that Abbot Ephraim of Vatopedi had been formally charged by Courts of Cessation for embezzlement. Russia's Putin refused to cooperate with the banking investigation, and Greece's government began transferring titles of properties in downtown Athens back to the people of Greece.

Kostas grinned. While he had been comfortable stealing codices from the wealthy for a hefty "finder's fee," he detested how the monks had stolen from hardworking Greeks. Father Yeorgi denied that his monastery had been involved, claiming they had numerous favorable donors. Putin?

Kostas stood and stretched. Abbots arrested and charged. His cousin's monastery was under siege by the military police. The Greek government pursuing their bank accounts. Why was he still doing business with them? If he found this scroll, what should he do with it?

Resuming his study, he identified one inner courtyard as resting above the power plant for the abbey—heat pumps, electricity, plumbing, and such—and the other two were above large *auras* or rooms. Each courtyard discreetly hid solar panels and venting, confirming his suspicion that the library and archives would be under each. He'd seen this in other libraries and private homes. Temperature and moisture control in humid climates requires a lot of electrical power.

He would enter as he had with the tourists. Then, he would follow the stairs near the high altar down to the old Roman ruins, the home of Saint Cecilia, and the original chapel and monastery. He would take the corridor from the saint's house to the nearest stairs and descend one more level. Archives would most likely be on the lowest level of the complex.

Alarms were an unknown factor. He had seen no evidence of any security system. Still, in these days of advanced technology, the nuns may have installed something he hadn't been able to locate yet. Kostas took several deep breaths. Unknowns always bothered him.

THIRTY-FIVE

I STANBUL

The two women slipped into the tent to escape the relentless sun. Taşbent pulled a cloth from her pocket and wiped her face, damp with sweat. "I'd never thought the public would be interested in my work. In what I do here."

Sofia smiled. "Now you know. We can't afford to be timid, Āminah. Not with the developers or with politicians. We must expand the dig to find everything we can on Olympias." The idea of this dig being abandoned before being thoroughly investigated sickened her. She doubted this would happen if it was connected to men's history.

Taşbent sighed. "I agree, but funding is a challenge."

"So, we get moneyed people interested." Sofia moved to a chair and sat. What had been bothering her finally came to light, why there had been little news of this dig. "First, we need your graduate students to help us set up a website and use social media to spread the word. We'll put their smartphones to work to save Olympias." She laughed.

"Maybe that's what we should call this. The *Save Olympias Crusade* and start a crowdfunding campaign."

Taşbent sat as well. "A what?"

Sofia explained what that meant. She had learned about crowdfunding from Brother Makarios, bless his heart. "We live in new times now. We take this project out to the broader public, putting pressure on politicians. Do you know any women in the government or wives of influential politicians that we might bring on board? Bring them out here to see what you're doing?"

Taşbent spoke hesitantly. "Well, yes, I think so." Her face brightened. "Yes, I do know several who ought to be interested. And several successful businesswomen as well. Would you be willing to speak with them of Olympias' letters you've unearthed?"

Sofia sat silently, gazing around the room at the table with microscopes, a scanner, and a laptop. Some of the parchment fragments rested nearby underneath the netting. She had already begun planning how to introduce Deacon Olympias' letters to her fellow scholars. After seeing the tourists' reaction to this site, she knew she would write an article for a more popular magazine, maybe National Geographic or The Smithsonian?

"Yes, I can introduce Deacon Olympias and explain her importance to women's history. All women's history, regardless of religious background. I'll also produce some PowerPoint presentations showing some of the letters and my translations." Maybe publicizing Olympias' letters would divert attention from what she held in Rome, buying her more time to figure that puzzle out. Or maybe acceptance of her unearthing the letters of Olympias will pave the way to announce her other discoveries.

Sofia turned toward her host. "Āminah, do you have a solicitor we can bring in to help us?"

"I hadn't thought about that. I could speak to my university."

"I suggest we bring in a solicitor not beholden to government or university. We must delay the developers until we know what their sewers will do to the site."

Taşbent excitedly said, "Yes, my family's solicitor. And I'd want to update the patriarch's office as well."

Patriarch Bartholomaios. Sofia was getting used to the idea of his involvement. Should she tell him about her other discoveries soon? She stood and approached the table, located a magnifying glass, and lifted the netting. She delicately picked up one of the larger fragments with long-nosed tweezers and examined it. "Clear strokes. The ink is in such good shape, I'd guess it was made from soot and gum."

"We haven't begun testing yet."

"Is this the first of the parchment fragments?"

"No. This is only from the last couple of days. I've got the rest stored in a temperature-controlled vault."

Sofia turned toward her host. "Good. And I look forward to seeing them." Her phone rang.

"*Yeia sou*." Takis. She listened. Her stomach gripped. "Oh, God. It's all my fault. Is she okay?" She barely heard what Takis was saying, her mind racing. With sweaty, shaking hands, Sofia ended the call.

"Sofia, what's happened?"

"I need to return home right away." Was she the reason Christina's home was broken into? Were they after her, or was this just a coincidence? "A family emergency." She did not want to frighten Taşbent, who might lose her courage if she knew. "I'll call you tomorrow to plan our next steps."

Sofia grabbed her briefcase and slipped out under the tent's flaps. She barely heard Taşbent call after her, "As-salaam." The sun glared. The air was dusty, and she struggled to breathe.

§

THESSALONÍKI

Sofia's taxi swung into the driveway of Christina's house, the head-lights flooding the entrance with harsh light against the black of night. When the cab braked, her head whipped forward and back. Her shoulders had tightened from stress, and her muscles were throbbing now. She knew she would be in pain the following day. Diving out of the vehicle, she ran to the front door, which swung open just as her hands grabbed the handle.

Christina's daughter, with a cranky baby draped, squirming, over her shoulder, greeted her. "Hi, Sof. Saw your headlights and didn't want you to wake mother."

Slipping through the entryway, Sofia caressed the baby's auburn hair and asked with a trembling voice. "How's Christina? Is she okay?"

"Mom interrupted the intruder. She's badly bruised. The doc-tor insisted on a sleeping pill, so she's sleeping soundly." Her cousin turned away and paced, trying to entice her baby to sleep. "It's so frightening. I don't think of this as an area with much crime. But you can talk to her in the morning."

"The police? Did they come?"

Her cousin glanced back. "Yes, they checked the house. The lock to the door near your office was broken." Sofia followed her cousin into the sitting room, her eyes hurriedly scanning the area. "Strange, nothing really taken that we could tell. All the silver, artwork, and antiques were left behind. Even some euros left on mother's desk were undisturbed. The strangest thing was that the intruder was down in the basement, and that's where mother was assaulted."

Sofia felt sick to her stomach.

"What I don't understand, Sofia, is what he was doing there. With all the stuff he could've stolen and didn't, what do you have in your office that he wanted?"

Her cousin's question felt like a sucker punch to the gut.

"Just my boring research." Panic slithered over Sofia.

"Not stealing ancient stuff for museums or private collectors?" Her cousin laughed and then tried to choke it off as the baby began to cry.

A pang that felt like hunger twisted inside her.

"I'm sorry Takis even told you. This could've waited until you returned." Her cousin was rocking the baby. "He said you were in Istanbul. You sure have been traveling a lot lately, especially for someone with no job."

Another left jab.

"Yes, I've been traveling a lot lately with projects I'd hoped would turn into full-time employment. As it stands, I'm probably headed to California." Sofia fought off fatigue. Guilt lodged deep in her gut. Only a very few knew what she was doing down in the basement.

"What's in California?"

"A job paying good money. Any idea who did this? Are the police following up?"

"Oh, I should think so. Takis will be changing locks and repairing the window and door downstairs." Her cousin began humming softly, rocking a baby resisting sleep. "Weird. Takis has been staying here the past few days. Unusual for him to stay put for very long. When this happened, he was off arranging for a security system to be installed. Like he had a premonition or something."

A surge of energy pulsed through Sofia, and she couldn't sit still. She slipped down to the basement to check her office. Flipping on the light, she immediately noticed the contents of her bookcases had been strewn about. She went cold. Damn. Fortunately, her treasure sat in

Rome. She plopped in her chair, feeling both buzzed and exhausted. She was grateful that her stunning discovery was stored in a safe place. But obviously, her nemesis was getting close.

These past days have been so strange. She combed her hair with her fingers, trying to figure out her next steps. Sofia glanced toward her computer station. Something was wrong. Rolling her chair closer, she scanned the surface. Her mail was gone. She opened drawers to find several thumb drives missing. A sinking feeling came over her. What could the bastard learn? Of Andrucci in Bologna and Santa Cecilia in Rome? She felt her chest constrict. Should she warn Andrucci? And tell him what? And Sister Meg? Certainly, she'd better warn Āminah. Her adrenaline disrupted her ability to think clearly.

§

Sofia rose at dawn after a fitful night. Her head felt caught in a vise, and she could barely move her neck and shoulders. While stretching, she noticed someone had cut the lock to her old trunk. She cringed. Nothing to find there, bastard.

Hearing her aunt's voice, Sofia donned a wrap despite tight muscles, grabbed some ibuprofen, and headed downstairs to the veranda. She squinted at the bright morning sun. She winced when her aunt turned her way. Christina's jaw and neck were a deep purple.

"Now, Sofia, dear, please don't look at me like that."

Sofia gently hugged her aunt. "I'm so sorry this happened." She could feel the tears fill her eyes.

"I'm fine, Sofia. Just a bit shaken. But why ever did you cut short your trip to Istanbul?"

"Because you were hurt, and it's my fault." Sofia dropped into a chair and rested her head on her hands.

"How could this possibly be your fault? You take on much too much responsibility for things in life."

"The reason why the intruder didn't steal anything of value—."

The two women heard the front door open, followed by heavy footsteps. Takis called out.

Her aunt stood, "Out here, Takis. On the veranda. Let me brew some coffee."

Sofia just realized how stiffly her aunt was moving, just like herself.

Takis passed through the doorway, followed by a guy in a utility uniform. "How are my two favorite women?" Then her cousin cringed at the sight of their aunt's face.

"I'll be fine. You two worry too much."

"This is Marinos. He's here to install a new security system. I'm sorry we couldn't get out here yesterday."

"I'm making coffee. Join us, dear?"

Takis kissed his aunt's cheek and announced coffee was on him. He headed toward the kitchen. Her aunt turned toward Sofia, favoring her right shoulder and neck.

"How was Istanbul? You're meeting with Professore Taşbent?" Both women glanced toward the kitchen and all the noise Takis was making. Sofia cringed, her head still pounding. "You look so worried, Sofia. It didn't go well?"

"Better than expected. But you've been hurt, Christina. I feel terrible about what happened to you." Sofia attempted to stretch her taut muscles.

"Dear heart, why do you think this was your fault?"

Why did her aunt minimize the seriousness of what happened? "Because I'm the reason this break-in happened."

"No, Sofia—."

Takis returned with a carafe and cups. He poured a cup for each.

"The thief was after what I took from Esfigmenou."

Her aunt sighed. "I guess that makes sense. I had warned you, Sofia. These men are hard and play dirty."

"I know, but I didn't think they'd come after me. I didn't think they'd figure out who I was."

"Oh, honey. You so don't understand how well you're known in certain circles. All they had to do was figure out who was working on early Christian women, and your name is everywhere."

Sofia gazed out across the veranda and the view beyond. Guilt threatened to overwhelm her, and she had many decisions ahead of her. Taking a deep breath and turning back toward her aunt, she said. "While working in the archives at the university, I had a near encounter with the monk who chased me to the boat. I think he, or someone he knows, traced me here and broke in, looking for what I took. But what he wanted isn't stored here."

Takis interrupted. "This is getting serious, Sof. I warned you that Esfigmenou was filled with crazy guys."

"I know, Takis. And until today, I would've said the risk was worth it, especially after my trip to Istanbul." Sofia struggled to contain her tears. "But I never meant to endanger either of you."

The three sat in silence. Takis fidgeted in his seat.

"I cannot let this go on, and I think Taşbent has shown me my next step." Sofia sensed a calm and peace within herself. "I need to move the scroll to Istanbul."

Confusion swept across her aunt's face. "Not Greece?"

"No. My discoveries wouldn't be safe here in Greece."

"Just what are you thinking, Sofia?"

"To ask the patriarch's protection." Sofia told them about Taşbent's dig.

"My goodness, Sofia. Even I know this is astonishing." Was her aunt smiling or grimacing from pain?

"You think the patriarch would help us?" Takis made no attempt to hide the grin on his face.

Us? Sofia smiled. Her cousin seemed to be taking some ownership of this. "Taşbent seemed to think so. He's provided support and protection for the dig. Once I figure out where the money will come from, I'll need to leave for Rome immediately and arrange to move them. I don't want Sister Meg to get hurt next." Sofia cringed again at the sight of her aunt's bruised face.

"How could they make the connection?"

Anxiety twisted in Sofia's chest. "Because the thief stole my thumb drives and even my mail. He'll learn who was testing the vellum and inks."

Takis pulled out his smartphone and began tapping. "Then I guess we leave for Rome on the next possible flight."

THIRTY-SIX

Kostas stood before the marble sculpture of Saint Cecilia, hands clasped and head bent as if in prayer. His eyes monitored the surroundings while listening attentively for movement. The nuns had finished chanting their prayers about twenty minutes ago, and the tourists were departing. He heard the guard, with a fistful of keys, begin the methodical process of locking gates and doors for the night. Glancing around, he noted that the guard's back was to him, so he edged around the statue and jumped over the low gate leading to the area below the high altar. He descended the steep circular marble stairs and slipped silently into the monastery complex.

Straight ahead was an ornate gate that led to the site of Saint Cecilia's family home, chapel, and the original monastery. Kostas pulled on tight-fitting leather gloves, popped the lock, slipped through, and closed the gate behind him. The shaft and grill above allowed natural light and fresh air to filter through the passage. He flipped on his penlight, its dancing shadows revealing stone-hewn walls and crossed under arched supports that cast dark shadows on the uneven ground. The ruins of the saint's house and remnants of the original chapel lay before him on either side.

Passing through the site, Kostas turned right into the old underground corridor and stepped softly through the dancing shadows. When he came to a solid stone wall, he bore left. Like many old monasteries and castles he had been in, this one contained ruins of old corridors and tunnels. Thus far, each wall and room were as he had studied it in the architectural plans. No undocumented changes.

Kostas, hearing voices, turned off his penlight and stepped back into a shadowed corner. Animated women's voices speaking in Swahili. He had assumed nuns went to bed after their last prayers like his cousin did. Did he have a problem? He remained quiet and still until the voices faded before moving.

A few more paces ahead and to his left, Kostas reached the first doorway to one of the *auras*, large enough to contain a library or archives if the nuns had yet to make any changes. And if this room did not yield what he sought, another aura was just beyond.

With more difficulty, Kostas picked the lock and slipped through, closing the door behind him. The sharp beam of his penlight cast upon neat rows of metal shelving. A wooden staircase that he assumed led to the main floor above divided the room. Beyond the stairs, the dancing shadow of his penlight revealed the tops of still more rows of metal shelving. He noted several long worktables to his left with a half dozen tall metal filing cabinets.

Stepping across the room for a closer inspection, he noticed that each row of shelving had a handle, no noisy cranking mechanism, to move one row—which would slow his search down. He sighed, realizing that each bookcase contained identical gray boxes, the kind he had seen in other archives, just like the one where the old book he had retrieved had been stored.

Kostas pulled the first shelving unit to expose the next area and began his methodical search. He knew the parchment was at least two meters long, so most of these boxes were too short. Using his penlight, he peered behind each row of boxes in case it was hidden.

A half-hour later, Kostas had finished his search of the near side of the room and moved beyond the staircase to begin his task on the other side. As he did so, the door at the top of the wooden staircase opened. He darted behind a row of shelving, away from the stairs, crouching close to the far corner wall.

"Let me know when Sofia is ready," a woman said.

Sofia? Was Papandréou here? The lights in the room came on, too bright for his comfort. He heard the scuffing of what he presumed was a stool, the power of a computer turning on, and the shuffling of what was probably books. Then, a voice from above called out. "Sister Meg."

"Yes?"

Kostas heard muffled voices, unable to hear what was being said. Odd, Kostas thought, she was speaking in English, not Italian. And why aren't they asleep?

"Great, I'll be up," the woman's voice said.

Then he heard footsteps fading with distance. The lights were left on, and the door above open. Waiting for a discreet length of time, he stepped out and scanned the shelving as quickly as possible, keeping an eye on the doorway above.

Kostas had to make a quick decision. Should he remain and search for the scroll now, risking exposure? Should he wait here until he can continue his work in peace? Maybe it would do the stuff-shirt monks some good to let this scroll get out into the public. Clearly,

Papandréou placed a considerable value on the scroll as it took a lot of courage to do what she did. He hated to leave a job unfinished.

Glancing across the wooden staircase, Kostas noticed several rectangular, waist-high metal cases on wheels tucked behind a long wooden table and file cabinets. Studying it, he realized that its five drawers were just the right size for the scroll.

He stepped across the cavernous room to take a quick look. Carefully pulling open one drawer, he noticed the cabinet was refrigerated and released a wave of brisk air. Fine silk netting covered parchment underneath. Lifting the net, he saw a sheaf of lambskin with the same odd script he had studied on his laptop's screen. This had to be it. Hearing footsteps and distant voices, Kostas closed the drawer and slipped through the nearby doorway into a corridor beyond. He stood with his back to the stone wall and steadied his breathing, listening to the sound of footsteps descending the wooden stairs, muffled by the cool stone of walls and floor.

Three pairs of feet descended the stairs, then the same woman's voice. "And Āminah has been able to confirm that it's Deacon Olympias' monastery that she's been uncovering? Not some palace or whatever deniers have been claiming all these years?"

Who is Āminah? Was she here? A new woman's voice. "I hope we'll more than succeed. I'm still thinking about how to present these discoveries to the academic world. But her connection to Patriarch Bartholomaios has given me a way forward. He has the global clout we need, and Āminah has an impressive vault in her office and university security to back her up. This seems to be the right direction for me to take."

Was this Sofia? Father Yeorgi told him his nemesis' voice was low for a woman but didn't mention that her voice sounded like liquid silk.

Now, some guy asked, "So where is this scroll that's got the under-world chasing you, Sof?"

"Let me show you," Sofia said.

Lighting moved about in the *aura*, and then he heard one of the long trays being opened. "Meg, you did a great job. The vellum is relaxing evenly," Sofia said.

The guy interrupted. "Wow, look at those bright colors."

"This is an early Ge'ez text from Ethiopia, in East Africa," Sofia explained.

"I don't understand what you just said."

"'Ge'ez' is like 'Orthodox,' and Christianity arrived in East Africa about the same time as it did in Greece. There were lots of Jews in Ethiopia like there were in Greece."

He heard two-wheeled stools squeak while being moved. The first drawer was closed, and another opened.

The guy whistled. "Do you know what it says?"

"Yes, I'm mostly finished with my translations. Dottore Andrucci has completed his first round of tests on the parchment. Next, we compare the results with other Ethiopian texts."

"Why?" the guy asked.

"Because what it says has never been seen in a surviving manuscript before. Maybe other books like this had once existed but have been destroyed or just lost."

"So, this thing is old? Like the other stuff you were looking at?"

"Yes," Sofia answered. "And some people won't believe this is real because it's in good shape. We expect old stuff to decay."

"Did you know that this was at Esfigmenou? Is that why you insist-ed on going there? Risking your life, by the way? That important to you?"

"Yes, Takis, it was worth it to me. But no, I didn't know I'd stumble into this."

So, the guy's name is Takis. Heard or saw that name when he ransacked Papandréou's office. They're somehow related.

"Takis," the nun interrupted, "you did a great service helping Sofia.

Kostas heard the shelf slide back in its place, and then he heard another shelf open. Apparently, this woman took more than Father Yeorgi told him.

"This looks different," Takis said.

Sofia answered, "You're right. Not from Ethiopia."

"Not Greek, either."

"So, you've noticed. Be careful, you might be tempted to give up horticulture for archeology," Sofia teased.

Horticulture? Is this the guy growing weed on Mount Athos? He stifled a laugh.

"So, who made this?"

"It's from the old empire of Armenia. And since it's essentially Syriac, I'm guessing before 500 CE."

The guy whistled. "I thought the Ottoman Empire destroyed everything of theirs."

"This survived. Somehow."

A clank, a thud, a meow, followed by the thumping of the cat's paws. Kostas breathed deeply to steady his nerves.

"Santa Chiara, behave yourself," the nun chastised the cat. "Thinks she's the abbess, I'm afraid."

Sofia laughed and said, "I've brought some special archival fabric to roll these in, along with several leather tubes that we'll slip these parchments into. Āminah came through with paperwork from her university to authorize my carrying these scrolls in case Italian security suddenly decides to do its job. Our flight is tomorrow early afternoon. I need to get this packed first thing in the morning."

Another university was involved now? He heard the cat jump up on a table, scurry across, and jump back down. Then, the cat started sniffing in his direction.

"Do you really think these scrolls are safer in Istanbul? Certainly, the patriarch could be an important ally. Maybe Taşbent as well."

"I think the creeps following me are more afraid of the patriarch than anyone in Italy."

Kostas smiled. Too bad the patriarch will never have an opportunity to view these. Still, the Patriarch's very name rankled his stuff-shirt cousin.

The nun spoke up. "We could call a press conference and announce your discovery to the world. No security like publicity."

The damn cat had passed through the entryway, approaching where he stood. He moved further into the darkness. The cat meowed.

"Santa Chiara, get back in here. No more mice hunting tonight," the nun called out.

Some muffled talk, then he heard Sofia say. "I will, but in Istanbul. Along with the patriarch."

Wow, this woman was serious, letting the world know what she had done. Wouldn't that rankle his cousin.

"The Patriarch doesn't have the money to build proper facilities, does he?"

Sofia answered. "No, he probably doesn't. And none of us knows anyone with piles of money that they'd share."

"Sofia, people with money love to have their name associated with a stunning discovery like this. I can think of a few. And I suspect Brother Makarios would also offer some leads for moneyed people."

Takis interrupted. "I still haven't figured out what's so astonishing about what you've got here. Why are these monks so afraid of you, Sof?"

The nun responded. "What little I've heard from Sofia says these scrolls will be politically explosive. Good for most of us. Threatening to some."

"Good, Sof. I think I like that. But sister is right. You need to stay safe."

Sofia sighed. "I'm not sure I care anymore. About me, that is. The Patriarch has both the Greek and Turkish police at his disposal. I want reputable scholars to see this. I want the debate to begin."

THIRTY-SEVEN

ARCHIVES, SANTA CECILIA ABBEY

Kostas scrambled to think through his options. He would need to grab the scroll tonight and get out of Italy right away. And he would find a safer way to deliver it to his cousin. Too many people involved for his comfort. His back had stiffened, and he feared a spasm if he had to stand against the cold stone much longer.

"Sofia, you're on the verge of something big," the nun said. "Your world will never be the same. Forget old ways of thinking. These scrolls will speak for themselves. You're wise to invite our colleagues to spend years arguing over this. And have fun doing so."

"Maybe it's time to tell the truth about where I found this," Sofia said.

A laugh. "Sofia, when was the last time a woman was arrested for camping on Mount Athos?"

Kostas smiled. Feisty women.

"Well, I suppose I could be the first. But I'd use my trial to challenge how Greeks treat women."

He heard drawers open, but he also heard swishing sounds like fabric rustling. The three talked quietly as these sounds persisted. Were they removing it now? He had to grab these scrolls and get out right away. His stomach gripped, and he began the quiet mantra he used to razor-sharpen his focus before any big job. Could he overcome all three of them? Then Kostas heard footsteps taking the wooden stairs up.

Sofia said, "I'll get the leather tubes to pack these properly, and then we'll leave you in peace." She laughed, "For a while, anyway."

He heard footsteps going up the wooden stairs but could only make out two sets. Someone stayed behind? For several minutes, Kostas remained motionless, his back against the stone wall, concentrating on the task at hand. Eventually, someone walked away from him. The footsteps grew distant. The nun? He couldn't wait any longer. Pulling out his penlight, he reentered the room as he moved toward the metal cases and scanned the room for anything to carry the vellum. He realized they had removed some of the scrolls, which were rolled up in fabric. Was this everything?

Kostas checked all the drawers, which proved empty. Grabbing a swath of cloth, he wrapped the scrolls inside and picked up the cylindrical package, cradling it in his forearm.

"Is that you, Sofia?" The nun seemed to be in a room beyond. More archives? The door above opened.

Kostas froze. Overhead, lights were switched on, and footsteps descended. He would need to pass before the staircase if he ran for the corridor. There was no exit behind him. Scanning the room, he moved behind the closest section of shelving units and near the corner of two walls, crouching and holding the bundle.

Peering through the shelving, he could see the nun who appeared to be searching the workbench and around a computer station. "Sofia, where are you? Why aren't you answering me?"

Kostas felt something brush against his leg and, in surprise, bumped against the shelving. He saw the four-legged devil, a brown mackerel tabby, dart off.

"Santa Chiara, are you causing trouble again?" the nun asked.

Kostas could see the nun step toward the cat. Peering around, she called, "Who's there? Sister Redemptrix? Scholastica?"

The nun glanced in his direction and then turned away. He breathed deeply. She picked up a cell phone and punched a key.

"Takis. We may have company down here. Call the guards." Her voice echoed off the stone walls.

Kostas remained still with heart racing. Noticing the nun walking down an aisle between two rows of metal shelving near him, he began walking in the opposite direction, hoping to clear the corner as she turned down the next aisle of shelves.

"Whoever you are, you won't be getting very far," the nun said.

He detected a quaver in her voice. When she glanced around the far end of the shelving, he moved around his end and proceeded along the wall.

The nun had not turned the corner. Instead, she had stopped. They made eye contact.

"Hey!" she shouted.

He began running alongside the wall, gripping the scroll. Kostas was seized by powerful hands, slowing his pace.

"You aren't going anywhere," the nun said, her breath heaving.

He swung his free elbow at her. She let out an involuntary gasp but still held her grip. He punched her in the sternum, his full weight behind his fist. He heard her slam against the stone wall as he passed through the doorway and turned a hard left into the underground corridor.

With every step, the corridor grew darker. His heart pounded, and he gulped air, trying to stay focused. His shoulder brushed the stone wall. Kostas slowed and scanned the walls and corridor with his penlight. He heard voices echoing behind him, and he began running again, his footsteps ricocheting off the stone walls. His light cast eerie shadows off the stone and metal sconce casings. He turned right, heading back toward the saint's home.

The glow of candles greeted him to his right. He never slowed to see if anyone was in the small chapel praying. Feet pounding on the stone, he reached the access door beyond and pulled on the handle. The door creaked open, resisting his efforts. Footsteps echoed behind him. Passing through, he pressed forward, scanning the wall to his left until he located the emergency door beyond.

His shoulder pressed against the red emergency exit bar. Kostas forced the door open, the siren sounding as he passed through and the fresh warmth of evening brushing his face. As he bore a hard left up the utility service alley, he heard cursing behind him, his pursuer getting closer. Ahead lay the gate and his freedom. Reaching the top, Kostas leaped onto the first bar and grabbed the next one with his free hand. Hands slammed down on his shoulders from behind, the fingers digging into his flesh with a painful grip. Agony shot through his muscles, leaving him unable to move his arms. He was thrown around, stumbling to keep his feet under him. He stared into the face of a tall, skinny Greek.

Kostas dropped his prize, and as his pursuer reached for the bag, he kicked the bastard in the stomach, hearing a sharp intake of breath and a grunt, and his pursuer dropped to his knees. As Kostas reached for the bagged scroll, the Greek grabbed his arms and threw him against the gate. A left hook sent his head into the bars. He saw stars.

The Greek turned and ran with the scroll. Kostas decided not to pursue the bastard. He wasn't going to risk prison. He scrambled up the gate, swinging over and down. Kostas ran and never looked back.

§

Sofia ran to Sister Meg, sprawled on the floor, her head at an awkward angle, her eyes vacant and unblinking. A small amount of blood oozed onto the stone. Sofia gently moved Sister Meg onto her lap, cradling her. Sofia began shaking, and tears flowed. She rocked back and forth, "I'm so sorry. I'm so sorry I did this to you." She began chanting in a low, soft voice, *Hágios ho Theós, Hágios iskhūrós, Hágios āthánatos, eléēson hēmâs.*

Sofia was barely aware that her cousin had returned. He knelt beside her and put his hand near Sister Meg's nose. Checking for breath?

He sighed, deep from his gut. Sofia felt his arm around her. He joined in chanting, *Holy God, holy and mighty, holy immortal one, have mercy upon us."*

"Sofia, this isn't your fault. That guy's a *bástardos*. And we'll find him. He won't get away with this."

Disbelief nearly overwhelmed her. Sister Meg's head had hit the stone at full force. Death was instant.

She didn't know how much time passed. But she heard the drawer to the refrigerator door open and close.

She barely registered that officials had entered the space, escorted by one of the nuns. Sofia resisted when the *medici* gently moved her aside and lifted Sister Meg onto the *barella*. A sob erupted from deep within as the *medici* covered Sister Meg with a sheet. Several nuns gathered around the *barilla,* one holding a lit candle, and began to chant,

Possano gli angeli portarti in paradiso.
Vengano I martiri ad accoglierti nel tuo cammino,
E condurti nella città santa . . .

She held onto the railing until the *barella* was lifted into the *ambul anza*.The two were escorted to an *aura*. Takis sat next to Sofia, holding her as the polizia interviewed the two of them, creating a sketch of the murderer. Waves of anger swelled up. She could barely focus on their incessant questions. Why aren't they out there grabbing the animal? Her jaw clenched, and her nostrils flared. Bless Takis; he did most of the talking. First, her aunt, and now her mentor. Who would be next? How does she stop this madness? She needed to call Taşbent as soon as she could.

The polizia asked what the guy might've stolen. Rare books and artwork? Takis deferred to the nuns to respond to those questions.

Later, the community gathered and insisted Sofia and Takis join them. The nuns were distraught. Sofia explained what they had been storing that the thief was after. She assumed Sister Meg's assailant was either a monk of Esfigmenou or someone they hired. After some silence, Sister Scholastica made Sofia promise to make these scrolls, whatever they contained, public. Let their abbess' death be for good. The sisters then began sharing stories of Sister Meg, and the nuns wanted to hear more of Sofia's history with their abbess. She talked more than she had expected, tears flowing nevertheless. And several times, she found herself laughing, the nuns as well.

Sofia did not sleep that night. Give up? No. She was more determined than ever to announce her discoveries to the world. Damn, the monks at Esfigmenou.

The following day, eyes swollen from crying, waves of anger sweeping through her, Sofia called Taşbent, hands shaking, and told her what had happened.

"Your Sister Meg is dead?" Taşbent's warm voice exuded shock and compassion. "This is terrible. Are you safe?"

Sofia's stomach gripped like a vise. "I never thought that they'd kill someone. These monks must be truly frightened by these scrolls. I cannot risk your life. I'll need to figure out another place to store these. Sister Meg was in contact with someone at the Vatican libraries. Maybe they'd take them."

"No, Sofia. Bring them here as we planned. We'll contact the Patriarch's office and get him involved."

"I don't want to put you in any danger, Āminah. I'll try to find another way."

"No, Sofia. Bring these scrolls. I'll have security at the airport, and you will stay with my family. We'll place them in the vault, and I'll notify security at the university."

"But –"

"I'll contact the Patriarch's office and arrange a meeting. And our solicitor will be involved as well. I think your Sister Meg would want you to be bold. You honor her by moving forward."

The two women wrapped up their phone conversation. Sofia would remain in Rome until after Sister Meg's funeral. Takis rebooked their flights.

§

An exhausted and numb Sofia and a bruised Takis arrived at Atatürk Airport and claimed their luggage. Approaching customs, she saw Taşbent waiting for them near a customs agent, accompanied by a distinguished silver-haired Turk in an expensive-looking gray suit. And a security guard as well. Taşbent waived them over, and passports were surrendered for scrutiny. Sofia stood holding the leather tube with her precious discovery. Would she be required to let them inspect its contents? To her surprise, Sofia and Takis had their passports back and were allowed through. No inspection.

They were ushered into Taşbent's Mercedes with its uniformed driver and whisked onto the highway. "Āminah, how did you get us through customs? Who was that gentleman?"

"He is from the Department of Antiquities and trusts my occasional but odd requests."

"Thank you for all your help, Āminah. I'm afraid I'm now putting you in danger, but I can't let these discoveries disappear again."

Sitting in the front seat, Takis turned toward the women in the back, a pained grimace on his face. "*Mou oraios*, it's not your fault. None of this is your fault. None of us, Sister Meg included, ever expected anyone to die. And if you stop now, those damned monks will have won."

Sofia noticed Takis gazing around at the traffic. Were we being followed?

"It's my fault for ever involving her or her abbey. I put them all in danger. I just didn't expect that crazy monk to find us." As the numbing effects of shock wore off, her stomach gripped, shooting painful spasms.

Taşbent looked her way, gently placing her hand on Sofia's arm. "You were right to contact me. I don't know what you've found, but we resist if someone will kill for it." She smiled. "I do not doubt that this Sister Meg was so proud of her former student. You allowed her an experience so few of us who teach ever enjoy. To see one of our students succeed beyond our own accomplishments."

"I do look forward to showing you what the scrolls contain." Sofia's hands shook. She stared out the window, struggling to think.

Taşbent squeezed her forearm. "Did you find these along with the letters of Olympias?"

Sofia felt a wall of sleepiness heading her way. "No. At another monastery on Agio Oros called Esfigmenou. It's been under siege by the Greek police."

Taşbent whistled. "I've read about this in the news. How did you ever get in?"

Sofia told her as the Mercedes exited from the shimmering waterfront, took a roundabout, and merged aggressively into city traffic. They traveled through old Istanbul with horns blaring, thick smog, drivers gesturing, glaring neon lights, and carts attempting to dart between cars.

"Will you be in trouble with your religious authorities when they find out?" Taşbent asked, concern woven into her soft voice.

Sofia felt another rush of exhaustion. "I'll know the answer to that when I reveal my discoveries to the Patriarch. At least I hope we can get him to come. The most controversial scroll will challenge him, but I trust that he seeks truth and integrity over religious politics."

Takis turned her way. "*Mou oraios*, everything is political. You know politics is a major Greek sport. Don't back down now."

Their car began to ascend a steep hill toward the university. Sofia thought of Father Theodor. Might he be an ally?

Leaving their luggage in the trunk of the Mercedes, Sofia carried the leather tube, Takis close beside her, as the three, accompanied by security, walked under a canopy of trees toward Taşbent's office. Arriving at heavy wooden doors, she pulled out a ring of keys and unbolted the door. Once inside, Taşbent rebolted the door. Flipping on light switches, her host led them up a set of stairs and along the corridor to her office. Sofia noticed that Taşbent locked her outer door after they entered. Taşbent's precautions comforted her. Their host flipped on more lights, and she and Takis followed the professor into the workroom they had visited before. Sofia saw the vault across the room from the doorway.

Spread out on the table were the maps of the archeological dig, which Sofia and Taşbent rolled up and set aside. Sofia put the leather satchel on a chair, unfastened it, pulled out the wrapped bundle, and placed it on the table. Taşbent donned reading glasses. With Takis bending over her shoulder, Sofia and Taşbent began unrolling the silk cloth, revealing the layers of parchment. Sofia sighed. She had been worried that Meg's killer had damaged the vellum. Her heart ached. She had preferred the scroll be damaged than her friend dead.

Taşbent followed Sofia's lead as she placed the scroll and calfskin pages in the proper order. Taşbent whistled. "Sofia, this is incredible. These scrolls are in amazing condition. One is clearly Ge'ez. Am I right in guessing this other one is from Syria or Armenia?"

"Armenia. I've completed my translations. Āminah, even I found what these say to be rather astonishing. But the longer I sat with their words, the more sense it made to me. The women's voices in these scrolls fill many gaps in our understanding of the early Christian movement. And given the other fragments I saw on Mount Athos, I was left with even more questions until I stumbled into these." Sofia sighed, numbed with grief.

"Deacon Olympias?" Taşbent gazed at her with both curiosity and compassion.

"Yes, but more. I had stumbled into an assortment of fragments in different libraries. I don't understand why the monks have been hiding all this over the centuries. And yet, I do. This one scroll can potentially change many of our assumptions about Christianity and yet can enliven and deepen our tradition."

"Wow," Takis exclaimed. "All that? And I don't even understand what you're talking about."

Sofia smiled. "I'll make sure you do before this is all over."

Taşbent examined the vellum. "This was no commoner's copy."

"Commoner's copy?" Takis asked, holding one of the engineer's lamps at a helpful angle.

"Yes. This is an exceptional quality of calfskin. The best was saved for special royal documents and official histories for the Imperial Library. For Christians, Jews, and Muslims, copies of sacred texts meant for public proclamation used the best vellum available," Taşbent said.

Sofia stood up and stretched her back. "That's what I was thinking. This is a copy meant for a special client who understood its importance and took good care of it."

Taşbent looked at her. "And someone did."

THIRTY-EIGHT

U NIVERSITY OF ISTANBUL
Sofia slept late, arising near noon—her neck, shoulders, and head throbbing. Too much was happening too fast. And she still struggled to grasp that Sister Meg was gone, leaving her with a cavernous emptiness. Where was Sister Meg's killer? Had he followed them here? Her nemesis, Father Yeorgi, must be terrified of the world learning of her discoveries.

Sofia donned a raw silk, royal blue suit, hoping to exude professionalism and authority. Taşbent trusted this archpriest, personal aide to Patriarch Bartholomaios, but her stomach still gripped with anxiety. The Greek Orthodox Church had long been known for being stalwart and unmoving. But this Patriarch had shown himself far more open, and she had lauded his defense of the environment. Then, she had met some monks on Agio Óros who seemed open to the possibility of change. A taxi delivered her and Takis to Taşbent's office.

Passing through the doorway, Sofia heard the thud of the door and the bolt's lock. Takis made a great security guard. The two women hugged. "Your face is sad, Sofia. Were you able to sleep?"

"Somewhat." Takis handed her a cup of coffee. Food looked nauseating to her, but coffee might clear her head.

Taşbent invited them to sit. "I spoke with Father Andreas this morning, and he should be here within the hour. Apparently, he has his own news about battles with our Antiquities Authorities and the dig near Hagia Sophia."

Sofia's stomach fluttered. Revealing her scrolls was risky, but she had to begin somewhere.

"Who? What?" Takis spoke through a mouthful of pastry.

"Father Andreas has been my contact with Patriarch Bartholomaios' office regarding the dig at Hagia Sophia. He is the most effective person to bring Sofia's discoveries to the attention of the Patriarch." Smiling, Taşbent picked up a wad of keys. "And Sofia, we have an appointment with our solicitor tomorrow. We'll add the challenges around your discoveries to our meeting."

Taşbent's secretary called down and announced the arrival of Father Andreas as a tall, thin priest with black shoulder-length hair, bright blue eyes, and a thick but groomed beard swept through the doorway, his sostikon flowing loosely about him. Sofia struggled to recall why he looked so familiar. Taşbent introduced them. The priest smiled at her with a mischievous grin.

Sofia said. "We've met before, but I'm struggling to remember where."

"The Balkans. Your work reclaiming and preserving manuscripts at Kruševac. I recall that you took on the United Nations and several governmental authorities trying to claim ownership of the nun's property."

Takis smiled. "An adventure you forgot to include me in?"

"That was Naupara Monastery. I'll remind you later, Takis." Returning her gaze to the priest, Sofia asked. "You know Brother Makarios, don't you?"

Father Andreas sat and accepted coffee and pastry, skillfully balancing the small plate on his knee. "Of course. Doesn't he know everyone?" He smiled. "But the patriarch's office appreciated how you defended our nuns and their heritage."

Sitting, Sofia felt her face grow warm. This guy knew of her work. He knew Brother Makarios. He had been aiding Taşbent with the dig. An ally in the Patriarch's office? She would never have thought that possible a few months ago.

"Āminah, you've caused some consternation with the Antiquities Authorities. They've been receiving phone calls and emails from an interesting assortment of women from America." Father Andreas smiled. "Enough that they've put a halt on closing your dig while you present your case to them. What have you unearthed?"

"Sofia may have found the evidence to support my claim that the site is Deacon Olympias' monastery."

Father Andreas looked her way. Sofia calmed her breathing and gripped her coffee cup. "The letters of Olympias to John Chrysostom. I've been pursuing them for years. I suspected they were in the libraries on Mount Athos. And they are."

Father Andreas whistled. "After all these centuries? I didn't realize the university stumbled into anything like this."

"They didn't, Father. They're only interested in the illuminated manuscripts and liturgical texts. I found them."

The priest's eyebrows shot up, surprise on his face. "You? How?"

Ignoring his uncomfortable question, she responded. "Father Theodor at Hagia Theotokos held some of her letters off in a mostly unused part of his monastery library, complete with dirt floors and walls. Apparently, he thought others knew of the letter's existence. He is convinced that several other monasteries also hold some of them. I am awaiting digital copies once he locates them. However, I've translated the letters I have, and they fit in with Chrysostom's letters. I sent fibers from several of them to a colleague at the University of Bologna. He places the fibers around the eighth century CE."

"Before the monks arrived at Agio Óros?"

Sofia nodded. "My best guess is that Deacon Olympias' successors, when driven from their monastery to expand Hagia Sophia, eventually sent the letters to the monks for protection." How she wished those venerable women had held on to them. These letters were women's heritage, after all.

The priest was studying her. "Makes sense. We've only had Chrysostom's letters to her, so why the silence all these centuries? I find it hard to grasp that her letters have been on Mount Athos all these centuries, and no one said anything. Surely they're not all that controversial?"

"That depends on one's perspective. The letters will bring up some sensitive subjects, but I think Christianity will be able to handle this."

Takis interjected. "What problems, Sof?"

"The usual. Power, money, governments interfering in matters of faith, and the place of women in the church. Olympias was busy defending Chrysostom to the Imperial powers and reminded them of their corruption."

Sofia watched the expression on the archpriests' face grow pensive.

"Do we need more trouble now?"

"This kind of 'trouble' would be healthy for us and maybe make Christianity more relevant to my generation. The debate would draw their interest."

Father Andreas seemed hesitant. "Maybe –"

"Scholars need to see them."

"Sofia will oversee the preservation and translation of the fragments we've unearthed at Hagia Sophia," Taşbent said.

Sofia smiled. If only the two women could find the money to provide herself with a salary. "Father Andreas, Āminah invited you here at my request. I've put her in an awkward position, and I'm asking for your support. I'd like to show you some scrolls I've discovered," Sofia said.

"Olympias?" Father Andreas stood and followed the women to the floor below where the vault was located.

Opening the vault, the two women brought out the scrolls and parchment pieces. As they completed unrolling the raw silk, using leather-bound weights to gently hold the vellum open, Sofia moved to the opposite side of the table and faced the priest. The room became quiet as he studied her discoveries. Finally, Father Andreas looked across at her.

"I have digitized copies of the pieces of Olympias' letters. This piece reads:

> "I value your concern for my state of mind. The second trial, if possible, was more draining than the first. And I admit I am exhausted with my efforts to bring you home, the continued lies of Prefect Optatus's people, and the suffering I witness among my sisters. Your letters are encouraging, but I find myself burdened under a tyranny of despair..."

"I cannot endure Constantinople with your continued absence. I am continually pressured to support your nemesis, Archbishop Arsacius. I am concerned for the well-being of my beloved community of sisters. I have put my kinswoman Marina in charge of the monastery and am departing for Nicomedia with deaconess Pentadia. Maybe there I will find peace.... I find myself praying for release from this earthly life. . ."

Heavy silence draped over the room. His cheeks warmed. Father Andreas responded. "This is like hearing a voice from the past. I don't know what to say."

"The originals are scattered around Mount Athos, and I don't know if I have them all."

Pointing to the shorter parchment, Father Andreas said. "This appears to be Armenian. A rare example if it's authentic." Turning and pointing to the longer piece, "And this is Ge'ez. You've translated these, I assume."

Sofia nodded. "I have copies of my rough translations for you. With the meltdown of the economy in Greece and the rising demand for old manuscripts on the black market, I couldn't trust the security there. I actually took these to the Abbey of Santa Cecilia in Rome."

"Why Rome?"

"My dissertation advisor was abbess there. I knew she'd keep them preserved in a secure place while I arranged testing and figured out where we could store them. I hadn't met Āminah yet otherwise I would've come straight here." Sofia caught a near sob in her throat. "Sister Meg died protecting these."

"What? Who?"

Sofia explained what had happened.

"That's terrible. Black marketeers?"

"No, Father. The polizei are still investigating, but the assailant was trying to take these back on behalf of the monks at Esfigmenou."

"Esfigmenou? How could they possibly be involved in your work?" His cheeks took on the rosy heat of anger. His gaze returned to the vellum. "Just where did you find these?"

"Let's return to my office and let Sofia explain," Taşbent said.

Returning to Taşbent's sitting area. Sofia snatched a pastry and refilled her cup with steaming coffee. She was stalling, and yet she wanted to get this over with. She suspected the Patriarch was not going to enjoy hearing about all this. Maybe Father Andreas will decide to be discreet and not give him all the details. Maybe.

Sofia looked at Taşbent and Takis, then at Father Andreas. She couldn't read his body language. She could hear Brother Makarios describe him as "relaxed formal" and not the "stiff formal" of too many of their British colleagues.

She began. Father Andreas remained in his "relaxed formal" throughout the telling of her story. His eyes bored into her, and his countenance expressed concern. He occasionally glanced at Takis until she mentioned "Esfigmenou," and his back stiffened. "You entered Esfigmenou? That's crazy." His words like daggers.

"That's what I told her, but I'm afraid my adventurous cousin suffers the family 'crazy' gene just like me." Takis grinned.

"You could've been hurt. Those monks are ruthless. Anywhere else you would've been escorted off the peninsula, but—"

Sofia cringed. "Yes, I know. But everything I heard among the monks on Agio Óros told me I'd find a treasure there. And I did."

Father Andreas appeared to struggle absorbing all that Sofia was telling him.

"You know you violated sacred space. It's their home, and it's how they choose to live. But how ever did you manage to deceive so many monks? Or did they know and accept your presence?"

"I was with her, watching her back." Takis smiled in her direction, taking another pastry.

Setting her cup down, Sofia explained how she prepared herself and mostly stayed out of everyone's way. "The only librarian I talked with was Father Theodor, who was helpful. I suspect —"

Father Andreas laughed. "Oh, he knew. Father Theodor is quite renowned. You hadn't heard of him at the University of Thessaloniki?

"Only the archivist, Georgios Hatzidakis, had mentioned his name." Not my university anymore, she reminded herself.

Father Andreas gazed at her with animated eyes.

"His Holiness probably won't condone what I did."

"I should think not. And he'd be upset over the death of your friend. But, despite the monks' claim that no woman has ever entered Agio Óros for the last thousand years, that's just propaganda."

Takis grinned. "That's what I told Sofia."

Father Andreas continued. "Some women explorers of the Victorian era wandered onto Agio Óros and even stayed at one of the guesthouses. During Greece's Civil War of the early 1960s, the monks housed families."

"Then why couldn't someone like me, a scholar, work in the libraries there?" Sofia was nearly shouting. Anger and pain pierced her heart and went deep into her soul.

Father Andreas sighed. "You already know the answer to that. It's their home, and they make their own rules. Only with schismatics on Agio Óros, like the monks at Esfigmenou, will His Holiness intervene."

"That needs to change." Sofia's gut twisted deep within. "It's wrong that scholars like me cannot conduct research there."

The priest gazed intently at Sofia. "Other ways to allow women to access the libraries are already underway. You must've noticed the graduate students digitalizing manuscripts. Be patient."

"That's not enough. Only someone with my training and background would've noticed and appreciated what I saw. Even Father Theodor didn't think to make Olympias' letters known." Her anger roiled; her nails cut into the palms of her hand. She stretched her fingers, attempting to calm down.

He sighed. "Your friend, this Sister Meg, her death is tragic, Sofia. The Patriarch will hear about this. Do you think her assailant was one of the monks from Esfigmenou? Many have been evicted, but we cannot watch their movements."

Sofia felt tears brim her eyes.

Takis put his arm on Sofia. "The intruder was a professional, moved too quickly for a monk."

"My guess is that Father Yeorgi hired the guy to retrieve what I'd taken."

Father Andreas said something under his breath that sounded like a juicy curse. "We know of Father Yeorgi. He and Abbot Methodius are a dangerous pair. I'm afraid he was arrested and escorted to Athens, but, like most evicted monks, he is free to do as he pleases once off Agio Óros. We'd need evidence to arrest him."

Takis shuffled. "The Italian police are investigating. Hopefully, they'll nail the bastard."

Sofia leaned forward. "Father Yeorgi considered these so explosive that they dug into the side of Mount Athos and built a secure hiding place separate from their regular library. What I don't understand is why he didn't simply destroy them, given the impact on Christianity they'll have."

Takis' phone rang. Sofia jumped at the unexpected interruption. Her cousin headed toward another room. All she could hear was the word, *polizei*."

THIRTY-NINE

Sofia needed to convince Father Andreas of the importance of her discovery. She wanted the Patriarch on her side to protect these scrolls from Father Yeorgi. Damn, she was desperate to get back into the cave at Esfigmenou. Would that ever be possible? So many old parchments she had been forced to leave behind.

Her stomach clenched. Takis hadn't returned to the room. Had something else gone wrong? She leaned forward. "Father Andreas, I don't understand why the monks at Esfigmenou ever saved these scrolls. Some people will consider their message explosive. For others, it will be the best 'good news' we've had in two millennia."

"What do you mean by explosive?" Father Andreas asked.

Sofia felt herself blush. The more time she'd pondered her discoveries, the more convinced she was that her generation was ready to receive their message. "These scrolls appear to be letters or epistles, and one might be more of a gospel."

"No, Dottore Papandréou, not more of this. Not in times when we must put our attention to the literal destruction of Christianity here in the Middle East."

"What we've unearthed, between Āminah's dig and what I uncovered on Mount Athos, will support Christianity's importance to this region. Might even interest some Christians in returning to the lands of their ancestors." She shifted in her chair. "Like many of my colleagues, I'd always felt that Christianity had gotten short-changed by all that the gospels and early texts failed to tell us. Early Christianity was primarily a women's movement, but even the voices of too many men were lacking."

"Of course, we want to know more. The New Testament leaves us with more questions than answers." Father Andreas appeared impatient.

"Same with most of our surviving texts from early Christianity. More questions than answers. Big gaping holes, just like the letters between Olympias and John Chrysostom." Sofia was nearly out of breath. She needed to slow down and not frighten off her one shot at the Patriarch's support.

Taşbent interjected. "Sofia raises an interesting question that I'd think Patriarch Bartholomaios would be interested in receiving an answer. Why go to such lengths to hide these scrolls rather than destroy them?"

"Good question. We've never been able to get inside their monastery without causing great scandal. Still, I'd heard Esfigmenou had little use for books as they were too holy for study." Father Andreas' voice dripped with sarcasm.

Sofia glanced up as her cousin entered the room and shifted in her seat. "Another well-cultivated piece of propaganda. Their library is huge and suspiciously impressive. I noticed several medieval texts on their shelves that I believe belong in Vienna. Father Theodor also rejected their claims of disdaining books and scholarship. He was adamant that Esfigmenou held some of Olympias' letters, although I didn't find them."

They all fell silent for a moment at the sound of the muezzin's call to prayer.

Father Andreas sipped his coffee, gazing at Sofia. "You raise a good question. Do you have any theories on why these scrolls were saved?"

"None at this time." Sofia turned as Takis had returned to the room. "Is everything alright?"

Takis leaned against the wall. "The Italian police discovered a break-in at some professor's lab in Bologna."

Her chest constricted. "O, my. Andrucci. Is he alright?"

"They didn't say."

Sofia felt a flush of irritation at her cousin. Why didn't he ask? She turned toward the archpriest and explained. "Andrucci ran the tests on the fibers from these scrolls." What was there to find? Did they think the scrolls were stored there?

Her cousin continued. "A couple of low-life thugs are busy singing to whatever tune the *polizia* want. But they haven't found the guy who killed Sister Meg. They figure he's left the country by now."

Would it take long for Father Yeorgi or the creep to discover she was in Istanbul? She breathed deeply. "Father Andreas, how do we protect these scrolls from such people? I don't want them to disappear again." She shifted in her seat. "I'm asking for the Patriarch's protection. I want scholars to see and study them for themselves."

Taşbent interjected. "If you'd like, Sofia, the scrolls can remain here. You can invite appropriate scholars to come and conduct their own investigations. We can coordinate the study of these scrolls with our work at the dig and the small pieces of parchment that you'll begin overseeing."

Sofia's mind went in so many directions. Taşbent's security seemed tight, but she knew that once word got out, things could get explosive. The security around the Dead Sea Scrolls in Jerusalem was incredible. Might something like that be possible here?

Father Andreas seemed to be studying her. "Sofia, just what do these scrolls say that has Esfigmenou so determined to retrieve them? Even worse, to kill?"

She stood, stepped over to her case, and pulled out a file she handed the archpriest. "Here are my translations."

He pulled reading glasses out of his pocket, donned them, and began reading. The room grew still. Sofia observed the priest as he turned the first page, one eyebrow raised. He exhaled sharply as he looked up at her. "Are you assuming this 'Maryam" is the Magdalene?"

"Yes. Maryam is the most common form of Mary."

Father Andreas glanced at Sofia. "And Johanna? We've never known the name of Simon Peter's wife, so where does this come from?"

"With so much of our early history lost, that shouldn't come as a surprise. But again, Martha was a common enough name in Jesus' day."

"And who is this 'Hannah'?"

"Before you continue reading, let me read you something I didn't expect to find at Megistris Lavras. A letter from the Venerable Makrina to a young Olympias,

> "My daughter, I am pleased you aspire to greater
> things. May your petition to avoid the burden of mar-
> riage and pursue the joys of the ascetic life be success-

ful. Our community here in Pontus thrives. Women join us, but others come for days of teaching and return home to spread the message... [faded text] ... in these challenging times, we need the voice of women in leadership. We carry a wisdom complimentary but different from men. My brothers have certainly taught me this truth ... [tear in papyrus] ... as my health fails me, I lean ever more on the words of Hannah, who calls us ever more to embrace Wisdom.

"Hannah, again." Her heart seemed to dance, knowing he was getting to the most controversial texts.

"Keep reading, Father Andreas."

He turned to the next page. He appeared confused. His countenance grew serious. He adjusted his glasses and looked at her, his voice growing louder as he spoke. "This is audacious. Hannah, again? This is unacceptable. Sounds more gnostic, yet you believe what this seems to say?"

The accusations have begun. A clock nearby tolled the half hour. Sofia steadied her breathing. She could hear her heartbeat. "Yes, I do. At first, this document appears truly radical. Still, as I thought about the disappearance of women from the early records, the ones those who distrusted women could find and destroy anyway, this began to make sense to me. And too many accusations of Gnosticism flew around the Empire."

Father Andreas gazed at Taşbent, who nodded in affirmation. He looked quizzically at her. He reread her translations, slammed the pages on his lap, and removed his glasses to wipe them.

"This is simply too much – "

"You know I've dedicated my career to unearthing women's voices from the early Christian movement. First, some liturgical texts, and now Olympias. This fits in with the pattern of suppression. Leaders compromising Jesus' radical message to fit in with Roman society." She noticed her oddly behaving cousin left the room again.

"Obviously, you and Āminah believe these to be authentic, that I should take them seriously."

"Yes."

He pointed to the papers. "Please show me where on these scrolls you find these words."

Sofia smiled; the debate had begun. They stood and returned to the basement. Sofia picked up a pointer and started to show Father Andreas word for word.

Sofia pointed to the shorter text. "I believe the original was created sometime between 58 and 62 CE, before the death of Saint Paul and certainly before the destruction of the Temple in Jerusalem in 70 CE. Andrucci and I believe this copy has been stored in one of the monasteries along the Nile for the past few centuries. How this came to be in Africa from Asia Minor is merely conjecture at this point," Sofia explained.

Father Andreas turned and peered at it again. Silence crept into the room. Worry slithered in like a dense fog.

"And this longer one, the Ge'ez?"

Sofia sensed in him a mixture of disbelief and curiosity. "Seventh Century. As I'd mentioned, the fibers and the detritus lining the fibers indicate Ethiopia but possibly southern Sudan. The scroll may have moved between monasteries over the centuries."

"Please show me these words." This sounded more like a command, but one she was willing to follow.

Sofia began pointing out words, at times stopping to explain some oddities of phrasing. "I have some questions for an Ethiopian scholar I know, but my take is that this was a translation from Aramaic or Syriac, and the translator struggled with interpreting foreign concepts or words into early Ge'ez."

The archpriest looked across at her. "Meaning?"

"It will take several linguists to work through this, to figure out which language the text was in that the translator used to create the Ge'ez version. Translators always struggle with interpreting concepts or words foreign to the language they're trying to express them, so that should give us some clues."

"Clues?"

"Language will tell us where this has been before Ethiopia."

Taşbent interrupted. "Ethiopia was one of the ancient Christian churches. Correct? Christians were there long before Muslims arrived."

Sofia answered. "Yes, but we have few surviving texts before the eleventh century. Probably a form of Hebrew that predates Ge'ez."

"Frankly, I find this absurd. Why haven't we heard even a hint of something like this? I cannot imagine how such an explosive document has been hidden all these centuries." The archpriest sighed, shaking his head. "This just seems like a fabrication of some sort."

Sofia felt her neck warm. This has been a question that left her feeling disturbed. "Father Andreas, you know as well as I that Imperial armies destroyed many libraries. You know about the battles between bishops over what was orthodox and what wasn't. I can name several early bishops that would've ordered this destroyed, especially when Christianity began to be legalized and power became associated with the priesthood."

"That was more of a Western thing. We, of the east –"

Sofia interrupted, "also suppressed one another. I know it's hard for you to believe this could be real. That it says what it says. But think of this like a puzzle piece. We need scholars besides me to examine how this might fit with surviving texts. And yes, possibly prove that it's a fraud."

Father Andreas sighed. "At best, Dottore Papandréou, you have an old fraud."

Sofia felt her neck tighten. "What would've motivated someone to create a 'fraud' like this in Ethiopia or Syria? What might've been the motivation back then? Those are valid questions for scholars to pursue. I am asking for the Patriarch's protection and to let scholars investigate and challenge me. If it's a fraud, let them prove it."

Taşbent asked, "Father, might the patriarch appoint someone trustworthy to go to Esfigmenou's library and see what else is there?"

"Yes, and especially the underground cavern I stumbled into. I saw lots of other scrolls." Sofia realized she was talking faster and faster, something she did when she got excited. "I don't have them with me, but I did take photographs of this cavern, which would show you how many more scrolls are stored there."

Father Andreas stood gazing at her, then back at the scrolls. He delicately fingered the edge of the Ge'ez text. Sofia sensed a shift in him.

"You are right. This is worthy of investigation, given its age. But this must be kept quiet. I am concerned with what this would do to Christendom if the faithful heard about this. It could tear us apart," he said.

"I suggest it would bring new vibrancy. Just imagine the number of young people, long alienated from Christianity, whose imagination will be captured by this. Even the debate will draw them to reconsider a faith they long thought irrelevant." Sofia had been struggling for weeks over this question. If she brought the scrolls' existence to the public, it would alert her nemesis to its location and bring some protection once this scroll's existence became known.

Father Andreas shifted his gaze among them. The silence felt like a relief.

Finally, he spoke. "We have a church under siege in Syria, Christians martyred every day, and a Turkish government trying to squeeze the Orthodox church out of the country because of our efforts to assist Syrian refugees." He shook his head. "Most of the refugees we aid are Muslim, their own people."

Sofia heard the exhaustion and even near-desperation in his words. "Might the news of this scroll support your efforts, reminding the world of ancient Syrian and Armenian culture? Of why the destruction of so many monastic libraries in Syria is cultural genocide?" Thank God The Hill in Minnesota digitized most of those precious manuscripts in Aleppo before the civil war began.

"I'd expect the Turkish government doesn't want to be reminded of the Armenian genocide," Father Andreas said.

How did we get onto this topic? Why must this be so hard?

Taşbent interrupted, "That may be our way forward. My government protects these scrolls housed here in one of our universities to show the world that we have moved forward from our horrendous past. The presence of our dig and of these scrolls will also put pressure on my government to cease its quiet persecution of Christians here in Turkey."

Father Andreas returned to the sitting area, sighing as he sat down. Sofia and Taşbent followed him. Sofia glanced around. Where was Takis?

He continued. "This seems incredulous, yes, even insane. But what Father Yeorgi did is even worse. And for reasons I cannot fathom, he kept these scrolls for God knows how long. Why? We'll know when we find him." He shifted in his chair. "As for your archeological dig, Āminah, I will put the weight of the Patriarch's office behind this. I remind you, Dottore Papandréou, that you don't know what these are, only what they appear to be. I warn you against declaring these scrolls legitimate too hastily. If it's real, if it's of God, then the world must know. But you know as well as I that history is filled with discoveries soon revealed to be frauds. Because Āminah trusts you, therefore I trust you as well."

His doubt discouraged Sofia even though she fully understood that these scrolls must appear fraudulent to any non-specialist.

Her voice nearly quavered, a lethal combination of exhaustion, grief, and fear. Where was Takis? "I appreciate your willingness to risk supporting this project. Please put pressure on Interpol to find Father Yeorgi."

Takis entered the room with a grin on his face.

Forty

UNIVERSITY OF ISTANBUL

Sofia looked expectantly at her cousin. He slipped his phone into his pocket as he watched Father Andreas depart.

With a confused expression on his face, he asked. "Why is he leaving? Is the Patriarch going to help us?"

Sofia's heavy heart warmed. "Us," he had said. In his own way, he had made her mess his own project. At least she had two genuine supporters. She needed to track down Brother Makarios once she returned to their rooms.

"He made no commitment either way. I'm not really surprised. Not only is the Patriarch busy, but Father Andreas doubted the legitimacy of my discoveries, something I think will be the reaction of many people."

"Why? You're smart."

Sofia smiled. Taşbent handed each of them a thin glass of *raki*, Turkish ouzo. Taşbent clicked the bottom of her glass to each of her guests in traditional Turkish fashion and tossed her head back, downing her glass. Sofia followed her example, allowing the anise-flavored liquor to burn her throat.

She returned to her seat, asking. "What news, Takis?" Sofia felt her chest warm, easing a bit of her anxiety. Taşbent refilled her glass.

Takis shot back the *raki* and began. "First, I was talking to one of the polizia in Bologna involved in interrogating those guys who broke into that lab."

Sofia gripped her glass. "Andrucci's lab."

"Yeah, and the guy who hired them was a Greek monk and wanted them to find some old scrolls. And it seems that the Carabinieri are very interested in this monk and these scrolls that weren't there."

Sofia downed her glass.

"And that led back to the nun's Abbey, why Sister Meg was killed, and what we had stored down there." Takis shifted in his chair. "So anyway," Takis pulled his smartphone out of his pocket and began tapping the screen, "That guy told me that the Italian Ministry of Culture's Department for the Protection of Cultural Heritage—isn't that some title." Takis chuckled. "Well, they're now involved in this case. We're gonna have company."

Her cousin leaned forward to show her a picture of a well-dressed guy who seemed Greek. Her stomach gripped. "This is the guy I fought. I think so, anyway. It was dark and all. Look familiar?"

Sofia took his phone with shaky hands. "The guy who killed Meg?" She studied his face. Had she seen him before? Anywhere around the university? Do you think he's the one who attacked Aunt Christina?"

"Hadn't thought of that. Will send Christina this photo. Interpol seems interested in him, and they think he may be on to you."

She nearly dropped the phone. "Do you think he knows where we are? Did you tell the police where we are?"

"*Mou oraios*, they know we're in Istanbul and nothing more. The *polizia* want to get their hands on this guy but keep you safe."

Taşbent took the phone and gazed at the photo.

Sofia poured herself another glass of *raki*. She hadn't planned on Interpol getting involved. Did that help or hurt? Maybe they would protect her discovery.

Taşbent spoke up. "This would be the Works of Art unit. They're quite effective."

Her cousin asked, "But Sof didn't find artwork."

Taşbent returned his phone. "This still falls under antiquities, especially since they now know the age of the vellum. From what the two of you have told me, the intruder was a professional. I'd expect the authorities to be hunting down trafficked manuscripts."

"Like some of the books I saw at Esfigmenou that I'm rather certain belong elsewhere. Especially Vienna and Saint Gall in Switzerland."

Taşbent continued. "Interpol has an office in the new part of Istanbul. We can insist on meeting them there with our solicitor present. Sofia, we need to think about your safety. I want to move you deeper into the Muslim neighborhood. That will keep you safer than in a tourist hotel."

"Or maybe I need to return to Thessaloniki and keep you safe," Sofia whispered.

Her host countered. "No, we go see our solicitor tomorrow."

§

Sofia awoke to the baleful sounds of the muezzin's call to prayer. The *raki* had left her with a heavy head but the blessing of a night's deep sleep. She was now the guest of Āminah Taşbent and her rather large family. Did Āminah expect she'd blend in here? Sofia heard a knock at her door, calling her to ready herself for breakfast and the day's task. The solicitor awaited them.

The two women entered the Mercedes, same driver as before, with Takis in tow. Taşbent's mother had covered Sofia's hair and shoulders with a lovely silk scarf in pure white, draped so as not to appear like a ḥijāb, which was outlawed. To blend in? To disguise her appearance? Sofia felt comforted by this gesture.

As they pulled away from the curb, Sofia rechecked her old cell phone.

"Is something concerning you, Sofia?"

She glanced across at her host, concern in her voice. "I've left several messages for a friend, Brother Makarios, and he hasn't returned my call. I'm afraid he may have crossed the border into Syria again."

Takis turned toward the two women sitting in the rear of the car. "What would he be doing that for?"

"He'd been helping Syrians hide the books in their libraries, especially monastic libraries, from terrorist groups that are hell-bent on burning them."

"I hope he left his real phone at home. He should be using a burner phone," Takis said.

Why does her cousin know about this kind of stuff? "Then how would anyone locate him?"

Centrifugal force pressed her toward the door as they rounded a sharp corner. Horns blared.

Takis righted himself, a slight grin on his face. "That's the point. So, no one can locate him if he doesn't want to be found. And if his phone were stolen, no personal information could also be taken."

What she loved about Brother Makarios also infuriated her. He was too willing to risk his personal safety for ancient manuscripts. Sofia chuckled. She did the exact same thing. She noticed the others' curious glances her way. "I want Brother Makarios to be among the first scholars to see and study the scrolls."

The car made a sharp left down into an underground parking garage. The three exited the Mercedes, the driver leaned on the trunk, seemingly content to stay with the car. Sofia took the elevator and felt her stomach lurch as the elevator made its ascent. She was not fond of tall skyscrapers, and it seemed their solicitor's office was near the top of this building. The three exited into a modern office area with marble floors and stunning Turkish rugs. Modern art graced the walls above the leather furniture. Sofia began to wonder just how expensive this solicitor was going to be. Where would she ever find the money?

The three were escorted into a conference room with large windows on two sides. Video conferencing equipment with a large flat screen occupied much of the third wall. A woman's voice, deep in that Marlene Dietrich-way, greeted them from behind. Taşbent made the introductions.

Grasping Sofia's hand, Azra Güneş smiled. "So, you're the stunning archeologist that Āminah has been raving about

Güneş's dark skin was set off by a beautiful emerald-green silk suit. Her large brown eyes dazzled with intelligence and feistiness. A lioness in court, Sofia surmised.

"I'm not really an archeologist. That's Āminah." Sofia removed her scarf, moved toward a chair, and sat. "My area is early Christianity, and I've been fortunate to work with ancient vellum and parchment. I'd been working in a monastery on the border of Turkey and Syria before entering Mount Athos."

"Mount Athos? Isn't this forbidden?" Their solicitor smiled. No wonder Āminah trusted her.

"Yes."

"Impressive." Güneş updated Taşbent on the government's case to close the dig. An injunction has been granted, and we await updated reports from Taşbent. "We have a period of grace to build our case, and the Antiquities department requires a timeline for when your work will be completed."

Sofia interrupted. "Would the government allow this to become part of the museum complex, teaching tourists about women's history?"

Güneş gazed at her. "This is possible if we could provide funding to create your exhibits. And if this museum doesn't distract from the beauty of Hagia Sophia."

"Rome has several museums that are essentially underground. Same in Greece," Sofia answered.

"Yes, provided we find funding. It's always about the money, Sofia."

Taşbent explained the significance of Sofia's discovery of the Olympias documents for the dig.

"The two of you seem to be fomenting a revolution here. I like this," Güneş said. "But right now, Āminah tells me you two have more pressing concerns."

Güneş was a gentle presence, remaining clear and concise in their conversation. Sofia's confidence grew. She told Güneş her story from the moment she entered Mount Athos until now. "And now Interpol is interested in my discoveries and will arrive here in Istanbul soon."

Güneş gazed at Taşbent and Takis, then back to her. "I'd most certainly expect the Carabinieri, as well as our own Antiquities departments, to be interested. Trafficking in antiquities is a ruthless business. And presently a major source of income for terrorist groups. Does anyone in the Greek government know about your discoveries?"

Sofia squirmed. She sensed an edge to Güneş's voice. "No. Very few people know about any of this."

"And is Patriarch Bartholomaios extending his protection to these discoveries?"

"I've presented my case to his archpriest, Father Andreas, who hasn't made any commitment. I don't know if the Patriarch knows about any of this," Sofia answered.

"His support could prove helpful." Their solicitor turned as her aide entered, carrying a tray of Turkish coffee. They were each served in small, delicate porcelain demitasse cups. "Or his awareness of this could cause us trouble."

Sofia choked on her coffee. She hadn't thought of that possibility. "Trouble?"

"Yes, Sofia. He could claim the right of ownership, take these scrolls away, and they might never be seen by other scholars."

Taşbent interjected. "Surely—."

"Where men in power are concerned?" Güneş challenged. A clock chimed the half hour. "Your presence here suggests that you're an honest person. No trafficker would seek my services."

Sofia felt deflated. Why hadn't she thought of that possibility? Then a glimmer of hope emerged, deep within like a child's whisper. "Esfigmenou. The monks there have been an angry and infected thorn to the Patriarch. At a minimum, he'll want to know what they were hiding under the mountain and why. And I have several witnesses to the existence of these scrolls

Güneş smiled. "Good. So, our most pressing concern is to attempt to establish a legitimate domain or legal possession of these scrolls, at least for now. Turkish courts can drag matters out into the next millennium if need be."

Taşbent set her cup and saucer on the table. "What do we need to prove that Sofia is a scholar and not a thief?"

Sofia cringed. "Maybe a better question is how do we keep possession of these scrolls at the university? That I don't have these stored in a private vault but rather at a university would help build our case."

Güneş said, "I don't think I need to remind either of you. Too many scholars have proven to be thieves when the desire to possess is greater than their integrity. The fact that you've placed these scrolls in the university vault helps our case. I must file some papers with our government through the Antiquities Department to ensure the scrolls remain here until this matter is settled."

"These scrolls cannot disappear again. Some are Armenian, and some are Ethiopian. Each country has a strong claim on their respective scrolls," Sofia said. Would church authorities in Armenia or Ethiopia successfully claim ownership of these? And who, besides Brother Makarios, did she need to entice here to examine them? The more scholars who see them, the less likely the scrolls will disappear.

"Sofia, who besides Āminah can vouch for your integrity? People who have known you for some years?"

Sofia winced as she thought. Would Father Theodor come to her rescue? Georgios Hatzidakis, once she explained what she had done, and he finished laughing or raging, would certainly vouch for her. She would ask Brother Makarios to call their solicitor when he finally returned her calls. Where is he? "As it turns out, Father Andreas knew of my work in the Balkans. But I can gather some names and contact information for you."

"I don't expect us to prevail in court over issues of domain. Unless politicians sway our judges otherwise, the courts will order these scrolls be returned to the Greek Orthodox Church, given the independent status of Mount Athos."

Sofia silently agreed with Güneş's assessment. So, she must win the Patriarch over. And survive the pursuit of a vicious monk and his henchmen. Another conviction grew strength within her.

"Sofia, I'll make the appropriate contacts with the authorities and arrange a meeting in my office. Do not answer any questions from anyone without my presence."

Takis asked, "And so, who will win?"

The tiger lady looked his way, "We will, of course."

Forty-one

Father Yeorgi sat in the darkened Church, grateful for the silence and solitude. The vigil lamp shimmered next to the icon of the *Theotokos*, the Bearer of God, a continued source of strength in these challenging and dangerous times. Taking deep, steady breaths, he sought divine focus and pondered these past weeks. His cousin had disappeared, possibly with this dangerous codex. If so, it would be the last act Kostas would ever commit. The security guards at the University of Bologna had called in the Carabinieri before he could slip away. Seems his cousin had been nearly caught and had slammed a nun hard against a stone wall, killing her. Stupid. Thoroughly stupid. Father Yeorgi had refused to answer any questions—admittedly, feigning ignorance wasn't much of a stretch since he didn't know what his cousin had done until the news came out—and he would locate his cousin before the Carabinieri. Kostas would talk to no one else.

He crossed himself again. Why hadn't the Blessed Mother allowed him to grab the thief before she stole that boat? What was She up to? She to whom Agio Óros and his entire life had been dedicated to serving? He began rocking again, bent over in agonizing prayer. That dangerous codex must be kept from the world. Why hadn't he destroyed it once he learned what it said? More heresy—and from his own Orthodox tradition. The drumming in his head intensified. Pride and lust for beautiful old books, his greatest sin. He had kept it as an ancient curiosity. Heretical, but curious. Did women really think they had a place in the leadership of Christendom? Did they believe, even back then, that they could write themselves into a position of authority? The *Theotokos* was and remains the only woman worthy of veneration. But She, the Blessed One, confused him sometimes.

What slid into his gut like venom was the thought of his abbot. Father Yeorgi had never revealed the existence of this codex to Abbot Methodius, knowing the abbot would order it to be immediately burned. If the apostates occupying the other monasteries on Agio Óros ever learned of the codex, they would reveal its contents. His own sin might well wreak havoc upon the world and, worst of all, upon the remnant of true believers. Father Yeorgi beat his chest again.

His hands kept massaging his prayer cord, his prayers of late leaving burn marks on his fingers, and his prayers issued from his lips like the beat of the semantron. His investigation of this woman Papandréou revealed an impressive scholar—she had earned his begrudging respect despite her violation of holy ground—such a waste on that useless gender. He had ordered several young monks to observe the woman's home and the university archives and report immediately if she appeared. Nothing but silence thus far. Father Yeorgi also sent several others to watch his cousin's familiar haunts.

His instinct, maybe the Holy Spirit's guidance, told him to find Papandréou. He absolutely had to. Where would she flee?

A door opened behind him, and steady steps, leather on stone, approached him from behind. A young voice beckoned to him. "Father, I think we've located the woman."

With a lightning bolt of hope, Father Yeorgi rose and followed the monk, his hand continuing to massage his prayer cord. He needed to remain calm and focused. He was taken to a computer with two screens attached and sat.

"This is a new website, uploaded in the last week or so, regarding an archeological dig at Hagia Sophia."

Father Yeorgi studied the images as the monk continued his explanation.

"Someone is claiming this site is the early monastic community of the Venerable Deacon Olympias."

The word "venerable" grated on his nerves. "Of course, it is. Most non-believers are amnesiacs when it comes to Church history."

"Yes, Father. But—" the monk scrolled down and pointed at the screen, "here one Āminah Taşbent is listed as the lead archeologist and, I believe this is who you are searching for, one Sofia Papandréou is listed—"

Father Yeorgi leaned in. "—as an expert on the writings of Deacon Olympias who oversees the papyri and parchment fragments unearthed at the site." His heart pounded. He grabbed the mouse from his fellow monk and shoved him aside. He scanned the entire site. The dig was under the jurisdiction of the Turkish Antiquities Authorities and the auspices of *İstanbul Üniversitesi*, with special protection extended by His Holiness, Patriarch Bartholomaios. The heretic, damn him. Father Yeorgi felt the muscles in his neck tighten. His task might be more complicated now if the heretic knew of this codex. Why did he ever do it?

Father Yeorgi leaned back in his chair. The university might make its vast resources available to protect his codex. Well, maybe not if they knew they were protecting stolen property. Accusations of black-market activities work both ways. Taşbent had long been a challenge to his work, but not anymore. He would call their solicitors next. Accuse Taşbent of the very activity which she had long charged others.

§

Father Yeorgi arrived in Istanbul with two trusted companions, Brothers Stephanos and Petros. He would not leave without the codex, even if it meant destroying it to protect the faithful. Brother Stephanos drove them to Hagia Sophia. They arrived as the Muslim call to prayer sounded from a nearby minaret. He noted the white canvas tents near the far side of the apse and some orange netting being utilized as fencing beyond the tents. He exited the vehicle and headed across the front of Hagia Sophia toward the site, flanked by his two companions.

Approaching, he could make out the sounds of some male voices, barely audible above the screeching racket some call music. How do people live with all this noise? His nerves were on edge. Heading toward the orange netting, he glanced over and noticed several young men working—but no women. The dig was deeper than the pictures he had seen on their website. They were moving at a fast pace. He turned and headed toward the tents.

Father Yeorgi opened the flap on the nearest tent despite not having heard any voices within. The interior smelled of dirt, although the shade provided cool in the growing heat. He saw standard archeological dig equipment for sorting and cleaning anything unearthed. A microscope and older computer equipment sat at the far end of the tent. An organized mess. He turned and moved toward the farthest tent, where he had noticed the shadows of a person within.

He signaled his companions to remain outside and alert him to interruptions as he flipped the tent's flap open. A woman stood before a long tray; her hands partially hidden under fine netting. Parchment pieces, he presumed. She gazed toward him, and her eyes darkened in recognition. Good.

Father Yeorgi stared up toward the woman. "Papandréou. You know what I've come for, and I'll have its return today."

The woman turned, straightening her spine. Her countenance stiffened, and her pupils constricted. Yet she remained silent and strong. A worthy opponent.

"The scroll. Now."

"Really?" The woman took several deep, slow breaths. "Do you really expect me to simply hand it over?"

"I appreciate your honesty, but we will go together to retrieve everything you stole." His voice slid into a hiss. "You violated holy ground."

"The only woman allowed on your precious peninsula is the *Theotokos*. Not the rest of us."

His gut gripped, and his breathing grew shallow. She dared mock them.

She replaced the netting over the tray and stepped away. "My translations are completed. I only have a few questions for a scholarly friend whose Ge'ez is much better than mine." Her expression changed. "Hannah upsets you, doesn't she?"

He heard the mocking sarcasm. Moving toward her, he was surprised that she did not back away. "I presume you've placed the scroll somewhere at the university."

"In a high-security vault with proper temperature and humidity control, just as you'd expect."

The woman gazed at him. He felt chills up his spine like he was being undressed. Vermin.

The woman continued, "You believe the scroll to be authentic, don't you? That's what terrifies you. Hannah's message will be revealed to the world, and the Church will finally be forced to grow up and become what She was always meant to be."

He felt his muscles tighten and tremble. He released the prayer cord in his pocket and raised his chafed hand. The fool didn't fear him.

"Why don't you press charges against me? Trespassing onto Agio Óros, breaking into your monastery—not an easy task, I'll admit—and stealing your precious scroll. Oh, you can tell the authorities all about the other vellum sheaves I found as well."

His face grew hot, his stomach knotted. He reached out and grabbed the woman's upper arm. She flinched and tried to pull away. He tightened his grip. He was getting desperate, but he needed to maintain control.

The witch pulled her arm up in defiance. He pulled her closer. "I also found Deacon Olympias on Agio Óros as well. My translations are soon to be published. Questions will arise, and I'll reveal where I found them. Fortunately, there are saner monks on the Holy Mountain than the likes of you. I expect Father Theodor will confirm my findings and translations."

Her mention of Father Theodor concerned him. That one was a scholar too many underestimated.

Her eyebrows furrowed. "Why do you fear Hannah's message? Or even Olympias?"

She was confusing him. He must be strong. Any hope of restoration of an authentic Christianity depended on his success here. "There was a reason her letters were destroyed centuries ago to protect the faithful.

You merely lie and conjecture. Your fraud will be exposed." A pained expression crossed her face.

"How could Olympias ever threaten you? Her words were words of comfort and encouragement to a man of integrity who had taken on the Imperial Empire." Her expression changed, and sarcasm spiced her words. "Oh, yes. She was a leader who exercised her power with ease. That's what bothers you."

The truth of her words stung him. "No more of this." He pulled her toward him, and the woman resisted.

"Let go of me. Now," the witch demanded. "Āminah, call the guards," she yelled.

This would not be easy. He called out to his monks outside the tent. "Brother Stephanos, bring our car around. We'll be escorting this woman to the university." He barely heard the reply. Other voices were out there as well.

He tightened his grip. She flinched in pain. The woman glared at him—a powerful adversary. "You won't see the codex ever again. I've already shown it to several scholars and Father Andreas from the Patriarch's office. I've digitized every page and have copies stored in several locations."

Oh, God. His back stiffened. His nostrils flared. How could she do this? His nightmare intensified.

The woman pulled out a phone with her other hand. He slammed it down and away, hearing it crash against the leg of the table. He pulled her closer, and she jerked back and then slammed her foot into his shin. Pain shot through his leg, and he nearly lost his balance. He heard another woman's voice outside, calling to the woman. Father Yeorgi gripped her throat and forced her backward, repeating his demand for the return of the codex. The woman stumbled, but he held her upright by the throat. He moved them away from the voices outside. The two passed through another tent flap as the woman punched him while struggling to speak.

"The scrolls," he demanded in a low voice. He tightened his grip on her throat and continued pushing forward until she slammed against the outer wall of Hagia Sophia. His mind was clear. His focused energy all on the glory of God. "The scrolls."

"No," she barely hissed. She kicked his shin again. The pain energized him. Another woman's voice grew closer and louder. Men's voices were also heard, but he focused only on the woman. His sheer determination would grant him victory.

"I'll have my scrolls now."

He felt hands gripping him. The demon's minions?

The witch's face grew red. Her eyes bulged. She pulled and scratched at his hands. She made gurgling sounds. She kicked frantically, and he nearly buckled. Her body trembled. Then he felt hands, small yet strong, cut into his arm. The witch grabbed his beard and pulled his face close to hers. He heard voices but concentrated on the woman only. He must succeed.

He thought he heard the voice of the gardener, Brother Petros. Was he nearby? Far away? "Father Yeorgi, release her. You're harming her." Someone with a stronger grip was trying to break his hold on the demon. He heard screaming and people yelling. Why don't they value the silence he and his brother monks crave? Men's hands were pulling at him.

He squeezed her neck as if she, with his sheer effort, might cough up the scroll from her throat. A deafening thud, a lightning bolt of pain, and shards of discoloration before all went black.

FORTY-TWO

ISTANBUL, TURKEY

Sofia dropped to the ground, hitting her head on something solid. Her muscles limp and shaking. Her head, neck, and shoulders screamed with pain. She struggled to breathe, coughing and wheezing. Someone lifted her to a sitting position, and nausea overwhelmed her. She gripped her stomach. The room spun. People were yelling. She glanced up into the face of Āminah, etched with concern and anger.

Soon, men in uniforms hovered over her, all the talk and commotion like a vise squeezing her head. A medic flicking light into her eyes caused her excruciating pain. Soon, she was lifted onto a gurney and carried out into the daylight. She squeezed her eyes shut and flung her still limp arm over her eyes. She faded out as she heard the screeching noise of the ambulance.

Sofia awoke to the soft chant of a male voice. "In mercy, O Good One, cast Thine eyes upon the petitions of us who today are come together in Thy Holy Name, to anoint Thy sick servant, Sofia, with Thine oil divine."

She struggled to focus her eyes and realized that Father Andreas hovered over her, wearing his full black rason, stole, cross, and kamilavkon, his cylindrical cap on his head. He had placed the Holy Bible on her midriff. She smelled sweet oil. Was she dying?

Father Andreas began to intone, "O Lord who, in thy mercies and bounties, healest the disorders of our souls and bodies, do Thou, the same Master, sanctify this oil, that it may be effectual for Sofia who shall be anointed therewith, unto healing, and unto relief from every passion, every malady of the flesh and of the spirit, and every ill; and that therein may be glorified Thy most Holy Name, of the Father, and of the Son, and of the Holy Spirit, now and ever, and to the ages of ages. Amen."

Sofia's eyes began to focus better. Her aunt Christina stood opposite Father Andreas, holding one of her shaking hands. She struggled to clear her mind. She thought she saw tears in her aunt's eyes. Her body remained limp with exhaustion and pain.

Father Andreas continued his soft melodic chant: "Thou who alone art a speedy succor, O Christ, manifest Thy speedy visitation from on high upon Thy sick servant; deliver her from her infirmities, and cruel pain; and raise her up again to sing praises unto Thee, and without ceasing, to glorify Thee; through the prayers of the Birth-Giver of God, O Thou who alone lovest humankind."

Dying? She tried to speak, but her voice was hoarse, and she wasn't sure any noise came out.

The priest continued, "Look down, most pure Virgin, upon the supplications of your servant and crush the assaults of our enemies, delivering her from all afflictions. You are the only sure and secure anchor that we have, and you are our protection. Never permit us who call upon you, our Lady, to be put to shame. Hasten to fulfill the entreaties of those who in faith cry to you: Rejoice, O Lady, helper of all, the joy and protection, and the salvation of our souls."

Father Andreas began anointing her with chrism oil, first her forehead and then each of her hands, top, and palm. The oil felt warm and smelled sweet. He concluded with, "Amen."

"Sofia," Father Andreas softly called.

Sofia croaked out a response. "Am I dying?"

"No, dear," her aunt responded. "But you've suffered a concussion, and you were nearly choked to death. You're in hospital, and the doctors are monitoring you."

"The hand of God stopped that mad monk. I'm ashamed of his behavior. He's in police custody now," Father Andreas said. "Sofia, I believe God spared your life for a reason. And I suspect it's connected with your professional work."

"*Mou oraios*," Takis began, "I'm so sorry I wasn't there for you. I'm afraid I was distracted with the guys in the dig."

"No, Takis," Sofia croaked, "you've always been there for me."

Sofia rested her eyes as she listened to Āminah and Takis explain much of Sofia's adventures to Christina, and Āminah described Sofia's discoveries. She heard her aunt gasp several times, and despite the pain, Sofia smiled.

Father Andreas continued the story. "I've seen these parchments. I don't know what to make of your discoveries, but I will propose to His Holiness that he extend his protection to them and allow scholars to begin their work."

Sofia smiled.

He continued, "I will meet with His Holiness in the morning. I'll update him on all that has transpired." He sighed. "Esfigmenou must be dealt with firmly. We've been too patient with them. And I will insist that the authorities throw the full weight of the law against this monk."

Sofia smiled again. She grimaced with pain but refused the offer of more painkillers. She wanted her mind to be clear. Her instincts had been accurate. Yeorgi was as crazy as she thought. He probably believed the scrolls were authentic and couldn't bring himself to destroy a holy text, even one that went against all his narrow, rigid beliefs.

§

Father Andreas brought a pot of mint tea and a light breakfast to the office of Patriarch Bartholomaios. They began their days this way—unless they were traveling—and increasingly, their days began with news of more grief.

"Good morning, Holiness." Father Andreas set the tray down and, with shaking hands, poured each of them a cup.

"Father Andreas, you're upset. More bad news, I think."

"Yes, Holiness." He sighed as he sat. "You might recall my meeting with Āminah Taşbent and Sofia Papandréou, the talented Greek scholar. A monk from Esfigmenou nearly killed her yesterday afternoon."

The Patriarch choked on his tea. "What? What in God's name are you saying?"

Father Andreas began with a brief report of what happened, reminding His Holiness of the dig at Hagia Sophia and their protection of Taşbent's work there. "The culprit is one Father Yeorgi. He is in police custody."

"This is terrible news. How is she doing? She will recover?"

"Yes, Holiness. Bruised and shaken, a concussion, but I'm advised she should make a full recovery. I've also learned that hidden within Esfigmenou is a large library, apparently containing rare books, most were likely stolen."

His Holiness set his cup down. "This is appalling. Abbot Methodius had long ago renounced scholarship. They seemed quite proud of this."

Father Andreas noticed His Holiness' cheeks reddening as he recounted Papandréou's illicit adventure on Agio Óros, explaining her background and credentials, her interest in the early Deacon Olympias and her letters, and into what she ultimately stumbled.

The two sat in silence for a moment, both deep in thought.

"Her violation of Agio Óros is inexcusable. Yet understandable for a woman scholar." The Patriarch sat silently, staring across the room, then asked, "The lost letters of Deacon Olympias? They were hidden away?"

"Sofia Papandréou seems confident about what she found, as does Professore Taşbent. When appropriate, I'll make some contacts on Agio Óros. I don't know why our other monasteries were unaware of this. Or why they would've kept something like this secret. She found some other pieces as well." Gazing out the window, Father Andreas didn't want to deceive His Holiness, but he wanted his friend to see these discoveries for himself, then returned his gaze to the Patriarch. "I made no promises to Papandréou other than an open mind and possibly our support in encouraging certain scholars to study her discoveries. I regret my failure to be more supportive of her. We deny women—"

"No, the monks set their own policy. And you certainly didn't foresee this."

"I didn't consider violence a possibility, Holiness."

Silence that bore the weight of the world permeated the room. The Patriarch broke the silence. "This assault is tragic. And Abbot Methodius and his monks have now gone too far. Attempted murder. What is your assessment of these discoveries, whether fraud or not."

"The Olympias letters seem authentic from what we have of Chrysostom's surviving letters. But it's these other parchment pieces that enraged Father Yeorgi and drove him to attempt murder." Father Andreas shifted in his chair. "I don't understand how these got into Esfigmenou's hands nor why they were kept."

"We can ill afford controversy that might alienate more of the faithful."

"Yes, Holiness, and yet Papandréou feels their message might ignite the faith of believers and entice others to return to the Church. We can certainly use some good news." Father Andreas then informed the Patriarch of what happened in Italy.

"Murder? A nun?" The Patriarch sighed. "And the police?"

"They continue their investigation, but Father Yeorgi is under arrest for attempted murder. Numerous witnesses. Even one of the monks from Esfigmenou testified against him.

Distressed anger erupted. "Refuse any request for protection from us or the Greek government." The Patriarch gazed out the window.

Father Andreas drank some of his tea, wetting his dry throat. "I think we'll be faced with questions around stolen books and codices in addition to the money laundering schemes."

The Patriarch shuffled in his chair. "Order our people to cooperate with the Antiquities Authorities. And we will continue to refuse to defend any monastery involved in these

illicit activities. Scars on the Body of Christ. I will not tolerate any of this."

"Yes, Holiness.

The Patriarch sighed. His jaw tightened. "Place a call to the Premier."

§

ESFIGMENOU, MOUNT ATHOS

Orthodoxy or Death! Commander Leontis relished ripping down those damned banners that he had spent the past few years gazing at. One of his more adventurous men had climbed above and removed the poles that held these accursed things in place.

He heard the engines of jeeps and trucks rumbling down the hill toward the entrance to the monastery. As he had expected, monks from some other monasteries were arriving on orders of the Monastic Council. Once his men had finished sweeping Esfigmenou for any more renegade monks, his orders were to turn the keys over to this small group of amiable monks and depart. That was one of the sweetest sets of orders he had ever received in his long career. This tour of duty on the Holy Mountain had nearly driven him into early retirement.

Commander Leontis did not question his orders. These monks had been sent to ensure the finance office and library were sealed. He had been insulted at the notion that he or his men might steal from the monks, but hurt pride was a small price to pay for freedom from this hellhole of an assignment. Strange men with strange ways, he thought. UN duty in Iraq would seem pleasurable after this.

His personal march toward freedom began yesterday. Premier Karamanlís, carrying out instructions from Patriarch Bartholomaios, ordered the arrest of all the monks of Esfigmenou and affirmed that responsibility for the place belonged to the Monastic Council. Men moved with unusual speed for Greeks. Within hours, Abbot Methodius and his gang of minions were swept up and arrested. He assumed that the Italian nun's murder was what had triggered Patriarch Bartholomaios to finally approve this sweeping action. But then he had heard about one of the monks assaulting a woman at an archeological dig. Why? He knew these monks were pig-headed and irascible, but murder and assault?

Money laundering, real estate theft, and now murder and assault—all by monks allegedly dedicated to God. He pulled out his worry beads to calm his nerves. He hadn't bothered to tell anyone about all the cannabis plants his men kept stumbling into.

Orthodoxy or Death! Indeed, he thought. Commander Leontis allowed his men to burn the damn banners. The newly arrived monks looked on, grimaces on their faces, but not interfering with the well-deserved antics of his men. He had turned over the keys to Abbot Maximos, deciding that the police should stay a few more hours while this new group examined the monastery compound satisfactorily. No point in his men departing just to be called back if trouble erupted again. His headquarters at Karyés was several hours' drive away. A morning departure for Athens was soon enough.

Commander Leontis' curiosity was piqued by the two monks who climbed out of the battered truck. One was young, with a typical thick beard and an air of peasant. The monk carried a respectful and pleasant demeanor, Leontis thought. The other monk was frail, using two canes to walk. Why was he here?

"Commander Leontis? Brother Vassilis. This is Father Theodor." The young monk gently touched the older priest, apparently trying to steady him.

"How may I help you?"

"I'm getting too old for such adventures, young man. Just take me to this library that's been causing so much trouble."

The commander smiled to himself: was he or Brother Vassilis this "young man" to whom Father Theodor referred? The frail priest had a gentle expression on his face in marked contrast to all the surly monks of Esfigmenou that Commander Leontis had encountered.

"Father Theodor will not admit to being an expert on ancient manuscripts. Our abbot received a call from the Patriarch's office, ordering Father Theodor to oversee the collection," Brother Vassilis said.

"The Patriarch's staff advised me that a hidden room may contain rare and potentially explosive material. Imagine us on Mount Athos, the center of international espionage," Father Theodor said, laughing before a sadness swept across the kind monk's face.

"Then you've heard, Father. Of the murder of an Italian nun and then the assault on a young woman in Istanbul, all over a scroll that was once housed here."

"Tragic. I just don't understand how Jesus' message of love turned into hatred."

"I don't understand what His Holiness expects us to find here," the young monk commented.

"Whatever was such a threat that drove Father Yeorgi to murder had been stored here. The Patriarch also wants to know if there are more explosive scrolls down below. I think he intends on turning them over to the universities to hold and study," Father Theodor answered.

The young monk shook his head slowly in disbelief. "What could possibly be all that alarming?"

"Who knows? That Christ was really a woman?" the frail priest suggested, a gleam in his eye.

"Father," the young monk chided.

"Or that 'morose seriousness' is the 'sin against the Holy Spirit' we've all wondered about."

Brother Vassilis sighed in protest.

"Well, the library's all yours, Father. I've turned the keys over to Abbot Maximos, and my men will be leaving soon," Commander Leontis said, smiling.

Commander Leontis enjoyed these two monks. In fact, he liked every monk he'd met today. Why weren't there more like them?

"Thank you, Commander." The young monk assisted the frail Father Theodor through the gateway.

Orthodoxy or Death! Indeed. Commander Leontis laughed for the first time in a long, long while.

Forty-three

U NIVERSITY OF ISTANBUL

Sofia Papandréou stood in the doorway, next to Āminah Taşbent, and watched as the old Mercedes Benz entered the secure parking lot. Patriarch Bartholomaios climbed out and, after a gust of dry wind, straightened his skoupas. He headed toward them, Father Andreas beside him. Her heart pounded, and she felt the pressure building inside her. This was her "make or break" moment in so many ways. His Holiness held the future of her discoveries within his power. The Turkish government would not defy his decisions, and he had the authority to remove these scrolls back to Agio Óros. Father Andreas had made it clear to Sofia that His Holiness wanted to avert yet another scandal for the faithful. But the Patriarch was open to viewing her discovery at Father Andreas's urging, given that old Father Theodor traveled here to see these for himself. She hoped His Holiness was open to the possibility of the impossible.

Sofia extended a shaky hand in greeting. "Thank you, Your Holiness, for giving me some of your precious time. And for your openness to what I discovered."

He reached out and took her hand in both of his. Smiling as he gazed at her, "You have recovered fully? I was deeply disturbed to hear of your assault and the death of your friend. Scandalous."

"Thank you, Your Holiness. Sister Meg was my dissertation advisor. Her death hurts deeply."

"We pray for the both of you."

The Patriarch cupped Taşbent's in his, steadying them. "I've been following your work at Hagia Sophia, Profesőr Taşbent. I understand we've been given more time to complete your work at the site. This is good news."

The Patriarch looked across at her cousin.

"And this is my cousin, Takis, who has been of great help to me." Sofia watched her cousin smile lopsidedly as they shook hands.

"I'm not the family scholar. Just along for the adventure."

"I understand you're a frequent visitor to Agio Oros. Are you considering joining one of the monasteries?"

Sofia choked back a laugh as her cousin's neck reddened and, for once, was left speechless. Was the Patriarch serious?

Turning back to her, His Holiness said, "You understand I make no commitment regarding your discoveries. While I disapprove of what you did on Agio Oros, the Holy Spirit does move in mysterious ways."

"Yes, Your Holiness."

They all walked toward the elevator, which took them down a floor to the University's archives and rare manuscript lab. Passing through the vault door and into a well-lit and cool space, he was introduced to Brother Makarios Addicott. Papandréou explained his credentials. Also joining them was Profesőr Andrucci, who had conducted the testing on the parchment and inks. He then greeted his old friend, Father Theodor, leaning on a stool, canes nearby. Sofia introduced Doctor Gessesse, who, in Orthodox tradition, kissed the inner palm of the Patriarch's hand.

His Holiness gazed around the room. "Do I understand, Profesőr Taşbent, that fragments of what you've uncovered at Hagia Sophia are stored here?"

"Yes, Holiness. Sofia is working with the parchment pieces, but they are in disarray. The two codices are this way." She led the group around some long tables to the far end.

The Patriarch stood before the tables draped with fine silk cloth that obscured what was underneath.

Sofia and Āminah carefully removed the cloth from the first table and set it aside. Sofia barely breathed as she watched the Patriarch study the parchment before him. She was desperate for his support.

He looked up. "Armenian?"

"Yes, with strong Syrian influences." The feathery script was clear, with a couple of faded spots.

Andrucci, standing across from Sofia and the Patriarch, interrupted. "My tests of the vellum and ink estimate that this is a tenth-century copy." He went on to explain his procedures for verification.

She studied the Patriarch's face as he examined the scroll. She guessed he could read some of the Armenian as his lips moved.

His eyebrows rose. "You have seen these, Father Theodor? Your thoughts?"

The old librarian chuckled. "I just pray to live long enough to see what the young scholars come up with, especially with the second scroll."

"Interesting. And your translation?"

"There are a few troubling passages, but I'll read my rough translation." Sofia began to read.

> "On the first day of Unleavened Bread, when we Jews sacrifice the Passover Lamb, two of Jesus' other disciples had located an upper room for the feast. Mary, the Rabbi's mother, Joanna, Peter's wife, and I completed preparations for the meal, attempting to settle the children in all their excitement and anticipation. When evening was upon us, the Teacher arrived with the Twelve and the rest of their families.
>
> It was a festive occasion indeed. The Teacher's presence always seemed to bring out the best and worst in each of us. Mary, the Teacher's mother, welcomed each guest as she would greet her own family. Her eyes were filled with compassion for us, yet something more. His mother, really our mother as well, carried the sorrow of the tragic death of her eldest daughter, Hannah, and of her honorable husband, Joseph.

The Patriarch interrupted, "I am unaware that Jesus' sisters were ever named. This is most unusual. Continue, please."

Pushing down the rush of emotion in her throat, she continued,

> "With the lighting of candles, Mary's soft and resonant voice began the Passover prayers. Then Simon Peter and Johanna's youngest started the questions.

A ritual so familiar, yet a deep stirring in my heart told me new meanings awaited us. I felt that sense we women experience when we know, but without certainty, that we are with child.

When the meal was underway, Jesus said, "How I have longed to honor this Passover with you before my death. For I tell you, never again shall I eat it until the time when it finds its fulfillment in the Kingdom of God." Protests and confusion followed his strange words.

Death! My heart was pierced with hearing those words again. We live in such violent times. What does the Teacher know? Who threatens him? Yet when we encourage him to leave Jerusalem and even Judea, he rebukes us.

Sofia noticed Father Theodor lifting his glasses off his face, using the edge of his robe to clean them. He had a slight grin. Encouraged, she continued.

Joanna asked the Teacher about the coming of the Kingdom of God and whether there would still be priests and a holy Temple. Jesus instructed us, saying, "The Temple was given us when our faith was young and enemies threatened us. The time has come when priests and the rituals of the Temple will soon pass away. We will always have our rabbis, probing and wise teachers who serve as healing physicians with us. They keep us focused on the Kingdom to come."

Then He took a cup, and after giving thanks, he said, "Take this and share it among yourselves, for I tell you, from this moment, I shall not drink the fruit of the vine until the time when the kingdom of God comes." Jesus turned and gave me his cup to drink. After drinking, I passed the cup on to Peter.

Then he took bread, and after giving thanks, he broke it and gave it to us with the word. "This is my body that is given for you. Do this in remembrance of me."

Pouring more wine, Jesus again picked up his cup, saying, "This cup that is poured out for you is the new covenant of my blood. But see, the one who betrays me is with me, his hand with mine on the table."

My heart stung. Judas always resented the presence of women among the Master's friends. Often, he re-

fused to sit at table if we were present. Recently, he
had become enraged that the Teacher commanded
women to go forth and announce the coming of the
Kingdom. Always we lived with the threat of betrayal
and punishment, but we had hoped that the betray-
er would not be one of us, whom Jesus had called
'Friend.' Judas.

As dumb sheep are wont to do, the heated discussion
of the coming of the Rabbi's Kingdom deteriorated
into a fight over which of the Twelve should be considered the greatest. We women were furious."

Father Theodor chuckled. "Much hasn't changed in two thousand
years, has it." She continued,

"However, Jesus, ever gentle and kind, responded,
"Among the gentiles, the rulers lord it over others, and
those who have authority are given the title 'Benefac-
tor.' With you, this must not happen. No, the greatest
among you must behave as if you were the lowest, the
leader as if you were the one who serves. For who is
the greater: the one at table or the one who serves?
The one at table, surely? Yet here am I among you as
one who serves. You are friends who have stood by me
faithfully. I call you forth to find all my lost sheep and
reveal my Abba's love for them."

My fellow disciples expressed dismay and discontent. Again, the Master was commanding us to reach out to the untouchables and unclean.

Beware of the Evil One who sifts and shakes you all like wheat, but I have set leaders in your midst who will strengthen and encourage you when this present trial is past."

"Definitely the voice of a woman who was present. I like the humanity of this telling," Brother Makarios said.

My heart was pierced with love and dread when Jesus looked my way. He continued, "Woe to anyone who seeks to return the Kingdom of God to the deceptions and lies of the Temple ways. I say to you, pour your lives out as this wine to bring forth life to the Holy One's forgotten. Give your lives as we break this bread to bring forth captives to freedom. The way of the Prophets has always been one on behalf of the leper and the poor, the hungry and the slave. In the Kingdom to come, women and slaves, gentile and Roman will stand with the greatest of Prophets...."

Sofia felt the Patriarch's intense gaze at her.

"A Last Supper scene with women and children identified as present? This I could tentatively accept. Maybe even that Saint Joseph had only recently passed away." He raised an eyebrow. "But these names for women, which we've never known before? Just who do you suggest this "Hannah" to be?"

"I found a reference to Hannah in one of the letters from Makrina to Olympias—"

"The venerable Makrina?" the Patriarch asked.

"Yes, Your Holiness. I found it in Megístis Lávras." A tremor of nerves ran down her spine as she needed His Holiness to protect these. Even Father Theodor couldn't stop the Patriarch from suppressing these scrolls.

Brother Makarios cleared his throat. "Sofia and I, and other colleagues, have studied scattered pieces of parchment found around the Middle East, pieces that clearly have women's names on them. In many ways, this parchment, while still incomplete, answers some of our questions. Of course, women were present—"

"Yes, yes, that I understand. And even the presence of children. This was Seder, after all. Only later did Christians refer to this sacred event as the Last Supper, despite Our Lord's warnings," the Patriarch said.

Sofia noticed the Patriarch's cheeks warmed, and Father Andreas stood silent. "And the presence of women's names is hardly controversial."

"The inks used to script this were common in Armenia and Syria, the strokes consistent with what we've found elsewhere," Andrucci said. "My tests fail to find any evidence of fraud here."

The Patriarch removed and cleaned his glasses. "Just who do you think wrote this text?" He put them back on.

"Scholars will debate this question for some time. The later portions appear to be the voice of a woman. I believe it's Mary of Magdala," Sofia said.

"Profesőr Andrucci, Brother Makarios, do you stand by the authenticity of this scroll?"

"We need time to study this. We know more minds need to study this besides ourselves. We hope you allow us to open this to other respected scholars," Brother Makarios said.

Andrucci added, "I stake my reputation on my findings. The parchment, the inks, and the scripting style all coincide with the 10th Century or earlier. Not later."

"Unless this is a fraud created in the 10th Century. Not unheard of," the Patriarch responded.

"Yes, which is why I want to make these available to scholars to study and to begin the debate. Not like the Dead Sea Scrolls, which were seen and studied only by a small group of men." Sofia felt her chest constrict. "Regarding your question of who Hannah is, we must move to the other scroll."

Forty-four

The two women replaced the netting and then moved to the second scroll and removed the netting. Taşbent adjusted the lighting as the Patriarch moved and bent over the document, examining the words. "Ge'ez? Most unusual."

Sofia felt her body vibrating with tension and fear. "And well-preserved. I understand Father Yeorgi's attraction to this."

"Have you contacted anyone in the Patriarch's office in Addis Ababa?" His Holiness stroked his beard thoughtfully.

"Not yet, Your Holiness. I'm hoping Father Andreas would contact and identify several scholars who would join us in studying this." She wondered where the funding for this would come from.

"I should certainly think that appropriate. Your translations?" His Holiness asked while continuing to study the scroll.

Sofia began to read, made difficult by her dry mouth.

"I, Maryam, companion of Salome andher husband
Joseph, and of Mary our Theotokos, greet the faithful

of Jerusalem. I am unworthy to be called, by the will of God, servant to the Followers of the Way and apostle to the Apostles. Warm greetings from the community of believers here in Ephesus.

It has come to our attention that dissension has arisen among Followers of the Way. I am disheartened. We hear that believers place themselves in camps, saying *I am of Cephas Peter*, whom Jesuah[1] called 'the Rock.

The Patriarch, his face a portrait both puzzled and curious, asked, "Do you suggest this was also written by Mary Magdalene?"

"Portions are clearly in her voice. As you'll see, some challenges for us to figure out, including that the word 'Jesus' in the Armenian document is rendered 'Jesuah' here." Sofia continued,

Do you not realize that Jesuah was teasing his fickle friend? Then we hear, I am of Hannah, the Second-born and the Wisdom of God. Others say, I am of Maryam of Magdala, whom the Elders call 'First Witness to the Resurrection.' Who am I but a lowly yet loyal friend? And some say: I am of John the Baptizer. He was protector of the Second-born and our Way-shower, yet he declared that he was not wor-

---

1. Jesuah is the proper translation from the Hebrew for Jesus of Nazareth.

thy. Hannah, the Second-born of the Compassionate One, would tease her brother-cousin by calling him Thunder-of-God!

"Hannah again? The same person?" The Patriarch let out a harsh breath. "What do you make of this 'Second-born' or 'Way-shower' phrase? Why did you translate the Ge'ez this way?" the Patriarch asked. "A younger cousin or sister of Our Lord?"

"I expect lots of questions, your Holiness, but maybe it's best to finish reading, and then the questioning can begin." After hours of anguished thought, she remained convinced this is authentic.

I beseech you, do not divide the Way of Life. Do not compromise the Good News. We are one body of Incarnate Love. To divide the body of believers is to risk death. We who serve the One are of singular heart. Did I not give testimony to the gracious happenings at the First-born's tomb? Did I not share his words of comfort and intent? Did I not proclaim all Hannah's words of consolation and promise with you?"

"And your response? You divide into camps, fighting with one another. Is it stupidity or fear? Do you truly want to be called leader, one whom Messiah – Jesuah and Hannah – will call to the strictest account? Our salvation will return soon, and yet you waste precious time bickering. We must go forth to preach salvation and redemption. We must invite all to embrace the gift of life and not behave like petty politicians.

Worse yet, I now hear some preaching a denial of Hannah, the Second-born of the Compassionate One. Is YHWH[2] of half a mind? Can God be divided? Can the Messiah be split in half as if God were mere mortal? God promised the fullness of salvation. God's promises are trustworthy and abundant.

The Patriarch's cheeks warmed. "This sounds gnostic."

Father Theodor said, "That was my first reaction, but no gnostic text uses some of these words, which are clearly Hebrew in origin. And our Coptic brethren are fiercely loyal to their Hebrew roots. I do think this is worthy of your protection. Studying this will serve Christianity well."

As I proclaimed to you before, I say again: Jesuah and Hannah have defeated death and are present in our midst until the fullness of salvation. Death can no longer separate us from the Divine. That is why Jesuah and Hannah have crossed the threshold to encour-

---

2. Reader's note: Jews do not pronounce the name God gave Moses on Mount Sinai. YHWH is traditionally translated in three ways: *I am who I am*, *I will be whom I will be*, and *I will be gracious to whom I will be gracious*.

age those of us blessed with visitations. Jesuah, the
Anointed One, and Hannah, God's Abiding Presence, came to declare God's favor. Do not err in rejecting half of God's gift."

The Patriarch let out a deep sigh, stopping Sofia. "Enough. This
sounds like you're saying the Messiah is two people. Now really! I
can accept that Jesus had an extended family. Some women may have
been called 'sister,' but this is going too far." The Patriarch had slipped
into Greek rather than the English they had used for Āminah and
Andrucci's benefit. Brother Makarios translated for them.

Sofia gazed at His Holiness, her cheeks warming, then took a deep
breath to calm her nerves, her body vibrating with tension and fear.
"Yes, Holiness. Right now, this document rattles us. But what will I
find when I piece together the fragments found at the archeological
dig? What will Father Theodor learn as he examines the loose collection of scrolls that Esfigmenou was hiding?"

She looked down at the scroll and continued reading.

"God's day of deliverance was proclaimed in the fer-
tile darkness of Theotokos' womb. The angel Gabriel
gave Mary the names of her anointed children: Jesuah, meaning YHWH saves, and Hannah, meaning YHWH is grace. And they are called Immanuel,
God-Is-With-Us. How can our lives proclaim anything less?

Where the rabbis taught Jesuah was dābār, the Word of God, so they declared to us that Hannah was chokmah, the Wisdom of God. Dābār is rightly preached to the Gentiles to be the fulfillment of their aspirations, LOGOS.[3] But LOGOS is nothing without SOPHIA. Wisdom is the maturation and fulfillment of the Word that gives life."

The Patriarch sighed and stepped back from the table.

Brother Makarios spoke up. "I love a good mystery, and this qualifies. But, given my life's work, I expect puzzle pieces to come together as we work on this. Does Ethiopia hold similar pieces and don't realize the impact they'd have on the rest of Christianity?"

"What?" Father Andreas asked.

"If we don't know to look for something, then we can fail to see it when it appears. Is it possible that my fellow monks in Ethiopia hold something similar but don't share it, given how much we've stolen from them over the years?"

His Holiness stood still and gazed around the room.

"This is a possibility I hadn't considered, Your Holiness," Father Andreas admitted.

---

3. Reader's note: LOGOS is Greek for "Word." Early in the Christian movement, Jesuah, as the Twin of Hannah, was equated with the Greek logic notion of WORD. The early believers equated Jesuah as WORD incarnate. Hannah was equated with the WISDOM of God incarnate.

"When the angel Gabriel ordered Mary and Joseph to flee our lands for Egypt, the holy parents placed their daughter Hannah with the prophet Anna. There, Hannah spent her first years in the realm of the Temple and in the presence of hearts given to prayer. In Anna's last days, the prophet handed the babe to Elizabeth and Zachariah. Hannah grew to adore her cousin and playmate, John. They fought and laughed and wandered the countryside together. John was good at slipping by the occupying troops so they and their friends could go out and play.

Hannah was destined for a difficult life. Such is the work of salvation. The women of the Temple, prophetic contemplatives, undertook her formation and education. When her cousin John felt the call to the desert and began residing near the Essene community in the Judean region of Qumran. . . "

Fingers of fear curled an icy grip around Sofia's heart. The room was too quiet. She needed His Holiness to support this. "As you can see, there is fading here, and we need access to a computer to read it."

"... she would visit him and teach the women. Soon, she followed him, remaining there. Her visits to Nazareth and Jerusalem were as frequent as evading the Roman troops permitted. She and her brother, Jesuah, spent long hours alone in conversation.

When Jesuah began his public ministry, he rebuked any of his followers who mocked or degraded women. Detractors attacked Hannah for not serving quietly in the home. Ever since Jesuah playfully called his sister his beloved disciple.

Both Andrucci and Brother Mac chuckled. "Well, that's a new take. But I like it."

Hannah, having reached the fullness of her proclamation of the truth, died at the hands of the Roman centurions who ravaged the countryside, desecrating women. I will not remind you how she died. Jesuah was in the garden near Gethsemane, a place he favored for prayer, grieving the recent death of his sister when he was arrested. In the aftermath of Jesuah's crucifixion, Hannah appeared to me, speaking words of comfort and ordering me to gather some of the women and rush to his tomb."

"Wow," an excited Takis exclaimed. "They killed her?"

"And another post-resurrection story," Andrucci added.

"No wonder Father Yeorgi was willing to kill to get these back. But why did he ever preserve them, to begin with? These documents will shake the world from its complacency. A good thing, I might add."

His Holiness shot a piercing look at Father Theodor. "You take this seriously when this has the potential to split the church."

Sofia interrupted them, desperate that the Patriarch hear the complete translation, and pressed on,

> "And of Hannah's own message? She often called herself the moon's reflection of her brother's message. Where he is Light, so I am darkness. I dwell in the shadow where the defenseless anawim[4] shiver with fear. I am the moon's reflection, so sharp and true, encompassing and embracing. My brother and I often proclaimed, yea even commanded: there is no slave nor free, Greek, Roman, nor Jew, male nor female, for we are all One. In the fullness of time, all things shall be brought to completion. When we become one, so all things are brought to completion. When will we return? When religious division and slavery have ceased. When refugees are at home, and hospitality is extended to all. When the anawin of our world are recognized as the face of YHWH.

> Where my brother Jesuah is called to reveal, I am called to nurture. Where my brother rightly leads, so I am called to bring depth. Where my brother is called

---

4. Reader's note: *anawim* is a rich and complex concept in Judaism and early Christianity. The anawim are those who have no one else to speak on their behalf, such as lepers, widows and orphans, slaves, and prisoners.

Light, so I am darkness. To his ray, I am a shadow. Trust the promises of shadow. I declare that darkness is the tending place in which your longing and desire for healing, justice, and peace grow and come to birth.

Where some call my brother Jesuah great, so I am little. In my darkness are the hidden things of God. As yet-to-be-born babes are nurtured, fed, and protected, so the wisdom of God dwells.

"I don't know how you ever expect to make sense of this," the Patriarch interrupted.

Doctor Gessesse spoke up, "Your Holiness, I would like time to investigate this parchment, as shocking as it is. It's existance may be important to my people. And we may have parchments of a similar period that would help us figure this out."

A scream collapsed in her chest. She pressed on,

Where my brother is called to challenge the public authorities and risks being called "great," so I embrace the shattered. I am called to those trampled by the troops of war, driven from home by those whose god is Greed and Ruthlessness, whose god is made in their own image and likeness. I proclaim the Good News to women who have been beaten and raped. I seek out the leper and the disdained, all whom the Merciful One yearns to heal. When your heart grows faint with despair, look for the sign of my continued presence.

You will recognize me in the rose, the simplest of
thorny scrub brush.

The Evil One lurks about, seeking to destroy the Holy
One's creation. He will call good the trash that rots
the human heart, enticing foolish sheep to crave the
garbage heap that is his inheritance. The war against
women?[5] This evil is in our midst. The Evil One
assaults women's bodies, the source of life. He lurks
about, seeking every opportunity to ravage and rape
and degrade God's chosen vessel to bring forth life.
Satan's war is against the womb. He sent occupying
armies to crush any signs of new life."

Father Theodor took a deep breath. "The Evil One does assault
women with a particular viciousness."

The Patriarch started around the table, but Takis was in the way. "I
will not allow the faithful . . ."

Anxiety clawed in Sofia's chest. "Please let me finish."

"Do not be ashamed of how Hannah died. She chose
to die in the same manner that too many of her sisters

---

5. It is possible this is where the confusing statement in the Gospel
   of Mark 3: 28 ("but whoever blasphemes against the Holy Spirit
   can never have forgiveness, but is guilty of an eternal sin) origi-
   nated.

died. Do not be ashamed of how Jesuah died. He, too, chose to die in the same manner as many of his fellow rabbis died.[6] They chose horrific deaths to again stress the oneness of the One with humanity in all our creatureness. Do not be ashamed of the manner of John's dying; he submitted to the corrupt rulers of our day, meeting folly with quiet strength. He said he must stand aside for Jesuah and Hannah to complete their work of reconciliation. I, the one who survives, live to tell you of the great deeds that happened in poor, rural villages.

As Hannah taught us, the Source of Life is free to act in our uncertainty and unknowing. Darkness serves to heighten our hearing, our sense of smell, and even our playful intuition.

The Patriarch's face reddens with anger. "I expected better of a scholar of your renown. Certainly, eye-witness testimony would have survived to suggest this."

"Will you trust my credentials to finish listening to my translations?"

Father Andreas gasped.

---

6. Reader's note: Jesus was one of nearly three hundred rabbis to be crucified for refusing to compromise Judaism with the Roman religions.

Our salvation is the restoration of intimacy and friendship with the Holy One. Our salvation is the declaration of the fullness of our humanity. There is no greater or lesser, nor freed or slave. Just as Jesuah taught us to turn the other cheek in declaration of our equality with all, so abuse is not to be tolerated.

And when will Jesuah and Hannah return? When there is no more slavery and the anawim have taken their rightful place in the human community? When the innocents are treasured, no longer torn from their mother's wombs or left to die. When women are raised to stand next to men. When the nations are one, there will be no more domination. When war has ceased and hunger a mere distant memory. Believe me when I tell you: Hannah and Jesuah intend the fullness of the Kingdom of God here on earth and no mere imitation.

I (Maryam) exhort you to reject this misbehavior and live your lives worthy of the Good News. Make our Messiah – Jesuah and Hannah – proud to call you friend. You may trust: Hannah's message will rise again...in many lands and through many women and children, slave and free.

I bid you my fondest farewell. Ruah, the Breath of God, calls us East toward the rising sun. The proclamation of God's truth must go forth until the fullness of completion. My love to J (FADED AND TORN)"

"Enough. Please do not ask me to accept a never-before-seen scroll that declares that Our Lord had a twin. How could this possibly be?" He started across the room, shaking his head. "This is blasphemy."

"Holiness . . . "

FORTY-FIVE

S ofia whispered a heartfelt plea, *Hannah*, Jesus, and *Mary Theotokos*, please help me now, as she rounded the table in pursuit of the two clerics who had passed through the doorway. "Holiness, Father Andreas, please wait."

Father Andreas turned his head back toward her, sympathy written in his eyes, as the Patriarch strode away.

"Your Holiness, why didn't Father Yeorgi destroy the Hannah scroll if he believed it a fraud? Why was he willing to kill Sister Meg to get it back?" Sofia pushed down the rush of emotion in her throat. "Why did he ever go to such great lengths to hide it?"

Patriarch Bartholomaios stopped and turned toward her. "I expect better from a scholar of your obvious gifts."

"Father Yeorgi believed the Hannah scroll to be authentic while fearing it," Sofia said. She sensed the others gathering behind her. Their presence was a comfort, knowing each wanted these scrolls to be adequately studied.

"Enough," weariness wrapped around the Patriarch's words.

Father Andreas glanced across toward her. "Because he lusts for books."

"Yes," Sofia said. "And he's a rigid fundamentalist who believes his interpretation of Orthodoxy is the only valid perspective. He thinks you're the heretic." Sofia noticed a cringe of pain on the Patriarch's face. "That's why his monastery has been fighting you all these years and shaming Orthodoxy in the process."

"True," the Patriarch responded. She sensed his anger receding.

"I saw lots of liturgical books and volumes of early Patristic theology. So why did he save the Hannah scroll? What drove him to kill Sister Meg and try to kill me? What hand kept him from destroying the scroll immediately, especially if it's dangerous to believers?" The Patriarch's eyes conveyed pain.

"At least talk to him. Send Father Andreas to the prison where Father Yeorgi's being kept and ask him. Grill him if you must."

Father Andreas looked toward the Patriarch. "I'd like to hear the monk's response to that question. I could go with one of our solicitors."

The Patriarch looked at her in silence, his eyes revealing a thinking mind.

"He didn't destroy this because he feared it was what it seemed. That Hannah was part of our salvation story." Sofia knew she was pushing the debate prematurely but was desperate for his support. She was desperate for other scholars to see this.

The Patriarch's cheeks reddened.

"Your Holiness, at a minimum, the Hannah scroll will entice my generation to seriously reconsider our faith. Women will feel included rather than the centuries of exclusion that has been our reality."

"Dottore—" the Patriarch's voice sounded a warning.

Her heart thumped. "We have been suppressed and excluded. These scrolls explain why the early desert ammas were so comfortable moving beyond gender in search of the Divine. And the Jewish monastic community outside Alexandria was also quite comfortable with the Divine Feminine."

His Holiness retorted sharply. "As we Orthodox have been comfortable with the Divine Feminine if you knew your theology. My concern is pastoral. What effect will this have on the faithful?"

"There is risk here," Father Andreas began. "If we don't support this, we cannot guide the process nor contribute our chosen scholars. It's rather evident that Papandréou will not permit this to go away. We must be involved."

Sofia bristled. Why isn't she considered one of "their scholars." Don't these men even notice how they perceive women? Thank goodness she had uploaded all her files.

"I am concerned that our silence might come across louder than our willingness to participate and debate any findings," Father Andreas suggested.

"Yes, and I want scholars to study these scrolls. Invite your friend, Pope Francis with his Biblical Commission, to sponsor a conference to debate what these are. Or better, hold it in Ethiopia under the Coptic pope's authority." Few outside Orthodoxy and the Papacy knew that the Orthodox Church referred to the Coptic leader as "pope."

Father Andreas asked. "Do you accept the possibility that these are a fraud? Especially this 'Hannah scroll,' as you've named it?"

Sofia's confidence grew. "Yes, I must. Otherwise, I wouldn't be an honest scholar." As she took a deep breath, her back arched. "Do you accept the possibility that these won't be proven fraudulent?"

The patriarch gasped.

Her body vibrated with tension and fear. She had to win them over. "If a fraud, then scholars will ask why someone created a fraud more than a millennium ago. And in Ge'ez."

"Questions could go on and on," Father Andreas said.

Sofia felt a cool breeze brush her neck. The air purifying system must have kicked on.

"Yes, healthy debate. I would be interested in including scholars specializing in gnostic texts." Eight of the twelve gospels were considered gnostic, meaning "secret knowledge."

"Were some of the gnostic writings referring to the Hannah scroll when we thought it was something else?"

The Patriarch let out a long breath. "And in the meantime, the faithful will be scandalized."

"No, Holiness. They will be curious and interested in Christianity again. When women ask about this, we will refer them to the many women of early Christianity long forgotten. They will read Olympias' letters—."

"You intend on publishing the letters of Olympias?" Father Andreas asked.

Sofia looked his way, "Yes, and soon, especially given the archeological dig Āminah has been overseeing. Scholars will ask to see the originals I've digitized. Father Theodor must handle those requests since they're still on Agio Óros." She glanced his way, smiling. "And when my articles are published, curiosity about forgotten aspects of Christianity will erupt."

"Do you intend to publish your translation of the Hannah document?" Father Andreas asked. She sensed in him an astute politician's mind.

"Not at this time. I really want more scholars to see them, and I want a healthy debate. You can help me with this. You believe these are frauds, so choose your preferred scholars to join us in studying them."

Patriarch Bartholomaios gazed at her in silence. "Father Theodor and I will discuss this matter." He gave his blessing and departed.

Sofia stood, her energy depleted, but hope swelled like a dam ready to burst. She turned to gaze at her advocates, all smiling.

Takis slid the stool next to Father Theodor as he nearly collapsed, chuckling. "Sofia, dear. You just won the Patriarch over to this quest of yours. But we must be careful in planning next steps."

"Agreed. The politics could get nasty, but I'm all in," Brother Makarios said.

"I was serious about pursuing my own studies of this. And I'll contact His Eminence Abuna Mathias in Addis Ababa as well as His Holiness Tawadros in Cairo. I am certain they will want to be involved."

"These discoveries are safe here, Sofia," Āminah said as she replaced the silk covering over the Hannah document.

Excitement quickened in Sofia's chest as she gazed around the room. "I need you to check everything pulled out of the cave at Esfigmenou. Maybe Hannah is mentioned in some of the documents."

"I think we should move it all here for examination and protection. Can you make room for more, dear Āminah?"

"Yes, we must. And Sofia may find something useful in all the fragments from the dig."

Andrucci looked at Āminah. "I'll make my lab available to test any fragments you want. We need to establish a range of dates."

Brother Makarios grinned. "Addis Ababa? Interesting. But I look forward to our work ahead."

Sofia leaned against the wall, drained of energy. "It could be Rome if Pope Francis takes us seriously. I'd prefer His Holiness Abune Mathias and meeting in Addis Ababa. After all, that's where Hannah was found."

Author Note

My alter ego, Sofia, searched for the letters of Deacon Olympias, documenting the suppressed history of women's involvement in the early Christian Church. Deacon Olympias (365–409 CE) was a member of the Roman Imperial family, a philanthropist who carefully gave her wealth away—through deacons who saw to the care of widows, orphans, and prisoners, and to fund churches and monasteries. She built a monastery for up to 250 women—dedicated to chanting the Divine Office, studying Scripture and other texts, and extending care for the poor in their neighborhood. Two churches and her monastery were taken down to build Hagia Sophia, which was completed in 537 CE. She was close friends with John Chrysostom (yes, meaning *golden tongue*), who was driven into exile because he confronted corruption in the Church and government. John's letters to her survive, but hers to John do not. So, I crafted them by shadow-reading what was going on in her life at that time. Olympias literally died of grief over John's slow death.

Mary of Magdala (aka Mary Magdalene), "author of the Hannah Document," was one of the earliest followers of Jesus of Nazareth and is mentioned in many of the New Testament Gospel stories. She was not a "reformed prostitute," a mix-up in the Middle Ages with the unnamed woman who anointed Jesus with expensive nard (and why do we assume SHE was a prostitute?) and Mary the Egyptian. Many scholars believe she was a successful businesswoman who supported Jesus' ministry. From the earliest days of the Jesus Movement (not called Christianity for about another 60 – 70 years) she was venerated as *The First-Witness to the Resurrection* and *The Apostle to the Apostles*. Some scholars suggest that the rumor that she had been a prostitute was a power play to marginalize her followers. In fact, she was revered by her contemporaries on par with Simon Peter.

Makrina the Younger, known as *the Sage of God*, did write a letter to a young Olympias encouraging her to stand firm against the Emperor. Makrina was a formidable leader in the early Christian movement. She lived from 327–380 CE in Cappadocia (present-day Turkey). It's important to note that scholars, including those in the Orthodox tradition, now recognize Makrina, not her younger brother Basil, as the founder of Orthodox monasticism. When Basil documented all that he had learned from his older sister, the *rule* became known as *The Rule of Basil*, which is still followed by monks and nuns in the Orthodox tradition.

There are several Susannas, one of whom is in the gospel of Luke and the other in the Patristic texts. It was a common name as were Hannah, Joanna, and Mary/Miriam/Myriam. Too often, women were not named in early texts, and sometimes, we give them names, such as the woman at the well (John 4: 5 – 30) who became known as Photini. She was a great evangelist to the Samaritan people. Doctor Tim Vivian, scholar of early Copt and Christian history, painfully tells us that 90% of classical Greek and Roman literature is lost to us. How much of that involved women?

There is **no** evidence that Jesus of Nazareth had a twin sister (siblings, yes).But I played with the idea of *"what if"*. I asked myself: If Jesus did have a twin, who would then also be the messiah, what would her message be? And they would certainly be the *ying/yang* to each other. Thus, consider the final discovery as midrash—a form of storytelling—a long-venerated tradition in Judaism. The "Hannah document" is pure fiction but does reflect some of the early Jesus movement ponderings of what was expected of the longed-for Messiah. But it's fiction.

My locations are authentic, but the use of these spaces and many of the characters who inhabit them are products of my imagination. Mor Gabriel, near Mardin, in southeastern Turkey, was founded in 397 CE by Mor Shmu'el (Samuel) and his follower Mor Shem'un (Simon). It is the oldest continuously lived in Syriac Orthodox monastery in the world, and is still inhabited by several monks and many more nuns. You are welcome to visit and even stay in their guesthouse.

Agio Óros/Mount Athos (*Agio Óros* to Greeks and Mount Athos to the English-speaking world) is a peninsula in northeastern Greece strictly reserved for (male) monks of the Orthodox tradition since 1054. Mount Athos enjoys a semi-autonomous status (from the Greek government), is self-governed through its Monastic Council, and is under the authority of Patriarch Bartholomaîos, the spiritual leader of the Orthodox world. Mount Athos is home to twenty established monasteries of differing cultural origins as well as numerous solitaries on the peninsula.

Karyes is the administrative center. Men may come, after receiving written permission, for retreat or solitude. Catholics, Protestants, Muslims, Jews, Buddhists, and seekers of no particular faith are welcomed—but not women. Nothing female (so the monks claim—but yes, hens were finally permitted after 800 years—for eggs!). Hikers find their way onto the peninsula, including women. In the1950s, a law was passed in Greece forbidding women from entering Agio Óros with the possibility of a prison sentence if discovered. Mount Athos' website https://mountathos.orghas become quite sophisticated.

While I've named several monasteries that do exist on Mount Athos, I've invented their layout, as I'll never be permitted to enter. But Hagia Theotokos is entirely a creation of my imagination, as are any monkish characters encountered in *The Hannah Document*. The monks have graciously allowed their manuscripts and other valuables to be digitized. For the purposes of my story, this digitizing began around 2010 CE, a few years before Sofia "entered" Agio Óros.

In 2008, an investigation into real estate dealings involving Vatopedi monastery and its abbot revealed that several governmental ministers under Prime Minister Karamanlis had arranged for a land swap: low-valued rural land owned by Vatopedi for prime real estate in downtown Athens worth one billion euros https://orthochristian .com/50721.html. This was a complex case where charges were filed, dismissed, and then charged again. Eventually, the abbot and one of his monks were arrested in 2011 and brought in for trial. As of 2017, this legal situation seems to have settled without the settlements being publicized. Hopefully the citizens of Greece got their valuable land back. I referenced to this in Sofia's story to establish social context and build her frustration at slamming into so many stone walls.

Sofia passed herself off as "Brother Pachomius of Ipapandi." Ipapandi is one of several fascinating monastic sites in Meteora in central Greece. These are monasteries "in the sky," built on crags and peaks, often requiring the monk to climb a rope ladder to reach their home. Meteora is now a World Heritage Site https://whc.un-esco.org/en/list/455/.

Patriarch Bartholomaîos has been an extraordinary religious leader: reaching out to Christian, Jewish, Muslim, Buddhist and other leaders of faith communities. He's been a staunch defender of the environment, cares for refugees worldwide, and, more recently (2022), a defender of Ukraine over Russia's unlawful invasion. See *Global Initiatives of Ecumenical Patriarch Bartholomew: Peace, Reconciliation, and Care for Creation* and *Cosmic Grace, Humble Prayer: The Ecological Vision of the Green Patriarch Bartholomew I*. I hope I showed respect in using his name and spirit in telling Sofia's story—but his actions and words are my invention.

The breakaway monastery of Esfigmenou. Wow! I pared down a complicated situation to better serve my story. Troublesome monks residing at Esfigmenou forced Patriarch Bartholomaîos to declare this breakaway faction "heretical" (schismatic), requiring them to vacate the monastery. They refused. The monks recognized by Patriarch Bartholomaîos and the Monastic Council have been residing in Karyes while the police have been trying to evict the heretical monks. I did not invent *Orthodoxy or Death!* The schismatic monks did—hanging a banner with the words on the entrance. As of this writing, it is still there. The monks continue to reside there illegally, although Patriarch Bartholomaîos requested that the military police depart. You won't find them on the official Mount Athos website, but you will find some basic photos online.

The characters I created, including Father Yeorgi, who resides in Esfigmenou, are my imaginative creation, as is the hidden second library underneath. My understanding is that the schismatic monks are proud of their small library. While committed to praying the full Divine Office and honoring certain relics, they are proud of their rather anti-intellectual stance. The library Sofia stumbles into is strictly my dreaming far and wide.

My characters often mention "the Hill," a reference to The Hill Museum & Manuscript Library https://hmml.org in Collegeville, MN. This institution, dedicated to digitizing sacred and historic texts from various cultures and faith traditions worldwide, holds immense historical significance. It strategically focuses on preserving libraries most at risk of destruction, such as Aleppo, Syria, where my "shadow character" Adelie was based. The Hill's efforts to scan most of the manuscripts before Assad's troops bombed the city are a testament to their commitment. The hope is that they managed to relocate the precious manuscripts to safety in the mountains before the buildings were destroyed.

The Hill is an excellent resource for researchers. The Hill holds the Saint John's Bible https://saintjohnsbible.org, the first commissioned hand-calligraphied and illuminated Bible, using medieval methods, in over 500 years. It's well worth exploring. While Father Columba Stewart, OSB, is the executive director and the late Dr. Getatchew Haile (d. 2021) was the Curator of the Ethiopian Study Center, my characters (Father Simon and Dr. Gessesse, respectively) are my creation, and any resemblance is accidental. I do encourage my readers to visit these online sites.

The Abbey of Santa Cecilia, located in the Trastevere district of Rome, plays a significant role in my novel. Originally the home of the martyr Cecilia, a church was built in the 3rd century, and monastic communities came to occupy the space over the centuries. Benedictine nuns were invited to occupy the Abbey in 1527 and expanded the buildings. I have visited Santa Cecilia and met the nuns there. What I have seen is accurately portrayed in the novel; the rest I have imagined. I encourage my readers to explore their website at https://www.benedettinesantacecilia.it to further connect with the rich history of this place.

For many of us in Western Europe and the Americas, the world, culture, and spirituality of Eastern Orthodoxy may seem foreign and exotic, despite their presence in our midst. There is currently a notable resurgence of interest in the spirituality and liturgical traditions of the Orthodox or Byzantine world. Alongside western chant, musicians and performers are now showcasing chant traditions from the east, readily available on many platforms. New music is being composed and performed, openly influenced by these ancient Eastern chant traditions. There is also a renewed fascination with icons, which are written, not painted, and some contemporary artists are creating new images and interpreting human realities in thoughtful ways.

For readers interested in accessible introductions to orthodoxy, I recommend *Eastern Orthodoxy through Western Eyes* by Donald Fairbairn, *The Orthodox Way* by Kallistos Ware, and *Elements of Faith: an Introduction to Orthodox Theology* by Christos Yannaras. Why the concern to save ancient and medieval manuscripts? Read *History in Flames: The Destruction and Survival of Medieval Manuscripts* by Robert Bartlett. For readers interested in understanding the richness and mystery of icons, I recommend *The Mystical Language of Icons* by Solrunn Nes.

About the Author

I am passionate about recovering the stories of women long ignored, women who made significant contributions to culture and spirituality, and making their contributions known to a broader reading audience. My intent is to restore women to the stories being told. I've written several books on neglected aspects of women's history that have been translated into 12 languages, as well as on aspects of Benedictine spirituality. These include *The Forgotten Desert Mothers: Sayings, Lives, and Stories of Early Christian Women* (Paulist Press); *The Wisdom of the Beguines. The Forgotten Story of a Medieval Women's Movement* (BlueBridge, 2016); *Engaging Benedict. What the Rule Can Teach Us Today* (2005 / 2025); *The Benedictine Tradition* (Liturgical Press); as well as chapters to other collections. I have other nonfiction projects under construction.

I love opportunities to tell women's stories in workshops and retreats, I meet with wonderful people for spiritual companioning, and maintain my monastery's archives. I am a voracious reader of diverse material and do not apologize for the stacks of books in my bedroom and office. In my "spare" time, I spoil my grandnieces and nephews (with lots of books!).

If you enjoyed The Hannah Document, I would appreciate a review on your favorite site.

https://lauraswanosb.com/
https://www.bookbub.com/authors/laura-swan
https://www.youtube.com/@BenedictineLauraSwan